The Gin Lovers

Also by Jamie Brenner

writing as Logan Belle

Blue Angel

Fallen Angel

Naked Angel

Bettie Page Presents: The Librarian

The Gin Lovers

THE SERIAL

The Gin Lovers
Little White Lies
Society Sinners
Vice or Virtue
Dangerous Games
Hell Hath No Fury

Jamie Brenner

St. Martin's Griffin
New York

This is a work of fiction. All of the characters, organizations, and events portrayed in this novel are either products of the author's imagination or are used fictitiously.

This book is dedicated to my father,
Michael Weisman

Acknowledgments

Unlike the writing of other novels, there were no examples for me to follow in creating an e-book serial. *The Gin Lovers* was truly a group effort. Thank you to my publisher, Dan Weiss, whose innovation in e-book serials gave me the opportunity to combine my passion for novels with my lifelong love of soap opera—I'm grateful for your vision and for your support. Thank you to my tireless editor, Vicki Lame, who read every episode many times and nurtured each scene with a brilliant editorial hand and unflagging enthusiasm. Finally, to my agent and partner, Adam Chromy: If it weren't for our endless conversations about narrative and your refusal to accept the words "I can't," this book would not exist. You make my dreams come true.

Part I

The Gin Lovers

There are people who have money and people who are rich.
—Coco Chanel

Prohibition has made nothing but trouble.
—Al Capone

Chapter 1

"It's the party of the year, and it's a funeral."

Charlotte Delacorte overheard the comment outside Saint Thomas Church on Fifth Avenue. She didn't recognize the woman who made the callous remark and could only assume she was one of the new breed of vile gossip columnists who had descended upon New York like locusts.

"The world is going to hell in a handbasket," her newly deceased mother-in-law had often said.

Now, all of New York had turned out to pay its respects to the late Geraldine Delacorte. The line of people waiting to get inside stretched from the corner of Fifty-third Street to as far as Charlotte could see, and the avenue was a virtual parking lot filled with the finest Packards and Pierce-Arrow roadsters. The dark cars were like matching accessories to the crowd dressed in black, navy, and gray. Charlotte herself wore a black crepe mourning dress by Jean Patou. The French designer had offered to send over a matching chiffon veil, but Charlotte decided the veil would be more appropriately worn by blood relatives. Instead, she wore her long, glossy brown hair up in an elaborate chignon. She wished she'd had time to sneak on a bit of rouge—her fair skin was paler than usual, her wide gray eyes pinched with fatigue.

"Mrs. Delacorte, we really must expedite moving guests inside. Perhaps if you and your husband stepped inside and weren't greeting everyone . . ." Mr. Smyth, the director of the service, sweating in his heavy suit, was clearly overwhelmed. Charlotte was a little anxious herself but had learned that as a Delacorte, she could never let that sort of thing show. She tried to imagine what her late mother-in-law would want them to do with the bottleneck of guests.

"I think . . . it's important that we acknowledge each of the guests as they arrive. It's the proper thing to do," Charlotte said.

It was a comfort to Charlotte that the most important people in New York had turned out in tribute: The Vanderbilts, the Goulds, the Carnegies, Fricks, Astors, and Rockefellers were all represented on that gray Saturday morning. Charlotte's mother-in-law would not be impressed so much as she would have been satisfied.

The social clout of the family into which she had married was something Charlotte had almost come to take for granted. Certainly, she had not seen it exhibited in such a public way since her lavish wedding four years earlier—an almost overwhelming affair, planned and executed with near-military precision at the strong hand of William's mother. Charlotte had been so caught up in the excitement of William's whirlwind courtship, she had willingly gone along for the ride.

"Charlotte, my dear, you look lovely even on such a sorry occasion," said Mayor Hylan's wife. She took one of Charlotte's gloved hands into her own. "Such a loss. The city won't be the same without Geraldine."

This was true. Manhattan would not be the same without Geraldine Delacorte's endless petitioning against everything from the women's suffragist movement to the motor cars "ruining" New York City, to the "bad element" taking over Midtown.

"It's those nightclubs," Geraldine had said.

"Oh, people just need to have a little fun sometimes," Charlotte had replied.

"People? What people? Loose women and bootleggers!"

Charlotte couldn't help but think that Geraldine Delacorte's sudden death from heart failure had something to do with her constant meddling into what other people were doing.

Charlotte fanned herself with a scarf, beginning to sweat inside her dress. Her nerves were getting the best of her. Perhaps Mr. Smyth was right. It was time to get things moving.

She tried to catch William's eye, but he was oblivious, engrossed in conversation with the mayor.

"This crowd is simply overwhelming," said Amelia Astor, appearing seemingly out of nowhere. Charlotte had seen her arriving at the church, dressed all in black, her eyes red-rimmed and brimming with tears. Any casual observer would think that Amelia was a grieving daughter, not a mere school friend of the grieving son. "Do you need help ushering people indoors?" she asked Charlotte, a little too sweetly.

Amelia was one of William's oldest friends—part of the smart set that had all gone to the same private schools from the time they were in their first walking shoes. Charlotte had attended the best schools in Philadelphia—even after her father had lost most of their money they still managed to keep Charlotte afloat. But none of that mattered in New York. If you weren't a member of the Four Hundred—social arbiter Ward McCallister's list of the *true* members of New York society—you might as well be fresh off the boat. It was her mother-in-law who told her about the list— perhaps to remind her of her place. Charlotte asked, why the number four hundred? And her mother-in-law said breezily, "No more than that can fit comfortably in the Astors' ballroom."

"Thank you, Amelia. But I've got it under control," said Charlotte. "Perhaps the best thing you can do is go inside yourself.

People always *do* seem to follow your lead." It was just enough of a compliment to make the dismissal acceptable.

Charlotte crossed the stone entranceway to speak to her husband, who was now in a heated conversation with an underdressed, rather scruffy-looking man.

"William," she said, reaching for his arm.

"Not now, Charlotte." He shook off her hand. The strange man glanced at her, then quickly walked away.

"Who was that?" she asked.

But before William could answer her, a car came skidding to a stop at the corner, a garishly painted Model T. The vehicle was a shade of green Charlotte had never before seen on an automobile. The car was filled in both the front and back with passengers.

The horn bleated rudely, eliciting loud laughter from the backseat.

Charlotte turned back to William and found that he was staring at the car. It only took her a few seconds to realize he wasn't just distracted by the noise; he was entirely focused on the passenger disembarking from the backseat.

She was a stunning brunette, with a perfectly chic, slim figure, the short, boyish haircut that was all the rage, and wearing a sleeveless pink sheath dress that fell just below her knees. Her face was concealed by her pink cloche hat.

Charlotte was alarmed to see William cut through the throng of guests and make his way to the curb, where he immediately took the woman roughly, but intimately, by the arm.

Chapter 2

CHARLOTTE'S HEART POUNDED at the sight of her husband so familiar with a strange woman. But then the brunette turned her heavily rouged face in Charlotte's direction, and she realized it was, unbelievably, her young sister-in-law, Mae Delacorte.

The girl was nearly unrecognizable.

In the few short months since Charlotte had last seen her, Mae Delacorte had cut her long brown hair into a severe bob with bangs and dyed it nearly black. Her pretty face was dramatically transformed by kohl pencil around her eyes, rouge on her cheeks, and dark red lipstick. She wore a short dress, fringed, and sparkling with hundreds of shiny beads. It was like nothing Charlotte had ever seen outside the pages of a magazine. At nineteen years old, Mae Delacorte looked far more worldly and sophisticated than Charlotte.

"Mr. Smyth," Charlotte called, summoning the director of the procession back outside. His perspiration was now seeping through the underarms of his jacket. "I believe you are right. Can you please move everyone indoors? My husband and I will be in shortly."

Having dispatched Mr. Smyth to minimize the witnesses to what was sure to be an ugly confrontation between William and his sister, Charlotte made her way to the corner to join them.

A man climbed out of the car to join Mae on the sidewalk, and the car sped off with another jarring bleat of the horn, amid more laughter from the backseat.

Even from a few feet away, Charlotte was struck by the man's good looks.

"Hello, Charlotte! Don't you look fetching in black," said Mae with a smile. She emanated the overpowering smell of cigarette smoke and Joy perfume. "You should wear it more often." It was she who looked fetching. Charlotte could barely take her eyes off her. And William was clearly furious.

"Would you excuse us for a moment, please?" he said. Charlotte wasn't sure if he was speaking to her, or to Charlotte's companion.

"Certainly," said the man, removing his hat. "And Mr. Delacorte? My condolences." The man was very tall, with broad shoulders and shiny dark hair that was in need of a trim.

William ignored the comment; he was too busy dragging Mae halfway down the block, leaving Charlotte standing awkwardly with the stranger.

"Jake Larkin," he said, holding out his hand. Charlotte hesitated a moment before giving him her own. When he touched her, she felt something close to a shock.

"Charlotte Delacorte," she managed to say. He had strong brows, dark eyes, and a smile her mother-in-law would have called "charming," but not as a compliment. But he was handsome— good lord, was he handsome.

"I'm sorry for your loss," he said. His eyes were so dark they were nearly black and seemed to lock onto hers. She quickly glanced away, not so much out of modesty but more out of a sense of self-preservation. She reminded herself that she was supposed to say something.

"Well, thank you. Um, Mr. Larkin, if I may ask, how do you know my sister-in-law?" As soon as she asked it, she realized that she wasn't asking to be polite, that she actually felt an urgency to understand his relationship with Mae—to know everything about him.

"Oh, we're old friends."

"Old friends?"

"Yes," he said. "We go way back."

"From school?" Charlotte offered.

He laughed. "No, ma'am."

Even from the distance, she could hear William and Mae arguing. Charlotte wondered if she should intervene, and this reminded her where she was—and who she was.

"Mr. Larkin, is it your intention to accompany Miss Delacorte to the service for her mother? Because quite honestly, I don't think that would be the best idea given the circumstances."

"Isn't that up to Mae? She did invite me, after all."

The nerve!

"Mae does not always employ the best judgment," Charlotte said. "Now, my husband has just lost his mother. His sister has arrived at the funeral looking rather . . . inappropriate. Tensions are high. This is not the best time for us to be making the acquaintance of one of her suitors."

Unbelievably, the man laughed again.

"I'm not a suitor, Mrs. Delacorte. Like I said, we're just old friends."

His eyes held hers, then swept down as if to take her in completely. Charlotte felt her breathing quicken. It took her a moment to find words.

"I don't want to be rude. But I'm going to have to ask you to leave."

Jake Larkin reached for her hand, and this time, he kissed the back of it. His hand was large and rough, his lips surprisingly soft against her skin. Something deep inside of her twitched.

"Mrs. Delacorte, while I can't imagine there's any man on this planet who would want to upset you, I'm afraid I can't leave. I came here this morning to escort my friend, and that's what I'm going to do."

He turned and walked right into the church.

Charlotte stared after him, her heart beating fast. Then, with one more glance at her husband, she also walked inside, prepared to do whatever was necessary to make sure the ceremony went off smoothly.

People would expect no less of her.

BEVERLY "BOOM BOOM" Lawrence closed the door to her basement office. As the owner of and larger-than-life personality behind Midtown's Vesper Club, Boom Boom lived by the "late to bed, late to rise" edict. She knew it wasn't making her healthy, but it was sure as hell making her wealthy.

The only problem with starting her day just as most people were having lunch was that she was perpetually late catching up with the daily news. At twelve thirty in the afternoon, she was just having her morning coffee and reading the paper. And the headline that day made her choke on her Maxwell House.

THE PARTY'S OVER, SAYS BUCKNER: NEW U.S. ATTORNEY TO START PROCEEDINGS AGAINST PROHIBITION VIOLATORS.

"Fuck me," she said, lighting a cigarette.

In his first official statement as U.S. Attorney for the Southern District of New York, Emory R. Buckner has declared, "One of my first duties is to bring injunction proceedings against fourteen of the most prominent and exclusive cabarets in my district."

Boom Boom heaved her large frame up from the chair and walked to the filing cabinet where she kept her ledgers. She felt certain she'd done her monthly payoffs to Prohibition agents, but for the first time in a long time, she wondered if that was going to be enough.

The phone on her desk rang, startling her.

"Who the hell is calling this early," she muttered. "Hello?"

"May I please speak to Beverly Lawrence?" a female voice asked.

"Yeah? Who are you?"

"Oh, hello Miss Lawrence. This is Greta Goucher from the *New York Sun*. I'm sure you've heard that the funeral for Geraldine Delacorte is taking place today."

"I'm not on the guest list, lady."

"That's why I'm calling: Everyone knows Geraldine Delacorte was very active in trying to shut down establishments such as your own. Do you have any comment?"

Boom Boom hung up the phone. She could care less that the rich old bag had finally kicked the bucket. Except . . .

She pulled out another drawer from the filing cabinet and checked a different book. Sure enough, Geraldine's daughter, Mae, owed an outstanding tab of $2,025.00. Boom Boom never thought twice about letting her run up a bill like that because the Lord knew the Delacorte name was good for it. But she had to wonder, with Mama moneybags out of the picture, who was going to pay the bill?

Boom Boom made a note in her calendar. It was time to collect on young Miss Delacorte. She just hoped, for Mae's sake, her mother had thought kindly of her when drawing up the will.

Chapter 3

MAE DELACORTE RELUCTANTLY followed her older brother up the stairs of their mother's Beaux-Arts mansion, which was filling with mourners coming to pay their last respects.

The second floor afforded them some privacy, and from the look on William's face, she could tell they were going to need it.

He gestured for her to go to her bedroom—"Where no one will bother us."

The room was in its usual state of disarray, littered with dresses, shoes, postcards, magazines, and records. Her bed was unmade, and the window was still ajar from when she leaned out to smoke a cigarette after she put on her evening makeup. She probably should have felt self-conscious about the mess, but after so many years of William's and her mother's disapproval, she felt somewhat immune to the disgusted glare he was sending in her direction.

She looked at her brother, annoyed by their physical resemblance. They were like photo negatives of one another. While they had the same facial features—aquiline noses, high cheekbones, and wide-set eyes—William had their mother's nearly blond hair and hazel eyes, whereas Mae had her father's dark hair and eyes as dramatically blue as a Siberian husky's. There were rumors of some "black" Irish in the family, but her mother had always insisted their bloodline was pure Dutch.

Mae crossed her arms defiantly.

"You're either going to have to change your clothes, or leave," William said. "It's bad enough that you showed up at the church dressed like you just rolled out of a nightclub. I'm not going to have you parading around downstairs like that and disgrace Mother's memory."

Mae rolled her eyes. "Stop being so dramatic," she said. "Besides, you can't order me out of my own house." As if to emphasize the point, she sat on her bed.

William gave an odd laugh. "This was Mother's house, not yours. What do you think? That she left one of the most extravagant homes in Manhattan to a nineteen-year-old who has done nothing in recent memory but embarrass the family?"

"No, I assume she left the house to *both* of us, her two children."

"Well, you assumed wrong."

That got Mae's attention. She looked at him sharply. "What are you talking about?"

"Maybe you should have shown up to the reading of the will."

"I overslept."

"Well, allow me to bring you up to speed: Mother has left this house to the Women's Literary Alliance—something she created that she is actually proud of."

Mae paled. "So what does that mean . . . exactly?"

"You have two weeks to move out."

"I don't believe you."

"I'd be happy to have you talk to Mr. Paulson yourself. He can fill you in on all the details."

Mae jumped up. "Then I need to have my inheritance released to me as soon as possible so I can get my own house." The expression on William's face made her stomach ball into a knot.

"There will be no inheritance, Mae. At least, not for a while. You get nothing until you turn twenty-five. Until that time, I am your guardian, and I'll give you an allowance as I see fit. And I do mean *as I see fit*."

"You're a liar!" Mae screamed.

William closed the distance between them with a few quick strides and grabbed her arm roughly, jerking her up to a standing position.

"Keep your voice down," he hissed. She'd never seen him so worked up. "All of New York society is downstairs. Again, the lawyer will happily verify all of this. So I suggest you reevaluate your love life. And quickly."

CHARLOTTE WAS FAILING her first major test in her new role as the reigning Mrs. Delacorte.

It was evident to her that many of the people filing into her newly deceased mother-in-law's home had not been invited to the postfuneral reception. She had to wonder if they were there to pay their respects or merely seizing the opportunity to get a firsthand look inside the sprawling Beaux-Arts mansion. The last time Charlotte had been to a major reception at the mansion, four months ago at Christmas, it hadn't been nearly as full. And Christmas had been one of Geraldine Delacorte's largest events on the social calendar.

Amelia Astor had suggested that she post someone at the entrance to check arrivals against a master guest list, but Charlotte had rejected the idea. It wasn't as if they were hosting a ball. Who on earth would show up to a funeral for entertainment? But she had misjudged. As an outsider—to New York and to its high society—she still didn't fully comprehend the public's fascination with the Delacorte family. She had not considered the fact that some New Yorkers had witnessed, in 1893, the construction of the red brick and limestone house on the corner of Fifty-seventh and Fifth—the largest private residence in Manhattan. She had not taken into account that the annual Christmas decorations drew visitors from all over the country, or that the home displayed as much art as some museums. To New Yorkers, families like the Delacortes and the Astors were the closest thing they had to royalty.

As a result of her miscalculation, she could do nothing but put a smile on her face and watch the throng filing into the formal entrance, a great hall done entirely in cream-colored limestone. To the right of the entrance was a salon in the style of Louis XVI, and a billiard room with a spectacular Augustus Saint-Gaudens fireplace.

She was reminded of the first time she had seen William, at a party in a home nearly as grand as the one they were gathered in that morning. She had been a sophomore at Vassar, visiting her roommate for Christmas break. Charlotte's mother had started suffering from headaches and fatigue, and her father had encouraged Charlotte to spend the holiday with friends; the attempt to have their usual Christmas at home would only add to her mother's stress.

And so Charlotte spent her first week in Manhattan, never imagining she would ultimately live there, presiding over society parties like the one that had so intimidated her at age nineteen. Only William had managed to make her feel at ease that night despite the fact that he was elegant and handsome and very much a part of the strange and insular world that was so alien to her.

She realized, long after the fact, that he had probably been drawn to her because of the very outsider status that made her so uncomfortable. Their marriage had been, perhaps, his one act of rebellion in his otherwise by-the-book life.

"Quite a turnout," Amelia said. Charlotte looked to see if she was making oblique commentary on the fact that she had, in the end, been right about the checklist at the door. But Amelia's face was unreadable.

Charlotte saw her husband crossing the room, his eyes meeting hers across the crowd. He looked distressed, and not just from grief. William was clearly aggravated. She hoped this wasn't to be his permanent state now that his mother was not around to take care of everything.

"Excuse me," Charlotte said. She made her way across the living room but was intercepted by an unfamiliar woman. She was tiny, slightly horse-faced, and of indeterminate age.

"Mrs. Delacorte," said the woman, blocking her path with surprising ease and efficiency. "My condolences."

"Oh, I . . . thank you. Do we know one another?"

"Greta Goucher," the woman said, extending her hand. Charlotte noticed that she did not wear any jewelry, not even a single ring. "Is it true that Geraldine Delacorte didn't bequeath this house to the family but to one of her charities?"

Charlotte was taken aback. At first, she wondered what person could possibly be so ill-mannered, so downright crude. Then she realized that the woman must be a gossip columnist. Oh, how she hated it when Amelia was right!

"I must ask you to leave," Charlotte said, looking around to see if anyone had overhead their exchange.

"I'm here to pay my respects, Mrs. Delacorte. Your loss is all of New York's loss, don't you know? Now if you could just answer the question . . ."

William appeared by her side.

"I need to speak with you," he said, taking her by the arm.

"I'm sorry," Charlotte said to the woman, "I must again ask you to leave."

"Is there a problem?" William said.

"Not at all," said Greta Goucher. "I was just asking your lovely wife about the future of this jewel of a home. I know my readers wonder about its fate."

"Your readers?" William said.

"Greta Goucher, the *New York Sun.*" She extended her hand. William ignored it.

"Thank you for your interest, but I have to ask that you not make inquiries of my friends or family. This is a memorial reception. Please respect our privacy."

William steered Charlotte to the back staircase, where they were able to find some measure of quiet.

"What a horrid woman. I can't believe people have such nerve," Charlotte said.

"Forget about that gossip. We have bigger problems."

Charlotte looked at him. "What?"

"Your father is here."

Chapter 4

CHARLOTTE STIFFENED. "I don't see why that's a problem. It's the right thing for him to pay his respects."

But that wasn't entirely true; she was well aware why it was a problem. The last time John "Black Jack" Andover had shown up for a Delacorte party, he'd gotten outrageously drunk and made a pass at William's third cousin, Hortense. The unattractive spinster had been delighted at the attention though the rest of the family was a bit put out. Charlotte asked her father to please leave the flasks at home the next time he visited.

Five years into Prohibition, Black Jack still had enough alcohol stashed away from before the law went into effect to technically get around the Volstead Act. Prohibition had given many long-suffering wives the hope that their husbands' excessive drinking would finally be curtailed. But ironically, the men who most needed the government-imposed limits on their consumption were also the most adept at skirting the rules. And certainly, Prohibition had come too late to save her father's once-lucrative businesses.

"Where is he?"

"The parlor."

"There's nothing to worry about. I'll look after him."

Charlotte walked away, but William called her back. "What is it?" she said, anxious to find her father. She was not worried about his behavior—she simply wanted to see him. She realized, with a pang of guilt, that it had been at least a year since she'd been to visit Philadelphia. How had she let that much time pass? For all his trouble, for all the disappointment, time spent with her father still delighted her.

"Charlotte, now that Mother is gone, everyone will look to

you to set the tone for this family—maybe even to set the tone for New York society. From now on, everything is a potential cause for worry. It's not just about you or me anymore. It's about the family. Do you understand?"

"Yes," Charlotte said, though she doubted anyone would be looking at her as the next Mrs. Delacorte. It was more about William's rising to the head of the family. And this new reality was clearly sending him into a tailspin. "Where's Mae?" She suddenly realized she hadn't seen her sister-in-law at the reception.

"I asked her to leave."

"Leave the reception for her own mother? William, you can't do such a thing."

"This is exactly what I'm talking about. Of course I can—I did, and I'll do it again and again until she stops being an embarrassment to this family. Can you imagine if that Goucher woman got ahold of her? That's why I can't have your father falling down drunk, or worse—telling his tales and boasting about his daughter's marrying up. You need to ask him to leave."

"He's my father," Charlotte said.

"And you're the new Mrs. Delacorte."

"Oh, for heaven's sake!" Clearly, William had lost all rational thought. It wasn't worth getting into an argument. Maybe her father wouldn't mind being let off the hook instead of standing around making small talk for hours. "Fine. I'll ask him to leave."

FIONA SHAUGHNESSY—KNOWN to mostly everyone in Manhattan nightlife as Fiona Sparks—was rudely awakened from her early-evening beauty rest by a knock on her door. Since she worked most nights until the earliest hours of the morning, any sleep she was able to get before the start of her cocktail-waitress shift was crucial.

Annoyed, Fiona removed her black satin sleep mask and

walked in a daze from her bed to the front door. Since her apartment was the size of an average closet, it wasn't much of a walk. It took her far more time and effort to undo the elaborate system of locks and chains on the door itself. Although her neighborhood wasn't nearly as bad as the one she had grown up in, she'd flirted her way into having the landlord install a few extra safeguards.

"Who is it?" she called out.

"It's Mae."

Fiona's long fingers ran through the locks quickly and opened the door just enough to let her visitor step inside. "This is a surprise," said Fiona.

Mae didn't often visit the apartment on Orchard Street, and really, who could blame her. Fiona spent as little time there as possible herself. No, it was much preferable to visit Mae's mother's Fifth Avenue mansion, where Mae practically had her own wing.

Mae walked in, and Fiona closed the door behind her. Fiona knew she owed Mae an apology, but saying she was sorry was not one of Fiona's strengths. Where she was from, you could lie, cheat, and steal—and were expected to. But Mae came from a mannered world. It was the world Fiona was gunning for, so she knew she'd better learn how to play the part.

"I'm sorry I didn't make it to the funeral," Fiona said.

"That's okay," Mae answered, dropping her wrist-strap bag on the small table near the door. "I didn't last long there myself. My brother asked me to leave the reception at the house."

"He's such a wet blanket," Fiona said.

Mae pulled Fiona's hand down to her breast. Their eyes met, and Fiona saw the raw need in Mae's aristocratic blue gaze. She casually brushed her thumb over Mae's nipple, straining against the thin fabric of her dress.

Fiona stepped back and sat on her bed. She lay back on her elbows and spread her legs, revealing to Mae that, as usual, she wasn't wearing any underwear.

Mae kneeled in front of her and pressed her lips to Fiona's bare leg.

"Sometimes, when we're apart for a long time, it feels like this isn't even real," Mae said, her voice almost a whisper. "Like I could just show up at the club one night and realize I imagined you."

Fiona pulled her cream-colored satin teddy over her shoulders and down to her waist. It gave her great satisfaction to see Mae's eyes sweep over her breasts, to sense that her breathing quickened almost instantly. It gave her an unparalleled thrill to know she had such an effect on the newly minted Delacorte heiress.

"I wish everything were as simple as it is when it is just the two of us," said Mae.

"It's not that complicated." *Especially now that your mother is out of the picture,* Fiona thought. Fiona had never slept as soundly as she had when she snuck into the mansion, then curled up in that four-poster bed, with the silk sheets and the Louis VIII crystal chandelier overhead. It was there that she'd first experienced love with a woman, and while she never expected herself to fancy that—really, she was just along for the ride— somehow in that bedroom fit for royalty, it had felt like the most natural thing in the world. Great sex with cash benefits. If that wasn't the definition of true love, she didn't know what was.

Of course, there was that unpleasant business the night old Mrs. Delacorte caught them. Fiona could honestly say she'd never seen someone so angry. But it was a very contained fury—none of the yelling and throwing things she'd had in her house growing up. No, Mrs. Delacorte's anger was quieter but somehow scarier.

Fiona stopped going to the mansion.

Now that Geraldine was dead, Fiona imagined that not only would she be back to the mansion, she might even move in.

"But it *is* complicated. All the lawyers, my brother . . . my life will be like prison."

"A very lovely prison on the best stretch of Fifth Avenue."

Mae shook her head. "The house is gone."

Fiona sat up, her body suddenly rigid. "Don't tell me she gave it to your brother."

"No—worse. She left it to her charitable foundation."

Fiona searched Mae's face for any hint of a joke—it would be just like Mae. But she felt her stomach drop when she realized from the blankness of Mae's expression that she was telling the truth. It took Fiona only a few seconds to come up with a response that would assert her place in the equation.

"Well, then, we will just have to find you your own house. With your money, and my taste, that shouldn't be a problem."

Mae started to say something, but Fiona silenced her with a rough kiss. Then she sprawled out on her back, pulling Mae's gleaming dark head between her legs.

The editors of *Vogue* magazine had no idea that one of the women on their "most stylish" list was happiest while in bed with another woman—the daughter of a factory worker from the Lower East Side.

From an Irish tenement to Fifth Avenue in one generation. God bless America.

Chapter 5

CHARLOTTE KNEW SHE shouldn't eavesdrop, but William had been behind closed doors with his lawyer for over an hour. Although they spoke in hushed tones, she could still detect the heatedness of the conversation—and she distinctly heard the word "money" bandied about. She wondered if it had to do with her late mother-in-law's will. The reading had been the day before the funeral, and some of it had come as a bit of a surprise.

First, there was the way Geraldine had left a large portion of her financial estate and her grand house to her literary organization instead of to the family. And she had locked up the bulk of Mae's inheritance—except for a monthly stipend—until the girl turned twenty-five! Charlotte couldn't imagine her own parents being so stingy, but then, her own parents hadn't done a very good job of holding on to their money, so who was she to judge? And really, she and William couldn't complain; he inherited Delacorte Properties, the real estate business his father had turned into an empire, *and* they owned the mansion that Geraldine had bought them as a wedding gift. She had never expected any more but had to wonder if William felt the same.

The conversation stopped. Charlotte, heart pounding, jumped away from the door and retreated to the sofa. She rushed back to the sofa and picked up the *New York Sun*; her friend Isobel had told her she *had* to read Greta Goucher's latest gossip column. Charlotte flipped through the pages until she found the woman's byline:

GRETA'S GOTHAM: BY GRETA GOUCHER

The Queen is Dead, Long Live the Queen: With the recent passing of socialite Geraldine Delacorte, tongues are wagging about who will emerge as the new doyenne of Manhattan? Will it be her heir apparent, or—as some suspect—a dark horse waiting in the wings . . .

Charlotte closed the paper in disgust. She couldn't believe people could print such trash. She was just thankful she hadn't said more than a few words to the woman.

The parlor doors opened, and William and his attorney, Charles Paulson, walked into the room.

"Charlotte, a pleasure to see you again." Mr. Paulson nodded to her.

Their butler, Rafferty, showed Mr. Paulson out. Charlotte straightened her long skirt and crossed the room to follow her husband. She looked to her husband for any clue as to his postmeeting state of mind, but he was unreadable as usual.

"Is everything okay?" she asked him.

"Yes, fine. Nothing for you to be concerned about."

She followed him up the stairs toward their bedroom.

"I'm not concerned—just . . . curious."

William looked at her with an expression she couldn't quite interpret. "You better watch that."

"What? My curiosity?"

"Yes. It killed the cat, you know."

Charlotte looked at him, startled.

"What's that supposed to mean?" she said.

"Nothing. Forget it."

In their bedroom, William's clothes were organized and spread out on the bed next to his open suitcase. In a few hours, he would be leaving for a business trip to Boston. Charlotte couldn't imagine what was so urgent that he had to travel while he was still mourning the death of his mother.

"Too bad I can't go with you," Charlotte said. "It would be nice to get away."

William looked at her sharply. "You know that's impractical, Charlotte. No one's wives go on business trips."

"I know. But most women have children to look after. We don't have that issue yet. I wouldn't be a bother. I could sightsee during the day, or shop . . ."

"You live on Fifth Avenue. Why would you need to travel to Boston to shop?"

She ignored the question. Why couldn't he understand that she was bored—and lonely? Maybe she would feel better if she did have a baby to care for, but that didn't seem to be in the cards for them, at least not yet. At age twenty-four and after four years of marriage, her childlessness was a source of increasing anxiety for her. Her late mother-in-law had not hesitated to chime in on the situation.

"The Lord blesses us when and how He sees fit," she told Charlotte. That was all well and good for the Lord, thought Charlotte. But it was little comfort to her.

"Charlotte, have you heard a word I've said to you?" William said.

"What?" Charlotte quickly started folding William's clothes into his suitcase.

"I was saying, spend some time working on the library. Don't just sit in the house gossiping with Isobel Whiting. That would be enough to drive anyone mad."

The library.

While her mother-in-law had generously bequeathed her a few pieces of jewelry from her Van Cleef & Arpels collection, she had also left her a monumental job: Geraldine Delacorte had put Charlotte in charge of the project to turn her mansion into a library.

"I do have a board meeting scheduled for the Women's Literary Alliance," Charlotte said.

"Good. You can tell everyone about the plans for the library."

Charlotte hesitated. "Actually, I think I might keep that news to myself for a few weeks—at least until I've started planning. Once I tell the board, there will be no going back—everyone will be pressing her own agenda on the project." *Especially Amelia Astor,* Charlotte thought but did not say.

But she could tell William had stopped paying attention to what she was saying. He moved close to her and pulled her to him. She could smell the woodsy scent of his pipe smoke still lingering on his clothes, and she willed herself to feel the desire she'd once felt for him.

She didn't know why her feelings for William had changed. It happened so gradually, she had barely noticed it. But it had been a long time—more than a year—since she felt attracted to him.

Charlotte had been a virgin when they met and married. She hadn't waited until her wedding night, but close to it. That first time, his touch had been the most exciting thing she'd ever experienced. If she hadn't felt the physical fireworks she'd read about in romance novels, well, that was probably just the way it was in real life. But to be with a man—a man who had asked her to become his wife . . . it was thrilling. And for the first few years of her marriage, she was content. But after a while, the rules and rigors of being a Delacorte—dictates handed down by Geraldine and followed unquestioningly by William—had made her feel more like another Delacorte sibling than like a wife in charge of her own home. Maybe that was why lately, she preferred to curl up in bed with a novel instead of with her husband.

His hand slipped under her dress, cupping her bottom over her crepe de chine bloomers before tugging them off.

Charlotte lay down on the bed, still wearing her blue silk velvet afternoon dress. She knew their routine and pulled the skirt of her dress above her waist. William, dropping his trousers and underwear, climbed on top of her and began the methodical thrusting that was as predictable as spring rain.

After a few minutes, he shuddered silently and pulled out.

"I'm going to wash up," he said. She didn't know why he bothered to announce it every time.

William walked into the bathroom and closed the door.

Charlotte heard the sink faucets running. Once she was certain William was occupied for a few minutes, she reached her hand down between her legs to touch the throbbing part of her that ached. Moving her hand quickly, she finally felt her own tremors of satisfaction.

Chapter 6

CHARLOTTE SURVEYED THE living room, set with lavish bunches of posies, trays of tea sandwiches, and small bowls filled with dates, salted nuts, and candied ginger. She moved a seat slightly apart from the rest and pulled a small table beside it so she could read her agenda for that morning's Women's Literary Alliance meeting.

"Your first guest is here, madame," said Rafferty.

Charlotte looked up in surprise. She thought she had more time.

"Charlotte, doesn't this room look just like heaven," Amelia said, striding quickly across the peacock-tail carpet and kissing Charlotte on both cheeks. She was dressed impeccably in a navy blue dress with a shawl collar ending in a bow, bishop sleeves, and a layered skirt. She wore a matching blue velvet hat with an asymmetrical brim decorated with pink taffeta roses.

"We do get a lot of sunshine this time of day," Charlotte said.

"Indeed," said Amelia. Charlotte took a seat, but Amelia walked around the couch, pausing to look at the many photos in silver frames. She picked up a portrait of William and Charlotte on their wedding day, looking at it intently. Amelia asked, "Is this a Tiffany frame?"

"Um, yes. It is."

"The engraving is quite smart."

"It was a wedding gift," Charlotte said uncomfortably.

She heard the front doorbell ring and was relieved when Penny brought more members of the board: Isobel Whiting, Susan Hamilton, and Margaret Cavendish. While everyone greeted one another and exchanged compliments on dresses, hats, and the last dinner each had hosted, Charlotte glanced at the brief agenda she had written the night before.

When the group was fully assembled, and Penny had poured everyone a glass of her famous mint iced tea, Charlotte stood.

"Thank you, everyone, for coming. And thank you for your condolences. My husband and I appreciate it. We are comforted by the fact that we at least have Geraldine's work to carry on, and I know you will all . . ."

"It's so difficult to imagine the future of this group without Geraldine," Amelia interrupted. To Charlotte's surprise, she, too, stood. "But I suppose we can console ourselves with the fact that the best tribute to our dear Geraldine is to nurture and grow this organization as Geraldine nurtured all of us." She dabbed at the corners of her eyes with her handkerchief before sitting down.

Charlotte glanced at her friend, Isobel, and resisted the urge to roll her eyes.

"Thank you, Amelia," said Charlotte. "Now, the last time we didn't get to a few items on the agenda because we ran out of time. The summer book drive is . . ."

"I hate to interrupt, but don't you think we should spend our time today on bigger issues of the organization," said Amelia.

Everyone looked at her.

"I'm not sure what you mean," said Charlotte.

Amelia smiled sweetly from her perch on the couch. "Don't you?"

Charlotte felt her stomach tense. It was as if she were in the back of a car that had stopped short. "No, I'm sure I don't," she said.

"The library, of course! Aren't you going to share the news?"

Charlotte looked around the room at the expectant faces turned toward her. But her mind was pulled in too many directions to speak. She didn't know what made her more upset, the fact that William had told Amelia about his mother's library plans or that he did not admit as much to Charlotte during their conversation about the library the night before he left.

"Yes, of course," Charlotte said. "I was . . . I thought I'd save the good news for last."

Rafferty stepped into the room. "Madame Delacorte, your attention is needed in the front hall," he said. Charlotte looked at him and considered telling him that if it was a delivery, simply accept it. But on second thought, she could use a few minutes to compose herself.

"Excuse me," Charlotte said.

Chapter 7

"Is it a delivery?" Charlotte asked Rafferty. It took her two steps to keep up with every one of his long strides. That's what she got for having a butler who was scarcely older than she was. Rafferty was the son of the Delacortes' longtime servant, Eamon. When Charlotte and William married, Geraldine bought them their house. ("If you're going to have an unrefined wife, you at least need a proper home," she had told William at the time—or something to that effect. Right in front of Charlotte.) Geraldine had also assigned Rafferty as their butler. Charlotte knew that her husband would have preferred to find someone older and more experienced. For the first year, she knew he was just waiting for Rafferty to slip up and give him an excuse to fire him. But Rafferty had not given him one.

"No, madame. It's Miss Delacorte. She seems to think you are expecting her."

Mae?

Charlotte couldn't imagine what would inspire an unannounced visit.

"Mae—what a surprise," Charlotte said, thankful that William was not at home. Clearly, his outburst at the funeral had done nothing to dissuade Mae from her flamboyant ways. If anything, she looked more decadent than ever, wearing a black-sequined bandeau across her forehead.

"Really? You didn't know I was coming?" Mae said, walking right into the house as if she owned it, the usual scent of her Joy perfume trailing after her. It was then that Charlotte noticed the two large suitcases.

"I'm afraid not," Charlotte said, still distracted by the fact that Amelia knew about the plans for the library. "William isn't here, and he didn't tell me you were set to visit. But come in, of course. I'm just in the middle of something in the living room."

Mae looked at her as if she were speaking a foreign language.

"Charlotte, my brother didn't tell you?"

"Tell me what?" Charlotte said, her mind racing to remember anything William might have mentioned about his sister.

"I'm coming to live with you," Mae said, her voice heavy with resignation.

Charlotte tried to conceal her shock, but from the look on Mae's face, she was unsuccessful. "How typical of William to leave me to spring this on you," Mae said.

"I . . . he must have told me, and it just slipped my mind," Charlotte said. "Come in, come in. Nothing to worry about. You know you're always welcome here."

"I doubt that's true."

"Don't be silly," Charlotte said with discomfort. "Why don't you come upstairs, and I'll get you settled in the guest room. I think it would be the most comfortable for you. There's a larger bedroom down the hall, but it's not made up right now. I'll have Penny prepare it for you."

"The guest room is fine," Mae said. Even in her state of obvious discomfort, Mae had never looked more beautiful—her eyes bright, her lips painted a deep matte crimson.

"I like your lip rouge," Charlotte said, partly because it was true, partly because she wanted to put her sister-in-law at ease.

"Thanks," Mae said. "The color would look good on you, actually."

"Oh—no. I don't think so," Charlotte said.

"Let me guess: William doesn't like for you to wear makeup."

"Well, he's not terribly modern," said Charlotte.

Mae snorted.

Charlotte led her up the stairs to the second floor.

"Sorry for the interruption," Charlotte said, rejoining the group in the living room.

"Is everything okay?" Amelia asked.

"Oh yes, fine," Charlotte said. "My sister-in-law just dropped by for a visit." Her mind raced. Was it possible to call William at his hotel in Boston? She couldn't recall his mentioning where he was staying. Maybe his office could give her the number. Although she was certain he would be furious with her for bothering him on a business trip, it was his own fault for failing to tell her about Mae.

"Have her join us," Amelia said, standing.

"No!" Charlotte said, and the sharpness of her response made the others look at her strangely. "I mean, she's still in mourning. She probably came here for some peace and quiet."

The others murmured their understanding. Charlotte resumed her place in front of the group.

"As I was saying before the interruption, I have some good news," Charlotte said, speaking almost mechanically. All she could think is that she had to get in touch with William. How could he have forgotten to mention Mae to her? And why would Mae have to move in with them? Surely, the monthly stipend left to her was enough to afford a place of her own. She considered broaching the subject with Mae, but just as quickly dismissed the idea. She would only get the real story from William, and any attempt to talk to Mae about it would only make the poor girl feel that Charlotte was trying to find a way to undo the situation.

"Ladies, would you excuse me for just one more minute?"

Charlotte avoided Isobel's concerned glance, and she hurried out of the room. In her rush to the telephone in the sitting room, she nearly collided with her housekeeper, Penny.

"Oh! I didn't see you!"

"Can I help you with something, madame?"

"Yes. Please bring coffee to the living room." Charlotte closed the door to the sitting room. She hesitated before reaching for the telephone. She wasn't used to William's being out of touch, and she wasn't sure he'd appreciate her bothering him.

"Pauline, this is Mrs. Delacorte. I was wondering if you could give me the number where I can reach my husband at his hotel."

"Oh, I'm terribly sorry, Mrs. Delacorte. I don't have that sort of information." Charlotte found it odd that Pauline didn't know where to reach him. If he was away on business, wouldn't he need his secretary to be able to keep him apprised of what was going on in the office? She told herself not to worry. William would be home soon, and all of this would make sense.

Chapter 8

FIONA SPARKS SLIPPED inside the door of the Vesper Club on West Forty-eighth Street and breathed in the heady, smoke-filled air. The jazz music played loudly, she could smell the earthy tang of red wine, and she was surrounded by banter and drunken laughter.

Of course, she was late again for her cocktail-waitress shift. She was not, however, overly worried about her tardiness. If there was one thing she'd learned after a year at the Vesper, it was that beauty made up for a multitude of sins. In fact, the first day she tried to get a job at the Vesper was an audition for the chorus line. The club's owner, Boom Boom, had been all too quick to tell her that she had no talent, but looks were more important anyway. She was hired on the spot though only as a cocktail waitress.

Fiona had been introduced to bars early in life; by the age of ten, she was running to the corner pub with an empty pitcher and a handful of coins from her grandmother. That was before Prohibition, and the old lady would wake up at midnight and tell her it was time to go "rushing the growler" as she called it. All the bartenders soon recognized her, and by the time she was thirteen, most wouldn't let her leave with the full pitcher of beer until they got a kiss.

Fiona handed her leopard jacket to the coat-check girl even though staff was not supposed to use the coat check.

At nine at night, a circuslike atmosphere at the Vesper had taken hold. As always, within seconds of entering the lavish, Rococo-inspired space, Fiona forgot about the outside world. She never even worried about raids anymore; Boom Boom was paying off the right people, and the alcohol flowed freely.

And then she saw Boom Boom heading toward her, her brightly dyed hair as yellow as an egg yolk, her large frame barreling through the crowd.

"Where have you been?" the big woman said, taking Fiona by the elbow.

"Slow down, Mama Bear. I'm not in the mood to be manhandled right now," she said.

"Well you better get in the mood. I have a table of VIPs up front, and they are asking for you."

"For me? By name?"

"Yes. By name."

"Hmm. Sounds like I'm as big a draw as the dancers. Maybe I should be getting a raise."

Boom Boom handed her a silver tray. "Why don't you worry less about squeezing me and focus on getting a dime off them."

Fiona started heading toward the tables, but Boom Boom again grabbed her by the arm, more forcefully this time.

"Where's your little friend?"

"What friend?"

"Don't play dumb with me. I know you're not usually playing when you act dumb, but we both know exactly who I'm talking about."

Fiona's cheeks burned, but she kept her expression neutral. Boom Boom took her hand off Fiona's arm.

"If Mae Delacorte shows up tonight, tell her I want to see her."

CHARLOTTE STOOD OUTSIDE Mae's room. The door was closed. Charlotte rapped lightly.

"I'm busy."

Good heavens, what kind of manners does this girl have?

"It's Charlotte. I wanted to see if you need anything."

Silence. Charlotte waited, wondering if she should leave. Just as she was about to retreat, the door swung open.

"I'm fine, thanks," Mae said.

The smell of tobacco smoke was overwhelming, so much so that Charlotte took a step back. She composed herself, and said, "I'd like to come in for a moment, please."

The room was in a state Charlotte never could have imagined. Every surface was covered with dresses, scarves, stockings, ropes of beads, hats, and high-heeled shoes. One of the windows was opened completely, but even the breeze couldn't conceal the cigarette smoke.

"Mae, we are happy to have you here. But you simply cannot smoke in this house. This is our home, not a speakeasy," Charlotte said.

Mae sighed and turned her back on Charlotte to—unbelievably—pull even more clothes from a suitcase.

Charlotte walked deeper into the room, marveling at the short, colorful dresses. She ran her hand along the edge of a short red silk dress with beaded fringe on the bottom. It was decadent and elegant at the same time. It was difficult to believe that women now lived their lives in clothes like this, but now that one of those women was living under her own roof, it was impossible to deny.

"Did my brother send you in here to spy on me?" Mae asked. Charlotte pulled her hand away from the dress, suddenly ashamed for admiring it.

"Certainly not. You are our guest, Mae. I'm here to make sure you are comfortable."

"I'd be more comfortable if you gave me some privacy," she said.

Charlotte was speechless.

Mae walked over to the door and held it open for her. Not knowing what else to do, Charlotte walked out.

CHARLOTTE AWOKE TO a noise in the hallway.

Her first thought was that it was morning, and she'd overslept, and Penny was coming to wake her. But no, the room was pitch-black, and she soon realized it was still the middle of the night.

Her heart began to pound, and she lay perfectly still, listening for a repeat of the sound. Instead, she heard a thud on the first floor.

Charlotte couldn't simply lie there and wonder what was going on in her own house. She wished William were there. Why did he have to travel so often lately?

She slipped into her house shoes and pulled on a robe. Slowly and quietly, she opened her bedroom door. The house was still. She glanced above her, listening for sounds on the servants' floor. Nothing.

She inched down the hallway to the guest room, where Mae was sleeping. The door was slightly ajar. Inside, the room was dark.

Charlotte told herself she had imagined the sounds. That was what happened when she slept alone: She was jittery and nervous, and now she was hearing things.

And then there was the distinct sound of the front door closing.

Charlotte turned and rushed down the stairs, nearly taking them two at a time. When she reached the front door, she peeked out of the side windows just in time to catch the rear view of what appeared to be a taxi.

Slowly, Charlotte climbed the stairs. Instead of returning to her room, she once again stood outside the door of the guest room. She listened for any sound, but the house was so quiet, Charlotte could imagine she was deaf.

She pushed the door open wider. The room smelled of cigarette smoke despite the open windows. With the curtains pulled back, enough moonlight filled the room to make it clear that the bed was empty.

Charlotte inhaled sharply. Where had Mae gone at that ungodly hour?

She sat on the pristinely made bed, still set with the decorative pillows that Penny always painstakingly organized. It was clear that Mae had not even attempted to sleep. Charlotte reached over and turned on the bedside lamp. The sudden light made her close her eyes for a second. When she reopened them, she adjusted to the room and focused on the objects scattered on the small table. Mae had left an open pack of Lucky Strikes, a gold-and-ruby ring, and a matchbook. Charlotte briefly considered confiscating the cigarettes; she knew that was what William would want her to do. But she couldn't bring herself to go through with it. Instead, she picked up the matchbook and examined it. It was black with a coat of arms on the front, and in silver lettering it read, THE VESPER CLUB. Charlotte slipped it into the pocket of her robe.

She surveyed the mess of dresses, hosiery in every imaginable color, shoes, hats, and bags everywhere. And what bags! She picked up a black, crocheted, wrist-strap bag with looped fringe and satin lining. It was covered in dark glass beads.

And then she spotted the sleeveless, fringed, red dress still draped over the desk chair.

Charlotte walked over to it, touching it the way she had earlier that day when Mae couldn't wait to usher her out of the room. This time, no one was around to see her or to stop her. The feeling of being alone with that dress was exhilarating.

What if she tried it on? But no, she couldn't do that. Yet she found herself untying her robe and pulling her nightgown over her head.

She stood in front of the antique full-length mirror. It was oval and framed in wood and had once stood in her mother-in-law's childhood bedroom. She had given it to William when he and Charlotte moved into the Fifth Avenue town house. In fact, most of the antique furnishings had been passed on to them from Geraldine Delacorte.

Charlotte looked at her naked body. It was slim and firm, and she had always felt good about it. But now, with the new boyish silhouette being so in vogue, she realized her breasts were perhaps too large. She had read an article recently that the new cupless brassieres would actually flatten her breasts to make them fit better under the more modern dresses.

Without another moment's hesitation, Charlotte pulled the dress from its perch on the back of the wooden desk chair. Slowly, almost with reverence, she undid the zipper, and stepped into it.

Slowly, she turned her eyes to the mirror, and what she saw made her smile. She gathered her long hair in one hand, then draped it so that it looked as if it were only chin length. The shorter style seemed to flatter the lines of her face and jaw and called attention to her large gray eyes. For the first time in as long as she could remember, Charlotte felt beautiful.

Chapter 9

CHARLOTTE SAT UP and looked around the room bright with sunlight. Her breath came in shallow bursts. The dream was still fresh, clinging to her like sweat: She was in the backseat of a car, and it was littered with matchboxes and discarded clothes. Charlotte lay on her back, the straps of her red dress pulled down so that her breasts were exposed. The man from the funeral, Jake Larkin, was stroking her bare skin, teasing her nipples with his light touch. He kissed her mouth, then her neck, and she felt the roughness of his unshaven jawline against her breasts. His hands slid down her body, pulling up her dress. But someone was banging on the car door . . .

"Mrs. Delacorte? Are you awake?" Penny called, knocking on the bedroom door. "I'm sorry to bother you, but there is a phone call."

"Just a minute," Charlotte called out. It was then that she realized her hand was between her legs.

"I don't mean to disturb you," Penny said. "But Mr. Delacorte is on the telephone."

"Thank you, Penny. I'll be right there."

Charlotte quickly pulled on a robe, shaking off the dream, and hurried down the stairs to the sitting room. She noticed, on the way, that Mae's bedroom door was once again closed tightly. Charlotte knew she had left it ajar after her middle-of-the-night visit, so at least Mae had, at some point, returned home.

Sunshine filled the room, a space that was used less formally than the parlor. It was the only room with pieces of furniture Charlotte had brought from her life before she married into the Delacorte family: a chestnut end table, an antique clock. This was also the room that held the books she'd been collecting since she was a girl.

She gathered her long robe and sat on the chair nearest the telephone.

"Hello?" she said, surprised at her nervousness.

"Charlotte, were you still asleep? It's nine in the morning," William said.

"No—I'm awake," she said. The sound of his voice grounded her reality. The silly dream seemed much less important. Still, the thought of it made her feel guilty.

"My office said you rang yesterday. Is everything all right?"

"I told Pauline not to trouble you," Charlotte said.

"Well, she did. Now what was so urgent?"

"Your sister arrived yesterday."

Silence. Then, "I'm sorry. I wasn't expecting her for another week."

"I wasn't expecting her at all," Charlotte said.

"I *apologized,* Charlotte," he said. "Things have been busy lately, and I'm managing everything the best I can."

"Is it true that she's going to be living with us?"

"For the foreseeable future, yes."

"But why?"

"I need to keep an eye on her. She's bound to bring scandal on the family with the way she behaves. And now that Mother is gone, it's more important than ever that I maintain our reputation and our business. We can't afford any negative attention. So I need your support on this. Did she go out last night?"

Charlotte hesitated for a moment. "I don't think so," she finally said, uncertain why she lied.

"Good. Please keep an eye on her until I return."

Since she didn't particularly relish the idea of being awakened in the middle of the night again, she decided she would have a talk with her sister-in-law.

CHARLOTTE SPREAD THE architect's drawings over the living-room coffee table. Penny had set out tea sandwiches.

"Do you see how walls will have to be added in order to provide shelf space?" she said to Isobel, whom she had enlisted for the library project. If she was going to spend the foreseeable future doing the bidding of her late mother-in-law, she would at least have a friend by her side.

"I think one of these rooms needs to be preserved as it is for table reading."

"You're right." Charlotte made a small mark in pencil. She could feel her friend's eyes on her.

"Is everything okay?" Isobel asked.

"Yes—I can give the architect notes. He works for me, after all."

"I don't mean about that. You don't seem yourself."

"I'm just tired. I didn't sleep much last night."

Hours after Charlotte had returned to her bed, she had sat awake, waiting to hear Mae's return. And when she finally did fall asleep, she had that unspeakable dream.

"Is someone else here?" Isobel said. Only then did Charlotte hear the voices in the hall. She was certain it was Mae, finally awake. But who on earth was she talking to?

"Will you excuse me for a minute?"

Charlotte strode quickly to the doors, swung them open with as much authority as she could muster, and was startled to find a beautiful redhead in her hallway. Her face was very pale, her hair long and loose over her shoulders. Mae was hanging on her arm, wearing a hot pink velour negligee trimmed with ostrich feathers. Her own eyes were smudged with dark cosmetics she'd evidently worn to sleep, and her short-cropped hair was askew.

"What is going on here?" said Charlotte.

"My friend was just leaving," said Mae.

The redhead looked at Charlotte brazenly, her catlike green eyes meeting Charlotte's with disconcerting directness.

Charlotte assessed the situation, confused at how the girl could have come to the house for a visit in the middle of the afternoon and Rafferty not alert her that they had a visitor. Then she took in the spangly gold dress, the girl's evening bag . . . and Charlotte realized that Mae's friend had spent the night.

"You must leave," Charlotte said uncomfortably, opening the front door. And then, to Charlotte's utter shock, the redhead leaned over and kissed Mae, her mouth lingering on hers as if she were tasting something delicious. Charlotte noticed how Mae's entire body seemed to wilt with desire. Charlotte was both appalled and strangely aroused by the brazen display.

Charlotte cleared her throat. The redhead didn't even glance at her on her way out the door.

Charlotte slammed it closed.

"Why must you concern yourself with everything I do?" Mae said before turning to run back upstairs.

Charlotte took a minute to collect herself, then followed her.

"Mae, I don't know how you were conducting yourself when you were living with your mother, but I can't imagine that she was condoning this behavior." She heard William's voice in her head, *she's bound to bring scandal on the family.* . . .

"Jesus, Charlotte. I mean, if you want to live your life like it's still 1890, that's your business. But you can't tell me how to live mine."

With that, Mae returned to the second floor, leaving Charlotte staring after her. It took a moment for Charlotte to remember that

Isobel was waiting for her in the living room, and she immediately said a silent prayer that nothing had been overheard.

She took a deep breath and told herself that William would be home in two days to deal with Mae. As far as she was concerned, she was done.

Chapter 10

ROGER WARREN OPENED the bronze-handled door of the new art deco building on the corner of Nineteenth Street, bought and paid for by the taxpayers of New York City. Bright and modern and imbued with the sheen of importance, it wasn't a bad place to report to work. Unless, of course, you worked under a boss who had become messianic.

Not for the first time, Roger lamented his misfortune to be a staff lawyer in the U.S Attorney's Office during a term when the U.S. Attorney had it in for Prohibition-enforcement agents.

"They're bigger fucking criminals than the bootleggers," Emory Buckner said.

No shit, Roger thought. Everyone knew that the whole city was rotting from the head.

Determined to avoid the corruption that had plagued his predecessor's time in office, Emory Buckner had the brilliant idea to handpick half a dozen staff members to go undercover and infiltrate the city's nightclubs. He believed in the initiative so strongly, he paid for it with his own money. They were calling it Operation White Lightning.

And so, instead of filing paperwork and spending their days at the courthouses, Roger's colleagues were infiltrating the clubs of Manhattan every night, looking for leads that would bring them to the rum runners and distributors at the top of the illegal booze trade. Roger, only two years out of law school and a new father, had avoided the insanity. He fought the good fight from behind his desk, where he belonged.

Roger took the elevator to the eighth floor. His briefcase was filled with casework. With every passing week, the courts became more and more clogged with Volstead Act violations. Prosecuting the cases was like killing a roach on his kitchen floor—a temporary sense of accomplishment, then the depressing reality of finding five more where that one came from.

"Morning, Anne," he said to his secretary.

"Good morning, Mr. Warren."

Roger opened his office door and almost jumped back in surprise.

"Good morning, Warren," said Emory Buckner from his perch in Roger's chair, his feet up on his desk.

"Did I miss a meeting? Am I late?" Roger said nervously. He had never seen his boss in his office, and he wasn't happy to start now.

"You are right on time," said Buckner, standing up. "Keep your coat on. We're taking a little ride."

A government-issued black Ford was idling outside the building, Buckner's driver at the wheel. Roger sat in the backseat, alongside his boss.

"Where are we going?" Roger said.

"New Jersey."

That was not what Roger wanted to hear.

One of the biggest lines of rum running was off the New Jersey coast. He also knew that liquor brought in from Cuba to southern Florida was loaded onto false-bottom Pullman train cars. The cars, headed to New York, stopped in Secaucus, where the liquor was unloaded.

Buckner was silent for the half-hour ride. Roger didn't ask any questions because he didn't want to know the answers.

Roger wished he had a cigarette on him. His wife had made him quit. She had some crazy idea it was bad for the baby. Who ever heard of such a thing? Roger's buddies said motherhood makes women half lose their minds, and he was seeing that was an understatement. Not to mention the fact that since the baby was born, physical relations between them had all but stopped. None of his friends mentioned that particular phenomenon, and he wasn't about to be the first one to volunteer the information.

The car pulled off the highway and followed a local road for a mile and a half.

"Do you want to go up the drive or wait for the other cars?"

"Wait here." Buckner consulted his watch. "We're early."

Roger looked around nervously. Sure enough, a few minutes later, a fleet of marked police cars passed them at high speed before turning right a few yards past them.

"Go!" said Buckner. The driver took off at high speed, and Roger gripped his seat.

Chapter 11

THEY SPED UP at dirt driveway, and after they cleared a wide patch of land and pine trees, a large brick building came into view. It was surrounded by the police cars, which were manned by officers braced behind open front doors, down on one knee, their Thompson submachine guns fixed at the building's entrance, exits, and windows.

"Jesus, Emory. What are we doing here?" Roger said. What he meant, of course, was what am *I* doing here?

"Lenny Sugarfield. He's been running a flat-bottom skiff through Raritan Bay, then off-loading to this warehouse."

"Is this . . . surveillance?"

Buckner looked at him like he had a few screws loose.

"Do I do surveillance?"

"No."

"Do you?"

"No."

"So why the hell would I bring you here to do surveillance?"

"But this isn't even our district. I don't get why . . ."

"Warren, do rum runners stay in designated little districts?"

"No," he said, yet again.

"And where does most of the alcohol end up?"

"Manhattan," Roger said.

"That's right. So I don't give a goddamn about districts. None of us do. We're all working together. And it would be nice if you would get with the program. Now, when our guys come out, we go in next. We need to be quick because the guys on the ground will get any of his men on the premises. But other people could show up. So in and out." He reached below his seat and handed Roger a large sack, the kind a mail carrier might use. "I want any papers you can get your hands on: ledgers, calendars, notes, letters— don't think about what means what, just get it all out of there."

"We have a warrant?"

Buckner shot him a look. "Take anything you can get your hands on."

Roger kept his eyes on the warehouse. Even from the distance of the car, he could hear shouting. He thought it was the height of stupidity to wait in the car like sitting ducks. He didn't want to go into the building, but it might be better than being a waiting target.

"Keep your hands where I can see them," he heard the officers yelling. One by one, men filed out of the front door, their hands folded behind their heads with their elbows out to the sides.

Buckner jumped out of the car. "Where's Sugarfield?" he said.

"They got him," called one of the officers. "Took him out the back."

"Is it clear?" Buckner said.

"Go in," said the officer.

Buckner waved Roger along. Roger felt his heart beat fast. He slammed the car door and trotted up behind Buckner.

"Remember—take anything you see, and do it quick. In and out."

At first, all Roger could see were bottles of liquor—crates of it, shelves of it, bottles in rows on tables and bottles tagged on the floor. The inventory was being tended by the officers. Buckner steered Roger to steps leading to the second floor.

"Look for an office."

They filed up the narrow stairway and down a hallway that only got light from the floor below. The hallway was open to the interior of the warehouse, so that if Roger leaned over the ledge, he could fall to the first floor below. Still, Roger felt a sense of claustrophobia in the narrow walkway.

The hall divided. Buckner went left and pointed for Roger to go right. Almost immediately, Roger saw light coming from an open doorway. He stood close to the wall, then slowly peered around the corner of the doorway. He saw a desk, a phone, and piles of paper. No one was inside.

Roger opened his sack and swept the contents of the desk into it. He found a small filing cabinet and emptied it.

The phone rang, and Roger nearly jumped out of his skin.

Ring. Ring. Ring.

He froze, praying for it to stop, as if the phone were a beacon that would lead anyone still in the building directly to him. He knew it was irrational—who would run to answer a phone in the middle of a raid? Still, he didn't move until the phone fell silent.

Roger found a small trash bin and emptied its contents into the

sack. There was a map of the United States on the wall, but he left
it there. Then he noticed faint pencil markings on it and decided
to err on the safe side. He pulled it down, tearing the edges, and
folded it in half before shoving it in the bag.

And then he heard the shots.

Instinctively, Roger dropped to the floor. He tried to crawl
under the desk but couldn't fit his entire six-foot-two frame. More
shots.

"Man down," he heard someone yell from the first floor, and
Roger was certain it was the voice of one of the officers.

"Warren!" Buckner called from somewhere down the hall.

Roger couldn't respond. He'd never heard live gunshots before, and it sounded like they were right on top of him. He pressed
himself closer to the desk, clutching the sack of papers for dear
life.

Chapter 12

AGAIN, CHARLOTTE WAS awakened by a noise on this stairs in
the middle of the night. But this time, she was ready for it.

Pulling on her robe, Charlotte rushed into the dark hallway.
Without bothering to check Mae's bedroom door, she hurried down
the stairs, where she found Mae standing at the front door in the
dark, looking out the window.

"Waiting for your cab?" said Charlotte.

"Jesus Christ, you scared me!" Mae spun around, putting her
hand over her heart.

"How do you think I feel being awakened in the middle of the
night?"

"I'm sorry, Charlotte."

"This has to stop. Your brother won't stand for this." Charlotte didn't know what made her more angry, the fact that she was again awake at some ungodly hour or that Mae had so little respect for her. She felt pathetic having to invoke William as some sort of threat, but clearly she had no authority of her own.

A car pulled up to the curb. Even in the dark, Charlotte could see that it was the same absurdly colored Model T that had deposited Mae at the funeral.

"I have to go," Mae said.

"Mae, I forbid you to leave this house."

Mae ignored her and hurried to the curb. Charlotte left the door ajar and ran after her.

Heart pounding, she reached the car just as Mae closed the passenger-side door.

"Mrs. Delacorte! We meet again. Great to see you," said Jake Larkin from the driver's seat. He wore a snap-brim hat and the same insolent smile she remembered all too well from the day of the funeral. And those intense, dark eyes . . .

She was on her back, the straps of her red dress pulled down so that her breasts were exposed. Jake was stroking her bare skin, teasing her nipples with his light touch. . . .

Charlotte wished that she'd had the time to put on an overcoat. She held her robe closed and crossed her arms over her chest. *Say something,* she told herself. She shifted uncomfortably.

"Do you have any idea what time it is?" she said, then immediately felt foolish. She sounded like a schoolmarm.

Jake turned to Mae at his side. "What time is it?"

"Time to go," said Mae, pulling out a compact and applying more lipstick.

"I apologize for the disturbance," Jake said, his eyes bright with mischief.

They stared at each other, and her heart beat fast. She was furious.

"This is unacceptable, Mr. Larkin,"

"Have a good night." He tipped his hat at her, then drove away. Charlotte stood helplessly at the edge of the street.

This was outrageous. And she would never be able to fall back asleep.

Charlotte returned to the house with a sense of resignation, but by the time she reached her bedroom, her anger had returned.

She didn't know what to do, but she did know that she couldn't sit in the house a minute longer. She was going to finish the conversation she had started with Mae.

Charlotte dug her hands into the deep pocket of her robe and pulled out the matchbook she had pilfered from Mae's room. She turned it over, reading the silver lettering on the front and the back.

And then she quickly got dressed.

A BRIGHT PINK neon sign marked the Vesper Club on Forty-eighth Street and Broadway. Outside, women clustered in pairs and groups, dressed in colorful dresses, as flamboyant as wild birds. Their cigarettes created a cloud of smoke, and from somewhere came the sharp riffs of a trombone.

"Good heavens," Charlotte said before stepping out of the cab. She walked through the people on the crowded sidewalk.

At the door of the club, she was met by a gentleman in a dark suit and wearing a fedora.

"Good evening, madame," he said. "May I check your coat?"

She smiled. It was so civilized! Was this what all the fuss was about—the corruptive nightclubs?

"The *couvert* tonight is five dollars," the man said to her.

"Excuse me?"

"The admittance fee. Five dollars."

Charlotte opened her purse, her heart pounding. She only had enough money left in her wallet for the return cab ride home.

She handed the man her last few dollars.

The man opened the door, leaving Charlotte to walk self-consciously out of the vestibule into a crowded room filled with the rich sound of a saxophone, smoke, and giddy laughter. The walls were a sugary pastel pink, and overhead hung a Rococo iron-and-crystal chandelier. But what struck her immediately was the wall covered with an enormous reproduction of William-Adolphe Bouguereau's *The Birth of Venus*. It was an unmistakable painting, with its nude Venus front and center, standing on an oyster shell, her long red hair flowing behind her as various centaurs, angels, cupids, and nude maidens surround her.

And everywhere: mirrors. Mirrors on the walls, mirrored tabletops, and in one room she passed through, a mirrored ceiling. These made it impossible to miss the fact that the patrons were all—every last one of them—drinking alcohol.

It was like a scene out of a movie.

Room after room was filled with beautiful people talking in animated groups, couples huddled with their arms locked around each other. Waitresses in short dresses carried trays filled with colorful drinks. No one paid her any notice. It was as if she were invisible.

She told herself she would just find Mae, tell her she had to leave, and they would return home. As she walked through the club, the electrifying riffs of the jazz band grew louder. She spotted another Bouguereau painting featuring nude women, this one *Nymphs and Satyr*. Here and there, couples danced alongside tables and in the middle of the floor. Charlotte scanned the crowd, and finally spotted her sister-in-law's slender frame and short dark hair. Mae, talking to a woman holding a tray of cocktails, looked radiantly happy. Charlotte realized Mae was talking to the same woman she'd brought to the house.

Charlotte took a deep breath and marched over to them. She tapped Mae on the shoulder.

"I need to have a word with you," she said.

Chapter 13

MAE LOOKED AT her blankly for a moment, as if it didn't quite register that it was Charlotte. Then she covered her mouth with one hand.

"Good lord! What are you *doing* here?" Mae said.

"I came to find you."

"Well, you've found me. Now you can go back home."

"I'm not leaving without you."

Mae shook her head and took Charlotte by the hand, tugging her impatiently to a back corner of the room.

"You can't *be* here, Charlotte. Do you want Greta Goucher to write about you in her column? My brother would positively murder you if he found out about this."

"So let's go home."

"And, Charlotte, what on earth are you wearing? You're lucky they let you inside wearing that getup."

Charlotte looked down at her gray ankle-length, draped-silk velvet evening gown with a boat neckline and silk floral embroidery. She had left the house feeling very smartly dressed but could see now that it was all wrong. All around her, women frolicked in short dresses—black and silver and gold. They wore diamond pendants and beaded necklaces, and their short hair was adorned with headbands with beading and feathers. Mae was perhaps the brightest, shiniest, star of them all: She wore a beaded, black lace dress that fell just below her knees and plunged low in the back. She wore a red chiffon scarf and a red silk flower on her hip. Ropes of pearls fell down her back across her bare flesh.

Mae took her by the hand and tugged her toward a bar near

the back of the first room. They sat down on two padded bar-stools. "Jimmy, give me two sidecars."

"Who's your pretty friend?" Jimmy asked, smiling at Char-lotte. "I know I haven't seen you here before. I'd remember."

"Oh, this is"—Mae looked Charlotte up and down—"this is Grey. My friend Grey."

"Pleased to meet you, Grey. How do you like our little party, here?"

"It's really something," Charlotte said.

"Two sidecars, coming right up," Jimmy said.

Mae turned to Charlotte. "I can scarcely imagine what brought you out here tonight—or how you found me. But you really have to leave after this drink. You're just going to get yourself—and me—into trouble."

"You're the one who is going to get *me* in trouble," Charlotte said. "William doesn't want you running around at all hours like this, and while he's away, you're my responsibility. So after this one drink, we both leave." She looked around to make sure no one nearby could hear her. "And for the record, I don't understand how this place gets away with serving alcohol out in the open like this."

"There are ways to keep Prohibition agents happy—and si-lent," said Mae.

Jimmy reappeared, handing them both yellow cocktails, the rims dusted with sugar and garnished with wedges of orange.

"Cheers," Mae said. Charlotte touched her glass to hers. Mae took a long swallow, but Charlotte didn't dare take a sip.

"Oh, Charlotte, live a little. If you're not going to leave, you have to at least have some fun. Otherwise, you'll ruin my good time."

Charlotte brought the glass to her lips, then licked some sugar off the rim. The sweetness emboldened her, and she took a small sip of the drink. It was sweet and sour and filled her throat with a warmth that made her feel giddy. It was her first taste of alcohol since the champagne her father had brought to her wedding.

She felt a pang at the thought of her father. It had broken her heart to ask him to leave the reception following Geraldine's funeral. But he had understood. Oh, her father! He hadn't done much for the Andover name or the Andover fortune—what was left of it. But he was the most handsome, charming, downright roguish character she'd ever met. And while her mother had encouraged her to marry a different sort of man—a safer man—Charlotte doubted that her mother would have done anything different with her own life given a second chance.

"Do me a favor and don't get crocked," said Mae.

"What? Of course not." Charlotte put the drink down on the bar. "So where's your friend?"

"Which one?"

"The one who drove you here."

"Jake? Oh, he's not here. He hates the big clubs."

Charlotte was shocked by her disappointment.

A large woman with yellow hair peaking out of a gold lame turban sauntered over to them. She waved her cigarette in Mae's face.

"I need a word with you, Miss Delacorte," she said.

"Save my seat," Mae said to Charlotte.

Even as they walked away, Charlotte could see that the over-sized, brassy blonde was telling Mae something she did not want to hear. Mae stopped in her tracks, and the woman grabbed her by the arm brusquely. Mae shook off her hand and returned to Charlotte.

"Let's get out of here," Mae said quickly.

Confused, Charlotte jumped up from her seat and followed Mae to the door. Along the way, Mae tapped on the shoulder of a statuesque woman wearing a short dress fringed with peacock feathers.

"Betty, are you off yet?" Mae said to her. "I need a ride to the juice joint."

The woman looked at Charlotte. "What's with that getup? Did you come from a costume party?"

"Don't mind her," said Mae. "She was just leaving. Grey, this is where we say good night. I'll help you find a cab."

Charlotte didn't know what a "juice joint" was, but she did know that she had zero intention of going home without Mae.

"I'm going with you," she said.

Chapter 14

IT SEEMED UNLIKELY they would find a club on the dark and quiet street. The sleepy Greenwich Village block seemed to house nothing but closed storefronts. And yet Betty—the woman in the peacock-feathered dress—parked the car and turned off the engine.

"Nothing seems open," Charlotte said, stepping out of the backseat. Mae rode in the front alongside Betty.

"Oh, it's open all right. If you know where to look," said Mae.

Charlotte followed them to a building at the edge of the street. On the corner was a cigar store. Then just beyond it, a sign advertised a tailor shop. They went around the side of the tailor shop, into an unlit alley, and down a flight of stairs. Mae reached for Charlotte's hand to guide her. Before she reached the last step, Charlotte could hear the sound of jazz.

Mae knocked on the door. It opened a few inches but remained chained. From behind the door, a male voice asked, "Who is it?"

"Giggle water," said Mae.

Charlotte looked at her.

"Password," Mae explained.

The door opened.

Charlotte, utterly confused, let the other two walk in front of her.

It was a single room, with dark sheets covering the windows and a red sheet stretched across the ceiling in what Charlotte could only assume was a makeshift attempt at decoration. And the source of the loud music was a crowd of musicians seated on the sparse and ramshackle furniture. The air in the room was heavy with smoke and smelled slightly sweet. The musicians were colored.

One of the men stood in the center of the room playing the trumpet. He was clearly the focus of everyone's attention.

Charlotte knew she should leave, but the idea of wandering around the quiet side street alone looking for a cab was unthinkable. She would have to convince Mae to leave with her, and she knew that was easier said than done.

"It's getting late," she said.

"So get a drink and relax," said Mae. She tugged on Betty's handbag to get her attention. "Take Grey to the bar."

"Come along," said Betty. "Stop being such a flat tire."

Charlotte felt certain that police would be banging the door down any moment. If Mae wanted to put herself in this kind of situation, there was nothing Charlotte could do to stop her. But she certainly wasn't going to go down with her. Maybe she should ask Betty to help her find a cab.

The "bar"—if you could call it that—was a long wooden table set in front of a basin sink.

"What are you having?" Betty said. "They don't have all the fancy stuff like at the Vesper, but it's good and stiff. I'd stick with the gin if I were you." She pulled out a barstool, and Charlotte sat down next to her. The bartender, his back to them, was busy shaking a cocktail in a metal mixer.

"After you order a drink, do you think you could help me get a cab?" Charlotte said to her.

"Horsefeathers!" Betty said, slamming her hand on the bar.

Charlotte took that as a no.

Aside from dashing her hopes of making a quick exit, Betty's outburst got the attention of the bartender. He straightened up and turned to them.

"Well, well, well, look what the cat dragged in," he said.

Charlotte nearly lost her balance on the stool.

"I guess I'll put manners first, drink order second," said Betty. "Jake, this is our new friend, Grey. Grey, this is Jake Larkin. And I'll have my usual."

Jake pulled a bottle from underneath the table, dropped some ice in a glass, and poured until it was full. All the while, he kept his unnerving dark eyes on Charlotte.

"Welcome . . . Grey, is it?" Jake said with a knowing smile. Charlotte said nothing. She knew now was the time to get out of there—just to save herself any further embarrassment or trouble. But, suddenly, she didn't want to go.

"You're not here to ask me to leave my own establishment, are you, *Grey*?"

"What an odd thing to say." Betty laughed flirtatiously. "You slay me."

"This is your place?" Charlotte said.

But Jake didn't respond. He was busy pouring a drink for the trumpet player, who was now standing with them at the bar.

"When do you leave for Chicago, Louis?" said Jake.

"As soon as the missus packs our bags," the man replied. His face was round, and his hands were enormous.

"Mr. Armstrong here plays for the Fletcher Henderson Orchestra," Jake said to Charlotte. Or maybe he was talking to Betty. "But we're losing him to the Windy City."

"Oh, you simply can't go," said Betty, as if she were deeply invested in this issue. "There is no city like New York. I have been all over, and take it from me, Mr. Armstrong—you might leave for now, but you will be back."

Jake put a drink in front of Charlotte. She took a small sip.

"Mr. Armstrong, do you know that fellow over there with the guitar?" Betty said. "I like the look of him."

"I would be happy to introduce you," said the trumpet player, and they left the bar, drinks in hand.

Charlotte and Jake glanced at one another, but neither spoke.

"I should be going," she said uncomfortably.

"I would imagine so," he said, again with that infuriating smile.

Charlotte shifted uncomfortably.

"I feel silly asking you this, but do you think you might help me call a cab?" she said.

"I'm afraid I can't do that," Jake said.

"Why on earth not?"

"To put it simply, I don't want to draw attention to our little party here. Believe it or not, there are some folks who don't approve of our fun-loving ways. You can understand that, can't you, *Grey*?"

Charlotte looked down at her drink.

"But I'll tell you what. Since I already know where you live, I'd be happy to drive you home myself."

She was in the backseat of a car, and it was littered with matchboxes and discarded clothes. She lay on her back, the straps of her red dress pulled down so that her breasts were exposed. He was stroking her bare skin, teasing her nipples with his light touch. He kissed her mouth, then her neck, and she felt the roughness of his unshaven jawline against her breasts. His hands slid down her body, pulling up her dress. . . .

She swallowed hard, averting her eyes. "You're not serious."

"I am serious—especially about not wanting a cab showing up here."

"How can you leave if you're . . . working."

"Anyone can pour a drink. There's not a person here who doesn't know his or her way around a bottle. So are we going?"

"I . . . yes, okay. Thank you for the offer," Charlotte said, warmth flooding her body.

"See if Mae wants a ride, too."

Charlotte, inexplicably, felt a stab of disappointment.

"Of course," she said, almost stammering.

She found Mae lounging on a dilapidated couch, smoking a cigarette and laughing.

"Are you ready to leave? Jake is giving us a ride home."

Mae looked at her, glassy-eyed.

"No, I'm not ready to leave. Fiona is meeting me here when she gets off work. And what do you mean Jake is giving you a ride home?"

Charlotte felt herself blush. "He's giving *us* a ride home," she corrected.

"Since I just said I'm not leaving, he's giving *you* a ride."

"He doesn't want me calling a cab," said Charlotte.

Mae laughed. "I'll bet. Go—don't worry about me."

"Don't bring Fiona back to the house," Charlotte said.

Mae leaned forward and gestured for Charlotte to bend down to hear her. "I think you'd best just worry about your own company tonight," she said.

Chapter 15

CHARLOTTE FOUND JAKE waiting for her at the door, his keys in hand. He tossed them to Charlotte, and she caught them.

"I'm driving," he said. "Just testing your reflexes."

"Mr. Larkin, on second thought, I think it's best if I stay a bit. Mae isn't ready to go just yet, and I can't very well leave her here."

Jake smiled. "I think you worry too much," he said.

"I'm not worried. It's simply that Mae is my responsibility."

"I think it's the other way around. From what I've seen, Mae can take care of herself. You, on the other hand . . ."

Charlotte shook her head. "Why must you always insult me?"

He laughed, and Charlotte felt the blood rush to her cheeks. "Glad to be your source of amusement," she said, walking away. He grabbed her arm, and as soon as she felt his touch, she didn't want him to let go.

"Now don't go off in a huff," he said. "As long as you're going to hang around a while, you might as well enjoy yourself. Let me introduce you around. And I'm not using that silly alias you came in here with. There's no need for that here. There are people in this joint with much bigger names than yours."

And as Charlotte allowed Jake to lead her around the room, making introductions, she found that what he said was true: There were indeed much bigger names than her own. There was the long-haired painter, Georgia O'Keeffe, and her new husband, Alfred, who took photographs. There was the Italian fashion designer, Elsa Schiaparelli, who was complaining to Charlotte that her husband never went out at night with her. And then, unbelievably, there was actress Marion Davies, huddled with friends in a corner of the room. It was clear she didn't want to be bothered, and who could blame her, given her scandalous relationship with William Randolph Hearst.

As for the musicians, she didn't recognize any of them. There were piano players, saxophone players, guitar players, and even someone on the banjo. They were all men, mostly Negro, and it was evident they preferred to play their instruments rather than waste time with conversation. Jake assured her that although she had never heard of them, someday their names would be recognized all over the country, if not the world.

Charlotte felt embarrassed that she had no talent to speak of:

She didn't paint, she didn't design clothes, and she didn't write or play music. And yet everyone seemed fascinated with her all the same.

"You have the one thing no one else here has," said Jake. "Money."

Charlotte looked around the room, suddenly feeling even more like an outsider. She gulped her gin.

"Surely, these talented people make money."

"They make artist money—not heiress money."

"I'm not an heiress," she said.

"Well, most people would think that's bull. But I don't care how much dough you or anyone else has. I just like people who are interesting."

Emboldened by the contents of her glass, Charlotte said, "And do I make the cut?"

He looked her up and down, his face locked in exaggerated concentration.

She instantly regretted the question.

"It's a little early to call the game," he said.

Charlotte set her drink down and walked away. She was tempted to glance back and see if he was watching her, but she resisted.

She found Mae still sitting on the couch, smoking a cigarette with one hand and holding a drink with the other.

"Have you seen Fiona?" Mae said. Charlotte sat down. Mae offered her a sip of her drink, and Charlotte took it. It was straight gin, barely chilled. Charlotte forced herself to swallow. The slow-spreading warmth in her throat was worth the hard taste.

"I don't want to go back to that house," Mae said, staring at the crowd.

"Well, don't take this the wrong way, but no one forced you to move in. I don't understand why you showed up here this week, but I suppose that's a conversation I should have with my husband."

"I'll save you the trouble—since my brother clearly has no

interest in keeping you *au courant*." Mae focused her big blue eyes on Charlotte. "I have no choice but to live with you. As you know, the home that I grew up in is going to become some ridiculous library. And I can't buy a place of my own: Mother left my entire inheritance in a trust until I'm twenty-five. I have to rely on William to give me an allowance—as if I'm a child!"

"He didn't tell me." Charlotte put her hand on Mae's arm. She didn't understand why William had kept that from her. "But I can talk to William, get him to advance you some money so you can have some independence."

Mae shook her head, a strange smile on her lips. "You don't get it. They don't want me to have independence. Mother wanted William to control me. Lord knows she was never able to." Mae put her cigarette out in a glass and promptly lit another. "But there is something I need money for—and quickly."

"Of course. Just name it."

"I have a two-thousand-dollar debt to the Vesper Club. Maybe a little more. That's what the owner was yelling at me about tonight."

"Mae! How could you spend so much money there?"

"Very easily, trust me," she responded, shrugging.

"I'll talk to William. I know he has money to give you every month, but it might take some time to convince him . . ."

"I don't have time; Boom Boom is threatening to tell the gossip columns about Fiona and me."

Charlotte took a sharp breath. "And what is there to tell, Mae?"

Mae rolled her eyes. "Don't you know?"

Charlotte looked away. "I'll talk to William," Charlotte repeated. "Does he know about your . . . friend?"

Mae shrugged. Then, like a sun-shower clearing, her face broke into a smile. "She's here."

Charlotte didn't have to ask who she meant. She looked through the crowd, and, sure enough, Fiona Sparks was making her entrance. With her red hair tumbling over her shoulders and her red-beaded dress, she was impossible to miss. Charlotte turned to talk to Mae, but she was already gone.

Fiona, barely out of her coat, was already the center of attention. Along with two other women, she formed a makeshift chorus line, kicking up their legs and passing a bottle back and forth. Mae joined in, and the crowd in the room arranged itself for maximum viewing. A few of the saxophone players started up to offer the girls a jaunty tune, and couples got out on the floor. Jake tried to wave her over, but Charlotte pretended not to see him.

One of the colored men and colored women broke into a fast-moving, mesmerizing dance she had never seen before. At first, it looked like the Charleston—but then the woman did a backflip over the arm of the man. Charlotte gasped, and in her complete absorption in the show the couple was putting on, she failed to realize that Jake was standing next to the couch.

"Come on," he said. "You can't just sit here."

"Oh, I'm not going to dance."

"Look, the only price of admission here is participation. Now let's go." He held out his hand, and Charlotte—noting that the number of people on the dance floor was surpassing the crowd of onlookers—reluctantly took it.

"What is that dance they're doing?" she said, letting Jake twirl her slowly.

"The Lindy Hop. Just let me lead. You'll pick it up."

Charlotte did her best to follow Jake, but the moves were nothing like the quadrilles or waltzes she had been taught. She tripped over her dress, and suddenly the shorter frocks worn by the flappers seemed less for shock value and simply a matter of practicality. It seemed impossible to get it all right, so she just gave up and moved her feet as quickly as she could to mimic Jake's turns and stomps, trying to trust him enough to lean back or twirl when needed.

"Now you're on the trolley!" he said, smiling at her broadly. She smiled back, not caring how much she was botching the steps: It felt fantastic.

When she was completely breathless, she pulled Jake's hand to go off to the side.

"It's so warm in here," she said, finding her purse on the couch and retrieving a handkerchief. She wiped at her damp brow.

"You're a regular Oliver Twist," he said.

She shook her head. "I could barely keep up with you."

One of the musicians passed Jake a glass of gin, and he passed it to her. She took a gulp, then sank back onto the sofa. She closed her eyes, and the room tilted.

Chapter 16

"CHARLOTTE, GET UP. It's morning!"

Charlotte felt herself rocking, as if she were on a boat. She opened her eyes slowly although doing so intensified the feeling of a weight crushing her skull.

"Don't shake me," Charlotte said, her mouth so dry her tongue could barely form the words. In front of her, Mae blinked with concern.

"We have to leave," she said.

Charlotte didn't know why she would have to leave her bedroom, especially when she felt so ill. And then she looked around the room—distressingly shabby in the stark light of day—littered with discarded bottles and strange people draped over furniture or passed out on the floor.

"Oh, my good Lord. What time is it?"

"It's nearly ten."

"We have to get home," Charlotte mumbled. And then she had a thought that made her liquor-soured stomach tighten into a knot: Was it possible that this would be the day that William returned home? He had said a day or two. When had that been? Yesterday? Two days ago? She was so disoriented, it was as if she had been asleep on that couch for a week.

"I went upstairs to Jake's apartment," Mae said calmly. "He's getting dressed now and will drive us."

At the mention of Jake, Charlotte's first thought was that she must look a fright. And then she realized the absurdity of that concern considering the situation she was in. She forced herself off the couch and looked around the floor for her handbag.

"Ladies, I hope you slept well. I always consider it a successful night when it concludes the following morning," Jake said, strolling into the room, looking fresh and showered and as if he had had twelve hours of sound sleep. His dark hair was damp, curling around his shirt collar. Even in her exhausted and distressed state, Charlotte had the urge to touch it. And this made her even more irritated.

"How could you let this happen?" Charlotte said, as loudly as her headache would permit.

"It's not his fault," Mae said.

"Fault?" said Jake. "I consider it part of my duty as host to accommodate any guests who are in no condition to make it home. And you, my dear, were certainly not in any condition to leave last night."

"Do you have any idea how this looks?"

"Come on, let's just go, Charlotte. Wasting time blaming Jake won't get you home any faster."

The morning was bright and almost warm, the light stronger than it had been in months, heralding the imminent arrival of spring. For a moment, Charlotte felt a surge of happiness, an almost déjà vu sense of when she had been a girl, and her father took her out to explore their gardens. Or the days when she was a bit older, and her father took her to work with him. For Charlotte, mornings always felt like freedom and possibility.

They piled into the green Model T. Charlotte climbed into the backseat, following Mae. If someone had told her on the day of the funeral, when she first saw the obnoxious vehicle, that she would soon be traveling in it herself, she would have called them mad.

"What am I, a chauffeur? One of you come sit in the front," said Jake.

Mae, who was already settled into the far side of back, declared that she wasn't changing spots.

"Oh, for heaven's sake," Charlotte said, moving to the front passenger seat.

Jake maneuvered the car through the busy streets with more speed than she was used to. She wanted to tell him to slow down, but she was, at that point, more concerned with getting home than with her own safety. The city was bustling, each street seeming busier than the next—and each a rebuke to her irresponsibility. And yet, the closer they got to Sixty-fifth Street, the more Charlotte felt a growing sense of loss. She was Cinderella the morning after the ball, but there was no glass slipper left behind, no proof that for one night she had lived someone else's life.

But then her house came into view, and any thought of the previous night's gaiety disappeared in one heart-stopping moment.

There, parked out front, was William's Rolls Royce. And behind it, two police cars.

Chapter 17

CHARLOTTE JUMPED OUT of the car and opened the backseat, pulling Mae with her by the hand.

"Go!" she yelled to Jake.

"I'm not leaving until I'm sure you two are all right."

"You're just going to make things worse. I'm begging you—drive away."

The fog of her hangover dissipated. It was clear to her what had happened: William arrived home, found her missing, and called the police.

She fumbled in her purse for the house key and burst through the door. Rafferty stood in front of the stairs, seemingly not fazed by their bizarre arrival. She was reminded of something her mother-in-law once said: A good servant hears nothing, sees nothing, but knows everything.

"Where is Mr. Delacorte?" Charlotte asked, so anxious that she was out of breath and could barely get the words out.

"In the parlor, madame."

"Please—go tell him that I'm home. There was no need for him to call the police." She didn't want to face William herself—not until she'd had time to change her clothes and fix her hair.

"I'm more than happy to announce your arrival, madame. But Mr. Delacorte didn't call the police."

"What do you mean, he didn't call them?" Charlotte said.

"Mr. Delacorte arrived home not an hour ago, and the officers weren't far behind him."

Why on earth would the police come to the house?

And then Charlotte realized that the visit by the police, ironically, might have prevented her from getting caught in her own little crime: If William had not made it up to the bedroom, he hadn't discovered that she wasn't home when he arrived.

As if reading her mind, Rafferty said, "It all happened so quickly, Mr. Delacorte didn't even make it upstairs."

Their eyes met until Charlotte looked away.

Two officers and a man in a suit bustled into the entrance hall, one of them nearly colliding with Mae on his way to the front door.

"Excuse me, ma'am," said the man in the suit, while the officers looked her up and down, taking in her wrinkled evening clothes and disheveled hair, regarding Charlotte with a bit less than the respect she was usually afforded as Mrs. William Delacorte.

She wanted to ask them what they were doing there, but she had learned a few things from her father, and one of those things was that when it came to the police, it was best just to keep your mouth shut.

Rafferty saw the men out of the house, and Charlotte rushed through the parlor to William's office. The door was closed.

"William." She knocked. No response. She tried the doorknob, but the door was locked.

She backed away slowly.

CHARLOTTE DRAINED THE bathwater.

She heard movement in the bedroom. She quickly toweled off and changed into the floral-print day dress she'd brought into the dressing room. She ran a comb through her hair and pinched her cheeks to give herself some color. Anyone who knew her well would see that she had barely slept.

"William? Is that you?"

He was sitting on their bed, his suitcase in the corner of the room, half open. He looked more tired than she felt. She walked toward him to put her arms around him, as she usually did when he returned home from a trip. But then she stopped.

"When did you get home?" she said.

"Early. I didn't want to wake you."

"I knocked on your office door, but you didn't answer," she said. She didn't mention the police; surely, he would bring it up himself.

He stood and crossed the room to stand in front of her.

"Is everything . . . all right? I saw the police," she said, unable to wait a second longer to talk about it.

William ignored the question, instead reaching for the buttons on the front of her dress. At first, she thought William was securing them because she had left the dress too open in the front. Then she realized he was undoing them.

Her dress fell to the floor, and William led her to the bed. He pressed her down on her back and tugged down her bloomers as he stretched out beside her, still fully clothed.

William ran his hands roughly over her breasts, then between her legs. His touch was more assertive than she was used to. She knew this should excite her, but it had the opposite effect. It took all of her effort not to push him away.

She closed her eyes and tried to welcome her husband's affections. But his fingers felt foreign and out of place between her legs, pressing and poking as if searching for something. And it became worse when he pulled his pants down to his ankles and climbed on top of her. He thrust in and out, the friction rough like sandpaper against her tender flesh. William's thrusting grew faster and harder, oblivious to her discomfort and detachment.

She thought about Jake Larkin. He was the one on top of her. They were on the couch, at the speakeasy. . . .

William finished quietly and rolled off her.

"I'm going to run a bath," he said. "When you go downstairs, tell my sister I want to speak with her."

Chapter 18

"I THINK YOU'RE being too hard on Mae," Charlotte said. The lunch table was set with William's favorite dish, beef Wellington. The sight of the meat made Charlotte's sour stomach turn.

Penny poured them both mint iced tea. Charlotte sipped hers slowly.

She had been able to steal an hour of sleep on the couch while William closeted himself yet again in his office. She woke up to the sound of his argument with Mae.

"I'm disappointed that you would say that," William said. "I need your support, Charlotte."

"She won't learn how to be responsible if you treat her like a child. She at least should have some money to save or spend as she sees fit to plan for her future."

William shook his head. "This is the only way to keep a firm hand with her. Trust me, there are things about my sister's . . . nature that you don't know—and I don't want you to know. It was bad enough that my mother was burdened with it. It was probably the death of her."

Charlotte thought of how aroused she had felt when she saw the chemistry between Mae and Fiona.

"I've had the chance to spend some time with her this past week, and she's not as bad as you make her out to be. I think you'd see that if you gave her half a chance."

"Stay out of it, Charlotte."

How was she going to convince him to give Mae an allowance to start paying off the Vesper Club debt? If she told him about the threat of the gossip columns, he might give her money, but then he would never let Mae out of the house again. Charlotte didn't know what had gotten into him, but it was clear that rational discussion was not going to be possible. She would have to use the one area of leverage she had.

"I'm making progress with the library," she said slowly.

"That's good news."

"Yes. But I'm going to need a bit more than I anticipated for the contractors this month."

"How much more?"

"About two thousand."

"If you need to go past the agreed-upon budget, you'll have to go to the Women's Literary Alliance treasurer."

"The treasurer? Since when is there a treasurer?"

"Since Mother died. This isn't just a little hobby of hers anymore, Charlotte. It's a corporation. The board members are officers of that corporation."

"Your mother named me as head of the library project. The treasurer should report to me, not the other way around."

"Checks and balances, my dear. It's what makes America work. And it's what's going to keep this project on track."

"So who is the treasurer?"

"Amelia Astor," William said.

"Greenwich Village," Charlotte told the cab driver.

She wasn't sure of the street name, but she would recognize the cigar shop on the corner. When the car was within a few blocks of their destination, Charlotte could hardly believe she had just left the neighborhood that morning. And up until the minute William left for yet another late meeting, she hadn't been sure she'd actually have the nerve to return.

But William hadn't given her much choice.

"Right here is fine," Charlotte said.

She waited until the cab was out of sight, then she rounded the corner and found the tailor shop. She followed the alley to the flight of stairs and descended them as she had last night in the dark.

This time, there wasn't any music coming from inside. And when she knocked on the door, no one asked for the password.

She waited a minute, then knocked again. It felt silly to be standing there, alone at the bottom of a staircase, when she should have been at home getting ready for dinner. The absurdity of the visit struck her, and she told herself she would knock one more time, then leave if there was no response.

The door swung open. "I know you're new to the scene, but things really don't get started around here until after midnight," Jake said with a grin.

Chapter 19

HE HELD THE door open, and Charlotte walked past him, trying to ignore the small flip in her stomach.

The room was as shabbily and sparsely furnished as she remembered, though considerably cleaner. She glanced at the worn leather couch where she had spent the night. If she closed her eyes, she could smell the smoke, hear the music, taste the gin.

"So what brings you by, Mrs. Delacorte?"

"Are we back to formalities now?" she said.

"You tell me. People can be funny about those things in the harsh light of day."

"I think we are beyond formality," she said, wishing she hadn't dressed up quite so much.

"Sounds good to me. Care for a cocktail?"

"It's not even five."

"There's no clock in here," he said, gesturing to his bare walls. "And a drink is usually the reason people pay me a visit. Unless they're looking for a place for a good jam session. And I see you haven't brought any instruments." He winked at her.

"Listen, Jake—I have a problem. Actually, Mae does, but now it's my problem. I didn't know who else to talk to, and I figured with the business you're in, you must have some . . . discretion."

"I like to think so," he said. He pulled out a wooden chair at the card table and gestured for her to sit. "What's the problem?" He sat across from her. His gaze unnerved her, but she pressed on.

"Mae told me she owes quite a bit of money to the woman who owns the Vesper Club. I was hoping you knew of someplace I could borrow it so she could pay it off."

"You and Mae need to borrow money? You're two of the richest women I know."

"My husband controls the money."

Jake laughed. "I don't understand you rich people. In my family, if one person has money, we all have money."

"Well, that's an easy thing to say when no one has any. When there's great wealth, things get more complicated." She tried not to look at his mouth, and the humiliating memory of the way she thought of him during sex with William made her cheeks burn.

"What makes you think I can help you get that kind of cash? You must see me as a real shady character."

"Not shady. Just . . . knowledgeable."

"Well, I hate to disappoint you, my dear, but I don't do that kind of business. That's what gets a guy in a lot of trouble. Or gal, for that matter."

Charlotte felt like a fool. Why should she have asked him for help? She barely knew him.

"If Mae needs money, why doesn't she just get a job?" he said.

"Mae can't get a job—it wouldn't look right."

"What the hell does that mean? There's no shame in working for a living. At least she'd have some independence."

"There's no job that will pay the kind of money she stands to get as a Delacorte heiress. Forget it. I'm sorry to have bothered you," Charlotte said, standing up to leave.

"Look, this isn't really my business. But since you brought it up, when you do get the money, take it to Boom Boom directly—I don't think Mae is the most reliable."

"Are you done lecturing me?"

"I do have one more thought, now that you ask: You should talk to your husband about this money situation. You're married—you have a right to get cash if you need it."

Charlotte was suddenly, inexplicably furious.

"And what do you know about marriage?"

"Nothing," Jake said, standing up. "And I don't intend to ever really know."

"This was a mistake," she said, striding quickly to the door.

He followed her and grabbed her hand, drawing her close to him. She looked at him in surprise.

"Why did you really come back here?" he said. His eyes were dark, liquid pools, his mouth lush and so close to hers . . .

"Exactly why I told you," she said, reminding herself to breathe.

"I don't believe that. I think you wanted an excuse to see me."

"What? That's ridiculous."

"To tell you the truth, I was planning on finding an excuse to stop by your house tomorrow."

She stared at him in amazement. "You don't mean that."

"I never say things I don't mean."

They locked eyes, and Charlotte's heart raced.

She forced herself to turn away and left without another word.

AFTER WAITING AN hour and a half for a liquor delivery that never arrived, Boom Boom slammed her office door and picked up the phone. It was going to be a busy Thursday night, and she didn't have time for this shit.

She dialed Lenny Sugarfield's office as quickly as her long red nails would allow. The phone rang. And it rang and rang.

Slowly, she replaced the receiver.

So it was happening already. Damn that U.S. Attorney.

Boom Boom heaved herself up from her desk chair and hurried to the basement as quickly as her large frame and bad hip would allow. Once there, she counted the crates of gin, beer, whisky, and wine.

She figured she might have enough to be operational for two weeks without another shipment. Finding a new source—and quickly—was going to be tough in this environment. Not to mention costly.

"Fiona!" Boom Boom called from the top of the stairs. "Meet me in my office."

It took the girl more than five minutes to appear, and when she did it was with obvious impatience.

"Yes?" Fiona said.

She wore pink lisle stockings, a short, fringed, pink dress, and gold brocade T-strap heels. Her face was pale, her fair eyebrows almost invisible, making her painted red lips stand out as if they were lit in neon.

"Where do you go after you leave here every night?"

"I'm not sure that's your business," said Fiona.

"Everything's my business. That's why I have one."

Fiona shrugged. "I go to different places."

"Well, let me try to narrow it down: I'm guessing none of those places is an early-morning prayer service. So I'll take a leap and assume you troll around in some two-bit speakeasy. Since that joint is entertaining half my staff, I'd like to know where it gets its liquor. Find out for me."

"I can't make any promises."

"You get me a lead on a reliable new supplier, I'll give you a commission."

"How much?" Fiona crossed her arms in front of her chest. Boom Boom sighed with irritation.

"What do you care? It's more than nothing. Just get me a meeting with your guy."

"Is that all?" Fiona stood to leave, and Boom Boom grabbed her by the wrist.

"Where's Mae Delacorte been?"

"I don't know."

"Hmm. Well let's do a little detective work. For the past year, she's been here every night—give or take. Then three nights ago, I told her to pay up her tab, and she hasn't shown her face since. Seems to me like she's avoiding me."

"She's having family issues."

"And you can tell her they're about to get worse: If her account isn't paid in full by tomorrow night, I'm calling Greta Goucher and giving her an exclusive on a certain society girl and her cocktail waitress lover."

Chapter 20

IN THE MORNING, Charlotte lingered in her bedroom, reading *Harper's Bazaar*. She was in no rush to see her husband at breakfast.

At a knock on her bedroom door, Charlotte hid the *Harper's Bazaar* under the morning paper. Isobel had told her she just *had* to read the short stories by Anita Loos. And they were, as promised, quite scandalous. The woman in the story, Lorelei, seemed concerned with nothing more than collecting diamonds and lovers. And her boyfriend was married.

"Come in," she said.

"Sorry to disturb," said Penny. "There is a visitor at the front door for Miss Mae, but Master Delacorte said she isn't to have any visitors."

"Who is it?" Charlotte was already heading for the hallway, straightening her dress.

"She didn't say."

Charlotte felt a surprising sense of disappointment and realized she had been more than a little hopeful that the visitor was Jake Larkin. Instead, she knew she would be faced with the unpleasantness of getting rid of Fiona.

"Is Mae here?"

"I'm not sure, madame. I know Master Delacorte left for the office a few hours ago, and I haven't seen Miss Mae all morning."

Charlotte walked so quickly that Penny could barely keep up with her, and that was her preference. She wanted to speak with Fiona in private but didn't want to ask Penny to leave them alone. She was in the unenviable position of having to tread lightly with her own servants. Lately, she felt she needed them more than they needed her.

Fiona was seated on the red, silk-cushioned, antique bench just inside the entranceway. In her pink frock and matching hat, her hair falling over her shoulders in loose ringlets, she looked like she belonged in the pages of a magazine or onstage, not paying a morning house call. They were like a pair of peacocks, she and Mae.

"You can't come to this house anymore," Charlotte said.

"I need to see Mae."

"You are going to cause her trouble." Charlotte lowered her voice. "Didn't Mae tell you how things are right now?"

"No. How are they?"

"Difficult. And you are making them more so. Just let things be for a few weeks."

"Mae doesn't *have* a few weeks. Boom Boom says she wants the money tomorrow, or she's going to the gossip pages. You do know what I'm talking about, don't you?"

The girl looked so young and innocent. It was difficult to believe she lived such a scandalous existence.

Charlotte nodded. "Yes. I do. So thanks for the message, and now please leave."

Fiona fixed her remarkable green eyes on her. "You were out with us the other night. Mae brought you into our world. You can't have it both ways. You have to at least let me see her."

Charlotte shook her head, sighed, and gestured toward the stairs.

IT WAS THE height of impropriety to show up at Amelia Astor's home unannounced. But waiting for the next WLA meeting to ask for the additional two thousand dollars she needed was out of the question. No, Charlotte decided that an inelegant social call this morning was better than having her family name splashed all over the gossip pages the next.

She pulled her car into the driveway just off Seventy-ninth Street. The Astor home—not the primary mansion, but the secondary one that Amelia lived in on her own—was inconvenient for parking. Amelia had to employ a handful of valets just to make sure her guests didn't have to hike a city block every time they paid a visit.

"Morning, Mrs. Delacorte," said the valet, opening her door.

"Good morning," said Charlotte, stepping out of the car and handing him her keys. "I won't be long, so you can keep it nearby."

"I'll just put it right around the corner next to your husband's."

Charlotte froze. "My husband is here?"

"Yes, ma'am."

Charlotte felt a flash of irritation. What was he doing there in the middle of the day? Just when she thought Amelia couldn't insinuate herself any more into her business.

"Well then, no need for me to stay. He must be taking care of . . . what I needed." She sat back behind the wheel and, with shaking hands, closed the car door.

The valet knocked on the window. She rolled it down.

"Your keys, Mrs. Delacorte."

Chapter 21

FIONA WALKED DOWN the long hallway on the second floor of Charlotte's house, pausing to look at the antique tables with the crystal and silver and the framed John Singer Sargent portraits. She wondered how long it would take for her and Mae to get a setup like this.

She knocked on Mae's door.

"Go away," Mae said.

"It's Fiona."

The door seemed to spring open.

"What are you doing? You can't be here," Mae said.

Fiona had never seen Mae look so unkempt. Her hair was dirty and limp, she seemed to have lost five pounds she couldn't afford to lose, and her skin was dry and the color of paste. She smelled like stale smoke. If it weren't for the elegant Chanel robe, Fiona might not have recognized her.

"Yeah, so I've been told. What the hell is going on?"

"Come in so I can close the door," Mae said. She cleared a pile of clothes off a chair next to her bed. Fiona sat down, and Mae handed her a cigarette. "God, you're a sight for sore eyes."

Mae pulled her close, her hands running over her breasts, her mouth on hers with urgency. Fiona kissed her back for a minute, then pulled away.

"So what the hell is going on?"

"I tried talking to you about this the other day when I came to your apartment."

"No you didn't. All you said was that your mother left her house to some charity. You didn't say you were going to hide out at your uptight sister-in-law's place."

"I'm not hiding out, Fiona. I'm living here."

Fiona sighed. She'd heard that rich people were actually the cheapest bastards you'd ever meet, but this was ridiculous. "If you don't want to buy your own house this quickly, I'll help you find an apartment. You can't sit around here all depressed." She stood up to pull Mae to her. The expression in her lover's eyes was so bruised, it was almost a turn-on. "You should have called me, bunny," she said, kissing her neck. Sometimes Fiona forgot the two-year age difference between them. Maybe it was why Mae seemed like such a child to her. Or maybe it was because she grew up in places like that house, with servants and a mother telling her what to do all the time. Fiona hadn't had a mother since her own died in the Triangle Shirtwaist Factory fire. She barely remembered her. Maybe that was for the best if the alternative was for her to be a sniveling wreck at the slightest inconvenience later in life.

"I don't have any money to buy a place. I don't have any money, period."

Fiona took a step back. "What are you talking about? Your mother, from what I hear, had more dough than God. What did she do with all of it?"

"It's . . . tied up for now."

Fiona shook her head.

"That's not going to work."

"I'll figure out how to get it," she said, taking her hand. "It just might take some time. Besides, what are you so put off about? I mean, unless you were only with me for my money."

Fiona snatched her hand back. "I never thought I'd be involved with a woman. You're the one who came after me, remember?"

"I'm sorry. I didn't mean that."

"And it's not just the money. But you're acting real weird. Hiding out here . . .

"No one's seen you since the other night at Jake's. Maybe you're upset about the money, I don't know. But you could have come to see me."

"I've wanted to see you—you have no idea how much. It's killing me. Look at me! I can't even eat. But my brother is watching me. My mother must have told him about us, and he's told me very clearly that if I ever want a penny, I can't see you for a while. I can't do anything." Mae pressed herself against Fiona, and Fiona accepted her, stroking her hair and telling her it was all right. She barely knew what she was saying, but whatever she was mumbling seemed to calm Mae down. But Fiona's mind was rolling so fast she could barely process the thoughts. On the one hand, this was all probably a sign she should cut Mae loose. She had tried going down this road, had enjoyed it for a while, but now it was going nowhere. On the other hand, what if Mae had it all wrong? What if this brother of hers was full of shit?

If there was any way to shake the money loose, Fiona would figure it out.

CHARLOTTE RETURNED TO her house through the side entrance. It was never used except by the servants on nights Charlotte and William entertained. Upstairs, she heard furniture being moved around as Penny cleaned. She had no idea if Mae was still home or not.

She removed her shoes, and walked as silently as possible to

William's office. If she had any reservations about going through his books to find their bank-account information, it was quelled by the thought of his visit to Amelia Astor. What good reason could he possibly have to be there at this hour of the day?

If William wouldn't give Mae any money, and wouldn't give her any money, she was just going to have to take it herself. And it was high time she had access to their bank account. What if there was ever an emergency? And really, wasn't this an emergency?

Jake was right: She and William were married. There was no reason for him to treat her like a child on an allowance. And now that Geraldine was gone, there was all the more reason for her to be included in financial decision-making.

Charlotte turned the doorknob, but it didn't budge.

"Oh, no. This can't be." She'd never known him to keep the door locked. When was the last time she had gone into the office when he wasn't home? Maybe a year ago. It hadn't been locked then.

She could wait until he used the office later and try to sneak in before he locked it again, but that was too risky. Fiona said she only had until tomorrow to get the money to Boom Boom.

Charlotte tried turning the knob again, as if somehow the result would be different.

"Open!" she hit the door with her palm. And then she had a memory—a moment recollected so vividly, it was as if it were still happening: Her mother, tired of her father's returning home drunk yet again, locked him out of the house. Charlotte awakened in the morning to the sound of his pounding the front door. She opened her window and looked down at him.

"Charlotte, honey," he called. "Toss me a hairpin."

She pulled a pin from her hair and laughed as she tossed it down to him. It hit the snow at his feet, but he retrieved it and stuck it into the door lock. The next thing she knew, he was in the house, and her mother was hollering at him.

Later, he showed her how he used the hairpin to unlock the door.

"Charlotte," he'd said, "the most important lessons in life are the ones they don't teach you in school."

What kind of life had her father anticipated she would have that she would need to know how to pick a lock?

She pulled a pin from her hair, straightened it, and pushed it into the lock with a quick forward, then upward motion. The knob turned.

Charlotte closed the door behind her.

The office was neat and organized, just as she remembered it. William's desk was free of clutter: just a calendar, an engraved brass pencil holder, a typewriter, and several leather-bound ledgers. She flipped through one, but all she saw were columns of numbers and account numbers that made no sense to her.

She imagined he would keep his bank statements or checkbook in the desk drawer. But along the far wall, William had several tall wooden filing cabinets. If she had no luck in the desk drawer, going through the files could take some time.

Charlotte pulled at the narrow desk drawer. It was filled with pens, papers, and a few sheets of correspondence that appeared to be business-related, but nothing to help her access his bank account.

Closing the drawer, she turned from the desk to the first filing cabinet. It was as tall as she was, and she decided to start at the bottom. She pulled at the lowest drawer but realized it was locked. The drawer itself didn't have a lock, so she stood to search the piece of furniture. The top drawer had a round lock, and Charlotte employed the hairpin yet again. She heard a satisfying click and bent down to try the bottom drawer again. This time, it slid right open.

What she saw made her freeze: The entire drawer was filled with cash. The money wasn't organized into neatly bound bundles like banks distributed, but instead was loose and unwieldy in one enormous pile.

The lowest denomination she saw was a fifty-dollar bill.

She sank to the floor slowly, her mind racing. Where had all this cash come from? And why wasn't it in the bank?

Just one handful of the hundred-dollar bills was more than enough to pay Mae's debt. Quickly, Charlotte got up and slipped a bundle into her purse, telling herself that she would find a way to replace it as soon as possible. The priority was paying Boom Boom.

She eyed the second filing cabinet. While she knew she should just get out of there, she couldn't leave without knowing what might be hidden in there as well.

After a quick glance at the office door, she turned her attention to the round lock at the top of the cabinet, and as with the previous one, checked the top drawer first. It was empty. The second drawer, also empty. She crouched down and opened the bottom drawer.

"What the hell?" Disbelieving, she looked down at a black handgun.

What on earth is William doing with a gun?

And then she heard the office door opening behind her.

Part II
Little White Lies

I don't want to live. I want to love first, and live incidentally.
—Zelda Fitzgerald

Chapter 1

CHARLOTTE SLAMMED THE file cabinet drawer closed and turned around, her heart pounding.

"Is everything okay, Mrs. Delacorte?" said Rafferty, standing in the doorway.

Charlotte almost fainted with relief.

"It's just you," she breathed, standing up slowly.

"I don't mean to intrude, but I saw you come in here and thought you might need assistance."

Had he seen me enter the office? Had he noticed that I picked the lock?

"I don't need anything, Rafferty. Thank you, I'm—I'm fine." She couldn't get out of there fast enough, but the expression on Rafferty's face made her hesitate. "What is it?" she said.

"It's just—and I'm sorry if I'm talking out of turn—I don't think Mr. Delacorte likes anyone to be in this room."

Charlotte felt her pulse quicken, sensing she was about to hear something important but not necessarily something she wanted to know.

"And what gives you that idea?"

Rafferty hesitated. "Please tell me," she said, walking closer to him. His eyes were pale blue, and, she noticed for the first time, he was a striking man. She had never given a lot of thought to the people who worked in the house. The culture of servants was not one she had grown up in, and she dealt with it by keeping a respectful distance and not relying on them any more than was required of a woman in her social position.

"He told me that if he ever caught me in the office, I would be fired on the spot," Rafferty said.

"*What?*" Charlotte knew it wasn't appropriate for her to reveal that she was at odds with what William had told Rafferty, but she couldn't contain her surprise.

Rafferty shrugged. "It's not out of the ordinary. People need their privacy—especially where servants are concerned," he said.

"Okay, if you say so," Charlotte said. She imagined William walking in, catching them both in the office.

She started for the door.

"But he did make it clear he didn't want *anyone* in this room— including you," Rafferty added.

She turned back to face him. "How did he 'make it clear'?" she asked.

"He told me to tell him if the room was breached."

She stared at him, momentarily speechless. "And will you?" she finally said.

Those pale blue eyes met hers and held them.

"I didn't see anything to tell, madame."

BOOM BOOM COULD smell the money.

Thursday night at the Vesper Club, and it felt like Christmas and New Year's rolled into one. Some nights were like that: The booze was flowing, the women were dancing, and the men were tossing around dollar bills like confetti.

Still, she couldn't relax. She was never more than a few paces from the bar, and she could barely keep her eyes off the entrance. Of course, no one was sharp enough to recognize a Prohibition agent when he walked in the door, but she hoped her instincts would at least give her a few seconds to react before a raid.

Two women sauntered in, their curvy figures a striking departure from the flat-chested, boyish look all the fashionable gals were going for. No, none of that for these two: Their breasts were front and center, brimming over the tops of their low-cut, sequined dresses. But their hair was stylishly short, shiny and dark and skimming their jaws in perfect, identical bobs. Boom Boom rarely forgot a face, and she'd never have forgotten those tits: These women were new to the Vesper.

Boom Boom watched the women take in the room, and when they homed in on the table of men ordering tray after tray of cocktails, her antennae went up.

"I need more Luckies."

She was distracted by the whine of one of her cocktail waitresses. Boom Boom used to give the girls open access to the stash of cigarettes because they sold so fast during the night. But lately, the inventory didn't match up with the cash, and she had been forced to lock them up and dispense them on demand.

Everything was a hassle.

"How many packs d'ya have left?" Boom Boom said. And then, out of the corner of her eye, she saw something that made stolen cigarettes look like child's play.

The women, after just a minute of circling the table of high rollers, said something that made the men follow them out the door like children after the Pied Piper.

"Do you see that?" she said to the waitress.

"Yeah. That's weird. They just ordered a round of drinks."

"God damn it!" Boom Boom said, watching helplessly as the group disappeared into the night.

So this is what it was coming to: As if it wasn't bad enough that she had to worry about getting busted by Prohibition agents and finding a replacement for her supplier, who was currently sitting in jail, she now had to fend off poachers. Poachers!

Club owners were feeding on each other. Well, Boom Boom was not about to be the only guppy in the shark tank.

"Go find Fiona for me," she told the girl who was waiting for her cigarette stash.

The girl scampered off, and Boom Boom surveyed the room, looking for the magnificent redhead who might be more valuable to her than the entire stocked bar.

Fiona appeared before her, dutifully but with barely concealed irritation.

"Put down your tray and come to my office," Boom Boom said.

Boom Boom closed the office door. Fiona stood against the wall, her long legs crossed. She looked supremely bored.

"Congratulations," said Boom Boom. "You've been promoted."

Fiona wrinkled her milky white brow but said nothing.

"Don't you want to know your new job title?" Boom Boom prompted.

"President?" said Fiona dryly.

"Hostess," said Boom Boom, smiling as if she'd just handed Fiona a check for a million dollars.

"What does that mean? I greet people at the door? Doesn't sound like the kind of gig that makes for a lot of tips."

"You're not greeting people at the door. What I want you to do is keep an eye on the high rollers: the fellas who come in groups, get a table, order round after round of drinks. Or maybe it's just a lone guy throwing money around the bar, then watching the show. I want you to single out one guy or a group every night and make sure he stays happy. I'm tired of seeing our club attract the big spenders, then have them get lured away by some hussy from the El Dorado or the Fey Club."

"I can't stop people from leaving the club."

"No. But you can leave with them. And that will keep 'em coming back."

Fiona and Boom Boom locked eyes. Fiona looked away first.

"Do we understand each other?" said Boom Boom. Fiona nodded, then spoke slowly, as if forming the ideas as she talked.

"Just one thing: Since I might be cutting my night short by a few hours when I would be standing around getting waitress tips, I guess you'll be paying me a wage. I mean, this is a promotion, you said."

Boom Boom retrieved her gold cigarette case from her jacket pocket and lit one. She took the time to blow a perfect smoke ring before saying, "You're not as dumb as you look, you know that?"

"Is that a yes?"

Boom Boom paced silently, as if Fiona were suggesting something outrageous. In truth, Boom Boom had already anticipated the price of doing business.

"Fine," she said, finally. "Fifteen dollars a week."

Fiona smiled and opened the office door.

"I'd better get back to my shift," she said. She was halfway out of the room when Boom Boom called after her.

"Sparks!"

"Yeah?" Fiona turned around, her eyes bright with triumph.

"Get me that meeting with your guy who runs the speakeasy. If I don't get booze to sell, none of us has a job."

Chapter 2

CHARLOTTE ADJUSTED HER cloche against the bright morning sun and clutched her mesh handbag close to her body. It was unlikely that she would fall victim to a purse snatcher on Twenty-first Street and Broadway, a bustling corner of office buildings and

shops—but on a day she was carrying $2,000 in cash she had sto-
len from William's office, she wasn't taking any chances.

The family business, Delacorte Properties, had long operated
out of a modest redbrick brownstone in Greenwich Village. But
fifteen years ago, with a surge in fortune, the company constructed
a fifty-seven-floor Gothic revival building—the tallest building
in the country. Charlotte's late father-in-law, Atticus Delacorte,
had intended to pay for the 14-million-dollar project in cash. But
shortly after its completion, he was struck with the first of several
strokes that would eventually kill him. William became head of
the company and often complained that he was still paying off his
father's "ego-driven, overindulgence of a building."

She couldn't remember the last time she had visited her husband's office, and certainly couldn't recall ever having shown up
uninvited. But she walked into the marble lobby with as much confidence as she could muster. As always, she was taken with the sheer
beauty of the place, with the vaulted ceiling, mosaics, and stained-
glass skylight.

She was tempted to walk the ten flights of stairs to William's office; she still did not trust elevators. But the impossibility of such an
endeavor in her high heels made practicality win out over caution.

"Good day," the elevator operator said as he closed the gate.
Charlotte clutched her purse and resisted the urge to close her eyes
as the elevator car rose. With a slight shudder, it came to a stop.
"Floor ten," the operator called, and pulled open the gate, then the
door.

The Delacorte Properties office suite took up the entire tenth
floor. Charlotte opened the double doors and walked inside with a
sense of pride and trepidation.

"Mrs. Delacorte! What a pleasant surprise. I didn't know you
would be visiting today. I would have made sure the place looked
a bit more presentable," said Pauline, shuffling loose papers into a
quick pile.

"Oh, not to worry. Mr. Delacorte isn't expecting me. I was just hoping to catch him in."

Charlotte waited in the reception area. Someone offered her coffee, and she declined. All around her, she heard people tapping on typewriters and answering phones. She looked at the women behind their desks and wondered, not for the first time, what career she might have found if she had not married a Delacorte.

Charlotte wished she had a magazine to read. She glanced at her watch. How long had she been waiting? Five minutes? Ten? She couldn't help but wonder if William was making her wait on purpose, as punishment for showing up unexpectedly.

"Right this way, Mrs. Delacorte."

William looked up from his desk. If he was irritated by the unexpected visit from his wife, he didn't show it.

"Charlotte. What a surprise. Pauline, hold my calls."

Charlotte sat in a chair facing him. The room, with its dark wood floor and wide oak desk and ample windows with sweeping views of the city, spoke of power and success.

"Is everything all right?" William asked.

"Yes, fine. I just thought it would be nice to see you."

He smiled at her. She shifted in her seat.

William walked to the window, looking out over the city.

"What do you have on your calendar today?" he said, almost absently.

"Oh, just a few errands." She tried not to think about the contents of her handbag.

"You know, Charlotte, if the library project isn't keeping you busy enough, we could be entertaining more. Most of our friends host two functions a season. Amelia did three last fall."

At the mention of Amelia Astor, Charlotte stiffened. She hadn't visited his office to have the conversation turned into a discussion of her hostessing skills.

"William, why were the police at our house?"

He looked at her, guilty as a kid caught with his hand in the cookie jar. He stood and walked to the door, pressing it as if making sure it was really closed. Charlotte hoped he would take the seat next to her, but he returned to his desk.

"Is that what's bothering you?"

"You can talk to me, you know. I'm your wife." She thought of Rafferty's words, *He told me to tell him if the room was breached.*

"Thank you, Charlotte. And if it were anything worth concerning you with, I would. Now what I really need is for you to focus on getting that library finished. That's what I want of you as my wife—not worries about imaginary problems."

"I didn't imagine the police at our house, did I?"

The sudden rage on his face surprised her almost more than it frightened her.

"If you must know—if you really have to take up my workday discussing this—the police were at the house because apparently a few people who showed up to pay their respects at Mother's funeral are under investigation."

"Who? And under investigation for what?"

"I don't know, Charlotte! I didn't recognize a good number of people at the house that day. Or at the church, for that matter. You know not everyone was an invited guest. People just wanted to rub elbows with prominent New Yorkers, and they used Mother's funeral as a way to gain access."

Charlotte looked down at the floor, relieved that there was an explanation for the police visit but feeling guilty once again for not having maintained better control of the guest list that day. And it still didn't explain the reason for the hundreds of thousands of dollars stuffed away in his office. Or the gun.

She put her hand inside her bag, touching the bundle of cash. It would be risky to ask him directly about the money before she'd returned the amount she took.

"I feel like something is going on," she said. "Something is not right."

William sighed, looking extremely tired.

"Everything is fine, Charlotte."

It was obvious to her the conversation would go nowhere. Unless she was going to tell him outright what she'd seen, she might as well leave.

"You can't fault me for being curious," Charlotte said. He looked at her without so much as a blink. "Okay. Well . . . I'll see you at home tonight." She stood to leave.

"Yes. I'll be home at six. Tell the kitchen I'd like fish for dinner. And no need to worry about the menu for me tomorrow night. I'll be going out of town."

Again?

"Where to this time?"

"Back to Boston. Just for a night or two. Will you be able to make sure Mae behaves?" he said.

"She'll be fine. I don't think your sister is as much a problem as you imagine."

William got up from his desk and walked her to the door, his hand on the small of her back. He kissed her lightly on the cheek as he opened the door. "I'm glad to hear it."

Charlotte held her handbag close to her body. She couldn't wait to unload it so she had less to hide and could focus instead on figuring out why William was hiding so very much from her.

MAE DELACORTE FELT half a dozen faces turn in her direction when she walked into the firehouse on Lexington Avenue.

She knew she looked particularly attractive that afternoon. For the first time in days, she had dressed with inspiration, wearing a fuchsia georgette dress with gypsy girdle, bias-cut ruffles, and flounces. Her shiny dark hair was tucked behind her ears, short enough to barely skim her jawline. She had forgone wearing a hat; her only accessories that day were the ropes of pearl around her neck. Her lips were painted as dark red as she could justify in daytime, and even she could smell the liberal douse of Joy perfume she'd applied before leaving the house.

"Can I help you, miss?" one of the firemen asked, dropping a large rubber mat he had been hosing down. From the way he looked at her, she was pretty sure he'd have to hose himself down next.

"Yes, I'm hoping so." Mae walked toward him, stepping gingerly around a ladder and stepping over a wide coil of rubber hose. "I was looking for something to help with fire safety," she said. She blinked her eyes quickly to draw extra attention to them.

"Well, you've come to the right place," the man said jovially.

"I live in a big house, and I worry about getting to an exit in case of a fire. I was wondering if you have some sort of ladder I could keep in my bedroom that I could put out my window in case of an emergency."

"That's a very smart idea, young lady. Unfortunately, the only ladders we have here are the industrial ones we use on the outside of homes to get to the second and third floors. I believe what you want is maybe a rope ladder."

"A rope ladder," Mae repeated. "Do you have any idea where I could get one of those?" She leaned in close, giving him the best view of her *décolletage*.

"Try Lascoff Hardware," said another man from behind a desk.

She turned around, and he looked sheepish. Clearly, he had just been admiring her ass.

Mae smiled brightly. "I'll do that."

Chapter 3

CHARLOTTE FELT CERTAIN she was walking to her death.

She took the steps slowly, descending into the dim light of the Vesper Club basement, cursing the day she took it upon herself to help Mae. She couldn't imagine why Boom Boom would want to meet her in the basement and not the perfectly suitable front room unless it was because she was going to shoot her. *Isn't that what happened to people who didn't pay their debts?* Okay, technically it was Mae's debt. But she doubted someone like Boom Boom would split hairs over the matter.

She just wondered what photo of her they would run in the newspaper story. Maybe her wedding picture.

At the base of the stairs, Charlotte saw light shining from behind a partially open door.

"This way, missus," said her guide, an oddly shaped girl with an indeterminate accent who went by the name Horace. The girl knocked on the partially open door. "I 'ave a Missus Delacorte," she said.

The light was obscured as Boom Boom's wide frame filled the doorway.

"Welcome, Mrs. Delacorte. It's a fine day when high society comes to call." Boom Boom stepped around her desk and extended a hand. Charlotte shook it with tepid enthusiasm. "Please. Have a seat."

Horace retreated back into the darkness.

Though she had no interest in doing so, Charlotte obediently sat in a wooden chair next to Boom Boom's desk.

"I won't be long. I just wanted to take care of some outstanding business," Charlotte said, reaching into her bag. Her hand shook as she gathered the bundle of cash and handed it over.

"Ah, well, I knew the Delacorte name was good for it," Boom Boom said, immediately counting it out in front of her. When she was satisfied that the amount was accurate, she smiled at Charlotte, "Mae is lucky to have a relation such as yourself."

"Not at all," said Charlotte, getting up to leave.

"I can only imagine how burdened the family is by her . . . social life."

Charlotte couldn't believe she'd heard correctly.

"Excuse me?" she said.

"Of course, everyone's lips were sealed while Geraldine Delacorte was alive. No one would risk *that* woman's ire. But now she's gone, and tongues are a-wagging. If you know what I mean." Boom Boom winked.

Charlotte was momentarily shocked into silence but quickly recovered. "I'm sure I don't know what you're talking about. But I'll tell you this: Don't extend any more credit to my sister-in-law, at least not if you expect to be paid back. This is the last dollar you'll ever see from me."

She stood up, keeping her hands tucked under her arms. She did not want Boom Boom to see how they were shaking.

MAE CLIMBED THE five flights of stairs, and knocked on the door. She only had to wait a few seconds to hear the usual clicking and clattering of the multitude of locks being undone. Her heart raced in anticipation. The door opened, and a ravishing redhead stood before her, wearing a skimpy crepe de chine teddy. A black satin sleep mask was pushed above her forehead.

"You're lucky you didn't wake me up again," Fiona said, stepping aside for Mae to come in. "Your late-afternoon visits are wrecking my beauty sleep."

Mae looked at Fiona's alabaster skin, her rosy, bee-stung lips that never needed lipstick, and her wide eyes, the color of gray-green sea glass. "You don't need to be any more beautiful. I couldn't take it."

Fiona seemed not to have heard her and climbed back in bed on top of her sheets. She moved aside the latest issue of *Photoplay* magazine. Her idol, Clara Bow, was on the cover.

"When is your prison warden of a brother going to start letting you out at night?" Fiona asked.

"I think I've found a solution to that problem," said Mae, taking off her light coat, then unbuttoning her dress.

"I'll believe it when I see it," said Fiona.

Mae circled the bed, then perched on the edge, pushing up Fiona's gown. As usual, she was not wearing any underwear, and Mae ran her fingers over the thatch of russet-colored hair. Fiona sighed and closed her eyes, confident Mae would make the afternoon wake-up more than worth her while.

Mae stretched out next to her on the bed, her hand still moving with slow, practiced strokes between Fiona's legs. Mae loved the sound that Fiona made when she was touched. She was like a cat purring.

As Mae watched Fiona's fair skin grow flushed with ecstasy, she grew even more excited, her own skin becoming hot to the touch. Mae knew that she was the first woman Fiona had ever had sex with, but she had proven to be a fast learner.

Fiona cried out, shuddered, then looked at the ceiling, her body absolutely still. Mae watched her, enraptured.

Then Fiona sat up, kissed Mae on the forehead, and jumped out of bed.

"That's it?" said Mae, trying not to sound as disappointed as she felt.

"To be continued." Fiona smiled.

"Why are you rushing off?"

"I have to get dressed. Early shift tonight. I got a promotion at work," Fiona said, looking like the cat who swallowed the canary.

"What kind of promotion?"

Fiona shrugged. Something about the look on her face made Mae's stomach tighten.

"Nothing major. I'm just hostessing now."

Mae regarded her with suspicion. "I don't like you working there every night. All those men looking at you like you're a piece of meat."

Fiona shrugged. "Come on, Mae. You know as well as I that there's three types of women in the world: rich women, working women, and kept women. Maybe someday I'll know what it's like to be one of the other three. But for now—I'm a working girl. So you have to skedaddle."

Chapter 4

ROGER WARREN HAD not been the same since the warehouse raid.

He could not help but feel a deep sorrow that practicing law had, in this crazy, modern day, become a vocation in which he literally had to dodge bullets.

With a heavy heart, he thought of poor McLaren—a bullet to the leg. And with the office baseball league starting in a month.

Roger tapped the white glass keys of his typewriter, the sound ringing out to punctuate his thoughts. He couldn't wait to finish logging the evidence from the raid and put the entire episode behind him.

"Warren!" his boss yelled from down the hall.

Roger sighed, gathered the papers next to the typewriter, and shuffled down the hall.

Emory Buckner sat with his feet on his desk, a cigar in one hand.

"Let me see what you've got so far," he said.

"These are just names. I haven't cross-referenced with phone logs and . . ."

Buckner flexed his fingers in a gesture of impatience. "Just hand it over."

He removed his feet from his desk, stubbed out the cigar, and hunched over Roger's paperwork.

"Ah-hah!" he said, dragging his pen decisively over something he found on the second page. "Our first two-for-oner."

Roger leaned over, trying unsuccessfully to see what had Buckner so excited. His boss turned the page around. He had circled two words: Boom Boom.

"You're familiar with the Committee of Fourteen?" said Buckner.

"Of course." The antiprostitution group had made a big push a few years earlier, but anyone with any sense found their initiatives overreaching at best. Mayor Hylan thought they were a joke.

"They've issued a new report about some of the establishments in Midtown and Harlem, in particular. The findings are pretty damning."

"But prostitution is state jurisdiction," Roger said.

Buckner stood and paced the floor.

"Beverly 'Boom Boom' Lawrence is the proprietor of the Vesper Club on Forty-eighth Street. Boom Boom has been on our radar for years. She used to run a bordello on West Fourth Street but a lot of her business crossed state lines. Boom Boom doesn't do anything in a small way. She was busted a few times and finally closed up shop. Then she resurfaced with the Vesper Club. I need someone in there. I want you to keep your ear to the ground and find out who she hooks as her new liquor source, and I want to know if she's running women out of the club and the scope of the operation."

"That sounds like a big job," Roger said. "Maybe McBride would be better to . . ."

"I've got him in Harlem. McClaren just took a bullet. I'm running out of manpower. So it looks like you picked the short stick today."

"But—"

"It wasn't a suggestion."

Roger didn't know what made him more upset—the job, or the prospect of telling his wife he'd be working nights.

"Now listen to me, Warren: I don't care if some bimbo offers to leave the club with you one night, and another broad throws herself at you another night; I don't necessarily want the individual girls. I need the big picture. I want a pattern, and I want the people at the top."

"I need some time to adjust my schedule. . . ."

"You start tomorrow night."

FIONA WAITED IN a window booth overlooking Broadway.

Lindy's Deli on Forty-ninth Street had been around about four years and was one of Fiona's favorite places to eat out. It always seemed to be filled with interesting, if questionable, characters and always made her feel like she was really out in the world. It also had the city's best cheesecake. But tonight, its most important selling point was proximity to the Vesper. She would barely avoid being late for her shift if Jake let her get right down to business.

As soon as Jake strolled in, the other female customers immediately perked up. Jake Larkin was a handsome fellow, strikingly tall, with dark hair and serious dark eyes—if you liked that sort of thing. Which, apparently, the very-married Charlotte Delacorte did. Fiona wondered how Charlotte could stand by while her husband kept Mae locked up like a prisoner, when she herself was recklessly running around town, swooning at the feet of a bootlegger. Fiona wasn't a saint, but at least she wasn't a hypocrite.

She smiled at Jake as he slid into the booth.

"Okay, lovely Miss Fiona. What is so important?" Jake said. The waitress appeared instantly though Fiona had been sitting ignored for twenty minutes.

Jake ordered coffee and Fiona ordered a slice of cheesecake.

"I hope you're buying," Fiona said. "I'm starving, and I have a long night ahead of me."

"I'll buy if you talk. What's this all about?"

"Music and connections. And you're wasting both," she said. "You put together the best live music in town . . . but it's in some nothing basement apartment that no one knows about. If you want to play with the big boys and be their manager someday, you need to show them you can get them a big audience. And for the ones who already play at the big clubs, show them you can get them more money."

"It's not that easy, Fiona. If it were, everyone would be doing it."

The waitress served Jake's coffee.

"Can I get you anything more, sir?" she asked, sliding the cheesecake across the table without so much a glance in Fiona's direction. Fiona waited until the woman walked away.

"I can get Boom Boom to let you book some acts at the Vesper."

Jake smiled as if greatly amused. "And why would she do that?"

"A lot of reasons. She's always looking for talent and ways to make the club a draw. I could convince her you're a guy to make things happen."

"Well, you know I'd be indebted to you, Fee. Give it a shot. If anyone can work it, you can."

Fiona nodded, as if a profound thought had just crossed her mind. "The key is to make her feel you're *the* guy. Like she needs you."

"Ah, but she doesn't need me."

"You know what she does need? A liquor connection. Hers just got busted. If I bring you in, tell her you can get her in touch with your guy."

Jake shook her head. "I'm not getting involved in that."

"Why not?"

"Too big a game for me."

Fiona leaned forward, her elbows on the table. She set her green eyes on him with a focus she rarely gave anyone.

"Aren't you tired of watching everyone else make money? I know I am. This city mints a new millionaire every day, while people like you and me get the crumbs working as their window dressing and entertainment."

Jake nodded, his sexy dark eyes focused on her completely.

"You talk a good game, Fee. But what are *you* doing about all that?" he said.

"For your information, I just got promoted at work. But *this* is about you, Jake. And I'm handing you an opportunity. As the middleman for Boom Boom, you'd get a cut. For doing practically nothing. And she'd be indebted to you, and I guarantee, you'll get your musicians in there."

He sat back in the booth and downed his coffee. Then he played with the empty mug.

"You're an interesting woman," he said.

Fiona wondered if she should bother fucking him. Putting all her energy into Mae wasn't exactly paying off.

"Is that a yes?"

"I'll think about it," Jake said.

"You should. You better start making some dough. Your new girlfriend has expensive taste."

Jake laughed. "What girlfriend?"

"Princess Charlotte."

"You have quite an imagination, Fee. We're just friends."

"Yeah. And I'm just a cocktail waitress," said Fiona.

Chapter 5

"You're late," Charlotte said, standing impatiently outside of Saks Fifth Avenue.

Mae, having rushed through the crowded sidewalk tottering on impractically high heels, was breathless by the time she reached her.

"Sorry. I had to make a quick stop downtown. How did it go with Boom Boom?" Mae asked.

"It's taken care of," said Charlotte. "But that's the last time I'm doing it."

"Thanks, Charlotte. I owe you one. That's why I'm taking you shopping. There is no excuse for you to dress like a Victorian spinster. Besides—I need you to buy a few things for me."

One of the perks of being a Delacorte was Charlotte's house accounts at all the best stores in the city. William was stingy with cash but never questioned a clothing bill. It was the cost of keeping up appearances.

"It's just as important to look like a lady as it is to conduct oneself like a lady," Geraldine Delacorte always said, and William was willing to back that statement up with his bank account. It had taken a while for Charlotte to allow herself to shop without guilt. Growing up, her family fortunes had always been up and down—mostly down by the time Charlotte was a young woman. Her mother, Lillian, always sacrificed to make sure Charlotte was dressed elegantly—her mother wanted, more than anything, for Charlotte to marry well. Charlotte always knew that the clothes on her back came at great cost, and she rarely wore them with pleasure. But starting with her wedding dress, a couture gown by Jeanne Lanvin that her future mother-in-law had insisted on buying, Charlotte knew that dressing extravagantly—or, at the very least exceedingly well—was not a choice but a duty.

Charlotte followed Mae into the store. She tried to ignore the occasional curious glance directed her way by the other shoppers. After her mother-in-law's death a few weeks ago, the *New York Times* had been quick to declare a passing of the social baton: All eyes were on Charlotte as one of the emerging *doyennes* of Manhattan.

"If you would try behaving for a while, I could maybe convince William to loosen up on you a bit. And, for the record, I dress fine."

Mae rolled her eyes. "Did you learn nothing when you were out with me the other night?"

She had a point. Charlotte's impulsive first visit to a Manhattan nightclub confirmed what she had long suspected: The world was passing her by. While she was busy marrying well, dressing to please her conservative, widowed mother-in-law and rigid husband, most young women were running around dressing and acting like showgirls—and loving it.

"Good afternoon, ladies. What a pleasant surprise." Gloria, Charlotte's usual saleswoman, visibly brightened at the sight of the two Delacortes. Charlotte knew it was, no doubt, a surprise to see her. Typically, Gloria simply delivered things to the house. She knew what Charlotte liked—or, rather, what she *should* like—and that was the extent of Charlotte's shopping.

But now Mae was taking over. She told Charlotte that hemlines have come up and waistlines have dropped. "It's really that simple," said Mae.

Gloria, who must have been close to fifty years old, wouldn't raise her hemline if she were walking across a river.

The saleswoman crossed her arms, tapped her fingers, and said, "Let me show you a few things."

"Don't mind us," said Mae. "I've got it from here."

Gloria's mouth opened, but nothing came out. She stood immobilized, while Mae steered Charlotte into the wide hall of the dressing area.

"Start changing, and I'll just hand you things."

"This bossy side of you reminds me of your brother," said Charlotte. She closeted herself in the small room and removed her dress but kept her underwear, stockings, and shoes on. She glanced at her body in the full-length mirror before slipping into the cotton robe on the hook behind the door.

"Open up. These should give you a good start."

Charlotte cracked the door a few inches and took an armful of dresses.

"Come out and show me when you've got the first one on," called Mae from the other side of the door.

Charlotte shook her head and sorted the dresses on separate hooks. Two black, one emerald, one red. They were short; they had fringe, or lace, or beads. Hanging on the wall, they were like artwork.

Another knock on the door.

"And you need these to go with them," said Mae, handing her a bandeau, a few long, gorgeous necklaces with colorful, geometric-shaped beads, a chiffon scarf, silk flower, and Perrault gloves.

"Okay, this is enough for now," Charlotte said, closing the door sharply. She leaned against it as if to ward off any more "help."

When she felt confident there would be no more interruptions, she chose a black lace evening dress by Chanel to try on first. She stepped into it and pulled the straps over her shoulders. The dress fell to just below her knees, but what shocked her was the plunging neckline in the back. It was spectacular.

She imagined Jake Larkin seeing her dressed like this.

Despite doing her best not to think about Jake Larkin, he was never completely out of her mind since the night at his speakeasy;

perhaps never out of her mind since he had first appeared, accompanying Mae to her mother's funeral. She constantly felt his dark gaze on her, tracing her body. At first, Charlotte hadn't minded the slight distraction—even the fantasy—of him. But she knew it was inappropriate. How could she blame her husband for keeping secrets from her if she was keeping her own?

Another knock on the door.

"*What?*" Charlotte said.

"Come out and show me," Mae said. "Or I'm coming in after you."

"For heaven's sake, I'll be right there." Charlotte took another look at her bare back, draped a scarf over it out of modesty, and stepped into the common hallway outside the dressing rooms. There, she was able to stand on a little stool in front of a three-way mirror and get an even better view of the spectacular frock.

"Smashing," said Mae. She pulled the scarf from Charlotte's shoulders, folded it lengthwise, and tied it around her neck.

"Well, well, well," said a familiar voice. "I see someone's getting quite risqué."

Charlotte immediately stepped down from the stool. There, peeking out of another dressing room, wearing a floor-length brocade gown, was Amelia Astor. Charlotte now realized why Gloria had asked if there was an upcoming event.

"Hello, Amelia," said Charlotte.

"I had no idea you were so fashion forward, Charlotte. You look like a flapper in that *ensemble*."

"It's . . . I've become quite interested in what Chanel is doing for evening," she said.

"We all *know* what she's doing: convincing American women that it's okay to dress like boys by day and streetwalkers by night. Everyone's overpaying for a flash-in-the-pan designer. I can't imagine your husband would find that look attractive."

Charlotte wanted to reply that Amelia shouldn't be imagining what William finds attractive, but, of course, she wouldn't dare.

"You don't need to remind us how limited your imagination is, Amelia," responded Mae snarkily.

Charlotte retreated to the safety of the dressing room and changed back into her own clothes, her heart pounding.

Charlotte gathered the four dresses off the hangers and collected the accessories from the chair. She opened the door and handed the clothes to Mae. "I'll take everything," she said with a smile.

Chapter 6

FIONA DRESSED WITH special care for her first night as hostess. She wore petal pink, knowing it set off her coloring perfectly. The silk evening dress, trimmed with silver bugle beads, pink seed beads, and rhinestones, had been a gift from Mae.

The club was unusually packed, and the air vibrated with the electricity of a spring thunderstorm. Fiona had splurged on a cab to get her to the club, rationalizing it because of her raise. She wondered if she would ever lose the sense of panic she felt whenever she had to spend money.

"Hi, Becks," she said to the doorman, shaking off her umbrella. She shouldn't have gone through the front entrance, but taking the side door would have meant more time exposed to the punishing downpour. And she needed to look her best.

"It's a full house, Fee. I hope you're ready to make some bucks."

"Oh, I've never been more ready," said Fiona. But the truth was, she wasn't entirely sure what to do in her new role. Usually, she would grab a tray and start walking around with drinks. Maybe that was the best way for her night to begin, regardless of how Boom Boom intended it to end.

She made her way to the bar, aware, as always, of the multitude of hungry eyes watching her. The bartender, Jimmy, handed her a tray.

"Give me half a dozen gin and tonics. I'll see who's biting tonight," she said.

"Coming right up."

And then she saw him. He wasn't the handsomest guy in the room, and not even the best dressed. But her devoted reading of *Photoplay* magazine was finally paying off.

Fiona cut a clear path through the crowd, sidling up to the man's table.

"Are you gentlemen in need of a cocktail?"

"We're having sidecars," the man said. "Unless you care to recommend a house specialty?"

He had dark hair, a high forehead, and there was a clean-cut, very poised air about him. Fiona knew that they called him the "Boy Wonder" of Hollywood.

"Our bartender does have a drink you might especially enjoy," she said pointedly with a sly grin. "It's called the Mary Pickford."

The man looked at her more closely, knowing he was no longer anonymous.

"You don't say. And what might we expect of that?"

"Oh, a little rum. Pineapple juice. Grenadine. It's sweet, but unusual."

"Just the way I like 'em," the man said, his eyes meeting hers in a way that suggested her new duties were going to begin sooner than she thought.

"Make it a round," said the friend seated to his left.

Fiona smiled on her way to the bar, like someone with a delicious little secret. The rest of the club receded into the background, the laughter and music just a dull buzzing in her head, no more significant than the steady tick, tick, tick of a clock.

"Jimmy, I'm returning these." She passed the bartender the gin and tonics on her tray. "Give me four Mary Pickfords instead."

She felt a hand on her shoulder.

"Do you know who's at that table," said Boom Boom.

Fiona smiled the smile of someone who understands her own sudden importance.

"Of course. *Photoplay* is my bible."

"Well, now you got yourself a little miracle."

Boom Boom leaned in close. "Irving Thalberg makes fifty thousand a year. Make sure he spreads some of that around this joint for as long as possible tonight. Bring those drinks to the table, plant your ass in a seat, and don't move."

"Yes, ma'am," Fiona said with a mock salute.

She wondered if she could get her up to twenty-five bucks a week.

MAE HEAVED HER bedroom window open as high as it would go.

The cool night air blew into the room. She shivered in her lightweight dress but didn't want to be weighed down by a bulky coat. Ignoring the chill, she swung one leg out the window. Bracing herself against the sill, she double-checked the suspension hooks. She'd nailed them in carefully, just as the old man at Lascoff's Hardware had instructed her. The rope ladder was securely hooked, and the bottom half was nearly touching the ground below.

Her days as a prisoner of Fifth Avenue were over.

FIONA CARRIED THE drinks back to Irving Thalberg's table, expertly ducking anyone who might interrupt her.

"Gentlemen, introducing . . . Mary Pickford." Fiona handed the glasses around the table.

"Why don't you join us," said Irving. The man next to him pulled up a chair for her.

"Delighted to," said Fiona.

"I'm Irving," he said.

"I know who you are. *The Hunchback of Notre Dame* is one of my favorite movies."

The other men laughed, and one said, "Irv, you've got fans everywhere."

"Yeah, but not all are this beautiful," said Irving. "What's your name, honey?"

"Fiona."

"Fiona, I've got a new film coming out in a few weeks called *The Merry Widow*. You'll have to let me know what you think."

He put his hand on her knee. Fiona leaned close to him, talking so low she doubted anyone else at the table could hear. "I just know I'll love it." She wondered if he could smell her Chanel No. 5. It had taken her three months to save up enough to buy it, then she was hesitant even to use it. She was glad she'd splurged tonight.

"Oh, sweetheart, I wish all the critics were so open-minded." He laughed.

He offered her a cigarette, and when she looked up, she saw her first glitch in the evening heading toward her at full speed.

"Will you excuse me for a minute," Fiona said, jumping up from her seat.

Chapter 7

LOUD MUSIC. SMOKY air. Beautiful people. The Vesper Club enveloped Mae in an embrace. She was home again, back where she belonged, and nothing was going to keep her away ever again. Not even her uptight brother.

Of course, her escape hadn't been flawless. She had gotten a run in her stocking and cut her toe on a small rock or stick when she jumped off the ladder. But those minor hiccups were all but forgotten when she saw her.

Fiona, in all her cherry-haired glory, sat at a table, surrounded by men. She was laughing and smiling—a rare sight. And she wore the pink Lanvin dress Mae had bought her; that was heartening. Surely, it meant Fiona knew that Mae would indeed make it out that night as she'd promised.

Yes, Fiona had been waiting for her. Because as soon as she saw her, she jumped up from the table and rushed to meet her across the room.

"Lord, am I happy to see you!" Mae said, dying to throw her arms around her. She didn't dare, of course.

"What are you doing here?" said Fiona.

"I know—it's fantastic, isn't it? I told you I found a way to get out of the house."

"Yes, doll, that's keen. But tonight isn't really a good night."

Mae realized that Fiona was looking all around, everywhere but at her.

"What are you talking about? Not a good night for what?"

"Look . . . I'm working,"

"I'll just wait around until your shift is over, and we'll beat it to Jake's."

Fiona looked at her as if trying to muster the patience to deal with a small child. Then she took her by the hand and practically dragged her to the coatroom.

"Can you excuse us for a minute?" Fiona said to the coat-check girl.

"I'm not supposed to leave m'post," the girl said, her small eyes darting around nervously.

"Get the fuck out," Fiona said.

The girl scuttled off. Fiona closed the door, and Mae leaned back into a row of coats, sinking into a long mink.

"What's going on?" she said to Fiona.

Fiona kissed her, hard. Mae opened her mouth, the blood rushing between her legs. Fiona pulled down the strap of Mae's dress, her mouth moving to her breasts. Mae sighed deeply, closing her eyes, her hands in Fiona's tangle of long hair.

Fiona lifted her head, speaking quietly into Mae's ear as she slipped her hand into her bloomers and pressed her fingers between her legs.

"Listen, baby—I have to focus on work tonight. So I need you to be a good girl and duck out of here." Her hand moved in sharp, quick strokes, until Mae cried out. Fiona held her so she didn't lose her balance and fall into the coats.

Then she wiped her hand on the mink.

"I'm going back to work," Fiona said. "Do what I tell you, and I'll see you tomorrow."

Mae was caught too off guard to argue. She stood alone, nesting amongst the coats until she heard a timid knock at the door. Mae opened it.

"I got to get back to work," said the coat-check girl.

"It's all yours," said Mae. She thought about pulling a coat out of there for herself but decided against it.

She had no intention of going home.

THE CROWD AT the bar seemed to have doubled during the time Fiona had been in the coatroom.

"Excuse me." She pushed her way through the people milling around, ignoring the patrons who recognized her as a cocktail waitress and hailed her for a drink. She got within a few feet of Thalberg's table but couldn't catch sight of him. Wait, maybe that wasn't the table. Or was it?

Then she realized he was gone.

"He left," said Boom Boom, so close behind her she could feel her breath on her ear.

Fiona whirled around.

"What?"

"Two women came in, sat at the table, and within ten minutes, the whole group walked out."

Fiona's heart began to pound. She had visions of being fired, of moving back in with her grandmother. Of working as a maid.

"It won't happen again. . . ."

"Come with me."

Fiona followed Boom Boom to the back of the club, close to the side exit. Boom Boom said nothing; she simply stood there, waiting.

Fiona turned at the sound of a woman's yelling, the hum of the crowd and a sense of the room parting, dividing like a river when a boat causes a wake. Then the source of the commotion came into view: Two men from Boom Boom's security team were holding Mae by her arms, practically dragging her to the door.

Mae bucked like a wild animal, and in her furious state didn't notice Fiona, standing off to the side. Fiona resisted the urge to run over and tell them to get their hands off her. An hour ago, she would have. But she still held out hope that she would not be tossed out next.

Boom Boom opened the door, and the two men shoved Mae outside.

"It's all right, everyone. Some people just can't hold their gin. No cause for alarm," Boom Boom said to the handful of onlookers who were still paying attention.

She pulled Fiona aside.

"The next time you fuck someone in the coatroom, it better be a guy who's dropping some cash around here. Or I promise you will be back on the Lower East Side faster than you can say 'Irish whore.' Now get out and show up tomorrow night ready to make me some money."

She held the door open again.

Chapter 8

THE MORNING BEGAN with a downpour of rain, a seamless storm from the night before. Charlotte knew it was typical for early April, but it wasn't a pleasant way to start the day—especially since she had to get up and out the door to the mansion on Fifty-seventh Street.

She was sorely tempted by the new clothes hanging in her closet. It would brighten her mood to wear one of the dresses—two were suitable for daytime. But she knew that the Women's Literary Alliance meeting was not exactly the place to debut her updated wardrobe—despite the fact that Amelia Astor had already gotten an accidental preview. Instead, she dressed in a tailored, maroon silk crepe dress and cloche hat by Caroline Reboux.

Charlotte made her way through the marble entrance hall, an imposing space dominated by Favrile glass mosaics and a large fireplace. She was early and fully expected to be the first in the parlor, where she had instructed the board members to meet. It was one of her favorite rooms in the house—not overwhelmingly large, but captivating in its ornate, Louis-XVI-style décor. The room also featured a full-length portrait of Geraldine, circa 1890, painted in Paris by Carolus-Duran. It was a fitting backdrop to the group's first meeting at the house without her.

But Charlotte was not alone.

"Oh! I didn't expect anyone to be here yet," Charlotte said.

And certainly not her husband. But there he was, sitting across from Amelia Astor on the French settee with the carved Giltwood frame. It was a piece she and William had discussed bringing into their own parlor.

She had never seen William at a WLA meeting—not even when his mother was at her most active. Maybe this was his way of making an effort to connect with her. She could not be the only one unhappy with the distance between them.

Charlotte took a seat at a round, mahogany table. She spread out her notes, her heart beating faster than usual. "I'm surprised to see you here, William," she said slowly. "I didn't know you were interested in these meetings."

"I feel a responsibility to mother's memory," said William. "I just want to make sure that you are as invested in this project as you are, say, to shopping."

Charlotte looked up, her cheeks burning.

She glanced at Amelia Astor, but she was suddenly very busy with her own pen and paper.

That bitch!

"I'm completely invested in this library, darling. And certainly more than in shopping or, say, gossiping," she responded sweetly, a slight edge to her voice.

Isobel Whiting, Harriet Guinness, and several other board members filed into the room.

"Glad to hear it," William said. "Then I'll leave you ladies to it."

Charlotte watched him walk to the door.

"Let's begin," Charlotte said, standing to face the group. "I want to take time this morning to discuss the library's opening-night gala." The idea of planning a party in three months for all the notables of New York, from art to society to politics, had been daunting at first. But the night she went out with Mae and saw the atmosphere at the clubs, she realized that maybe it could be more fun than obligation. This wouldn't be a Geraldine Delacorte party—it would be a Charlotte Delacorte party. And her party would have a theme. "The social calendar is getting more crowded every year, and I think people are getting almost fatigued by the competing events." She looked pointedly at Amelia, who was by far the most egregious overscheduler. "In order to make the WLA event stand out—to make it something people are excited about—I suggest we plan the party around the theme of King Tut."

The room erupted in conversation. The discovery of King Tut's tomb three years earlier had captured the country's imagination. Personally, Charlotte had been obsessed by it. The very idea of ancient history being unearthed, close enough to touch. And those treasures . . . that gold burial mask. After five years in New York, being surrounded by all that money could buy, she was even more impressed by the wonders of history, the quest for discovery.

"The color palette will be gold, and while I think we will stop short of a costume party, I would certainly encourage Egyptian influences in dress."

Charlotte could tell that she had the support of the room, but when she looked for Amelia, to gauge her reaction, she was gone.

"It will be expensive," said Margaret Cavendish.

"I think everyone in this room has thrown more extravagant parties for less important reasons," said Charlotte. "We want to put this library on the map. I want every paper writing about it. I want tourists to think of it as a place they can't miss while in the city. And, most importantly, we want women to think of it as a place where they can indulge their own sense of discovery. Every book has the potential to be someone's King Tut's tomb."

"I love it!" cried Isobel, clapping her hands.

Charlotte continued to scan the room.

"Excuse me for a minute," she said.

Charlotte took a right turn out of the parlor and headed to the stairwell leading to the second floor. But she realized that if she looked out of the second-floor window, her view of the entrance would be blocked by the carriage porch. Charlotte changed direction, and hurried down a rear staircase to the wing that housed the dining room. From there, Charlotte had a direct view of the entrance. Sure enough, William's Rolls Royce was parked in front.

Next to the car, standing in the rain and leaning in the front passenger window, was Amelia.

Chapter 9

"MADAME DELACORTE?"

Charlotte sat up abruptly, startled out of her unplanned nap on the parlor sofa. The articles and photographs about the discovery of King Tut's tomb were still spread on her lap. "I'm sorry, madame. I didn't mean to wake you," Rafferty said.

"Oh, not at all. I was just resting for a minute. Planning, that sort of thing." She stumbled groggily. Ever since the incident in William's office, she felt self-conscious around Rafferty, noticed him more. The mistress-of-the-house/servant power dynamic had been upset. He had seen her in a moment of weakness, had something over her. And yet, she did not feel he would use it against her. If anything, she felt bad about having put him in such a position.

Rafferty's face was unreadable as he said, "Penny found this while cleaning Master Delacorte's office. She wasn't sure what to do with it, but I thought you might want it."

He held out a twisted hairpin. The one Charlotte had used to pick the locks on William's office door and file cabinets.

"Oh, goodness. Thank you, Rafferty. That must have fallen out of my hair. I'll . . . dispose of it properly."

Rafferty nodded, seemed about to say something, then refrained.

"I'll be more careful with these from now on," she said, then immediately wished she could take it back. But surely she had to acknowledge that he and Penny had spared her the disaster of William's finding it and putting two and two together. "Is that all?" she asked, trying to regain some measure of composure.

"You have a visitor in the front hall. A Mr. Larkin."

Charlotte kept her reaction neutral. After four years of being a Delacorte, she had at least mastered something.

"Fine. Please show him in."

She had been tormented for days about her misguided visit to his apartment to ask for help finding money to pay off Mae's Vesper Club debt. Not only had he looked at her like she was little more than slightly pathetic, he had seized the moment to tell her exactly how weak her marriage must be if she couldn't ask her husband for money.

Her one consolation had been that she would probably never see him again. And yet, here he was—about to walk into her parlor, unannounced, in the middle of the afternoon, while her husband was gone.

Charlotte stood and smoothed out her dress quickly. It was the same one she had worn to the meeting that morning. It was creased but still more presentable than one of the housedresses she might have changed into if she had known she'd be falling asleep. *Thank the Lord for small favors,* she thought.

"I apologize for not calling ahead," Jake said, his dark eyes immediately taking her all in.

Rafferty closed the parlor doors behind him.

Charlotte experienced a strange sensation at the sight of Jake. It was as if a balloon of happiness filled her chest, making it difficult to breathe.

"Have a seat," she said, knowing that her smile belied the nonchalance of her greeting. He sat across from her in a Jules Allard armchair. A small Louis XV table stood between them. "You know, normally I would not encourage you to come by this house. I'm sure my husband would remember you from your appearance with Mae at the funeral, and that is not the best association to have."

"I had it on good authority that your husband isn't home in the afternoons." He smiled slyly.

"And how did you learn such information?"

"From a conversation with Mae last night."

Charlotte looked at him in confusion. Last night? As far as she knew, Mae had gone to her room after dinner and never left. She would have heard Mae sneak down the stairs again. *Wouldn't I?*

"Well, thank you for your discretion. Would you like tea or coffee?"

"No, thanks. I can't stay long. I just wanted to apologize for the other day—at my apartment. It wasn't my place to tell you how to conduct your marriage. As I said—what do I know? And I didn't mean to be insensitive about your need to find money. I know you were just trying to help Mae get out of a tight spot. Anyway, I've been thinking about it, and if you still need money, I have an idea."

Charlotte's impulse was to tell him she didn't need his ideas—that she'd found the money herself. But it wasn't entirely true. She'd found the money, but she still had to replace it. As much as she wanted to save face and tell Jake she had it under control, she couldn't afford to.

"I'm listening."

"It's tough for you to get your hands on cash, but I imagine it's not tough for you to get your hands on stuff that is worth some cash."

"What do you mean?"

He looked pointedly at the diamond and onyx Van Cleef & Arpels bracelet on her wrist. She put her hand over it. "Sell my jewelry?" she whispered. It felt like a transgression just to say the words.

"It's just an idea."

"I appreciate your trying to help. But you don't understand: I can't walk into a store without being recognized. If I sold a piece of jewelry, it would be in the gossip columns the next day."

"I've already thought of that. That's why I came here in person. If there is a piece you want to unload, I'll take it and do it for you."

Charlotte looked at him, her voice a murmur. "Why would you do that?"

"I told you. I feel bad about what I said the other day. . . ." He looked down at his hands and back up at her searchingly.

"You could simply apologize—which you already did. Or just give me your idea. You don't have to volunteer to actually go out and pawn jewelry for me."

Jake seemed to consider this.

He stood from the chair and joined her on the couch, sitting far too close to be considered acceptable for casual socializing. Charlotte tugged at the collar of her dress, suddenly extremely warm as she looked down at his strong, rough hands so close to her. She could only imagine what they would feel like on her bare skin. . . .

"I think you should leave now," she said. "Thank you for your idea. I'll consider it. Hopefully it won't come to that."

"Charlotte, you're right: I don't have to get this involved. But frankly, I haven't been able to stop thinking about you." He took her hand gently, stroking it with his thumb. She closed her eyes, sinking into the slight touch, then opened them and looked at him.

His eyes were perhaps the darkest she had ever looked into, a lush brown that reminded her of velvet. But he had terrible manners. And he didn't have a proper job. And *she* was married. So why, oh why, did his words make her feel like the very ground beneath her was shifting.

Breathing and talking at the same time was suddenly difficult.

"While that is very . . . nice to hear, I'm afraid there's not much to be done about it," she said, pulling her hand away.

He nodded slowly. "That is how it appears."

Charlotte stood. "Rafferty will show you to the door."

ROGER WARREN BARELY recognized himself in the mirror.

His Washington Square apartment was quiet, his wife putting their son down to sleep. And instead of preparing for bed himself, Roger was getting dressed in a jazz suit.

His clothing that night, from head to toe, had been issued by the U.S. Attorney's Office. The blue suit jacket, single-breasted, was dramatically tight-waisted, with long back vents. The trousers were tight and narrow. His shoes were two-toned in white and black, with a fringed tongue.

Roger was amazed by his boss's commitment to this operation – to go so far as to put his own money towards a successful bust; he knew that the Committee of Fourteen had hit a wall in earlier investigations because they didn't have the funds to roll convincingly with the nightlife crowd. The fourteen directors came out of social work, law enforcement, and clergy—and none had the resources the Committee really needed. Just last year, their top investigator, Harry Kahan, gave up on busting the El Fey Club because he didn't have the funds to infiltrate it.

Roger had no such excuse to fail.

"Is this truly necessary," asked his wife, Elizabeth, standing in the doorway.

"Unfortunately, it is," he said, kissing her on the forehead. "These are the times we live in."

"Do you think you'll be terribly late?" From the next room, their eighteen-month-old son wailed his protest at being left alone to sleep.

"I do," he said. "Don't wait up." Roger had not been to church in over a month, but he silently prayed she would not ask what time the clubs closed.

He could not tell her that when the club closed, his night might just be beginning. Turning his back to Elizabeth, he slipped off his wedding band and put it in his nightstand drawer.

CHARLOTTE FLIPPED THROUGH the pages of *Vogue,* her eyes skimming unseeing over the words and photos.

She kept replaying the conversation with Jake in her mind, over and over, an endless loop of the conversation she still could scarcely believe had actually happened. Even in her fantasies, anything that transpired between them was wordless. She had never even dreamt that he would say something about how he thought of her, and so meaningfully. Despite herself, she longed to know how it felt to be in his arms.

She startled when William walked into the room. He usually spent an hour or two in his office after dinner.

"You're upstairs early," she said.

"I've got to pack," William said, pulling his suitcase out of his closet.

"Now?"

"I'm catching a train tonight. That gives me the full morning to work tomorrow."

Charlotte hugged her arms around herself.

"I wish you'd told me."

He looked at her sharply. "Don't be like that, Charlotte."

"Like what? I'm your *wife*. I have no idea when you're coming or going. I'm a complete afterthought to you."

He looked at her with undisguised annoyance.

"You're being childish. Do you have any idea what it takes to keep the company going? And now settling Mother's estate? And being responsible for my sister?"

"Maybe I could help you with these things if you didn't push me aside. And what was that remark you made this morning at your mother's house? You hope I am as committed to the WLA as I am to shopping? If you think I spend too much money shopping, you should have said something earlier."

"I don't have an issue with the money you spend shopping," he said, laying shirts and jackets out on the bed. "Why? Have you bought something new?"

Something tells me you know that I have, Charlotte thought.

"Yes, as a matter of fact. I picked up a few things at Saks yesterday."

"Well, let's see them," he said with a smile.

"Now?" Maybe this *was* his way of trying to connect with her after all. She smiled to herself; Amelia's little attempt at sabotage was going to backfire. She would try on the dresses, and he would see her looking beautiful, perhaps see her as he did when they'd first met. And he would make love to her, not like the other morning when it felt like she wasn't even in the room, but the way she imagined it could be, the way she knew somehow that it was supposed to be. "I'll be right back."

She slowly went to her dressing room and closed the door. The clothing was still wrapped artfully on the hangers. She ran her hands over each dress, wondering the best dress to model for him first, what he might like best. Perhaps the emerald green that fell just below her knees, with the rows of fringe at the bottom. William always loved her in green.

She stretched her arms behind her to pull up the zipper, then stepped into the matching pair of heels she had bought. Wrapping a bandeau around her hair, she paused for a moment. She had fantasized about wearing the outfit to the Vesper Club, but showing it off to her husband was more important. When William looked at her—*really* looked at her, not just passing a glance on his way to taking care of some piece of business—she didn't feel like the world was passing her by. She still felt alive. Unfortunately, those looks had become rare. But perhaps she was as much at fault for that as he was.

This time, if he made love to her, she would not think about Jake Larkin.

She took one final look in the mirror and felt beautiful. She smiled at her reflection, knowing she might make heads turn even at the Vesper Club. When she walked back into the bedroom, she felt a bit like a proud peacock.

William was still sorting through his closet. But when he turned to look at her, he reacted instantly.

"You look as if you're wearing a costume. Stop being silly and return those clothes."

Charlotte's hand went to her heart; she felt as if she'd been struck. When she finally spoke, her voice was barely audible.

"Half the women in New York would give a limb for these clothes."

"And there's a class of women who are selling more than 'a limb' on the street each night. Doesn't mean I want my wife dressing like them."

"I'm not returning these clothes," Charlotte responded quietly, shaking. "I like them."

"Then feel free to wear them around the house to amuse yourself. But don't ever let me see you dressed like that in public."

Chapter 10

As soon as he saw it, Roger realized that he had passed the Vesper Club many times during daylight hours and never noticed. But now, at night, lit in pink neon, it was like a beacon.

"Five dollars," said a man at the door.

Roger reached for his wallet. He couldn't believe he was dipping into his expense account before he even walked into the place.

A petite young woman with an accent checked his coat. After that, he wasn't quite sure what to do with himself.

The pink front room was covered with portraits of nudes, and the chandelier looked like it belonged in a Fifth Avenue ballroom—not that he'd ever been in one of those. But it was fancy, that was for sure.

After seeing that every seat at the bar was taken, Roger decided to get the lay of the land. He walked casually to the back, where he found an unoccupied stage surrounded by empty tables. He realized he probably should have shown up later. But he was already there, and so he needed to find a way to make use of the time.

He returned to the barroom and took a table for two. The couple laughing at the table next to him were smoking and throwing back drinks like they were at the world's greatest party. In fact, everyone seemed to be having an amazing time. And they were all dressed to the hilt. Roger was grateful to whoever had the foresight to supply him with some decent clothes.

"Can I get you somethin' to drink, sugar?" a pretty blonde asked him with a wink. She had brightly rouged cheeks and a beauty mark next to her red lips that might have been penciled on.

"Uh, sure," he said. "I'll have a bourbon on the rocks."

"Coming right up," she said. The edges of her spangly dress tantalizingly flapped against her thighs when she walked.

Roger shifted in his seat. He wished their operations budget allowed for him to have a buddy along. At least then he could talk to someone and not feel so out of place. But he knew the whole point was meeting new people and figuring out the key players. He glanced around the room. He'd never seen so many scantily clad beautiful women in one place. It was straight out of one of his sexier late-night fantasies. The kind of fantasy he didn't dare share with his wife.

And then he saw her.

Luminous, she exuded sex appeal. Her long, red hair framed her delicate porcelain features, and even from across the room, he could see she carried herself like a prize. Her short dress was a shade of pink that seemed to redefine the color. And with her pale limbs, she looked like a fragile doll.

She was talking to two men, and they hung on her every word.

"Bourbon on the rocks." The cocktail waitress reappeared, suddenly blocking his view of the redhead. Roger quickly handed her a few bills, far more than he needed to. All he wanted was for her to move away.

The redhead sat in one of the men's lap. He had his hand on her white thigh, and Roger felt an irrational surge of jealousy. It was all he could do not to get up and find a way to talk to her.

He angrily tossed back his drink.

His one consolation was that he wasn't being paid to fraternize with the patrons of the club. He would focus on the staff, and it would be all business.

He signaled the waitress for another drink and forced himself to look away.

CHARLOTTE TURNED OVER in the empty bed. Outside, the rain had finally stopped, and she found herself longing for the sound of it pattering against the house.

It was too quiet.

She thought about William on the train to Boston and wondered if he wished he were home instead. She hated to admit it, but the answer was most likely no.

Why all of this sudden travel? He was the president of Delacorte

Properties. His grandfather had been the founder; his father had helmed the company for decades of success. Even if all of this travel was necessary for the company—expanding its presence in other cities or whatever the reason might be—surely William could delegate some of it to an employee? He must want to be away a week or two out of every month, away from her.

What had she done? There was not one thing he had asked of her that she had refused. Was it her failure to get pregnant? Even his mother had been uncharacteristically understanding on that front.

Or was something else wrong—something that had nothing to do with her or their marriage? Did he have some problem he didn't feel he could share with her? She'd made it clear during her visit to his office that she wanted him to confide in her. That it was what a wife was for, after all.

She couldn't imagine what such a problem would be. She knew Delacorte Properties was not necessarily booming as it had been in the heyday of Atticus Delacorte's stewardship, but surely there wasn't an actual problem. And even if money was tight, the inheritance from Geraldine's estate would surely fix that.

No, the only logical conclusion was that he was avoiding her. He had taken a chance on marrying someone outside his circle, and it had taken Geraldine's death to make him realize he regretted it.

She thought of Amelia Astor, the way she always managed to be there when Charlotte messed up, or when William was particularly vulnerable to wanting things to be done "just so," done in a manner that was second nature to Amelia and still a concerted, learned effort for Charlotte.

Someone knocked on the door.

Charlotte sat up, pulling the covers around her body.

"Who is it?"

"It's me," said Mae. "Open up."

Charlotte felt around the floor, stepped into her slippers, and made her way across the dark room. She opened the door. Mae was dressed in a silver metallic dress and stockings studded with rhinestones. Her bangs were cut shorter, giving her an even more severe look. On her, it worked.

"Why are you locked in there like Fort Knox?" said Mae.

"I get nervous when William is away."

"Nervous? I say, hallelujah! Now get dressed."

"I'm in bed already," said Charlotte. "If you're going out, I'm pretending I don't know."

She started closing the door, but Mae stuck her foot out.

"Unacceptable," said Mae.

"Stop playing around!" snapped Charlotte. "Look, I don't know how you've been managing to sneak out of the house, but if you want William to start giving you more money, you have to behave."

"What makes you think I've been sneaking out?" said Mae.

"I know, okay? So just stop."

"Fine. I'll behave when my brother is around. But tonight he's gone, so let's take advantage of it. I'm going with or without you, so you might as well live it up one last time."

Charlotte hesitated.

"Come on. Get dressed," said Mae. "And don't even tell me you don't have anything to wear, because I know firsthand that you do."

Charlotte had to admit, it would be gratifying to go out on the town in her new clothes just a few hours after William had forbidden it. And she couldn't help but want Jake to see her in them . . .

Or she could lie in bed, tossing and turning and wondering why her husband didn't love her.

"I'll meet you downstairs," said Charlotte.

THE CAB LET them off across the street from the Vesper. A small line had formed outside the door.

"A line? Is that unusual?" Charlotte was eager to get inside. Tonight, she looked like she belonged. And more than that, she *felt* like she belonged.

"Not really," said Mae, oddly subdued.

She had been quiet during the ride, staring out the window and absently picking at one of the rhinestones on her stocking. Charlotte had to tell her to stop before she tore a hole. The exuberance Mae had shown when convincing Charlotte to leave the house was entirely gone. It was as if Charlotte had dragged her out instead of the other way around.

She thought Mae was just anxious to get to the club, but now that they were there, she seemed even more withdrawn.

They took a place at the back of the line.

"This will move fast," Charlotte said, trying to rally her. Mae nodded, staring straight ahead. When they reached the entrance, Charlotte handed the door steward ten dollars.

He refused the money.

"I'm sorry, ladies, I can't let you in. At least, not you, Mae," he said.

Mae looked around like a trapped animal, speaking in a low voice so others wouldn't hear. "Come on, Becks. She made her point, okay? I get it. I'll behave."

The man shook his head. "I'm sorry. Can't do it."

Mae began to tremble. Charlotte grabbed her hand.

"It's okay. We'll just go somewhere else. . . ."

"Can *she* go in?" Mae pulled Charlotte closer to the door.

"Yes. But not you."

Mae turned to her. "You have to go in and tell Fiona what's going on. Get her to come out here for a minute, so I can talk to her."

"Let's just go, Mae. I don't know what you did last night, but we should leave."

"I'm not going anywhere until I talk to Fiona. Please, Charlotte."

Her eyes were alarming in their desperation. Charlotte looked at the doorman, who had already moved on to the next group of people.

She should have stayed in bed.

"Fine. I'll try to find her. Hold my bag for me—and my jacket. Do not argue with this guy or try to come in after me. I'll be back in a few minutes."

Inside, Charlotte walked through the barroom as inconspicuously as possible. She hoped to high heaven that she wouldn't run into Boom Boom.

It took her less than two minutes to spot Fiona, her red hair and pink dress like a colorful flag waving everyone to attention. She breathed a sigh of relief, thankful Mae had been held outside: Fiona was sitting on some guy's lap, looking at him with rapt attention, while he ran his hand high up her thigh.

Charlotte maneuvered through the crowd. A cocktail waitress bumped into her, and a slosh of liquid streamed down her back.

"Sorry!" the waitress said. But Charlotte kept moving. A cigarette girl offered her a pack of Luckies.

There was no way to approach Fiona's table discreetly; the crowd was so rowdy and jocular that she was playfully pushed into one of the men standing nearby.

"Sorry, miss. You all right?" the man said, holding Charlotte by the shoulders so she didn't fall.

Fiona jumped up from her perch. "What are *you* doing here?"

The three men at the table regarded her with curiosity. The one she had collided with offered her a seat. "She's not staying," Fiona snapped. She sank back onto the man's lap, and he wrapped his arms around her.

"Can I speak to you alone for a minute?" Charlotte said, feeling like a fool. What had seemed like a relatively bad idea outside the club now felt like the height of stupidity.

"No," Fiona said.

That's it? Just . . . no?

"Mae is outside, and she'd really like to talk to you for just a minute."

"Go home, Charlotte." Her tone was so dismissive, it approached boredom.

Fiona lit the man's cigarette, and they resumed whatever conversation had been interrupted by Charlotte's appearance. No one at the table was looking at her any longer.

Charlotte turned away and walked slowly through the crowd.

ROGER WATCHED THE woman in the black dress stalk away from the redhead's table. He had been pleased to see the interruption. As soon as the woman appeared, the beauty in the pink dress had momentarily broken away from the man pawing at her like an animal. But she just as quickly melted back into him.

Whatever had been said between them, the woman walking away was not happy. Who was she? A friend? Sister? Rival?

Despite the woman's risqué dress, with its plunging back, there was something regal and almost reserved about the woman. And also something familiar. Where had he seen her before?

Roger stole another peek at the redhead. She was laughing as if she'd never been interrupted in the first place and resting her hand on the man's chest.

Roger waved the waitress over and ordered another drink. Then it hit him.

The woman in the black dress had been at the mansion the morning they questioned the real-estate mogul. He remembered her standing by the front door as they left. She had seemed completely out of sorts, as if she were the one who had done something wrong.

Charlotte Delacorte.

Roger looked back at the redhead. Maybe he had a reason to talk to her after all.

"FIONA ISN'T IN there," Charlotte said, pulling Mae away from the club and hailing a cab. It was suddenly very important to get Mae as far away as possible.

"She must be—she works on Thursday nights."

"Well, I didn't see her."

"Damn it!" Mae said. A cab pulled up to them, and Charlotte opened the door. Mae hesitated.

"Get in," Charlotte said.

They sat in silence for most of the ten-minute ride down to Jake's. Until Charlotte said, "You know, maybe with everything that's going on, you should cool it with her for a while."

Mae gave her a dirty look. "Oh, get off of your high horse. Why don't you cool it with Jake Larkin."

Charlotte shook her head. "There's nothing going on with Jake Larkin."

"Yeah, right. Then why was he asking me last night when William is or isn't at the house?"

"If you really must know, I was asking him for help finding the money to pay Boom Boom."

Mae sat up straighter. "William didn't give you the money? I thought you were going to say it was for the library?"

"It wasn't that simple."

"So where did you get the money?"

"Just leave it alone."

Mae sank back against the seat. "I don't know how you stay in your marriage."

"Well, Mae—it seems that if you want your inheritance, you might have to figure it out," she snapped.

Charlotte paid the driver. Mae didn't say anything during the

walk to the alley. But when she reached the top of the stairs leading to the basement door—when they could already hear the sounds
of the music from inside—she blurted out, "I love her."

Charlotte, already halfway down the stairs, walked back to
the top.

"Mae, I understand that you feel . . . strongly for her. But you
have to think about your future . . ."

"Fuck you."

Mae abruptly brushed past her and walked inside.

Charlotte sighed, sitting down on the step. *I'm just as bad as
William.*

I should find Mae and apologize. We need to stick together.

Inside, it was as noisy and smoky as she remembered. But this
time, the sight of the dark-skinned musicians, the makeshift bar,
and the ragtag furniture made her feel warm and welcome.

Mae had already claimed a spot on the sofa—the one on which
Charlotte had passed out the last time.

"I'm sorry," Charlotte said, but Mae turned away from her.
The woman next to Mae on the couch laughed at the rebuff.

The bar was crowded, but it was there that Charlotte found
refuge.

Jake was shaking up a cocktail and entertaining an audience of
half a dozen people. When he spotted her, he smiled.

"What a surprise. I didn't know the Delacorte girls were coming out tonight. What's your poison?" he said.

"Gin and tonic," Charlotte said. In the center of the room, a
man played a sax solo to a suddenly still, quietly wide-eyed audience. The man stood, his eyes closed, brow furrowed with effort to
sustain the notes. When he finished, the room erupted in applause.

"Who is that?" she asked.

"Coleman Hawkins. Best sax playing in the country. And you
can say you heard him here first." Jake squeezed a lime into her
drink and slid it across the bar.

"He's incredible," she said.

"There's more where that came from," he said. "Lots more."

She looked around the room. "Not here," he said. "I mean in the city. Have you ever been to a real jazz club?"

"Um, no," she said.

"Well, we can't have that," he said. "Get your jacket. I'll get one of these guys to cover the bar."

"Where are we going?" she asked, laughing, as he jumped over the bar and tugged her off her stool.

"Harlem," he said.

Chapter 11

JAKE OPENED THE passenger-side door to his garishly green Model T. The unnatural shade was completely unfitting for a car.

"I've wanted to ask you . . . why did you paint your car this color?" Charlotte said, climbing inside.

"I lost a bet," Jake said.

There was little traffic at that hour, and once they passed the nineties, there were virtually no cars on the road except taxicabs. Charlotte's skin tingled with the awareness of how alone they were.

Eventually, Jake parked on a side street, and they walked a block to their destination, their arms accidentally brushing as they moved. A sign out front said, THE KING CLUB.

A tall, extremely large black man stood sentry at the door. Charlotte wanted to just keep on walking, but as soon as the man saw Jake, he called out, "If it isn't the Lark. Where you been? And what you doing bringing your debs around here?" he said, looking at Charlotte.

"Bring my deb? She brought *me*. I thought maybe this joint was going soft."

"Don't give me no grief," the man said, laughing. He opened the door.

It was dark inside, and the limited light bathed the room in red. The air smelled of a sweet smoke she recognized from Jake's place that first night.

She heard music, but not the dizzying notes of jazz she had expected. Instead, a woman's mournful voice filled the room.

Jake took Charlotte's hand gently and led her to a table near the stage. They were the only white people in the club.

The woman onstage was tall and slender, dark-skinned, and stunning in her beauty. She had high cheekbones and thin, dramatically arched eyebrows. Her hair was wider than it was long, rebellious in its curls. She wore a long, beaded, blue dress that reflected light like a mirror.

"He done me wrrrong. . . ." she sang, her voice sorrowful. Charlotte couldn't take her eyes off her. Until Jake took her hand again under the table.

"What are you doing?" she whispered, leaning toward him.

"Sshh. Just listen," he said, and squeezed her hand. A woman brought them drinks. Charlotte hadn't even noticed him order anything, but she wouldn't be surprised if they just knew what he wanted. She took a sip from her glass and winced. Bourbon.

When the woman finished her song, the audience didn't applaud. Charlotte wondered if there was some strange protocol.

"Who is she?" Charlotte said.

"Rona Lovejoy," he said. "I think she's better than Bessie Smith, but she won't sing anywhere but this place. It's her brother's— Lawrence "the king" Lovejoy."

"She's amazing. And beautiful."

Soon afterward, a band took the stage and immediately launched into a frenetic number, dizzying in its composition. Jake listened with rapt attention, tapping out the song on the table with his fingers.

"You know this song?"

"Of course. That's the Duke."

"The Duke, the King . . . are we in Harlem, or England?"

Jake laughed. "Duke Ellington," he said. "This song is 'East Saint Louis Toodle-Oo,' That trumpet player is Bubber Miley. Listen to that." He closed his eyes.

"They sound really . . . different," Charlotte said.

"You have a good ear; they do sound different," Jake said, smiling at her. "They call their style 'jungle sound.'"

Charlotte felt overly warm and wanted to adjust her hair so it wasn't so heavy on her neck, but she didn't want to move her hand away from Jake's. She kept her eyes on the stage and tried to lose herself in the music. When the trombone blared at its highest sound level, she felt it run through her, and it made her heart race.

And then Jake rested his hand on her thigh. His touch radiated up her leg, a swift heat rushing up her until she tingled between her legs.

She pushed his hand away forcefully. And then immediately wished he would put it back.

MAE REMOVED HER high heels for the climb up five flights to Fiona's apartment.

After waiting for hours for Fiona to show up at Jake's, she finally couldn't take it anymore and hopped a cab down to the Bowery.

She couldn't believe that Fiona hadn't gone to work and hadn't shown up at Jake's. She must have been at the Vesper, and Charlotte had missed her. And then maybe she worked late and figured Mae wasn't out two nights in a row, and so she just went home. That made sense. And now Mae could remind her that she meant what she said: She wasn't going to let her brother keep them apart. She might not have any money for now, but at least they had each other.

Mae stood outside the door and knocked softly; she knew Fiona's neighbors were prickly about late-night noise. And considering how late she could be with her rent, her landlord didn't need another excuse to try to evict her.

She heard Fiona laughing. Alarmed, Mae knocked a little harder. The laughter stopped. Then silence. Mae knocked again, more loudly.

Nothing.

"Fiona, open up. It's me," Mae said loudly. The neighbors could go to hell.

"Ssshhhh," Fiona hissed from the other side of the door. Mae felt relief at the sound of the locks coming undone.

Fiona only opened the door about two inches.

"Hi, babe. Let me in," Mae said.

"Go home, Mae."

Mae knew she'd maybe had a few drinks too many—and maybe enough that she was hearing things wrong.

"Stop playing around—I'm too tired," Mae said. She shifted in her bare feet and dropped her shoes on the floor.

"Not tonight. I'll talk to you tomorrow," Fiona said.

Mae sobered up fast.

"What are you doing, Fiona?" She tried to push past the redhead into the apartment.

"Is there a problem?" said a male voice from inside the apartment.

Mae almost stopped breathing. "Who the fuck is that?"

"Quiet! You're going to get me kicked out of here. Just leave. I'll talk to you tomorrow."

Fiona slammed the door closed.

"Open this fucking door! I'm not leaving!" Mae screamed. "Who's in there?" She pounded on the door with the palm of her hand. The force of it stung, but she didn't stop banging until the police showed up and pried her away.

———

THE MAN ONSTAGE had slicked-back hair, a narrow, purple suit, and a voice like warm honey.

Charlotte still wasn't used to the way an electric microphone made the sound of the performers' voices fill the room. And with this man's deep velvet voice, singing slow songs of love and devotion, she was mesmerized.

"That's the King," Jake said, leaning in close during a break between songs.

"I think he just might be worthy of the name."

"Hey," the King called from the stage. "What you talking about there, Lark? Am I boring you?"

The crowd laughed and tittered.

"My friend here says you just might be worthy of your nickname," Jake called back. Charlotte covered her face with one hand.

"Glad to hear it, little lady. And just so you know, I am willing to take requests."

The room was silent, expectant. Charlotte looked at Jake, mortified.

"She's a woman of few words," said Jake.

"Well, that balances you out, don't it?" said the King. More laughter from the crowd. "I'll take a request from you . . . on the condition that you get up here on sax."

The room erupted in applause, and a few people hooted out, "Lark! Lark . . ."

"Is he serious?" Charlotte whispered.

"Yes, I'm afraid so. Would you mind?"

"No—of course not. Go."

She watched him join the musicians onstage. It was evident he had done this many times before. Jake and the King conferred for a few seconds, then the band—with Jake on saxophone—launched into an Al Jolson song Charlotte recognized.

With the musical intro in full swing, the King took the microphone.

"This little number goes out to a special guest tonight. It's her first time at the King Club—but hopefully not her last."

And then he launched into "The One I Love (Belongs to Somebody Else)."

Charlotte felt the rest of the room recede. She was alone, and Jake was playing to her. She felt it. "It's tough to be alone on the shelf. . . . It's worse to fall in love by yourself. The one I love, yes, the one I love, Oh, the one I love . . . belongs to somebody else."

The song ended to boisterous applause. Rona Lovejoy reappeared onstage and joined her brother in a duet. This time, it was a song Charlotte didn't recognize, but Jake again played the sax. She watched him, wondering how much more there was to discover about this man—keenly aware that she already knew more than she should.

As much as she enjoyed watching him, she wanted him back at the table. The space around her felt colder without him. This might be the last night she saw him; she didn't want to waste the time with a stage between them.

He looked at her just then, as if he understood her thoughts.

The song ended, and Charlotte stood while she clapped. Jake kept his eyes fixed on her as he took a bow and exited the stage.

When he reached their table, she impulsively threw her arms around his neck.

"That was incredible! I had no idea you actually played. I don't know anyone who does something artistic. I spend my life in homes filled the best sculptures and paintings and craftsmanship . . . but I don't know anyone who actually creates." She felt so excited, she could barely get the words out.

And then he kissed her.

She felt the kiss filter through her, a flip in her stomach that sent a tremor down to her toes. She'd never experienced anything like it.

He pulled back, his hands cupping her face close to his. "Let's get out of here," he breathed.

She nodded. He took her by the hand and led her through the maze of tables to the exit, deftly avoiding anyone who tried to talk to them along the way.

Outside, under the streetlights, she took deep breaths, as if preparing herself for a long dip in the ocean. Jake pulled her to him, one arm firmly circling her waist, the other hand brushing the hair away from her face. "Are you coming home with me?" he asked hopefully.

"I . . . can't," she said, looking up at him. She touched her hand to his jaw, feeling the faint stubble. She resisted the urge to press her lips against it.

Jake nodded slowly. "I get it."

"Get what?"

"It's okay, Charlotte."

"I'm married," she said.

He nodded. "I know."

He did not touch her on the way to the car. He opened the door, and she stepped in slowly, as if leaving something precious behind.

Chapter 12

CHARLOTTE WOKE TO knocking on her bedroom door.

"Okay, okay. I'll be right there."

She sat up slowly, still wearing her black Chanel dress from the night before. Her head was heavy from a restless, dream-filled sleep. She knew she should be thankful she had slept at all. After Jake dropped her off, she had sat in bed awake for hours, waiting to hear Mae come home. Mercifully, she must have eventually drifted off.

Charlotte pulled a robe over her dress and opened the door.

"Sorry to disturb, madame. There is an urgent call for you," said Penny.

"From whom?"

"The police, madame."

"Is something wrong? Is it William?"

"He didn't say, madame."

Charlotte brushed past her and rushed down the stairs to the sitting room. She picked up the receiver, out of breath. She desperately needed coffee, or maybe a glass of water.

"Hello?" Charlotte said.

"Mrs. Delacorte?"

"Yes, this is Charlotte Delacorte. What's happened? Is it my husband?"

"No, ma'am. It's your sister—sister-in-law? Mae Delacorte. She was picked up last night for disorderly conduct. She gave us your name as someone who would be willing to post bail."

Charlotte sat down, her head in her hands.

"May I speak with her?"

"Yes, ma'am. But the court needs to know if you'll be posting bail."

"Yes, yes. Of course. Please just put her on the phone."

Charlotte waited for what seemed an unnecessarily long time, then Mae was on the line.

"Charlotte, thank God! They haven't let me make a phone call, and I thought I was going to be here all day." She began to sob, still talking, the rest of what she was saying unintelligible.

"What in God's name did you do?"

"Nothing! I was just knocking on Fiona's door. . . ."

"Oh, Mae. Not her again. She's nothing but trouble, I told you. . . ."

"I don't need a lecture, Charlotte. Are you coming to get me, or what?"

Charlotte slammed down the receiver and took the stairs two at a time to her bedroom. She changed into a day dress and threw the Chanel onto the bottom of her closet. Then she rummaged through her bag for her wallet. William had left her a few hundred dollars before he left, and now she was going to need every penny of it to bail out Mae. But the money was gone.

She put the bag down and sat back on her heels. She couldn't have lost the money—it was impossible. She must have been robbed. But her bag hadn't left her sight all evening. Except when she asked Mae to hold if for her while she went inside the Vesper to find Fiona.

She sighed. Maybe William was right after all, and she was the one being played for a fool. Either way, if he found out Mae was in such trouble, he would hold Charlotte responsible. And where had she been when Mae was getting herself arrested?

She dropped her purse and found her toiletry bag in the bathroom. She pulled out the largest hairpin she could find.

Then she slowly walked downstairs to William's office.

FIONA KNOCKED ON Jake's door. A black man answered it.

Inside, half a dozen people were still asleep on the couch and on the floor.

"Looks like I missed quite a night," Fiona said. "Where's Jake?"

"Who wants to know?" the man said. She had seen him before and knew his name was Maxwell.

"Stick to playing your horn, honey," she said, pushing past him to the stairs.

Jake's apartment space was small, with a low ceiling. It was really a storage annex, but Jake used it as a sleeping loft, so the rest of the place could be used for the speakeasy.

It was dark, and Fiona fumbled around for a lamp. When she found it, she turned it on. Jake was asleep on the bed. Fortunately, he was alone.

"Hey, wake up, dewdropper," she said.

Jake stirred, opening his eyes halfway.

"What time is it?"

"Noon."

Jake sat up. He was shirtless, and for all she knew, completely naked under the sheets. If she hadn't had such a rough ride last night, she'd be tempted to have a look for herself.

"Are people still here?"

"Aren't people always 'still here'?"

"I guess." He sank back into the pillows. "What do you want, Fee?"

"I set the meeting for you and Boom Boom. Tuesday night at the Vesper." Jake crossed his arms behind his head, looking at the ceiling.

She sat on the edge of the bed. "Look around, Jake. You're a big man in a small sea. Do you want to jerk around with this shit for the next twenty years? Make some money, and open a real club for the guys downstairs. Or make some records. Do *something*."

"Thanks for the pep talk," he said sarcastically. "And what's your grand plan since you seem to know so much about it?"

"I made more dough last night than you'll make all month with your bush-league bootlegging."

"Gee, I wonder how. Performing brain surgery?"

"Who cares *how*? I'm in the game! And I'm giving you a chance. You think Charlotte Delacorte—or any woman who isn't a showgirl or a cocktail waitress or nightclub singer—would ever take a guy like you seriously? Her husband's an asshole, but at least he's a player."

She stood up. "Tuesday night. I'm telling Boom Boom you'll be there. I might be a whore, but don't make me a liar."

THE RIDE HOME from the police station had been silent. Whatever empathy Charlotte might have felt for Mae had disappeared along with the money in her wallet.

Back at the house, Mae had scampered up the stairs to her room, and Charlotte followed closely behind her to try to talk. But Mae closed the door, shutting her out.

"You're such an ingrate!" Charlotte had yelled, "I wouldn't even be so presumptuous as to expect a thank-you, but at least don't slam the door in my face."

Hours of silence had followed. Charlotte finally went upstairs to again try to talk some sense into her.

Mae paced the bedroom, biting her nails. "What was she *doing* with him?" She said for the countless time.

"We've been over this, Mae. I don't know. I think, for your own good—your peace of mind as well as getting what you really need, which is control of your trust fund—you should take a break from her for a little while."

Mae glared at Charlotte as if she had suggested Mae shoot her dog.

"And speaking of funds . . . did you take money out of my wallet?" Charlotte hadn't asked earlier, but she couldn't hold back any longer.

Mae at least had the decency to turn red in the face. "What possesses you?" Charlotte said. "Do you know how difficult you made it for me to bail you out?"

Charlotte heard the front door close. She glanced at herself in Mae's full-length mirror.

"That must be William. I'm going to go downstairs and greet him. You just stay in here until you can collect yourself."

Mae did not acknowledge that she'd even heard Charlotte. She just stood in front of the window, muttering to herself.

Charlotte left the room and closed the door behind her. She smoothed the skirt of her dress and descended the stairs, taking a deep breath.

William stood in the entrance hall talking to Rafferty.

"Welcome home," Charlotte said. She had anticipated feeling guilty when she saw him, but she didn't.

Instead of embracing her, he held her by the shoulders and kissed her on the cheek.

"I was just asking Rafferty if all was calm while I was away," he said with a smile. Charlotte glanced at Rafferty. "I'm glad to hear everything is running smoothly."

"How was your trip? Do you want me to have Penny draw a bath?"

"No, I've got to take care of a few things in my office."

Charlotte nodded, her mind running over every object in the office. Had she moved anything out of place? Would he count the money?

"What time would you like to have supper?" she asked.

"Don't bother—I have a late meeting," he called out to her.

Charlotte waited until he was out of sight before returning to Mae's room. She knocked on the closed bedroom door. No response. She tried the knob, but the door was locked.

"Mae, we're not done talking," she said. "Open this door."

Charlotte felt uneasy; the hair on the back of her neck nearly stood on end.

"I'm serious, Mae. Open this door right now." Charlotte spoke as loudly as she could without risking one of the servants or William hearing her.

"I don't think she's in there, madame," said Rafferty.

Charlotte spun around.

"I didn't mean to startle you, ma'am. Master Delacorte asked that I bring his luggage to your room."

"Oh, yes. Of course. But . . . what were you saying about Mae? You don't think she's in her room?"

"No."

"I just left her there ten minutes ago, and the three of us were standing at the base of the stairs. She couldn't have gone anywhere."

Rafferty had an odd expression on his face. It was the most emotion she'd ever seen him exhibit. "What is it, Rafferty? Please tell me. I'm worried for her."

After a pause, he said, "Follow me."

They walked to the rear of the house, through the kitchen, and out the back door.

Charlotte walked after him until they circled around the house and faced the back, where the bedroom windows looked out onto the small garden, fountain, and gazebo.

Rafferty walked to the edge of the house. Charlotte stood directly behind him. She examined the grass running alongside the house. It was where the ferns would grow in the summer, but there was nothing but weeds at the moment. Charlotte made a mental note to call the gardener.

"What are we doing out here?" she said.

"Look up."

And that's when she saw the ladder hanging from Mae's open window. It was such an outrageous sight; it almost didn't register with her. For a minute, she just stood looking at it, as if faced with a giant turd in the center of the hall carpet.

"Oh, my good Lord."

"Let me take care of this, madame. I'll remove it and store it somewhere."

She nodded, unsure of how to express her gratitude. He didn't wait for her to say anything but instead disappeared back into the house. She didn't know where Mae had gone this time, but when she returned to the house, Charlotte would make sure that Mae stayed in there until she got herself under control.

Charlotte followed Rafferty inside, wondering how much worse things could get.

Barely into the hall, Penny rushed over to her.

"Master Delacorte is looking for you," she said.

"WHAT MAKES YOU so certain someone was in here?" Charlotte said, trying to appear calm while sweat beaded on her upper lip. *How could I have been so sloppy?*

"I locked my office before I left, and I came home to find it unlocked."

Charlotte leaned against the closed door, her hand behind her on the knob.

"Is anything, um, missing?"

"I don't know, Charlotte. And I don't have time to look over every single thing. I'm late for a meeting as it is. Damn it! It was probably Rafferty. I never trusted him. And why did Mother saddle us with that lout? Now I have to go through the hassle of firing him and finding someone new. . . ."

"I think you're really getting ahead of yourself," Charlotte said. "Darling, isn't it possible that you forgot to lock the door? You've been so busy lately—I think you'd forget your head if it weren't attached!" She smiled and moved closer to him. "I know Rafferty was foisted on this household, but that wasn't his fault. And I do not believe for a second he would trespass."

William seemed to think for a minute. He shook his head. "I could have sworn I locked that door."

"We all make mistakes, darling. Don't be too hard on yourself."

"That's all you have to say about this?" he said.

Charlotte ran her hand through her hair. "I don't know what you want me to say."

"You made such a big point of coming to my office, telling me that I should come to you with any problems. Now I'm telling you we have a problem, and you're dismissing it."

"I . . . I'm just saying that maybe you're mistaken."

William's face froze, as if a ghost whispered in his ear.

"You're right, my darling. My thinking was all wrong. It wasn't the servants. It was my sister."

William stormed out of the office. Charlotte rushed after him and grabbed his arm when he reached the stairs. "Stop—you're making a mistake."

"Stay out of this," William said, pushing her aside so hard she stumbled on the bottom step and fell. He was halfway up the stairs before she caught up with him again. He turned the knob, found it locked, then pounded on the door.

"Open this goddamn door, you little bitch!" he yelled.

"I'll talk to her . . ." Charlotte said.

William grabbed her roughly by the arm and pushed her against the wall. "Do not let Mae leave the house. And that goes for you, too."

He dropped her arm.

She didn't start breathing again until he was out of sight.

Chapter 13

AMELIA ASTOR HAD never been what anyone would call a beauty. But now, just a few years shy of thirty, she was finally approaching what some would call "handsome." With her thick dark hair streaked with premature gray, her prominent nose and high cheekbones, and five feet nine inches of height, she rarely entered a room unnoticed. She was, anyone would say, a commanding presence.

She reminded herself of this when she was taken off guard with the sudden appearance of William in her parlor. She had not dressed for a visitor and had especially not dressed for the only visitor she even remotely cared to see.

"I'm sorry to drop in on you like this," he said.

"You know you're always welcome here, William." She smiled at him as her butler showed them to the parlor.

William sat on the sofa, looking up at the ceiling. His foot tapped quickly.

"Perhaps you could use something to relax," Amelia said. She opened a desk drawer, removed a key ring, and walked slowly to the large Henry VIII chest. She unlocked it and removed a bottle of whisky.

She poured two drinks and sat next to him. He accepted the glass from her with a warm and grateful smile.

"You always know just the thing, Amelia," he said.

"We are very much alike, you and I," she said, her mind already filling with fantasies along the lines of, *I've finally done it. I've left Charlotte.* . . . The timing made perfect sense. Geraldine was gone. He had realized life was short, and that he needed to carry on the Delacorte name in the best way possible, and he couldn't do it with that anchor of an interloper from Philadelphia around his neck.

It would be hard for him, of course. Divorce was a scandal, no matter how people tried to pretend it was somehow acceptable these days. But she would bear the burden with him. They would get through it together.

"There's something I need to discuss with you."

"Of course," she said. "You can tell me anything." She wondered if it would be acceptable to wear white at their wedding. It would be his second, but her first. Surely, etiquette wouldn't deny her a proper gown.

He sipped his drink. "It's about my mother's will."

"What?" Amelia asked, wondering if she had heard correctly. The deviation from her mental script was most unwelcome.

"Yes, I know—it's difficult to imagine I should have any reason to discuss Mother's will. But it's putting me in a bit of a bind, and Paulson isn't willing to take a second look because, well, you know he's been with Mother for fifty years. I got a second opinion from another attorney, but he was no help. I was wondering if your father might be willing take a look."

Barclay Astor, Amelia's father, was a highly esteemed estate lawyer and did the bulk of his work for their own tight circle of friends. But Geraldine Delacorte had felt it unseemly that someone in their circle should know the intricate details of the Delacortes' financial affairs, and had convinced Atticus to use her family attorney, Charles Paulson. Barclay had never considered it a slight, but Amelia's mother had always regarded Geraldine as a terrible snob.

"I'm sure he would. But can you tell me what's wrong?"

William stood and walked to the large picture windows. He looked outside and started speaking with his back to her.

"It seems that Mother, in her eternal wisdom, felt the need to put my sister's inheritance in a trust until she is properly married."

"Well, that was probably a good idea. I'm not sure you should ask my father to undo that, even if he could."

William shook his head. "I wasn't finished: Mother was so intent that Mae be married off—that she not continue to jeopardize the Delacorte name with her . . . behavior—she locked my money up as well."

"Are you telling me that you won't get your inheritance until Mae is married?"

William turned around, and the expression of anger on his

face was one she had never seen before in all the years she had known him.

"Oh, William. This is terrible. I mean, I can understand why Geraldine kept Mae's money out of reach—Lord knows that girl needs some carrot to rein her in—but why punish you for Mae's mistakes?"

"It's simple. She wanted to make sure I had incentive to get Mae settled properly," William said bitterly. "She probably thought if I had my money, what would I care if Mae ran off with some whore, never to be heard from again? And she was right."

William sat back on the couch and put his head in his hands. Amelia tentatively touched his back.

"What does Charlotte say about all of this."

"I haven't told her. I simply can't risk word of this getting out. I don't want anyone—not even my wife—to know what a vulnerable position I am in. I hope you understand how much I am trusting you with this, Amelia."

The conversation was not what she had imagined but was nearly as good.

"Of course. And my father will take a look and see what he can do. But in the meantime, you have to be tough with Mae and make it clear she has no options but to toe the line and do the right thing. She's a beautiful girl. And with the Delacorte name and fortune, any young man in the city would be happy to have her."

"Unless he knew the truth about her. Which everyone will the more she runs around. I've been explicit with Charlotte about keeping her under control, but it's no use," he said.

"You know, dearest William, there is nothing more dangerous than just a small amount of discipline. How can you expect Mae to take Charlotte seriously?"

William looked at her.

"I've seen how Mae behaves," Amelia continued, "and I've

held my tongue. But now that you've told me what's at stake, you must allow me to intervene: Bring your sister to live here. I'll set her right. Give me three months, and I'll have her engaged to the most suitable of men."

William looked at her with something close to awe. "You can't be serious."

"But I am."

William finished his drink, nodding his head slowly, as if listening to some inner voice to which Amelia was not privy. Finally, he said, "I'll consider your offer, Amelia. It's extremely generous. I'm just not sure it's appropriate to send my wayward sister to your household."

Amelia looked at his profile. She was so close to him; she would feel his breath if he turned to face her. She knew that other women, in that same circumstance, would use sex to sway the tide in their direction. But as someone who had never understood the appeal of physical relations, she certainly could not wield the promise of such things in the midst of a negotiation. No, for Amelia, the world was a place of logic and order. And she knew if she could provide this for William, he would turn to her eventually. Of this, she had no doubt.

Amelia had harbored no illusions about Charlotte Andover Delacorte. Every nerve in her body had prickled to attention when she first saw the fine-featured interloper from Philadelphia. From the minute Charlotte had walked into that Christmas party years ago, Amelia knew that if there was anyone she would have to fight to the finish line, it would be her. And it wasn't just the way William had looked at the girl that night; it was everything the girl represented. She was beautiful, of course—but there was no shortage of beauty in their Manhattan circle. No, it was her distinct *otherness*. She was not an Astor, a Vanderbilt, a Whiting, or a Frick. In choosing her, William was in a sense not making a choice at all. At the age of twenty-four, with the eyes of all major players of New York society waiting for his move, New York's most eligible bachelor bowed out of the game.

And he'd been paying the price ever since.

"Are you bringing Mae to the Waldorf dinner for the Walker mayoral campaign?" she asked.

"What?" he said, as if being jolted out of a dream.

"The dinner to raise money for Senator Walker's mayoral campaign?"

"I suppose. Frankly, it's more trouble than it's worth to make sure Mae's presentable."

"Bring her," Amelia said, standing up. "And pack her bags. Have your driver transfer them to my car before the end of the evening. She'll be coming home with me."

CHARLOTTE ONLY HAD to knock once before Jake opened the door. As always, the sight of him stirred something inside of her.

"You're full of surprises," he said, raising an eyebrow. "I thought we'd exhausted any potential conversation the other night."

Charlotte nodded and walked inside gingerly.

"I'm sorry to bother you," she said quietly.

"It's never a bother to see you, Charlotte."

"Well, you might change your mind about that: It seems I need to take you up on your offer to sell some jewelry for me."

She opened her handbag and put two pieces on the small table next to the couch. One was a white gold filigree brooch centered with a large emerald that had belonged to her grandmother. The other was a platinum pendant necklace of coral, onyx, and diamonds. It had been a gift from William on her twenty-second birthday.

Jake walked over and picked up the necklace. He turned it over to examine it, then set it back down.

"Are you in trouble, Charlotte?"

"No," she said.

He nodded as if thinking.

"Okay. I'm glad to hear it. And yes, I will sell this stuff for you. I don't know how much I'll get, but I'll negotiate as hard as I can."

"Can you do it immediately? Tomorrow?"

He looked at her closely. "If that's what you need."

She reached up and unthinkingly put her arms around him, her face against his shoulder. "Thank you. I knew I could count on you." She let herself sink into him, filled with such relief she wanted to cry.

He slid his hand up her back and held her tightly. She closed her eyes—she felt so calm. When she looked up he was staring at her, and she willed herself to just stay still, to lose herself for a moment in those dark eyes. Then she kissed him.

He kissed her back—hard. She opened her mouth to him and felt the kiss run through every part of her body. He cupped her breasts, and she felt her fullness fill his hands. She was suddenly thankful she wasn't a skinny little flapper. She had never felt more like a woman. Charlotte pressed herself against his body. He slipped one hand under her dress, over her underwear but between her legs.

Then his hand stopped.

"You don't have to do this, you know. I said I'd sell the stuff for you."

"What? I know—that's got nothing to do with it."

"Then what's changed since last night?" he asked.

The truth was, she didn't know, exactly. But she knew something had, and that was all that mattered to her.

"Nothing . . . everything."

He held her by the hand, and slowly led her up the stairs. When she reached the top, she let go of him and took a deep breath.

Jake glanced at her with a gentle smile, and reached for her hand again.

She hesitated only for a second before following him into the bedroom.

Part III

Society Sinners

The most courageous act is still to think for yourself. Aloud.
—Coco Chanel

Chapter 1

IT WAS BARELY a second floor—more like an attic. But there was a bed.

"You're so beautiful," Jake said, those dark eyes of his sweeping up and down her body. Charlotte's heart beat so fast she felt it must be visible.

She sat timidly on the edge of the bed, and he gently pushed her back. Charlotte looked at the ceiling, a faint crack running down the center. He touched her face, then ran his hand slowly down her front, brushing her nipple with his thumb through her dress. Reaching behind her neck, he undid the top clasp of her dress. She raised her arms and he carefully slid it off over her head.

He paused, looking at her inquiringly—she nodded breathlessly—and then pulled off her underwear.

He took in her naked body, his eyes filled with an awe and reverence she had never seen in her husband's.

Jake took of his shirt and his pants, and she closed her eyes, her breathing shallow. He stretched out next to her, his mouth on her neck, and then her breasts. He moved down, kissing her belly, and then between her legs. She'd read about people doing such things, but she didn't believe it was anything more than scandalous fiction. And yet there she was, unfolding herself to him, like a flower in bloom.

"Jake?" She put her hand on the top of his head, mortified but overcome with the sensation of soft heat in the place where she'd felt barely anything before. She knew if she was going to stop it, now was the time. But then he moved on top of her, and she would no sooner stop him than she would stop breathing. If anything else existed prior to that moment, she forgot it in the merging of their bodies.

She wrapped her arms around him, her face against his, feeling that she loved him. But no, it wasn't possible. It was a trick of her body, her body that was rolling with a pleasure that made her senseless.

"Oh, my god," she cried out.

He lay next to her and pulled her against him. She put her head on his chest and he stroked her hair.

She waited to feel ashamed or guilty, but instead she was overcome with a sense of relief. And she realized how numb she had become.

She pressed her lips against his skin, amazed that in the past hour, somehow this had become something she was able to do. For the first time in years, she felt like the girl who had left home for Vassar College, so naively certain that she would find happiness in the world and in love. Jake, with this simple, unexpected, crazy afternoon, had given her back the old Charlotte. It was like breathing life back into the dead.

She didn't know how she would be able to go home, how she would be able to return to her old life.

THE DINNER TABLE was set with blue and white Wedgwood china, the good silver, and hyacinths in a cut crystal vase. In the center of the table, a fresh salad brimmed with bibb lettuce and tomatoes that were nowhere near in season and must have cost a fortune.

Charlotte could do little more than push the food around on her plate. She shifted in her seat, the dull ache between her legs serving as a shocking reminder of what she had just done.

"Charlotte, is there something you want to tell me?" William said.

She dropped her spoon, and Rafferty moved quickly to replace it with another. As discreet as he was, she could feel her servant's eyes on her. Had he seen her sneaking into William's office?

Or maybe he had seen Jake Larkin drop her off.

It had been folly to allow him to drive her home, but she had been greedy for the last few minutes she could steal with him. Even then, sitting in the car outside of her own house, when the shame of what she had done should have propelled her away from him like a bullet, she could barely tear herself away. If it hadn't been for the urgent business of the envelope on her lap stuffed with thousands of dollars in cash—payment for the jewelry Jake had successfully pawned for her—she might still be sitting in that idling car.

Did she look different? Surely, everything that roiled inside of her must show on the outside. She felt the events of the afternoon were surely clinging to her skin like perfume, shining in her eyes and changing the very way she breathed.

But what did William know of any of it? Nothing, she told herself. He couldn't possibly know. She had replaced the money in his office. And as for the other . . .

Charlotte's hand shook as she poured herself water from the heavy crystal pitcher.

"Let me do that for you, madame," Rafferty said. He stabilized her pouring, and for just a fraction of a second she felt his hand on her own, as if telling her to be calm. But no, that was impossible.

She was losing her mind.

"I can't think of anything," she finally said, forcing herself to look at William. It was the first time she'd met her husband's eyes since another man made love to her. And still, she still did not feel guilty.

This, more than anything else, told her she needed to end her marriage.

"What is happening with Mae?" William said.

Mae. That was it? With everything that was going on, he was still obsessing about Mae's behavior? She almost laughed.

"Nothing," she said.

"She's out of control, isn't she? Why haven't you told me things are getting worse?"

She chose to say nothing, instead letting him go on and on. And then, when he took a break just long enough to take a bite of steak, she blurted out, "I'm going to Philadelphia to visit my parents."

She spoke before she'd fully realized she'd been thinking it. But of course, it made perfect sense. She would get away for a few days, and tell her parents that she planned to leave William. Her mother would take it hard but would ultimately understand. And her father, although he didn't offer the most practical life advice, somehow had a way of helping her not take it all quite so seriously. He, out of anyone in the world, would understand about Jake Larkin. It was unspeakable, of course. But she suspected that just being around someone who would, in theory, understand, might help her agonize less.

"Work is too busy for me to go with you," William said.

"Oh, that's a shame," Charlotte said quickly. "But I will be fine. Just a short visit."

"This isn't a good time, Charlotte. We have the fund-raiser for Senator Walker on the sixteenth. At the Waldorf. You didn't forget?"

"How could I forget," she said with a tight smile. "Amelia has been so helpful with her reminder notes and solicitations for donations."

The urgency she suddenly felt for the trip made her wonder how she would wait the day or two it would take to plan her travel.

Chapter 2

FIONA STOOD ON Sixty-fifth and Fifth, gazing up at the Delacorte mansion. Its classic grandeur was so imposing she almost turned around and left.

Almost.

"Can I help you?" As usual, the young butler answered the door. He was startling in his good looks. He reminded her of the boy she lost her virginity to when she was fourteen, Declan Joyce. She wondered if Charlotte ever thought about having sex with her butler. If she hadn't, she should. Fiona wished she had servants. If she did, they would all be gorgeous—the men and the women.

"I need to talk to Mae," Fiona said.

"Don't come here and be startin' trouble," he said.

"It's only trouble if the man of the house sees me. So why don't you do everyone a help and tell Mae to meet me at the tobacco shop on Sixty-ninth and Lexington."

"You'd better be leavin'," he said, his blue eyes bright with irritation.

Fiona put her hand out to prevent him from closing the door in her face.

"You know it'll be Mrs. Delacorte getting the trouble from my visit, not just Mae. And you don't want that, do you?"

The door slammed in her face.

But Fiona felt confident Mae would get her message.

MAE CHECKED HER reflection in the store window next to
Hanson Tobacco. She was not happy with what she saw. But what
could she expect after not sleeping for two nights? Nothing was
worse for her skin. And her bangs were a quarter of an inch too
long. That was the problem with the extra-short bob. It only
looked perfect for about a week.

But she had been summoned.

If Fiona hadn't shown up at the house, Mae didn't know how
long she would have waited to find an excuse to sneak out and see
her. The rope ladder was gone, and Penny swore she didn't know
anything about it. Mae didn't dare ask Rafferty, and she didn't
want to make Charlotte any angrier with her than she already was.
She doubted William was responsible for its disappearance—lord
knows he would have been happy to take the opportunity to yell
at her.

No, today she'd left the house the old-fashioned way: with a lie
about needing fresh air.

"Make sure you're back here in twenty minutes," William had
said from the breakfast table. Charlotte clearly knew Mae was up
to something, but remained silent. She looked in need of escape
herself, a prisoner surrounded by a moat of fresh fruit and pastries.

Mae peered into the tobacco shop, and the sight of Fiona flooded
her with joy. She wore white and her long red hair was gathered
carelessly at the nape of her neck with a satin ribbon. Mae could
see that she was in an animated conversation with the shopkeeper,
no doubt trying to talk him into selling her something on the
cheap.

The door rang with a small bell when she opened it. The shopkeeper and Fiona turned to look at her.

"There she is! Don't we look alike?" Fiona said with a wink,
striding over and throwing her arm around Mae.

"Your sister was just telling me that it's her birthday," said the man. He was stout and sported an unfashionable mustache.

"Look at this," Fiona said, waving an ivory cigarette holder in front of her.

"It's hand carved," said the man.

Mae dutifully inspected it, making the expected fuss over the intricate dragon adorning the back.

"He's selling it to us for quite a discount," Fiona said with another wink.

"A steal," he said.

They looked at Mae expectantly.

"I . . . didn't bring my purse," she said.

The man scoffed. "Well, that's going to make it difficult to buy your sister a gift."

"Excuse us for a minute," Fiona said, tugging Mae's hand to leave. Once they were outside, she said, "Do you really not have any money on you?"

Mae looked at her like she was out of her mind.

"Is that why you told me to meet you? To buy you something?" she said, almost shaking. Was it completely lost on this woman that she'd spent the night before last in jail?

"No. Don't be ridiculous. But that *was* a great-looking ciggy holder."

Mae crossed her arms. "Do you realize that I was arrested the other night?"

"I heard the police. You caused quite a ruckus."

"That's all you have to say about it?" Mae's voice was shrill.

A couple walking past turned to stare.

"My poor darling," Fiona said, leaning in and kissing her. Mae was momentarily startled out of her anger and indignation; they'd never displayed affection publicly before, and she knew she should pull away. But to touch and taste her was so intoxicating, it was worth the risk.

Fiona pulled back, and hooked her arm through Mae's so they could stroll. "I warned you to leave, but you didn't listen," she said.

"Who were you with?" Mae said, hating that she had to ask.

"It's not much of your business."

"We're a *couple,*" Mae said. "I'd say who you're with at one in the morning is very much my business!"

"Don't cause a scene," Fiona said. "You're the one who will be upset if we end up in the gossip pages."

Mae stopped walking. "You didn't think about that when you kissed me a minute ago."

Fiona examined fruit at a stand. She turned an apple around and around before saying, "Why do you make things harder than they have to be?"

"I love you, Fiona," Mae said. "But if we're going to be together, then I need you to promise me that what happened last night won't ever happen again."

Mae had never before made demands of Fiona, and going so far as to give her an ultimatum made her stomach clench into a tight little ball.

Fiona didn't respond right away. She put the apple back in the stand, and started walking again. Mae followed beside her, fighting the urge to fill the silence with more talking.

"Well," Fiona said finally. "You know I can't promise you that."

"What?" said Mae.

Fiona shrugged. "You can't be with me because of your family situation. And I can't make money if you follow me around like a jealous husband. So we probably shouldn't see each other anymore."

The words took Mae's breath away. She blinked back tears, wishing she had some way to hurt Fiona in return. But that was the problem with love—you didn't pick it, it picked you. And from that point on you were defenseless.

"That's it?" Mae said.

Fiona pressed something small, cool, and heavy into her hand. Mae looked at it: a silver cigarette case. It still had its price tag from the tobacco shop.

"Go back to your big, beautiful house, Mae. You've got nothing to cry about."

Fiona turned, her long hair a flash of orange and gold, and she walked away.

Chapter 3

CHARLOTTE LOOKED OUT the window of the train's dining car, the Pennsylvania countryside rolling by like a colorful moving picture. Although her breakfast order of poached eggs, asparagus, and iced tea had been served, she couldn't bring herself to eat.

Now that she'd admitted to herself that she wanted to leave William, her mind was a constant tumble of nervous planning.

She didn't know where she would live, or what kind of job she would find. But she did know that she couldn't count on getting a penny from William. No matter what divorce laws might be in her favor, the Delacorte lawyers would find a way around them.

What would it be like to give herself to Jake freely? She couldn't imagine waking up every morning knowing she could see him day or night . . . or even wake up with him already next to her.

She blushed at the thought.

"May I clear this for you, madame? We'll be pulling into Broad Street Station any minute now."

"Yes, thank you," Charlotte said, stirring from her reverie.

The train was enveloped in the darkness of the station tunnel, and Charlotte closed her eyes. The next time she was on the train, she would have already confessed her plans to her parents. And all she would have left to do was pack her things and tell William.

Minutes later, a porter carried Charlotte's suitcase from the platform to the station hall where she waited.

"Thank you. I've got it from here," she said, tipping him.

Outside, the afternoon was sunny but cool. She buttoned her Chanel coat, and looked around for her father's car. She had told him it wasn't necessary for him to pick her up, but he had insisted. And now he was nowhere to be found.

Everyone who had disembarked from the train with her had long cleared out of the station. She waited, shifting uncomfortably on the sidewalk. She glanced at the taxi cab line, and walked toward it slowly.

She might as well get used to doing things on her own.

THERE WAS SOME confusion at the front desk at St. Luke's Hospital.

The guard on duty seemed to think that visitors for room 206 needed special security clearance.

"I work in the U.S. Attorney's Office," Roger Warren said. The guard looked at him blankly. Then, as if struck by sudden inspiration, he held up one finger and smiled.

"I think I have a list here somewhere." He fumbled through a pile of papers. "Ah-ha. Here we go." He dragged his finger down the list slowly, as if reading Braille. "Are you family?"

"No," said Warren, glancing at his wife by his side. Elizabeth squeezed his hand, telling him to be patient. The guard shook his head.

"Then I'm afraid you're out of luck. This here paperwork says family only, or the District Attorney's office."

Roger rolled his eyes at Elizabeth.

"I *am* from the District Attorney's office," said Roger.

"Then why didn't you say so?" said the guard, giving a cursory glance at his identification and waving them through.

Roger held Elizabeth's hand on their way up the stairs to the second floor. As unpleasant as the circumstances might be, it was their first time out and alone together since the baby had been born.

"Thanks for coming with me," he said, squeezing her hand.

"Of course. I feel terrible about Paul."

Roger knew she would only feel worse if she knew he had been at the warehouse raid where Paul McLaren got shot in the leg. Now it was infected and Buckner said there was talk he might lose it.

Roger had known McLaren since the second year of law school at NYU. They had never been great friends, but had enough in common that they always found themselves talking about one thing or another. The last conversation they'd had before the shooting, McLaren told Roger his wife had started making noise about wanting a baby, and asked if it was true how exhausting it was.

"It's not only true," Roger had said. "It's more than true. Exhausting is an understatement. I don't think the right word has been invented yet."

A nurse was just leaving McLaren's room. "Only one visitor in the room at a time," she told them.

"I'll wait out here," Elizabeth said.

"There's coffee in the visitor's lounge down the hall, ma'am," said the nurse.

"I'll get you there when I'm done," said Roger. "I won't be long." He kissed her cheek, and hated to admit that the fleeting moment of contact flooded him with longing. At home, she never wanted to be touched. Once she put the baby down for the night, she essentially curled up in a ball on her side of the bed and was out like a light until their son awoke early in the morning.

Roger slowly opened the door to room 206. The lights were off, but sunlight sifted through the edges of the navy-blue window curtains. The room was overflowing with flower arrangements and next to the bed, on a small table, was a pitcher of water, a bible, and the latest issue of *Photoplay* magazine. Buckner had a subscription at the office; he thought everyone should be up on their Hollywood gossip for the sake of their nightlife conversations. He had even advised Roger to create an alias for himself as a film producer.

The man in the small metal bed sat up straight when he saw Roger in the doorway.

"Come in. I'm awake," he said.

"I brought you this," Roger said awkwardly, handing him the paper-wrapped crossword puzzle book.

"Thanks. You didn't have to do that. Here, have a seat."

Roger pulled a wooden chair to the side of the bed. He wondered how long he was supposed to stay now that he had delivered the small gift. "How are you feeling?"

"The pain's a killer," said Paul. "But the worst part is not knowing if they're going to be able to save the leg."

Roger looked down at his hands. "I'm sorry."

"This whole thing's fucking crazy," Paul said, shaking his head. "And for what? People are going to keep drinking. No law is going to stop it. And how many lives get ruined in the meantime?"

Roger nodded in empathetic agreement. What could he say? Was he going to make the intellectual argument, to a man who faced losing his leg, that their job was to uphold society to the letter of the law, regardless of how viable it was?

"I hear Buckner's got you working undercover."

"Started last week," Roger said.

"Don't get yourself in trouble," said Paul.

"It's not dangerous," said Roger. "None of the players are actually at the club, except for the owner. I just have to keep my ear to the ground and find out who they are. Get Buckner some names."

Paul nodded. "How's Elizabeth?"

"She's here—just down the hall. She sends her regards. She's very concerned and told me to tell you Mary-Beth can call on her any time if she needs anything. . . ."

"She's a good woman," said Paul. "Don't let Buckner's craziness mess that up for you."

Roger shifted uncomfortably.

"She understands the nature of my job right now," he said.

"I'm sure she'd be a lot less understanding if she saw what goes on in those clubs," said Paul pointedly.

Roger was about to disagree, tell Paul he was off the mark. And then he thought about the redhead and heat rushed through him. "I should let you get some rest," he said, standing to leave.

Chapter 4

THE TAXI PASSED through an arched, wrought-iron gate. In the distance, Charlotte saw the familiar Grand Allée of European linden trees. And just beyond that, on the tip of three hundred and fifty acres, rose the southern façade of Woodmere, the grand home of her earliest childhood.

"Don't drive up to the main house. We're going to the carriage house in the back," she told the driver.

He followed her instructions, and followed the path to a stone house in the shadow of the mansion.

"Can you please wait here until I go inside?" she said, tipping him generously. Since her father failed to pick her up at Broad Street station as planned, she wondered if she could even count on him to be home.

With the taxi idling, she knocked on the door to no response. She knocked again, and then walked around to the back to try the rear door. Still nothing. She left her suitcase in the door-way.

"I've changed my mind. Please take me up to the main house," she told the driver.

It had been seventeen years since her father, John "Black Jack" Andover, sold the house that he built for her mother to the Baxter family. The 350 acres had once been comprised of Quaker farms, but her father had been able to purchase the entire tract on the fortune he made in his first business, the fur trade. It was his work in the trade that brought him to London, where he met Charlotte's mother, a barrister's daughter named Lillian Caldwell. She agreed to marry him, but not to move to America. He then had prom-ised, if she would allow them to make their life in the United States, that he would build her a home to rival the best English country estate. He kept his promise with Woodmere.

Eight years later, his fortune failing, he had been forced to sell the mansion at a painfully low price to a man named Baxter, but under the condition that he and his family—which by that time included young Charlotte—could live in the carriage house.

Inscribed above the entrance were the words *PAX INTROENTIBUS – SALUS EXEUNTIBUS:* Peace to those who enter—good health to those who depart. Charlotte found it painfully ironic that her parents had been blessed with neither.

"Do I have to wait for you again, miss? Or can you actually get into this house?" said the driver.

"No, it's fine. You can go," Charlotte said.

She waited until the car was out of sight before announcing her arrival with the large brass knocker shaped like an eagle's head.

"Can I help you?" asked the butler who opened the door. He was new, at least new enough not to recognize Charlotte. For most of her life, the Baxters' staff had indulged Charlotte as a sort of bas-tard stepchild to the house. Mrs. Baxter had twin daughters, and

Charlotte was invited to their grand birthday party every year, where she was able to wander the grand rooms that had once been her own.

"I'm Charlotte Delacorte. My father lives in the carriage house. Is Mrs. Baxter at home?"

"I'm afraid not. But Miss Baxter is here."

Charlotte saw this as a test of her fortune of the day: If it was Serena Baxter, she would have a pleasant conversation and a good chance of getting a spare key to the carriage house. If it was Jocelyn, not only would she fail to get a key, she would be subject to Jocelyn's singular ability to make her feel just a few rungs lower than a housemaid.

Charlotte waited on the silk brocade settee just inside the door. The last time she'd been to the house, she still recognized most of the original furnishings. But already she could see into the front hall and notice the new modern wall coverings.

"Charlotte! What a surprise," said Serena Baxter. Charlotte would scarcely have recognized her, with her long hair cut fashionably short, her plain features now bold with kohl liner and lipstick. There was a freshness and light to her countenance that immediately told Charlotte she was in love. "And look at that coat. You are always so sharply dressed. It reminds me I should get to New York more often. As much as the stores here try to keep up, it's just never quite the same."

"Thank you, Serena. I have to admit, with the constant changes, I'm having a hard time keeping up with the fashions even in New York."

Serena laughed. "So tell me—what brings you back to the Main Line? It's been so long!"

"It's been *too* long, I'm afraid. I came for an overdue visit with my father but he's not home. We must have gotten our signals crossed and he wasn't expecting me until later. I was hoping maybe you have a spare key to the carriage house?"

"Heavens, I have no idea. And Mother and Father are in town for dinner tonight. Let me see if the houseman knows. Come in."

Charlotte noticed the large solitaire diamond on her left hand.

"Are you engaged, Serena? Congratulations!"

The girl beamed. Charlotte remembered the Baxters' invitation to tea when they heard of Charlotte's engagement to William. That visit to Woodmere had been the first one that wasn't painful. She had such high hopes that day for her future. Her family problems would be in the past, and the home that she and William would make for themselves would finally make the loss of Woodmere a distant memory. Her father, of course, had taken things one step too far.

"Perhaps your new husband will be on the market for a country home," he had said. Charlotte hadn't known what he meant until her mother turned pale.

"Don't be ridiculous, John," she had said. "The Baxters will never sell."

Charlotte looked at Serena, beaming as she talked about her fiancé and her upcoming wedding at the Philadelphia Country Club.

She suddenly felt overheated in her muslin coat.

"Oh, listen to me prattling on," Serena said. "Let me go see about that key."

"No—don't worry. I mean, I don't want to be a bother. I'm sure my father will be home any minute," Charlotte said, already walking to the door.

"Are you sure?"

"Yes—absolutely. And congratulations again. Regards to your parents."

Outside, Charlotte walked until she was well out of view. Then she sat at the foot of a beech tree, and put her head in her hands. She wanted nothing more than to get back on the train to New York.

Back to the apartment behind the tailor shop in Greenwich Village.

AMELIA ASTOR STRODE into the Delacorte house, ignoring the embarrassingly young butler. She couldn't imagine what Geraldine had been thinking, saddling William's household with such an absurd head of staff. She could only assume it had been punishment for Charlotte.

"What do you mean, Mrs. Delacorte isn't here? We have a meeting scheduled for this morning. Twenty people will be arriving shortly."

"She's out of town, madame. Visiting family. May I suggest you reschedule your meeting?"

"You may suggest nothing, Rafferty. *I* suggest that you show me to the telephone immediately."

Amelia followed Rafferty into the parlor, and dialed William's office. His secretary put her through immediately.

"Where has your wife run off to now?" she said.

"She's in Philadelphia, visiting her father. Is there a problem?"

"In her haste to run off, she seems to have forgotten we have a Women's Literary Alliance meeting set for this morning."

She could hear William's sigh across the line. "I'm sorry, Amelia. Just postpone the meeting until next week."

"It's too late for that. I am at your house and the rest of the board will be showing up shortly. I'm sorry to bother you with this, but Charlotte has put me in a terrible position."

Silence on the other end. Amelia smiled; she could only imagine his fury. "Why don't I simply run the meeting today?" she said.

"I hate to ask that of you."

Amelia gave a loud sigh, one she was certain could be heard on the other end of the line. "It's not work I was expecting to undertake today, but we both know how important this was to your mother."

"You're a saint," said William.

"I only ask that whatever progress we make at today's meeting won't be undone when Charlotte returns. We can't lose ground if we're going to have the opening night gala as scheduled."

"Of course. Thank you for taking care of this, Amelia. I don't know what I'd do without you."

She hung up the phone, smiling.

When she turned to the door, she found Rafferty standing there.

"Heavens! I didn't know you were still there," she said, pressing her hand to her chest.

"I'm sure," he responded dryly. "The other guests have arrived."

Amelia brushed passed him.

Isobel Whiting, Susan Hamilton, and Margaret Cavendish were seated in the living room. The housemaid was already busy serving coffee.

"Where's Charlotte," asked Isobel.

"It appears we've been stood up," said Amelia. "But I just spoke with William, and he's asked me to run the meeting."

"What do you mean? Is Charlotte sick?"

"No, Isobel. Obviously your friend doesn't keep you up to speed with all of her comings and goings. She's in Philadelphia."

Isobel shifted in her seat. "Then maybe we should just postpone this meeting until next week."

"Is that what's best for the library? I think not."

The rest of the room was silent, rapt by the exchange.

"Well, then: Let's get started," Amelia said. "Susan and I were just at the fund-raiser for Lenox Hill Hospital. . . ."

"I still can't get used to the new name," said Margaret. "Why does everything have to change?"

"You can't expect them to keep calling it the German Hospital," said Isobel. "Not since the war."

"Well, the war wasn't the hospital's fault," said Margaret.

"Let's stay on point, ladies. As I was saying, Susan and I went to the fund-raiser at the National Arts Club last week"—she glanced at Susan, who nodded at her—"and we both were struck by the simple elegance of the affair. It makes me wonder if the King Tut theme isn't a bit . . . gauche."

Isobel stood up.

"This is not a conversation we should be having without Charlotte," she said.

"I completely agree," said Amelia. "Unfortunately, Charlotte isn't here. So we have to just make do. As I was saying, the King Tut idea really isn't befitting the library opening. We need something more understated: Put the books center stage—and, of course, Geraldine's memory. I'm suggesting a Spring theme. The official flower for the month of May is Hawthorn, as you know. So we can encourage the women to take that into consideration with their dresses. And that can cue our palette for the décor."

"That's perfect!" said Margaret. "Hawthorn would remind people to think of the novelist, Nathaniel Hawthorne—did you think of that?"

"I love double meanings," said Susan. "So brilliant. Although, he did get his fame from writing about women with questionable morals. But I don't think Charlotte will have a problem with that."

Isobel pushed her chair back loudly, set down her coffee cup, and walked out. The women watched her go.

"I've often heard that the strength of an idea can be judged by the rigors of its naysayers," said Amelia with a smile.

Chapter 5

"I'M SO SORRY, Charlotte! I feel terrible," her father said, quickly unlocking the door to the carriage house. She stood from her perch on the front step, where she'd been waiting for close to an hour. "As soon as I realized I'd forgotten, I went straight to the train station, but of course you'd done the sensible thing and left on your own."

"It's okay, Dad."

Black Jack looked like he'd aged a year in the short time since she'd seen him at Geraldine Delacorte's funeral reception. A sense of guilt overcame her.

"Besides—I should be apologizing to *you* for taking so long between visits. Now where is Mother? I assumed she was with you. I can't believe she's out and about considering how she gets." In the past few years—since right after Charlotte's wedding—her mother had become forgetful to the point of getting confused doing the most routine tasks. The doctors just chalked it up to one of the many nuisances of getting older. The forgetfulness didn't concern Charlotte as much as her mother's seeming disinterest in the things she used to care about—including, unbelievably, her own daughter.

Charlotte shrugged off her coat and sat on the well-worn couch. The passage of time—and her exposure to the best of Manhattan— made the house and its furnishings appear shabbier than she remembered. She fought off sadness, a feeling that reminded her why she had stayed away for so long.

Her father sat next to her and sighed. "Charlotte, I've been putting off troubling you with all of this, but Mother is . . . not doing well."

"What do you mean? Where is she?" Charlotte's heart started to pound, her melancholy turning to panic.

"Put your coat back on. I'll take you to her."

AT FIRST GLANCE, the redbrick building, half covered in winding ivy, could have been the centerpiece of a small college campus. But once inside, no one would ever make that mistake. The Maple

Grove Home for the Elderly and Impaired was a labyrinth of sterile halls and remarkable silence. Everywhere, small reminders of life coming to an end.

Charlotte waited on a carved wooden bench in a sunny reception area.

"Mrs. Hargrove can see you now," said a pleasant woman at the front desk.

"Thank you," Charlotte's father said.

Charlotte followed him down the hall and into an office of dark paneled wood, oil paintings in soft colors, and vases filled with fresh flowers.

Mrs. Hargrove, a genteel woman of middle age, stood from her desk and smiled warmly at them.

"Mr. Andover. I'm surprised to see you back so soon." She crossed the room and extended her hand. Charlotte shook it warily.

"I've brought my daughter. Mrs. Charlotte Delacorte."

"Mrs. Delacorte, a pleasure," said the woman.

"I don't mean to be rude," Charlotte said, "but can you please tell me what's going on here? My father hasn't kept me apprised of my mother's condition, and this is all quite a shock."

Black Jack looked at the carpet, and the woman gestured for Charlotte to sit in one of the leather chairs across from her desk.

"I don't know how to explain it to her," Black Jack said. Charlotte had never seen him look so helpless and it terrified her.

"Mrs. Delacorte, your mother has been diagnosed with a disease called Alzheimer's," the woman said. "All of the changes you've noticed over the past few years are because of this disease. Unfortunately, Alzheimer's is a condition that deteriorates quickly. And there is no cure."

Charlotte looked at her father, tears filling her eyes until he was just a blur.

"Why didn't you tell me?" she said.

"It's all happened so fast." His voice broke.

"I need to see her," Charlotte said.

NO ONE HAD ever accused Jake Larkin of playing it safe.

The son of Jewish immigrants from Poland, he watched his father spend his life selling pickles on Orchard Street. His mother spent hours upon hours a day mending rich women's clothes; the tips of her fingers were so scarred and numb of feeling she could barely play her beloved piano.

Leaving Poland had been the one great chance they took in life, and after that, the passionate artists were bound by the day-to-day grind that it took just to survive and provide for their three children.

Jake was determined not live that way. The first casualty of this had been higher education, which he saw as a trap that would lead to a safe job, but one far from the world of music. The second was his relationship with a childhood sweetheart, because the responsibility of marriage and fatherhood would also require choices that would limit him.

So why, he had to ask himself, was he content to just run liquor out of his apartment and to play host to a handful of musicians—no matter how brilliant—that had an audience of only his close circle of friends?

He was embarrassed to admit that it had taken crazy Fiona Sparks to shake him out of his comfort zone.

"The cover is five dollars," said the man at the door to the Vesper Club.

Jake had been hearing about the club for over a year, first from Mae Delacorte. Then Mae brought her lover to his joint, because it was one of the few places she felt safe from people she might know and gossip. Then Fiona started bringing her co-workers, and soon his speakeasy became the de facto after-hours counterpart to the Vesper. And yet he'd never set foot in the place himself. The only clubs Jake spent any time in were the jazz clubs in Harlem, and even those were getting too crowded and glitzy for his taste.

"I'm here for a meeting with Boom Boom. Name's Jake Larkin."

The big man stepped aside. "Go on in. She's expecting you."

Inside, Jake was assaulted by pastel-colored walls, the smell of expensive perfume, and the sound of subpar music. It was jazz all right, but the type of compositions that felt fresh three years ago. And the saxophonist was weak.

But whatever the club lacked in ambience, it made up for in quality clientele. It was early in the night, and the room was nowhere near full. But every single customer—even these early birds who probably lacked the confidence to start their evenings later—were young, beautiful, and obviously flush with cash.

Still, in a room full of striking women, Fiona Sparks stood out. He spotted her right away, leaning over the bar, her short dress hiking up the back to reveal a long stretch of pale leg.

"Fiona," he said.

"Jake!" She turned around surprised. "Good. You're here. Follow me."

Seeing her reaction, he realized that she had doubted whether or not he would actually show.

It was nice to know that despite his shortcomings of late, at least he had not become predictable.

Fiona took him by the hand and led him through the club to a large room in the back with tables and a stage, where the band was playing. Jake got a good look at the musicians, and wasn't surprised that he didn't recognize any of them. None of his guys would sound like that even in rehearsal.

"Wait here. I'll get Boom Boom. D'ya want a drink?"

Jake shook his head. Fiona winked and disappeared.

He looked around, wondering what it cost to run such a big operation. The payola to Prohibition agents alone had to be more than he could imagine.

In the time it took for Fiona to produce Boom Boom, two other cocktail waitresses offered him drinks. He said no to both.

Alone in the room, his thoughts turned in a direction he did not want them to go. But it was impossible to stop thinking about her.

Jake had thought himself shockproof. But Charlotte Delacorte had proven him wrong.

The way she had kissed him, like the last breath of the dying. And his response had been automatic, but as soon as he touched her breast he expected to be slapped away. Instead, she had folded into him as if it were the most natural thing in the world.

"Mr. Larkin! So nice to finally meet the man who keeps my girls so well entertained until the wee hours of the morning."

Jake tried not to show his surprise at the sight of Boom Boom Lawrence, but she was a startling figure, with her bright yellow hair, large, pear-shaped body, and garish makeup. Her shiny, powder-blue dress was of an oriental design and cut so low in the front he saw more of her cleavage than he would ever care to see.

"Miss Lawrence. I've heard so much about you," he said, shaking her hand.

"I would tell you most of it is not true, but I'd be lying," she said with a guffaw. "Skeddadle, Fiona. We don't need a chaperone."

Boom Boom waited until Fiona was out of the room before sitting across from Jake at the table.

"No one offered you a drink?" she asked.

"They did—at least twice." He smiled. "I'm on the wagon tonight."

"I should do the same myself," she said. "I've got my figure to think about."

A drunken couple wandered into the room, laughing and knocking over a chair.

"This room's closed till eleven," Boom Boom said, waving them out. She turned back to Jake. "Maybe we should go down to my office."

"Lead the way," said Jake.

The stairs were steep and narrow, and the dark dampness of the basement level seemed more like a place to stash a body than to have an office. But sure enough, Boom Boom opened a door to a small but serviceable room with a desk, a phone, two chairs, and filing cabinets.

"So this is where the magic happens," Jake said, waiting for her to take her seat behind the desk before sitting in one of the chairs facing it.

"Ha! That's funny. Well, you and I both know it's not magic, Jake. This business is damn hard work, and getting harder by the day. But I'm thinking maybe you and I can make each other's lives a little easier."

"And what did you have in mind, Miss Lawrence?"

"Please—call me Boom Boom."

"That's quite a nickname."

"I've earned it," she said, lighting a cigarette. She offered him one, and he accepted easily. "What I had in mind is this: I know my gals are drinking at your joint seven days a week. Tell me: Is your source reliable?"

"It is."

"You're a fortunate man. And I'm wondering if I might be able to persuade you to share that fortune with me."

Jake sat back in his seat, drawing deeply on the cigarette.

"These are risky times to be doing favors," he said. "Even for a woman as charming as yourself."

"Oh, Mr. Larkin . . ."

"Please—call me Jake."

"With pleasure," she said, purring. "Jake, I wouldn't dream of asking for a favor. God knows I never do them myself. This is business. And I've been around the block a few times—enough to know a player when I see one. So why don't you tell me what kind of business *you* want to be in?"

Chapter 6

CHARLOTTE'S MOTHER HAD aged dramatically since Charlotte had last seen her. Lillian Andover had lost so much weight that her body seemed skeletal under the blanket, and her gray-streaked, chestnut colored hair was now completely white.

"Good lord. Is she in pain?" Charlotte asked the nurse.

"She's having difficulty swallowing," said the nurse. "You might have noticed the weight loss."

"It's shocking," said Charlotte.

"All to be expected, unfortunately."

Charlotte didn't know what her mother could have possibly done to deserve such a wretched fate.

"Does she know we're here?"

"Hard to tell," says the nurse. "The other day she seemed to recognize your father, but that appears to have been an anomaly."

Charlotte pulled a chair up to the edge of the bed. Her mother's eyes were closed, and it gave her the chance to study her, to search for the beautiful visage that Charlotte remembered. Charlotte had never recognized much of her mother in her own appearance; by all accounts, she took after her father. But she did have her mother's gold and brown eyes, the color of the stone cymophane, or "Cat's Eye." But she doubted, from the looks of things, that she would get to see herself mirrored in those eyes today, if ever again.

She took her mother's hand, and it felt as small as a child's.

"Oh, Mother. I'm so sorry it's taken me so long to come back and see you. I was so caught up in my own life. And now it's too late." She bent her head onto her mother's chest, and sobbed. She raised her eyes up to look at her again.

Her mother's eyes fluttered open.

"Mother! It's me. Charlotte."

But her eyes closed just as quickly as they'd opened. Charlotte bent her head and pressed it to her mother's hand. "Now that I know you can hear me," she whispered, "I can't help but wish you could tell me what to do."

JAKE CONSIDERED BOOM Boom's question. Of course he knew what kind of business he wanted to be in: He had thought about a moment like this—dreamed about it—for years. It was his break. His chance to get in from the outside. But somehow, he had never imagined the chance would come from a woman like Boom Boom.

"I'm in the music business," he said.

"Music's the blood of nightlife these days, isn't it? Amazing how important it's become. What d'you think of the fellas I've got playing tonight?"

Jake had never been one for blowing smoke up someone's ass, and he was willing to bet Boom Boom preferred honesty to niceties. "Not much."

"You think you could do better?"

"With my worst guys, on their worst night."

She laughed. "That's a bold statement, but you know what? I believe you. And even if I didn't, I'd be willing to help you roll out your business if you help me keep mine going. So what do you say you take my liquor order to your guy?"

Jake knew the flip side of opportunity was risk. He had always known that. And hadn't he already taken so many risks just to get to this moment? But the deal on the table was risk at an entirely new level.

"If you get busted, I'm totally exposed," he said.

She spread her arms out. "Do I look concerned about being busted? I've never had so much as a citation."

Jake nodded. "Times are changing."

Boom Boom heaved herself out of her chair and walked over to a filing cabinet. She unlocked a drawer and pulled out a folder.

"I pay more out to these Prohibition agents than I spend on my full-time staff," she said, tossing a list onto her desk. Jake picked it up and glanced at the names and the payout column.

"You think this makes you bulletproof?" he said.

Boom Boom sighed deeply. "I had no idea Fiona would send me such a nervous Nellie. Come here—follow me."

They left the office. The hallway was narrow and smelled like the basement of the tenement building of his childhood. When they were a few feet away from her office, she pulled her key ring from her pocket and opened a door to complete darkness.

"Step in," she said.

Jake looked at her skeptically. "Why don't I just stay here and you tell me what I'd find inside."

She looked at him. "I don't think you'd believe me."

What was the expression his mother used to say? In for a penny, in for a pound. He stepped into the room. But it wasn't a room—he could tell right away, even in the darkness, that the floor was unfinished. His instincts told him the space was very small, and sure enough, when he extended his arms, he could touch walls on both sides.

Boom Boom, directly behind him, lit a match. And when she did, he was glad she'd convinced him to take a look for himself.

"It looks like a tunnel," he said.

"It is."

"To where?"

"The kitchen of the restaurant next door. And from there, you can walk out onto the street."

"But why?"

"In a raid, I flee with the cash and don't get arrested. If I'm not on the premises when the 'crime' is being committed, I can't be personally nailed. They can padlock the club, but I'm in the clear. They won't have me in a cell, grilling me about my sources."

Jake nodded.

"Of course, we have the other safeguards, too: the bar shelves that rotate so they only have soda pop and juice on display. The drains along the floorboards to get rid of the poured drinks quickly. But the cops are catching on to all those tricks. If a raid happens, the best you can do is disappear and not go down with the ship. And I'm prepared to do that. My sources never worry about me or my club being a liability."

She blew out the match. "Shall we go back to my office?"

Jake nodded in the darkness. "Lead the way."

PROHIBITION HAD FORCED Kelly's Pub on Philadelphia's Walnut Street to remake its reputation on bangers and mash instead of Guinness stout. Still, the establishment had a loyal customer in Black Jack Andover. And it was here that he brought Charlotte after their visit to the home.

They sat at a table in the back, near a fireplace.

"God in heaven, I could use a drink," he said.

Charlotte felt the same.

"I wish you'd told me about Mother sooner," she said.

"I was going to call you this week, believe it or not. I didn't want to, but I knew I had to," he said. The waiter, a man about her father's age, greeted him by name and made a fuss about the pretty woman he was with.

"My daughter," Black Jack said, and even through his stress the pride shone through.

Black Jack looked at her across the table. "You're a sight for sore eyes, Charlotte. I'm so glad you chose this week to visit. It feels like an angel sent you."

"Oh, it wasn't anything that mysterious, Dad. I just wanted to talk to you and Mother about something. . . ."

"Charlotte, before you go on, I need to get something out of the way. I think this is partly why I dreaded calling you—not just with the bad news, but because I have to ask something of you, which I hate to do."

"What is it?"

"I need help in paying for your mother's care. I've tried to do it myself, but it's just too much. Perhaps you can speak to William?"

Charlotte swallowed hard, but held her father's gaze.

"Of course," she said, hoping he did not notice the tremor in her voice.

Her father squeezed her hand, and there were tears in his eyes when he smiled his gratitude. "Now, what did you want to talk about?"

"Nothing important," Charlotte said, opening her menu. "Nothing at all."

Chapter 7

THE VISIT TO see McLaren in the hospital had taken more of a mental toll than Roger had anticipated. But on the plus side, it meant Elizabeth finally agreed to turn over Henry, the baby, to her mother for a few hours. And now his mother-in-law, God bless the woman, had offered to just take him for the entire night.

"Why leave the baby with Mother all night? You're not even going to be home," Elizabeth had said.

"Don't you want a rest? And besides, I don't have to go out until ten."

She had relented, and so there they were, baby-free, and with two hours before he had to leave for the Vesper.

It had been over a year since Elizabeth had allowed him to approach her in the bedroom. Even he had often been short on ardor when the baby first slept in their room, then when Henry was always quick to wake up in the room next door. But now, mercifully, they were alone at last.

Elizabeth sat on the bed, folding laundry, most of which were baby nappies and towels. Roger picked out his clothes for the night— more office-issued, club-worthy attire—and hung it on a hook outside of his closet. He liked the gray fedora, something he wouldn't have picked out on his own.

He then turned to Elizabeth, but she was more interested in perfectly folded hand towels.

He sat on the bed, and picked up some of the garments to try to help her fold, but quickly realized he had no idea what he was doing.

"You're just going to make twice as much work for me," she said wearily, taking a towel from him with hardly a glance. The

skin around her eyes had the slightly bruised quality of the sleep-
less, and her lips were dry and cracked. Still, her body had returned to the figure that had so captivated him from the start: her
narrow waist, her breasts high and firm—although, to her endless
dismay, they had failed to produce enough milk. And now, even
though her bosom was of no use to their son, Elizabeth kept it
tucked away, off limits to Roger since the baby's birth.

"Elizabeth, put that down for a minute," he said, moving the
piles of laundry out of the way and sliding next to her.

"The faster I finish, the sooner I can go to sleep. I'm getting
Henry at seven in the morning so I don't miss his morning feeding."

"Stop," Roger said, taking her hands in his. She looked at him
in surprise. "Henry is with your mother. He is fine. He doesn't
need you right now. I do."

Understanding crossed her face, and it didn't exactly produce
an expression of delight. Still, Roger would not be deterred. He
pulled her gently toward him to kiss her. She responded, though
not with the greatest enthusiasm. Still, he was happy to take what
he could get; he eased her back and began unbuttoning her blouse.
Elizabeth lay very still, and he took this as encouragement. But
when he began to move up her skirt, her hand clamped down on
his wrist like a vise.

"What's wrong?" he said.

"Nothing. I just want to get the laundry finished." She sat up
and rebuttoned her blouse.

Roger stood up slowly. He glanced back at her, but she was
already tending to the pile.

He took his clothes off the hook and carried them into the
bathroom.

JAKE RETURNED TO the speakeasy to find the party had started
without him.

He saw his man Maxwell behind the bar, and Louis Armstrong playing the trumpet in the middle of the room. He smiled and waved him over.

"Excuse me, folks," Louis said to the small crowd, who immediately whistled and applauded.

"When did you get back in town?" Jake asked. Last he'd heard, Louis had no plans to leave Chicago once he got settled. Maybe he could persuade him to play a night or two at the Vesper—as Jake's first booking.

"Lil's aunt is sick. This here's a quick visit—just a few days."

"I'm glad you stopped by. How's the scene in Chicago?"

"Hopping. Everything it's cracked up to be. I know this ain't what you want to hear, but I don't miss New York."

Jake grinned and threw an arm around the man's shoulder. "I'm working on something that might make it worth another visit in a few weeks," he said. "Now don't let me keep you from playing a minute longer, or the room's gonna turn on me."

Armstrong shook his head. "This crowd is feeling no pain. But you don't have to ask me twice to get back on the horn—though I could use another drink."

Jake laughed and headed to the bar. "Coming right up."

He knew it was a longshot, but he scanned the group of women at the bar, hoping to see one improbable guest.

But Charlotte Delacorte was not there.

"It's about time you showed up. I was starting to think it was just a rumor that this was your joint," said Rona Lovejoy smoothly. She was perched at the end of the bar, luminous in a gray satin dress, the dark skin on her long limbs smooth as marble. Her big dark eyes consumed her face, not even rivaled by her wide, lush mouth, brushed with a red gloss. Now that Jake was in her orbit, he could feel that most of the eyes in the room were on her. But she was focused solely on him.

"What can I say? I leave for two hours and I come back to find a star-studded party. To what do I owe the unexpected pleasure of your company, darlin'?" He kissed her on the cheek.

"A little birdie told me that Louis would be playing here tonight. I missed him last time he was in town. I figured it was easier to travel to Greenwich Village than to Illinois."

"So you're here for the entertainment, not the company," said Jake.

Rona put her hand on his arm, squeezing it gently. "I figured Mr. Armstrong would be showin' the room one kind of entertainment, and you might be showin' me another."

A few weeks ago, this would have been something to jump at. From the first time he saw Rona at the King Club, he thought she was one of the most spectacular, seductive women he'd ever seen. And she had talent to boot. But a part of him couldn't help think that maybe Charlotte would show up.

"As much as I like the sound of that, when the room is this full, I'm all business, baby."

"Then I will be back. During off hours," she said with a suggestive smile.

Chapter 8

WALKING INTO HER beautiful house felt like a life sentence.

"I'll take your bags upstairs, madame," said Rafferty. "Did you have a good trip?"

"It was fine, thank you," said Charlotte. "And where is Mr. Delacorte?"

"His office, madame."

Charlotte shrugged off her coat. She might as well get it over with.

The sound of her shoes on the parlor floor echoed through the

silence on the way to William's office. She had a flashback to the
night she picked the lock on the office door to replace the money
she had borrowed with the cash she got from pawning her jewelry. The thought of all the cash stuffed in those drawers made her
stomach turn uneasily. But at the same time, it made it a little easier to ask what she was about to ask of her husband.

She knocked on the office door.

"William—it's me."

A long pause ensued before he opened the door.

Her husband greeted her with a bright smile, one that didn't
quite reach his eyes.

"Welcome home, darling. I hope your trip was satisfying." He
kissed her on the cheek, standing in the doorway in a way that suggested he was not inclined to invite her in.

"It wasn't quite what I expected," she said.

"Well, travel is unpredictable," he said, clearly distracted.

She took a deep breath. "William, there's something I need to
discuss with you. May I come in for a minute?"

It was evident how much he had to stifle his irritation.

"I'm just in the middle of something, Charlotte. Go to the parlor and I'll be there shortly."

He closed the door, and she wished to God in heaven that she
could have the conversation she had planned to have with him
upon returning from Philadelphia—something along the lines of,
I'm leaving. I've already packed my bags. . . .

Instead, she would be begging for her mother's financial life-
line.

She sat on the sofa, facing a John Singer Sargent portrait of
William's grandmother. The old woman seemed to be glaring at
her.

William emerged from the office, closing the door behind him.

"So what's so urgent?" he said, sitting across from her on one
of the Louis VIII chairs.

Charlotte looked down at her hands.

"I had a distressing surprise when I got to Philadelphia," she said. "My mother is very sick. It seems all the little things that have been happening over past few years—the memory loss, the moodiness, the inability to go out and do the things she used to do—are because she has a terrible condition . . . a disease. It's incurable and is only going to get worse."

"I'm sorry, Charlotte. I really am. You know I think Lillian is a fine woman."

Charlotte nodded, fighting tears. "Well, I appreciate that, William. Especially because I need to ask something of you."

She looked at him, trying to gauge his receptiveness, but his face was unreadable. He sat perfectly still—except for his foot, which was tapping quickly. He probably couldn't wait to get back to his office. Charlotte took a deep breath.

"My mother needs full-time care. My father has her in a . . . home, of sorts. It's the right place for her, certainly better than some sort of public institution. But he can't pay for it much longer without our help."

William crossed and uncrossed his legs. "I see. And how much does this care cost?"

"It's five hundred dollars a month."

"Good lord, Charlotte. They should be *curing* her for that amount of money."

Charlotte said nothing. William stood and paced the carpet. "You know, money is tight right now. Business is not what it used to be."

She glanced at his office door, and thought of the thousands of dollars in cash just sitting in his filing cabinet.

"William, we are married. I never ask you about money, and I never ask you *for* money. I never even asked what your mother left you in her will. But I'm asking you for this, and as your wife,

I think I am entitled—morally and legally—to use our assets to care for my parents."

William stopped pacing. He turned to her, and there was no mistaking the anger in his face. But his voice, when he spoke, was measured and calm.

"Yes, you are my wife. But you can't just pick and choose when you care to remember that fact. If you want the Delacorte money, you'd better start protecting the Delacorte name. And that means helping to keep my sister in line, and to give her a better example in you."

Charlotte nodded. "Okay," she said softly.

"Then we understand each other?"

"Yes," she said.

"I'll have a check for you in the morning."

He walked back to his office. The door closed behind him with a sharp click.

Charlotte's hands were shaking.

MAE IGNORED THE knocking the first time, but when it started again she roused herself from her bed. Anything to make the noise stop so she could return to the sweet oblivion of her dreams.

"What?" She opened the door and found Charlotte, dressed in a floor-length, beaded gown. Mae recognized her jade jewelry— the dangling earrings and the ring with a stone the size of a grape—as having belonged to her mother.

Charlotte had returned from Philadelphia a few days earlier, but since Mae was taking all of her meals in her room, this was the first she was seeing of her.

"Why aren't you dressed?" Charlotte said with a gasp.

"Because I'm not going," said Mae.

Charlotte walked into the room and closed the door. "James

Walker is probably going to be the next mayor of this city. You can't drop out of this fund-raiser. But more important, you can't spend the rest of your life locked up in this room. Rafferty told me you haven't been out since before I left for Philadelphia."

"It's really none of his business," said Mae. *Damn Rafferty!* She was certain he was the one who moved her ladder. No one else would have done it.

"But it is mine," Charlotte said, walking to the closet and sifting through the hangers. She pulled out a dark-blue silk gown. "Besides—I could use some company tonight. Someone who understands that I, too, would rather be somewhere else."

Mae looked at her in surprise.

"What? You think I want to go to this thing tonight? You think my mind isn't a million miles away?"

"Did something happen?" Mae said, feeling like the first bit of oxygen had entered her lungs since the moment Fiona left her on Lexington Avenue.

"Nothing that would make me forget that you and I can't run around doing whatever strikes us. It's the price we pay for our privileges. I know it's easy to forget that sometimes, but trust me—things could be a lot worse." She handed Mae the dress. "So please, keep me company tonight. Besides," she said with a wink, "there's nothing better for heartbreak than good food and live music."

Mae took the dress from her hands.

"We're in this together, Mae," Charlotte said gently. The words—intended to be kind—somehow brought Mae to tears. She sat down on her bed and put her head in her hands.

"It doesn't seem that way," she said, sobbing. "I feel completely alone."

Charlotte quickly sat next to her, and put her arms around her sister-in-law's shoulders.

"You're not! I'm here for you. I can't fix everything, but you have to know I understand. We need one another."

Mae looked at Charlotte, whose eyes were wide with concern. "I've lost Fiona. She doesn't want me with all these limitations."

"Listen to me: I know you got mad when I tried to talk to you about this before, but maybe it's for the best. You have to be smart about this for now. We both have to just play the game to get what we need, and for now, that's money. It would be a harder decision if Fiona was happily by your side. It would be impossible to push her away. But you don't have to make that choice. Now all you have to do is act the part your mother intended, get your inheritance, and then . . ."—Charlotte looked her directly in the eyes and smiled—"then you can make your *own* choices."

Mae took shallow breaths, her sobbing under control. "I don't know if I can do that."

"Take it one day at a time. For now, just get dressed. Meet us downstairs in an hour. The car will be waiting."

Charlotte patted her on the leg and stood to leave. Mae followed her to the bedroom door and closed it behind her. Then she went to the dark oak dresser, and opened the bottom drawer. She pulled her silver flask out from underneath her peignoirs and undergarments. It had been a gift from Fiona, and too obviously expensive not to have been stolen.

Mae opened it to make sure it held a little something to get her through the night, and was relieved to find it filled with gin. She strapped the flask to her leg, just below the knee, with a white garter.

And then she slowly got dressed.

WEAR YELLOW TO attract a fellow. It was something her mother used to say. Fiona hadn't thought of it in years, but now that she was wearing the first new dress she'd bought for herself in ages—a canary-yellow silk shift dress with beaded fringe—it came to mind. She wondered what her mother would think of her new career. Sure, it was easy to think she'd be none too happy. But wouldn't she? At the very least, Fiona wasn't working in a miserable factory, where she'd die in a horrific fire.

Of course, Fiona hadn't needed to take her job as far as she had. All Boom Boom had said was to watch the big spenders, make sure they don't get poached, and if they leave the club early, leave with them to make sure they're not hopping to a competitor. She never said Fiona had to bring them back to her apartment, and she'd never said she had to have sex with them. No, Boom Boom was too smart for that. But what did she think Fiona would do? After all, hers was a tip-based livelihood.

"Suzette called out sick so I need you back on cocktail shift to-night," Boom Boom said. Fiona didn't realize how much she hated lugging that damn tray around all night until she'd been able to give it up. She rolled her eyes in irritation.

"It's just for one night. How quickly we forget our humble be-ginnings," Boom Boom said, handing her a tray.

If she spilled something on her dress tonight, she was sending Boom Boom the dry-cleaning bill.

She approached the room clockwise, as she always did. She took the outer tables, and the more junior girls took the inner ones. Her first stop was a two-top occupied by a well-dressed guy wearing a gray, snap-brimmed fedora. He had sandy brown hair and a decent-looking profile. She'd have taken him for a banker or a lawyer, but his clothes were too snazzy. Something about him made him look out of place. Maybe it was the fact that he was alone, or that he didn't seem to be having a good time.

As she approached the table, his eyes lit up in surprise.

"You *work* here?" he said.

This was an unusual opening. Had she forgotten him from somewhere?

"Do we know each other?"

"No . . . but I saw you the other night sitting at a table. I thought . . . never mind."

"You thought what?"

"That you were a customer."

"How funny. Not quite. Now, honey, what can I get for you?"

The man was clearly flustered, and this amused Fiona more than it baffled her—though it did make her wonder about the guy. But she didn't have time to waste with one oddball.

When she brought him his gin and tonic, he paid her with a twenty and told her to keep the change.

"You serious?" she said.

"Always."

"Always?" she said, suddenly rethinking his oddball status. "That's a lot of time to be serious. I'm sure I could get a smile out of you," Fiona said with a wink. The man actually turned red!

She returned to the bar, laughing to herself, with Boom Boom right on her tail.

"Who was that you were yip-yapping with?" she said.

"Someone who is flush enough to hand me a twenty and tell me to keep the change, that's who."

Boom Boom looked over at the corner table. "He certainly knows how to dress. I saw him in here two nights ago. Keep him happy," she said.

"With pleasure," said Fiona.

Chapter 9

"AND NOW, FOR your evening's entertainment, I am delighted and honored to introduce . . . Mr. Al Jolson."

The Waldorf ballroom, filled with New York's most elite and arguably jaded denizens, couldn't help but burst into genuine and giddily enthusiastic applause. The twelve tables, set with white Frette linens and centerpieces of Casablanca lilies and roses set in vases of

Baccarat crystal, were populated by the social elite and more than a few head-turning celebrities: Dancer Martha Graham, playwright Eugene O'Neill and his wife, the writer Agnes Boulton, and Yankee baseball player Babe Ruth all added to the evening's cache.

But for Charlotte, nothing could top seeing Al Jolson. When he opened with his song "April Showers," Charlotte felt she would have done anything for Jake to be able to see him perform. Or maybe she just wanted him with her. But if she were with Jake Larkin, she would not be at the benefit at all. She had to get these things straight in her mind.

"I have to admit, this is a thrill," she said to William.

"I wouldn't overstate it, darling."

The music also provided a welcome interruption of Amelia Astor's prattle. But then, Charlotte was too optimistic on this count. The song had barely ended before she started in again.

"So I assume someone here can tell us why it's so certain Walker is going to prevail over our Mayor Hylan? So far as I can tell, his greatest achievement has been to legalize that barbaric sport," she said.

"How right you are," said Claud Miroux, smiling at Amelia. The scion of the shipping family recently moved to New York from San Francisco. Charlotte was amused by Amelia's response—a taut smile. To Amelia, nothing was more gauche than the West Coast.

"Keeping boxing illegal didn't help anything," said Albert Guinness. "It didn't get rid of boxing, and then add to that, a whole criminal element rose around it."

The table murmured in agreement.

"Couldn't the same argument be made against Prohibition, then?" said Charlotte. Everyone turned to look at her, forks frozen in mid-air.

"Certainly not," said Amelia. "Prohibition is already an institution. And any politician who doesn't want to commit career suicide knows it. Look at our Mr. Buckner. I guarantee that by this time next year, everyone currently running one of those godforsaken clubs will be in prison."

"She's right, you know," said a woman who was walking by the table. Charlotte recognized her, but she wasn't immediately certain from where. "Sorry—I couldn't help but overhear. But word on the street is that the District Attorney's office has spies in the nightclubs and speakeasies. They're all going down."

"And how would you hear about this?" said Amelia.

And that's when Charlotte realized it was the woman who had shown up uninvited to Geraldine's funeral reception—the gossip columnist.

"It's my business to hear about it," said the woman, extending her hand. "Greta Goucher, from the *New York Sun*."

"Excuse me," Charlotte said, not that anyone cared that she was leaving the table. They were too riveted by the gossip's long-winded account of the impending nightlife apocalypse.

Mae followed her to the powder room.

"Are you all right?" Mae said.

"Do you think it's true? That by the end of the year all the club and speakeasy owners will be in prison?"

"No," said Mae, lighting a cigarette. "But even if it is true, others will fill their place. Clubs and drinking are not going to go away." As if to make her point, she hiked up her dress and pulled the flask from its makeshift holder.

"Mae!"

"What?" she said, taking a swig, then holding it out to Charlotte. "You're welcome to have some."

Charlotte seemed to consider it for half a second, then, as if remembering herself, shook her head. "Don't get yourself into any trouble tonight—please," Charlotte said. "And as for the clubs getting shut down, that's not what I'm worried about."

"What then? Oh . . . Jake? He'll be fine. His place is beneath anyone's notice. I doubt they're after the small-timers."

"I hope you're right," said Charlotte.

JAKE RARELY MET with his supplier in person. Usually, there was no need: His order didn't change from month to month, and everyone preferred to keep as low a profile as possible. No one even used their real names: As far as Jake's "business associates" knew, he was Saul Larkinowski—a combination of his father's first name, and his surname before it was Americanized.

But the conversation about Boom Boom would take more than a mere phone call. So he asked O'Brian to meet him at the Broadway diner, the place where Fiona had first sold Jake on the idea.

"Thanks for taking the time for a face-to-face," Jake said as O'Brian slid into the booth. He looked exactly as Jake remembered him: tall, pockmarked skin, and a short, military-style haircut.

"I assume you'll make it worth my while," the other man said, ordering a slice of cheesecake and a black coffee.

"I have a potential new account for you boys." Not wanting to drag out the meeting any longer than necessary, Jake slid a slip of paper with the amount of Boom Boom's monthly order across the table.

O'Brian whistled. "That's too rich for my blood. Who's the buyer?"

"A big operation in midtown."

"Your numbers are over my head. You'll have to talk to my boss."

"I have to go to Boston?"

"I said *my* boss, not *the* boss," said O'Brian. This gave Jake pause. He wanted this to be simple, with no more involvement than it took for him to keep his own shelves stocked. But really, meeting one more person up the supply chain didn't mean anything.

"Okay. Can you set it up?"

O'Brian looked at him hard. "This is the game you want to be in, Larkinowski?"

Jake nodded. "I wouldn't be sitting here if it weren't, would I?"

O'Brian slipped the paper into his jacket pocket. "You sure your buyer's not playing us against someone for the best deal? If I set the meeting, you better be in."

Jake swallowed hard. "I'm in."

O' Brian looked at him, unblinking. "I'll let you know when and where."

Chapter 10

AMELIA WONDERED HOW long she had to listen to the interminable prattle of the man seated to her left. But then, she knew how long: until he decided to stop talking. Manners were manners.

"I'd be delighted to hear more about that library project of yours," said Claud Miroux.

"Oh, I'd love to tell you all about it, but Charlotte Delacorte gets quite possessive about the whole thing." said Amelia. "You really should ask her."

"But then, that would take all the fun out of it, now wouldn't it?" he said with a wink.

Amelia reached for her water glass, damning Prohibition for denying her a much-needed glass of wine. She knew that the attention from men like Claud Miroux was the price she had to pay for choosing to remain unmarried. And newcomers to New York were the most odious to deal with; they assumed Amelia was ripe for the picking. Manhattanites knew better.

She glanced across the table at William, who appeared about

ready to extricate himself from the conversation with Albert Guinness.

"Excuse me—I must visit the powder room," she said to Claud.

With a pointed look at William, she left the table and crossed the room slowly enough that he was able to follow her.

Outside the dining hall, in the empty room where the party had served the hors d'ouevres, Amelia was able to speak her first words to him since dinner was served.

"Did you give Mae's suitcase to my driver?"

"Yes," William said. "But I have to admit, I'm dreading the scene she's certain to cause."

"There's nothing to worry about; she's been getting up from the table constantly. We just need to intercept her out in the hall before she returns to the dining room. You'll have her coat and her bag is already in the car. You just have to stand firm, darling."

William looked at her, no doubt startled by the term of endearment. He smiled.

"I can always count on you," he said. "And knowing that truly eases the loss of Mother."

"She was a strong woman. And every man needs one of those in his life. Now. I should get back to the table before that insufferable bore comes looking for me."

"Who? The Californian? I hope he's not getting too familiar," said William.

Amelia smiled all the way back to her seat.

THE WHITE-GLOVED SERVICE cleared the dessert plates, and Charlotte waited for some signal from William that he was ready to leave. Mae was gone from the table yet again, spending most of the night drinking and chain-smoking in the powder room.

"I've been trying to talk to you all night," Isobel said, slipping into the empty spot next to her.

"I hate when they seat us at different tables," Charlotte said, squeezing her friend's hand. "At least we don't have to worry about that at our own parties."

"That's what I wanted to talk to you about," Isobel said. "Meet me in the powder room."

Charlotte, perplexed, watched Isobel discreetly slip out of the ballroom. Across the table, William was deep in conversation with Albert Guinness. Claud Miroux seemed to be talking Amelia's ear off. Charlotte left the table unnoticed.

But she wasn't so lucky when getting out of the dining room.

"Mrs. Delacorte—a quick word?" said Mary Winterbourne, one of the hostesses of the evening. "You're not leaving yet, are you?"

"No, of course not. Just going for a powder."

"We're so thrilled you and your husband could make it tonight. Your support is tremendously valuable to us."

"We're honored to be included at such an important event," Charlotte said.

"I know you're in the midst of a book drive to get your library up and running. I have, oh, maybe six boxes of books from Thomas's old estate that is just sitting in our country house. Would you accept the donation?"

"That would be lovely. Thank you so much. Please, just send them to our house."

Charlotte indulged in the necessary conversation before she could extricate herself. By the time she reached the powder room, Isobel was walking out.

"I'd given up on you!" she said.

"Sorry. I got hijacked by Mary Winterbourne."

They ducked into the bathroom. Sure enough, Mae was sitting at the vanity, smoking with a full ashtray in front of her.

"Good lord, you've spent more time in here than at the table," Charlotte said.

Mae shrugged. "Better company." Her voice slurred.

"Are you drunk?" Charlotte said.

"Pleasantly buzzed."

Charlotte sighed and turned to Isobel. "So what's going on? What's with the cloak and dagger?"

"You missed a WLA meeting while you were in Philadelphia."

"Oh, ducky, I know that. It was practically the first thing William mentioned when I got home. He wasn't too happy with me, but I told him we are ahead of schedule and one missed meeting won't hurt anything."

"But that's just it: We didn't miss a meeting. Amelia held it without you."

Charlotte looked at her. "You're not serious. Even she wouldn't overstep like that. She doesn't have the authority to run the meeting."

"William gave her the authority, apparently."

Charlotte pulled a velvet-covered stool out from under the vanity, and sat down. "I wish I could say that I'm surprised," she said.

"Oh, who cares," said Mae. "Let her run the stupid library. You didn't want the bother anyway, did you?"

"That's not the point," Charlotte said softly.

"She changed the theme of the gala," Isobel said. "It's not King Tut anymore. It's Spring—or something generic like that."

Charlotte nodded. "Thanks for telling me, Isobel. You're a good friend. Mae, come with me. I'm sure we'll be heading home soon."

Charlotte opened the door to the hallway, with Mae right behind her. They both almost collided into William and Amelia.

"I've been looking all over for you two," William said.

"Well, now you've found us," Charlotte said. William and Amelia exchanged a look. At first she thought she was imagining it, but it was unmistakable.

"I have your coat, Charlotte. It's time to leave," he said. Charlotte took her coat from him, ignoring his attempt to help her on with it.

"Do you have mine, too?" Mae said.

"We'll get yours on the way out," said Amelia.

"Oh? Are you coming home with us, too?" said Charlotte.

"No," said Amelia, with an odd smile. "Mae is coming home with me."

Mae laughed a drunken, irrational cackle.

"Has she been drinking?" said William.

Charlotte ignored him, turning instead to Amelia. "I don't know what you're talking about. But it's been a long night and you'll have to save your interfering for the next WLA meeting."

"Don't be a bother, Charlotte," William said, putting his hand on her arm and squeezing a little too hard. "Have you already forgotten our little talk the other day?"

Charlotte swallowed hard, and watched helplessly as William and Amelia ushered Mae out into the lobby.

Chapter 11

CHARLOTTE TURNED OVER in the darkness. Beside her, William fell into a loud, rhythmic breathing.

Finally.

She'd waited, lying stiffly on her side, for what felt like an hour. All she could do was replay in her mind the scene outside the bathroom and the look of devastation on Mae's face as Amelia led her away. Charlotte told William she was going to collect Mae in the morning.

"Stay out of it, Charlotte. I don't want to hear another word from you. You have no say in how I deal with my sister."

She could not stay in bed with him for another minute.

Charlotte moved as slowly as possible, putting one foot on the floor at a time. Then she tiptoed across the room. She lifted her

evening bag off of her dresser and retrieved the strappy shoes she
had worn that evening from the floor, and then slipped out into the
hallway.

Her eyes were adjusted enough to the dark to make it through
the hallway quickly. She ducked down the back stairs, and went
to the laundry room. The room was large and drafty. She switched
on the light. Sure enough, hanging beside piles of clean sheets and
white clothing, she found one of the dresses she'd worn in Philadelphia. It had been cleaned and pressed and was set to be returned
to Charlotte's closet.

Charlotte pulled off her nightgown, and stepped into the green
silk dress. It wasn't ideal for where she was going, but she couldn't
go into her closet without waking William. She'd considered bor-
rowing something from Mae's closet, but she felt so awful about
her sister-in-law's situation that she couldn't bring herself to go
into her room.

She stopped in one of the first-floor bathrooms and looked in
the mirror. Her face was too pale. She opened her bag, pulling out
the rouge Mae had lent her and dabbed a little on each cheek and a
dash on her lips. Then she pulled her messy hair away from her face.
She thought, not for the first time, that it was time to get a modern
haircut.

Quietly, she stepped into the hallway and closed the bathroom
door behind her.

"Madame?"

"Rafferty!" She nearly jumped out of her skin.

"I didn't mean to alarm you. I heard something down here and
I wanted to make sure everything was okay."

"Everything's fine. I'm sorry if I disturbed you. Please—go
back to sleep."

"Are you going out, madame?"

Charlotte hesitated. "Yes. I am. But please don't say anything.
I'll be back in a few hours."

"Do you want me to bring the car around?"

She smiled. "No, thank you. I'll get it."

"If you insist. And please—be careful, madame."

Charlotte didn't know if he meant that she should be careful out in the night or careful not to get caught sneaking out, but she wasn't afraid of either after what happened tonight.

ROGER TOLD HIMSELF the redhead—he had to stop thinking of her as that now that he knew her name was Fiona, gorgeous Fiona— was just a distraction and it was time for him to go home. The whole notion of him spending time at the club to glean information seemed less and less practical as the night wore on. No one talked about anything of significance. Boom Boom simply circulated all night, greeting customers and keeping her staff on the ball. Yes, there was the sale and consumption of alcohol, but that was an open secret and not the point. The bottom line was, he could hang out at the club from dusk until dawn for a year and never find proof of the supply and buy operation.

Roger paid his tab, left a generous tip, and headed for the front door.

"Now where are you running off to?" Fiona said, appearing at his side catching him off guard for a bit. He was so invested in lying while at the club, he couldn't even say the simple truth that he was going home.

"Um, I think I'll check out some other place. Can't just come here every night, right?" He stumbled over his words.

He noticed that Boom Boom was watching them.

"Want some company?" Fiona said with a smile. Roger was confused.

"Aren't you . . . working?" he said.

"It looks like my shift is over," she said with a wink. "Just give me a minute to get my coat."

———

CHARLOTTE FORGOT SHE needed a password to get into Jake's place at that hour of the night. This is what she got for running around without Mae.

"Tell Jake it's Charlotte," she said to the person who refused to open the door. She didn't hear a response, and waited uncomfortably in the dark. She could hear the music as loud as ever.

After a few minutes, Jake opened the door. It was as if he became more handsome every time she saw him.

"Sorry about that," he said. She wondered if he was as happy to see her as she was to see him.

Inside, she was overwhelmed by the crowd and noise. An hour ago, lying in bed at home, she had only imagined how it would feel to see Jake. She hadn't factored in the dozens of other people, the music, and the alcohol.

It must have shown on her face.

"You look like you need a drink," he said. When his dark eyes focused on her, it made her insides jump.

Jake took her by the hand, and led her to a seat at the bar. She felt calmed his touch.

"I do, no doubt. But I'm going to refrain," she said. "I can't stay long."

"Do you want to talk?" he said.

She hoped no one noticed them duck out of the living room and up the stairs to the second-floor loft. He closed the door, but the sound of the party below filled the small space.

There was nowhere to stand but in front of the bed. They looked at each other for a long time in silence. Charlotte ached for him to touch her, but he didn't. It was agonizing.

Unable to take another second without contact, she grabbed his hand. He looked into her eyes and her stomach felt as choppy as the sea. For a minute, the entire room seemed to tilt. And then he reached his hands behind her, and deftly began unbuttoning the mother-of-pearl beads in the back of her dress before it fell to the floor entirely.

She stood naked and trembling. Jake kissed her from her neck to her thighs with a slow patience that made her squirm. When she tried to pull him to her, he held her back, sweeping his fingertips over the places he had just touched with his lips.

"Don't tease me so," she said breathlessly. He finally gave in, pulling her down with him onto the bed and easing inside of her. She put her arms around him, her cheek pressing against his broad shoulder. With him, it was as if she had never had sex before. She felt completely at the mercy of his touch, her body unable to assert itself in any way other than following his lead towards the almost crushing sense of bliss. When she felt it, her mind went blank, as if it couldn't process anything more than the spasms of pleasure spreading through her body. She cried out in such a way that she didn't recognize her own voice.

Afterward, curled against him, Charlotte could almost forget the first half of her night.

Almost.

When her breathing had slowed, and the sweat on her body cooled to give her a chill, she pulled the covers over herself. He held her tightly.

"William sent Mae to stay with Amelia Astor," Charlotte said. Just saying the words made her feel like crying. Or maybe it was the intensity of the sex that had left her so emotional.

Jake stroked her hair. "Why would he do that?"

"He thinks she's out of control. Ever since his mother died, he's been consumed with the notion of how things reflect on the family."

He kissed her forehead.

"I know Mae. She's not a pushover. Why doesn't she just tell him to screw off?" he asked.

"He controls the money. Her inheritance."

"She doesn't need his money."

"It's her money, too."

Jake raised an eyebrow.

"Come on. Why doesn't she just get a job? It's 1925. Women have choices now," he said.

"There's not one job that will give her the money she's due as a Delacorte," she said. "Besides, it's not that simple."

"I think it could be," he said, sitting up.

"You think it's easy to walk away from money—the type of money that can solve problems—because you've never had it."

"I don't see it solving problems. I see it causing problems. And I see you letting it."

She looked down at her hands, nervously playing with her wedding band. "I should go," she said quietly.

Jake didn't argue with her.

Chapter 12

ROGER FOLLOWED FIONA up five flights of stairs, his heart pounding from the way her long hair fell over her pale shoulders, waving at him like a red flag.

He told himself there was nothing wrong with going to her place for a drink. And to refuse would be negligent in his job; clearly, this was a woman "in the know"—hadn't he seen her talking to Charlotte Delacorte that first night? And didn't the owner of the club seem to keep an eye on Fiona? And didn't the way both of them had jumped to alert when he paid the check to leave suggest that by taking her up on her offer, he was merely following the logical conclusion to the night?

"Make yourself comfortable," she said, opening the door. "I'll fix us some gin."

Roger had seen some small apartments in his day, but this one took the prize: just one room, the only furniture a queen-sized bed and two mismatched chairs. The "kitchen" was a small refrigerator, a sink, and a hot pot. It made his apartment on the West Side look like a palace.

He sat nervously in one of the chairs.

"I said make yourself *comfortable,*" she said, taking two glasses out of the sink. "I only use those chairs for something to hang my clothes on. Sit on the bed."

"I really shouldn't drink anymore," he said, not moving from the chair.

"Suit yourself."

She filled a glass for herself and sat on the bed. "Well, don't make me drink alone," she said, patting the space next to her.

She seemed to him the epitome of beauty, delicately luminous and bold at the same time. She was commanding, but also childlike, and his feelings toward her were almost protective. They had been from the first moment he set eyes on her.

"Do you need a formal invitation?" she said with a smile.

"Of course not." He didn't want to move from his seat, because it gave him the perfect vantage point to just look at her. But it would be awkward to continue to refuse her.

As soon as he sat next to her, she put one hand on his leg and squeezed. His breath caught. He inhaled her scent, a mixture of cigarette smoke and a flowery perfume. He couldn't help but compare it to Elizabeth's scent of late: stale milk and laundry soap.

"You still haven't told me what you do, Roger," she said.

Roger was grateful for the prep Buckner had given him for just such a question. He only wished he'd given more than a cursory glance at the issue of *Photoplay* floating around the office.

"I'm in the movie business," he said.

"Really!" Her big green eyes widened. "Do you know Irving Thalberg? He was in the club last week."

"Um, no. I don't."

"Well, if you run into him, tell him we miss him at the Vesper and that he should come in again," she said.

"I'll do that."

She finished her drink. "Excuse me for a minute."

He watched her disappear into what he could only assume was the bathroom. Or a closet.

There didn't seem to be a clock in the room. He wondered how late it was. He would give himself twenty more minutes, and then he would go. Fun was fun, but even his wife was aware that clubs didn't stay open until two in the morning.

"Good. You're still here," she said. "You're such a quiet little mouse, I couldn't be sure."

She had changed out of her yellow dress into a cream-colored peignoir set. Her breasts were visible through the sheer fabric, and the sight made him instantly hard.

"Jesus, you're beautiful," he said, shocked to hear the words come out of his mouth.

"Aren't you sweet," she said, sitting so close he could feel her breath on his face. Then she took his hands and put them on her breasts. He felt a buzzing in his head, his thoughts suddenly scattered like marbles. The pressure in his pants was unbearable.

She tugged on his jacket. "You really should take this off."

Then she reached into his pocket and took out his wallet. He knew he should care that she was removing a few twenties, but in that moment it merely registered as an annoying delay.

She replaced his wallet, tucked the cash beneath her pillow, and then shrugged off her robe. Slowly, almost teasingly, she eased down the straps of her teddy. He was awed, almost immobilized, by the sight of her.

Fiona lifted the nightgown over her head. She didn't wear underwear. This, almost more than anything else that had transpired, was shocking.

She lay on her back expectantly. Roger stood and fumbled with his belt, removing his clothes as quickly as possible. Even through the haze of his scattered thoughts, he knew he was crossing an unspeakable line. After tonight, he would tell Buckner that he was done at the clubs.

But for now, all he cared about was plundering the magnificent body that lay before him. Her flesh was so pale and flawless it scarcely looked real. He was tentative when touching her between her legs, but her body yielded to him in undeniable welcome. She didn't seem to mind his mouth on her breasts, the part of the body his wife had so long denied him. This was unbearably exciting, and he knew the only way to stand another moment in her presence was to be inside of her. He moved on top of her.

Within seconds, Roger felt sensations so exquisite, he knew he was lost.

Chapter 13

AMELIA WALKED INTO the newly occupied bedroom on the third floor. She didn't bother to knock.

She found Mae sitting in a chair, still in her nightclothes, staring at the wall. The toast, fruit, and coffee that Amelia had the maid bring up hours ago sat untouched on the tray. She knew she should be concerned that two days after arriving, Mae still refused food. But mostly, Amelia was just irritated.

"You're going to have to eat eventually," Amelia said. Mae showed no sign of having heard her. She did not so much as shift her eyes in Amelia's direction. And that's when Amelia realized she smelled cigarette smoke.

"Have you been smoking in here?" she said incredulously.

She heard the doorbell sound downstairs, though she wasn't expecting anyone.

"If you have cigarettes in this room, I suggest you get rid of them within the next five minutes. When I get back I'll be going through all of your bags."

Amelia slammed the door behind her.

The housemaid was already rushing up the stairs. "Mrs. Delacorte is here to see you," she said.

"Just what I don't need. Please get rid of her."

"Mr. Benjamin tried. He told her you were busy but she said she would wait." The housemaid winced at her words as if she expected to be struck.

Amelia didn't know what was more vexing: her butler's failure to get rid of Charlotte, or the housemaid's cowering fear in relaying the bad news. "Thank you. I'll take care of it."

Downstairs, she found Charlotte waiting patiently in the foyer.

"Charlotte, this is not a good time for a visit. While it's always lovely to see you, I have a very full plate today."

"Your plate is quite safe from distraction," said Charlotte. "I'm here to see my sister-in-law."

Amelia stepped in front of the stairs, and then realized how absurd it was for her to feel the need to physically block Charlotte from the second floor. This was her house. All she had to do was tell her to leave.

"How thoughtful of you. But really, Charlotte, it's not necessary. Mae is adjusting so nicely—I fear your presence would be a setback."

"I don't know what you and William think you're doing, but you can't stop me from seeing her," said Charlotte.

Amelia had to admit that all of this unpleasantness was almost more than she had bargained for.

"No need to be so dramatic, Charlotte," said Amelia. "No one is stopping you from doing anything. I should just think that if you want what's best for Mae, you'll let her relax here without seeing you act hysterical. Surely you can get along at the house without her. You really need to find ways to feel more useful."

She saw color flood Charlotte's face, but she barely had time to enjoy it because the doorbell rang again. "It's like Grand Central Station around here today," Amelia said, waiting for the butler to reappear.

"Are you expecting another guest?" he said.

"I was not expecting anyone today," she said. "Apparently, the simple courtesy of announcing has become too much to ask. When did this town become so uncivilized?"

The butler opened the door, and both women were surprised to see Claud Miroux.

"Ladies! What an unexpected bonus to find you both here," said Claud. Behind him, a valet held two large boxes, with another one at his feet. "I hope you'll forgive the unexpected visit."

"Don't be silly," said Amelia. "Do come in."

"I'm just delighted to know there is a good home waiting for these books. I overestimated the size of the library in my new house. The spaces are so much larger in California."

The valet followed him inside.

"Now, Mr. Miroux—didn't I tell you that Mrs. Delacorte was in charge of the library?"

"Oh, forgive me. I was under the impression the books should come here," said Claud, looking at Charlotte.

"Nothing to worry about, Mr. Miroux," said Charlotte. "We're just happy to have your donation."

Amelia pushed aside her fury at Claud's presumptuousness in showing up at her house, and instead recognized it as a blessing in disguise.

"Your timing is actually perfect," said Amelia. "Mrs. Delacorte was just leaving. Your valet can put the boxes right in her car. Now if you'll both excuse me, I have a houseguest to attend to."

———

Roger knew Buckner was trying to be helpful by giving him the day off, but the last thing he needed was more time at home—more time with a woman who wasn't Fiona.

He'd shown up at the office, bleary-eyed from lack of sleep, but fueled by a giddy, elated nervous energy. Despite his exhaustion, he felt more alive than he had in years.

But a half hour into a staff meeting, he could barely keep his head off the conference room table. Buckner pulled him aside.

"These late nights are a killer, I know," he'd said. "But it will all pay off in the end. Just keep your ear to the ground. And one day you soon you'll be back to just desk work and you'll miss all the action."

Of course, Buckner had no idea exactly how late those nights had become—and how much action Roger was getting.

"Go home and get some rest. There's nothing here that can't wait until the morning. And stay home tonight. You can check in at the Vesper on Friday."

And so, at one in the afternoon, still going on three hours of sleep, Roger sat at the kitchen table, reading through pages of a deposition.

"I thought this was supposed to be a day off," Elizabeth said with a small smile. Why did it irritate him so that she was still in her robe? He was certain Fiona wouldn't be caught dead in a garment that went from her neck to the ankles, with buttons running the entire length.

"I'm behind in my paperwork," he said, barely glancing up.

"The baby will be napping for two hours or so," she mused. Roger said nothing.

Elizabeth sat in a chair across from him and reached for his hand. "Roger, I know you've been . . . less than satisfied lately. And I know it's partly my fault. More than partly. But I don't want to go on this way."

He looked up at her, forcing a smile. "It's fine."

"No," she said. "It's not." She stood up and circled around to where he sat, and again took his hand, tugging gently to bring him to his feet.

For months, all he had wanted was for his wife to give him a little notice, to maybe even pretend to want him physically so that he could feel like a husband, if not completely like a man. And now, when he could barely stand to be in the same room with her. . . .

Roger let Elizabeth lead him to the bedroom. The bed was still unmade, and the ubiquitous laundry was piled in a basket on the floor next to two of his son's teddy bears.

He thought of the room last night—the smell of flowery perfume and cigarette smoke, the glass of gin on the floor, the sound of sirens outside. . . .

"What are you doing?" Elizabeth said. Roger jolted up, startled. He had unknowingly curled up on his side of the bed, already falling asleep, where he would no doubt dream of soft pale flesh and a tangle of red hair that fanned out across his chest.

"Going to sleep," he said. Her face was crestfallen. Well, now she knew how he'd felt for the past year. But what she didn't know was how completely, absolutely, and irrevocably everything had changed.

Chapter 14

CHARLOTTE DRESSED IN a fog for the morning Women's Literary Alliance meeting.

Why, she wondered, in an endless loop of things keeping her awake all night, had her late mother-in-law, who had never shown her one ounce of kindness or respect, appointed her head of the group and the future library anyway?

There was only one possible answer: So she could fail.

Charlotte stepped into a red Jacques Doucet dress with rows of flounces and pulled on the matching jacket. She took the time to pencil in her eyebrows as Mae had taught her, and applied bright lipstick. She wore her hair down, once again thinking she should chop it all off.

"Rafferty—can you please bring the car around?"

Yes, it all made so much sense now. She had been given a role in which she would obviously falter . . . or at least could be made to appear to be faltering. A role that someone else could easily— and by all appearances, heroically—step into. Charlotte had, unwittingly, played her part perfectly.

As had William and Amelia.

It was hard to believe it now, but there had been a time when Charlotte had her husband's support. When Geraldine denigrated her with her little quips and comments, William usually acted as a buffer. But now that Geraldine was gone, Charlotte's buffer had somehow turned into her staunchest critic. It baffled her.

When they had first met, she realized her differences from Geraldine were part of what attracted William. He was charmed by her outsider status, by her ignorance and indifference to the ways of the Manhattan smart set. She knew their engagement had been, in some ways, William's declaration of independence. Ironically, the union that for Charlotte was a concession to her parents' happiness, was for William, a rejection of his mother's wishes.

A wish that he marry Amelia Astor.

From the very start, William's mother had behaved as if Charlotte were breaking up a relationship in progress. But William had sworn to her that he had never so much as taken Amelia out on a date. "She's like a sister to me," he'd said. And she'd had no reason not to believe him. But what was the expression Geraldine had used? Of William and Amelia, she'd told Charlotte, "That train has already left the station, my dear. Of that you can be certain."

She'd relayed this little tidbit to William, who'd embraced her and said, "Wishful thinking."

How was it Geraldine was more influential in death than she'd ever been in life? It was as if in the very act of removing herself from the equation, she'd changed the entire value system.

And hadn't the stress she placed on their early courtship had the ironic effect of pitting William and Charlotte together against her, creating the cruel illusion of love?

"Would you like for me to drive you, madame?" said Rafferty. It was tempting; she was so tired it would be a relief to let someone worry about handling the car. But being chauffeured around was one luxury she had not yet learned to embrace.

"No, thank you, Rafferty. I'm fine driving myself."

"Very well," he said, his face appearing to fall a bit.

Was she imagining things, or did he seem disappointed?

The roads were clogged with cars. It seemed there were more on the streets every day. But it was just as well: Charlotte was in no rush to get to the house on Fifty-seventh Street.

So now what? She and William were in a loveless marriage that had begun with the best of intentions. She supposed it happened all the time. The only problem was, now she not only knew what love felt like, she knew that she had it—with someone who was not her husband. But the marriage that she had believed might be important for her own security and the well-being of her parents had now proven to be so, absolutely. To leave now would be the most selfish act imaginable. She wouldn't dare leave her parents without any resources, not when they needed it most.

She didn't blame Jake for being upset with her the other day; just thinking about it kept her awake at night. She spent so much time agonizing over the situation for herself, she had barely given a thought to what it must be like—and what it must look like—to him. For all he knew, she was happy to have her society husband and her bootlegger lover. But no, he couldn't really think that. He could see how she trembled in his arms, how she fought tears when she had to leave. She had to tell him the truth about her parents, about why she could never leave William.

Although "never" sounded like an awfully long time.

Suddenly, the thought of sitting through a two-hour Women's Literary Alliance meeting was unthinkable. And what difference would it make if she were there or not? If Amelia wanted to run it, let her.

She turned the car toward Seventh Avenue to head downtown. Now she wished she had taken Rafferty up on his offer so she didn't have to bother with parking—although she couldn't very well ask him to wait outside of Jake's apartment.

The parking spot, two blocks away, gave her time to mentally rehearse exactly what she would tell him. She could not say the words, *I love you*. She couldn't declare that she would leave her husband if she could. But when she told him the realities of her family, of her marriage, he would understand and know he was not playing the fool.

She knocked on the door to no response. Maybe he was still asleep? But then the door opened finally opened.

It was the beautiful singer from the King Club.

"Oh!" Charlotte said, startled. "It must have been quite a night if everyone's still here. Hi—I'm Charlotte. I'm here to see Jake."

"Not 'everyone' is still here," said the woman coyly. Charlotte remembered her name was Rona. "Just me. And Jake is in the shower."

Even if Charlotte mistook the meaning of her words, there as nothing unclear about the look in the woman's big, liquid brown eyes.

"Oh! Excuse me," Charlotte said, barely able to get the words out.

She walked quickly away from the apartment door, and as soon as she was out of sight, began to run back to her car.

"WHAT DO YOU mean, she missed the meeting?" William said.

"Just what I told you on the phone: We all showed up for the meeting and Charlotte never arrived." Amelia stood and glared at the parlor doors. "Where is our food? My house girl has got to go. I know you complain about your butler, but really, they're all the same."

"It's my fault for dropping in so suddenly. They weren't expecting to do tea service. But after your call, I just couldn't focus on the office."

"Of course not. How could you? It's all so troubling," said Amelia. "Your wife might just be a lost cause. Your sister, however, is not."

The tea and sandwiches arrived, and Amelia paused discreetly.

"Mae's been behaving here?" William asked, when they were once again alone.

"Well, she hasn't left her room."

"That's an improvement right there," William said.

"Quite. But, our goal is to have her become a respectable married woman—not a recluse."

"True," William said. "Still, I am so grateful for your intervention. I only wish Charlotte could have handled this discreetly in our own home."

Amelia set down her teacup, and moved from her chair to sit next to him on the sofa.

"William, I don't know how to say this, but as your friend, I feel I must: At a certain point, you have to ask yourself, what is it costing you to stay in this marriage versus what it would cost you to just be free of it?"

William drew a deep breath before responding. "Divorce is not an option for us, Amelia. The gossip, the scandal, the loss of respect . . ."

"Divorce is not such a scandal these days. And your mother, God rest her soul, is no longer here to tell you otherwise."

William shook his head. "I can't risk the scrutiny. Things are so difficult with business. I can not lose one inch of my standing in the community."

Amelia nodded, the picture of understanding. William looked at her with an expression that was so tortured, she was almost afraid to hear what he wanted to tell her.

She stood at the sound of the doorbell.

"Are you expecting someone?" he said.

"Yes," she said. "When you said you were stopping by, I asked my cousin Jonathan to join us."

"Jon Astor? What for?"

"I thought he'd be interested in meeting the most eligible young woman in New York"—Amelia raised her eyebrow—"but thought he should meet her brother first."

William smiled at her. "Do you think he will take to her?" he said.

"Jonathan isn't a saint—but he's very savvy. He knows he needs a proper appearing wife. But a truly proper young lady wouldn't have him."

"You're a genius," he said, taking her hand.

"Well, that may be so. But I need you to be smart about things, too. Think about Charlotte, would you? Consider your options."

William looked at her. "I already am," he said.

Chapter 15

"YOU HAVE A visitor in the parlor, Mrs. Delacorte," Rafferty said. His usually professional demeanor was punctuated by small smile as he took in her new appearance.

Charlotte glanced at herself in the hallway mirror. She'd finally done it: After seeing Rona at Jake's, she hadn't wanted to go home. With Mae no longer at the house, she couldn't stand the thought of being alone. Charlotte decided to go to the one place she was guaranteed she could spend an hour surrounded by company: the beauty parlor. And she told the girl at the salon, Anne Marie, who'd been styling her hair since her engagement to William, to cut it all off. "Like Louise Brooks," Charlotte had said.

She barely recognized herself, with her new jaw-length bob and bangs just skimming her eyebrows. And since she knew she had no doubt lost her appetite for good, she would soon be so skinny, and with her new hair and figure, she would look like a proper flapper. All that would be missing was mirth in her eyes. But that was lost to her now, too.

"Who's the visitor?" she said, shrugging off her light jacket. Rafferty took it from her.

"More book donations," he said.

Charlotte stifled a groan. She wished she had told everyone to deliver books directly to the Fifty-seventh Street mansion. But it was too difficult to make sure someone was there to receive them now that Geraldine's staff had been cut. Maybe everything should go to Amelia's now that she'd staged her coup.

She looked in the mirror one more time. Even in her miserable state, she had to admit the haircut did something magical with the lines of her face—her cheekbones were somehow more prominent, the curve of her jaw accentuated and dramatic, and her eyes seemed to have doubled in size.

It was a shame that Jake would never see her like this.

She kept playing the encounter with Rona over and over in her mind. Charlotte was certain she was not jumping to conclusions: There was no mistaking the look in Rona's eye, the way she shooed her out the door. And why else would she be there first thing in the morning?

Had she missed something the night Jake took her to the King Club? When he was up on stage, had a glance been exchanged between them? No—if something had been going on with Rona, Jake would not have brought Charlotte there. As much as she hated him at that moment, she had to admit he would not have willingly put the two women together in a room under those circumstances.

Charlotte wished she could talk to Mae. After she attended to the book donation, she'd call Amelia's house. That woman could hardly justify not putting Mae on the phone. She wasn't a prisoner, for heaven's sake.

She opened the door to the parlor, and stopped abruptly.

"You need to leave," she said.

Jake stood from a chair, and walked to her with great deliberation. He closed the parlor doors.

"You look beautiful," he said, his eyes taking her in from head to toe.

"I have no interest in hearing that from you right now," she said, her voice low. She walked into the room, away from the door so there was less chance of her being overheard. "I mean, really, Jake—there should be a revolving door on your bedroom."

"Charlotte . . ."

"I realize I have little ground to stand on here; after all, I'm the one who's married, right?" She knew her voice was shaking, and that she sounded more than a bit hysterical. But she couldn't control herself. "But I just didn't expect . . . I thought . . ."

"Listen to me, Charlotte. Come sit for a minute." He reached for her arm and she yanked it away, but she did follow him to the couch. She noticed a box on the floor.

"Did you really bring books?" she said.

"No. I don't have any books. I just needed an excuse in case William was home."

She sighed and crossed her arms in front of her chest, as if this was yet another affront.

"I didn't mean to hurt you with Rona. . . ."

"I don't want to hear about it." Charlotte fought back tears. How could she feel this badly about it all? What had she expected would happen with Jake? That he would simply devote his life to a married woman? And yet the pain was almost physical.

"You're married, and I assume you don't turn your husband away just because . . . you met me."

Charlotte felt her cheeks flush. "You can't think that I had any intention of being . . . intimate with both of you. After that happened between us, I knew my marriage was over."

"It doesn't look over. In fact, it became obvious to me the other night, when we were discussing Mae, that you had no intention of ever leaving your husband. You suffer with it, but you won't do anything about it. People like you never upset the status quo. If you really wanted to stay married and just have an affair, I could understand that. But I know that's not what you want, but it's what you do, and I don't respect that."

She stood up and faced the window. "Believe it or not, this is the conversation I came over to have with you this morning. I knew I owed you an explanation. But I was too late."

"You don't owe me anything."

She shook her head. "I married William with the best of intentions."

"I don't doubt it."

"Let me finish: I married him because I thought I loved him, but also because I knew he would give me the financial security I never had. My father and mother were madly in love, but when money was scarce, we all suffered. And now my mother is sick. She can't even feed herself. My father found a decent place that can care for her and keep her comfortable until . . . the end. But it costs a fortune. I can't help him pay for it without William's help."

By now, Jake was standing behind her. He put his arms around her, and kissed her shoulder. She didn't move, not shirking him, but not welcoming the embrace.

"I'm so sorry, Charlotte."

"Even if I left William and found a job, I would only be able to take care of myself—not my mother." Her voice broke.

Jake gently guided her back to the couch, and she sat next to him, feeling slightly calmer now. "I'm going to tell you something you have to promise not to tell anyone, okay?"

She nodded, hoping somehow he had something to say that would change the reality of their situation. But she knew that was childish; she could run around at night, she could cut her hair, she could dress in different clothes, and she could even fall in love: Nothing would set her free.

"I'm working on a big business deal that could change things for us."

"What kind of deal?"

"I can't get into details. But I might be making a lot more money soon," he said, drawing her close to him.

They sat quietly, holding each other. The house was still and silent, all she heard was the grandfather clock ticking in the farthest corner of the room.

She rested her head on his shoulder, breathing in his scent. She hoped it would rub off on her clothes, and stay with her.

The door opened and she jumped up.

William strode into the room before she could process what was happening. She didn't know how much he'd seen, but he headed toward them like he was shot out of a cannon.

Part IV

Vice or Virtue

The submission of her body without love or desire is degrading to the woman's finer sensibility, all the marriage certificates on earth to the contrary notwithstanding.
—Margaret Sanger

Chapter 1

CHARLOTTE FROZE, FEAR spreading across her face.

Her instinct was to grab for Jake's hand, but she stood perfectly still and stared at William with all the control she could muster. "Get the hell out of my house," he said to Jake.

"Well, seeing as I'm Charlotte's guest and not yours, I'm not going anywhere until she asks me."

"It's okay—just go," she said quickly. Jake turned to her before leaving the room. She met his gaze for a second, and that was all it took to know that he would be back for her. When the door closed behind him, she missed him already.

William stepped closer.

"What did you do to your hair?" he said, his voice barely more than a whisper.

"What?" She instinctively touched her head. The haircut—she'd forgotten about it.

And then she felt his hand heavy across her cheek, a shocking blow that sent her straight to the floor.

"It's bad enough I have a sister who shames the family. I won't stand for it from my wife!"

Charlotte looked up at him, willing herself to get up off of the carpet, but still too shaken to move.

"You have no right to raise a hand to me," she said, fighting back her tears. She refused to cry in front of him.

"I'm instructing the staff you are to have no visitors unless I approve them ahead of time. And please remember, Charlotte, before you have any more ideas about your hair, or your clothes, or your social life: I sent Mae away, and I won't hesitate to do the same with you," he spat.

"You think this is any way to have a marriage!?" she yelled, her voice suddenly just as loud as his.

"Is that what you call this?" he said icily. "Let me put it this way: Do you, or do you not, want me to write that check every month?"

They locked eyes. Charlotte looked away first. "I thought so," William said. "I'll see you at the dinner table. And please wear a hat so I can at least try to forget that my wife now looks like a schoolboy."

JAKE IGNORED THE few people hanging out on the first floor of the apartment, and rushed up the stairs to his telephone. He dialed the phone number off of a slip of paper he kept under his mattress. He never bothered to memorize it because it changed every month.

"O'Brian," the voice said at the other end.

"This is Larkinowski," Jake said, using his alias.

"What's with the phone calls lately? You miss hearing my voice? Maybe you need an old lady."

"I wouldn't have to call you if you'd set the meeting. Is your boss in or is he out? I need to get this thing moving."

"What's your hurry?"

"Either we do the deal, or someone else will," Jake said, although he had no reason to think Boom Boom was negotiating with other people on the side.

"The meeting is set: Friday night at seven. There's a restaurant few block from the Bowery: Cavanaugh's. My boss will be in the last booth on the right."

Jake found a stray pencil under his bed and scribbled the information on the back of a week-old newspaper.

"Does your boss have a name?" he said.

"To you, he's just 'Boss.' If he likes you and it's a go, then you'll hear from me and we'll set up the deal. Oh, and by the way, you better prepare Boom Boom to pay more than she's used to. Payola is going up, and so are prices for the customers."

Jake replaced the phone receiver. He tried not to be too concerned about whether or not "the Boss" would like him. He knew "like" meant "trust," and from one hustler to another, Jake would win him over. There was no reason why he'd be seen as a liability: He'd been running a tight ship for two years; he was handling the Boom Boom job discreetly. There was no reason not to get this deal in place.

And then he would bail Charlotte out of that marriage.

FROM HER BEDROOM window, Mae watched the afternoon fade into evening—the end of another twelve-hour stint in the prison of the Astor mansion. Soon it would be dark, and she would go back to sleep—her only escape.

She was starting to wonder if her inheritance was worth it.

Could being poor be any worse than being a prisoner of her brother or—more accurately now—of his lapdog, Amelia Astor?

What if she got a job like Fiona: working at a club, making tips, and scrapping it out? Now she wished she'd gone to college like some of her friends—or even like Charlotte. But how could she have known her mother would die, and then pull such a crazy stunt with her will?

Her biggest fear, as much as she hated to admit it, was that Fiona wouldn't want to be with her anymore if she weren't rich. But then, Fiona had already walked away from her. Mae was confident she could get her back if she was free and flush with cash. But how could she love Fiona knowing the truth about her bottom line?

But she did love her. It was the horrible, torturous truth of her existence. Something about that girl possessed her—and had since the first night they met.

It had been a week after her high school graduation. She and a few friends from the Spence School—Abigail Cornwall, Kiki Von Loring, and Sarah Strout—were having dinner in midtown when a group of fellas at the next table starting chatting them up. This almost always happened when Mae went out with The Group, as they liked to call themselves. They were an attractive bunch, all tall and lean, glossy-haired, and well dressed. They were the type of girls who didn't need to seek out male attention, and therefore they never failed to get it.

Mae, of course, had never been interested in that kind of attention—not that she would admit this to her friends. That she was a girl who liked girls had always been her little secret. The only one who had ever known was Paloma Dominion, her mother's housemaid's daughter.

Somehow, Mae—at just fourteen years old—had sensed that there was something different about Paloma. She only saw her one week out of the year, during her visit to the house at Christmas time. The way Paloma looked at her, shyly but directly out from under her thick dark lashes, signaled to Mae that it was okay to think the things she thought about the girl. And she did think about—not only during the weeklong visit, but all throughout her entire freshman year of high school. Every night before she fell asleep, Mae would lie in her big canopied bed, and touch herself while thinking about Paloma. She imagined what it would be like to have Paloma next to her, to be able to wind her hands through the thick plaits of dark hair, and then slowly move her hands lower to touch the breasts that were considerably bigger than her own. She wondered if Paloma ever thought about her; she wondered if the girl ever touched herself between her legs in a way that made her entire body vibrate.

She got her answer the following year when, during her mother's onerously large Christmas party, she and Paloma ended up naked together in the pantry. Mae finally knew exactly what it was like to hold those breasts, and she also realized Paloma had most certainly been touching herself—because she knew exactly how to make Mae's body spasm with pleasure. For the rest of the week, Mae and Paloma met up every night—a pre-bedtime ritual that was no longer just the stuff of fantasies.

But then it was over; by the following Christmas, Paloma's mother had retired from the Delacorte staff. And Mae never saw Paloma again.

Mae did not have those same feelings again for anyone until she met Fiona.

The night at the diner, the group of men invited Mae and her friends to follow them to a nightclub. And that was where she first saw her. . . .

"Mae, are you in there?" Amelia rapped loudly on the door.

Oh, for god's sake. Did it never end?

"Pretend I'm not," she shouted from her bed.

"There's no time for these games. I insist you open this door."

Mae rolled out of bed and trudged slowly to the door. She opened it no more than two inches.

"What is it now?" Mae said.

"You're going out tonight, so hurry up and get dressed. Like a lady; not in some crazy getup."

"Where do you think I'm going?"

"My cousin, Jonathan Astor, is taking you to dinner. I'm sure it will be someplace elegant." And then, as if noticing the look of absolute mutiny on Mae's face, Amelia added, "Maybe he'll ask you where you want to go. Regardless, you need to get out of that robe. You can't spend the rest of your life in this room."

Mae slammed the door.

"I'll see you downstairs in one hour," Amelia yelled from the hallway. "Don't make me call your brother."

Mae, heart pounding, swung open her closet. Fine—she would go out. She'd get some fresh air, buy some more cigarettes, and vent her frustration on this puppet doing Amelia's bidding.

And in the morning, she would move out.

Chapter 2

It felt good to have money.

For the first time in her life, Fiona Sparks didn't feel the underlying panic that usually ran her like an engine. She wasn't worried about losing her apartment, or that the meal she was eating might be her last. She finally understood what it was like to have some control. And she never wanted to lose it.

"I'm most likely to use it in bed, so it should go on that little end table there," Fiona said, directing the man installing her phone. Her own phone! Just the sight of it thrilled her, so streamlined and gleaming black, with the round dial inviting her to reach out to the world. "When will it work?"

"It works right now," the man said, picking up the earpiece and stretching the cord so she could reach it. "Just dial the number you want to call."

Fiona realized she only knew one phone number: Mae's, when she had lived at her mother's house. She felt a twinge.

She closed the door behind the phone technician after he left, and faced her empty apartment. She hated to admit it, but she missed Mae. She had thought—and would have admitted to anyone who cared to ask—that she was just with the heiress for the score. And when the money was suddenly out of reach, her interest cooled faster than a bath in January.

But now that the affair was over, she realized Mae gave her something no one else ever had: love. And now that she'd felt what it was like to be loved, it was difficult not to have it anymore.

She was startled by a knock at the door, and she had the fleeting hope it was Mae.

"Who is it?" she said, her hands already working on the elaborate system of locks.

"It's me—Roger."

Oh, for fuck's sake. What was he doing there? She opened the door and made no effort to hide her annoyance. At the sight of her, Roger's brown eyes lit up like a puppy setting sight on a bone.

"You can't just show up like this," she said.

Roger nodded. His dark hair, usually slicked back, was moppish, and his clothes were more casual than she was used to seeing. His Fair Isle sweater made him look almost boyish. She hadn't decided yet if he was handsome or not. He had good hair and nice eyes, but his nose was slightly too prominent. Overall, she would bet he didn't have a problem with the ladies—even when he wasn't paying for it.

"I had to see you. I won't be able to go to the club tonight or tomorrow, and I can't imagine waiting until the end of the week. . . ."

"Well, you're going to have to. I don't take house calls," she said, slamming the door.

She turned to contemplate her tiny closet. What was her sexiest dress? If Roger wasn't going to be at the Vesper tonight, she'd have to catch another big fish. Now that there was a phone bill to pay, she didn't have the luxury of a slow night.

MAE TRUDGED DOWN the wide stairway in her black, beaded, and extremely short Chanel dress.

She dutifully appeared in the parlor, and Amelia and an unfamiliar, fair-haired young man turned to look at her. The moment felt staged and overly controlled. But then, what else could she expect from Amelia?

"Mae—aren't you a vision," Amelia said, her smile more fake than a three-dollar bill. "That lipstick is so . . ."

"Red?" Mae suggested.

Amelia shot her a withering a look that the guest could not see from his vantage point. "Allow me to introduce you to my cousin, Jonathan Astor."

The man took her hand and kissed the back of it. He was handsome in a blond, patrician, bland sort of way. His nose was aquiline, his forehead high, with a hairline that she suspected would be receding before his thirtieth birthday. "Miss Delacorte, you are even lovelier than my cousin told me," he said. "And I had thought she was exaggerating."

Mae said nothing.

"Well, you two should be off. Have a good evening. And don't have her home too late, Jonathan."

The butler, Mumson, appeared with their coats, and the Astor cousin helped Mae on with hers. They did not speak again until they were seated in his Rolls-Royce.

"Are you hungry?" he asked.

"Let's just get this evening over with," she said.

"Oh, come now—it's not as bad as all that."

She looked out the window. It felt good, at least, to be out of

the house. But the smell of the night air—redolent with spring—
made her ache for Fiona all over again.

"Where do you want to go? Since you seem determined to be a
wet blanket, I'll let you choose."

"Oh—lucky me," she said. "Fine. Take me to the Vesper Club."
She waited to see if he would balk.

"Sounds good to me," he said, lighting a cigarette and offering
one to her.

Surprised, she accepted it. But when he tried to light it, she
snapped, "I can do it myself."

Jonathan Astor sighed. "I can see *someone* needs a drink."

THE BAND PLAYED a cover of Ted Lewis's "Show Me the Way
(to Go Home)."

"I like this tune," the man said. Fiona nodded, wishing she hadn't
noticed the man's hands: They were small with stubby, sausagelike
fingers. The thought of them on her body made her skin crawl. She
tried to push the image out of her mind, and focused on the hefty
billfold he pulled out of his pocket to pay for his drinks.

"You sure you can't have one, doll?" he said to her.

"I wish!" she said—and it was true. "But no drinking during
my shift."

He reached around and squeezed her ass. "What time are you
off duty?"

She considered her answer and as she did, looked up just in
time to see Mae breeze into the room on the arm of a dapper blond
guy. She looked more beautiful than ever, her hair a gleaming
black cap, her dress as dramatic as her severe makeup.

Boom Boom was certain to have a fit.

"Excuse me for a minute," she said to Mr. Sausage Fingers.

"Bring me a martini," he called after her.

It felt like it took forever to cross the room—like one of those dreams she used to have where she was swimming and swimming but couldn't make it to the surface. But then she was standing in front of her, and when Mae fixed those blue eyes on her, Fiona knew she wanted her back.

"You shouldn't be here," Fiona said. It wasn't exactly what she had planned to open with, but she was off her game.

"And who are you, sweetheart?" asked the fair-haired man by Mae's side.

"I wasn't talking to you," Fiona said. Mae smiled at her, and Fiona couldn't tell if she was happy to see her or amused by the exchange. And then she noticed Boom Boom heading for them. "See—here comes Boom Boom. Don't make a scene," Fiona said.

"What's a 'Boom Boom'?" said Mae's mystery companion.

"Boom Boom isn't a *what*," said Mae. "*She's* the owner."

Golden Boy nodded. Fiona wanted to smack his hand off of Mae's shoulder.

"I'm surprised to see you back here, Miss Delacorte," said Boom Boom. "Considering we had to escort you out last time."

"Boom Boom, is it?" said Golden Boy. "Jonathan Astor. A pleasure to meet you. I have to say, I've been spending all my time at the Del Rey, but Mae here insisted that the Vesper Club was the place to be. And I can see she was right. I'll have to spread the word."

Boom Boom looked him up and down, and her demeanor visibly softened.

"Well, any friend of Mae Delacorte's is a friend of mine. A pleasure, Mr. Astor."

He turned to Fiona. "Can you please get us two sidecars. And keep my tab open," he said.

Fiona, furious at being dispatched, didn't move.

"What are you waiting for, Fiona? A written request? Get the gentleman his cocktails," said Boom Boom.

Fiona looked at Mae, but she was focused on her date. Her date! It was going to be a long night.

Chapter 3

CHARLOTTE SAT STIFFLY on her side of the bed, ignoring William while she flipped through the pages of *Vogue*. She pretended to read, but her eyes didn't register a word. She couldn't imagine how she was going to sleep next to him all night; every cell in her body seemed to roil with repulsion. She could still feel the sting of his hand across her face.

He rolled over and turned out the light.

"I'm *reading*," she said.

He ignored her.

Charlotte threw the covers off of herself. "I'm moving into the guest room," she said.

"Are you asking me or telling me?" William said.

Charlotte considered her answer carefully, thinking about the monthly check to Philadelphia.

"Asking," she forced herself to say.

"I think that's a fine idea," he said. "I'll tell you when it's appropriate to return to the bedroom."

She still couldn't be certain of exactly what William had seen when he walked into the parlor earlier that day. She had pulled away from Jake as soon as she heard the door open. But it was very possible he had gleaned that they had been sitting closer together than was socially acceptable.

The hall was dark, reminding her of the times when Mae first moved in and Charlotte had been startled out of her sleep only to find the young woman on her way out for the night. It seemed so long ago; she was amazed at how innocent she had been.

She missed Mae terribly. Aside from Jake, somehow her

sister-in-law had become her one true friend. Charlotte felt a pang of guilt for allowing Amelia to prevent her visit.

Charlotte turned on the light in the guest room. There was no sign that Mae had lived there at all. The spectacular clutter that had overtaken the room immediately upon her arrival was gone. She paused in front of the full-length mirror. She didn't care what William said: She loved the short, bobbed haircut. She would never grow it out.

She opened the closet, and touched the bare clothes hangers. On the shelf, she found a matchbox from the Vesper. And somehow, the unmistakable scent of Joy perfume still clung to the small space.

Charlotte walked to the window, and looked out at the night. She craved fresh air, and leaned on the sill to open the window. Her palm was pinched by something sharp.

"Ouch!" She instinctively brought her hand to her mouth, and she tasted blood. The sharp hooks that had once sustained Mae's rope ladder stared back at her.

The rope ladder—the rope ladder William didn't know about.

Charlotte wondered if it was too late to go to the servants' quarters. She knew that technically, it was never too late. Still, she felt badly waking them.

But desperate times called for desperate measures, as the saying went.

She took care to be silent on the stairs, but if William heard her walking around, she would just tell him she needed fresh linens on the guest bed. Now that she'd thought of it, the linens would be her official reason for ringing the servants.

The hall in the rear wing of the house was dark, but she could see light under Penny's bedroom door. She pressed the bell.

Penny and Rafferty both appeared.

"Penny, I need fresh linens in the first guest bedroom," she said.

"Right away, Mrs. Delacorte." Penny looked pale and tired, and Charlotte felt guilty knowing that even though the light was on, the girl had been halfway to sleep.

Charlotte lingered in the hallway even after Penny set out for the linen closet.

"Is everything all right, Mrs. Delacorte?" said Rafferty. His blue eyes were bright and sharp. Charlotte couldn't imagine him ever at rest. She thought of the day he caught her in William's office, and she knew she could add Rafferty to the small list of people upon whom she could count.

"Remember when you confiscated that rope ladder from Mae's bedroom window?" Charlotte said. He nodded. "Do you still have it?"

"As a matter of fact, I do," he said.

"Tomorrow, after Mr. Delacorte leaves for the office, I need for you to put it back in the window. Make sure it's securely hooked."

"I understand," he said. "Consider it done."

She felt relief, the first minute since William walked into the parlor that she wasn't rigid with tension. And then came the tears.

Charlotte was mortified, but there, standing in the servants' hall, her entire body shook with sobs. Rafferty moved close to her. In the most shocking turn of the entire day, he pulled her into his arms.

"CHEERS," JONATHAN ASTOR said, touching his glass to Mae's. "To auspicious beginnings."

Mae rolled her eyes and took a hefty swig of her drink.

"Now then—I'm off to circulate," he said with a wink. "Time to work the room a bit."

"Work the room?" said Mae.

"Yes. There are some very attractive women here. Well done, Mae."

She looked at him like he was crazy.

"What? Don't look so insulted. You and I both know this isn't a real date. It's amazing what lengths we must go to in order to maintain the status quo, isn't it?" he said with a smile.

Mae suddenly saw him in a new light.

"So what's in it for you?" she said.

"The same thing that's in it for you, sweetheart. Appearances and all that come with it. Oh, speaking of money—here's cab fare. Don't get home too late. We want good old Cousin Amelia to be happy with our little union, now don't we?"

Mae took the handful of bills.

"Just how long do you intend to keep up this charade?" Mae said.

"I guess that depends on you." He winked again, and then disappeared into the throng of people at the bar.

Mae stuck the money in her bag. It was only then that she noticed Fiona watching her from across the room. Mae wanted nothing more than to walk over to her, but to do so would be giving up any progress she'd made that night: For the first time in as long as she could remember, Mae felt like she had the upper hand.

BOOM BOOM ROUNDED the corner, impossible to miss in a bright blue caftan and dangling feather earrings. Jake still was not used to the sight of her.

"Mr. Larkin—to what do I owe the pleasure?" she cooed, looping her arm through his and steering him to the back of the club.

"Why haven't you been answering your phone? I've been calling you all day."

"I'm a busy lady."

"All right. Well, I wanted to let you know I have a meeting set for Friday night. So let's get my boys scheduled in here to play."

"Friday night? Why is this dragging out so long? I'm running on fumes, here. Get it sooner."

"I'm not in control of these things, Boom Boom. We're dealing at a high level here."

"I know it's a high level!" she shouted. "Don't tell me about high level. That's the game I'm in; it's the game I've *always* been in!"

Marveling at her zero-to-sixty countenance, Jake could only imagine what Fiona had to put up with.

"Jeez—don't lose your skirt," he said. "I'll tell you what: You let me book my guys in here for music Saturday night, and I'll get the supply meeting moved up to next week."

"I already got a band booked for Saturday night."

"Unbook them," he said pointedly.

She looked at him, unblinking, for a good thirty seconds. He was careful to hold her gaze and not break contact first.

"Fine," she said. "I want the name of the band and the set list by Wednesday. I don't pay anything up front. Now you'd better make things happen quickly with your source—or you'll find yourself going from high level to no level faster than you can say 'two-bit speakeasy.'"

"No problem," he said. "Oh—and my source said to be prepared for a price increase."

"How does he know what I would consider an increase?"

Jake shrugged. "His exact words were, 'Payola is going up, and so are prices for the customers.'"

Boom Boom stormed off as fast as her wide and hobbled body would allow.

MAE SAW JAKE headed for the door. She finished her sidecar with one long swallow, set down the glass on the nearest table, and intercepted him.

"I'm surprised to see you," he said, looking around. "Who are you here with?"

"Not Charlotte, if that's what you're wondering. And I'm leaving. Give me a lift to your place?"

"Sure. So what happened? Rumor had it you were under house arrest."

"I am. Believe me, tonight is just a temporary reprieve. And I intend to take advantage of it."

"Well then, by all means—after you." He held the door open for her.

She knew Fiona was watching. At least now, if she wanted to see Mae later, she would know to find her at Jake's.

She followed Jake to his green Model T.

Maybe that odd Jonathan Astor was onto something. She shouldn't blow the whole thing up by rolling into Amelia's house drunk at two in the morning. If she was smart about this thing, she'd have many more chances to remind Fiona what she was missing.

"On second thought, drop me off at Amelia Astor's."

"I will. But do me a favor—call Charlotte in the morning. Tell her I'm coming to see her at eleven. If she thinks her husband will be home, tell her to just have the butler turn me away at the door."

"You two are crazier than I am," she said. "But I'll do it."

Chapter 4

WHEN THE DOORBELL sounded at eleven in the morning, Charlotte practically flew down the stairs in her excitement.

Rafferty answered the door as she was halfway to the front hall.

"I was surprised to get your message," she said to Jake, ignoring the surprisingly blatant look of disapproval on Rafferty's face.

"Are you kidding?" Jake said. "I've been worried sick about you since the minute William threw me out. I'm kicking myself for not getting here sooner. Are you okay?"

"I'm fine, but we have to be careful. Follow me."

Charlotte led Jake around to the back of the house.

"So now we'll be skulking around in alleyways?" he said with a wink.

"I want to show you something."

She led him to small patch of garden alongside the back of the house, and pointed up to the rope ladder handing from the guest bedroom window.

"What the hell is that?" he said.

"It was one of Mae's innovations," Charlotte said. "I had it taken down to save her from herself. And now I've had it put back."

Jake looked at her with a smile. "And why is that?"

"I've moved into that room," she said.

"Is that ladder my way in?"

She laughed. "I had been thinking of it as my way out."

"Well, you're a genius. I suspect it works just as well either way. Let me give it a try."

"Right now?"

He nodded and kissed her.

"Jake! Not here."

He grabbed the sides and stepped on the lowest rung, carefully with just one foot at first, testing his weight.

"Be careful," she said. He looked over his shoulder at her with a rakish grin and winked.

She watched nervously as he moved quickly up the ladder. At the top, he pushed the bedroom window open wider, and hoisted himself inside. Charlotte couldn't believe she was looking at him inside the house, with her down in the yard.

"Quick—lock the bedroom door," she said. She had a terrible

mental image of Penny walking in to straighten up and finding a strange man in the room.

Jake disappeared from view, then returned and leaned out.

"Come up—take your time. When you get to the top, I'll help you inside."

She swallowed hard, and grasped the sides of the ladder as she had seen him do moments before. She placed one foot, then the other, on the ladder, which swayed slightly from side to side. It was dangerous bordering on outright reckless, but it was better to try it out now, in daylight with Jake there, than alone in the middle of the night.

"Don't look down," he shouted to her when she was at the midway point. She kept her eyes focused on each rung. Finally, when the windowsill was within reach, Jake put his arm out and encircled her midsection, pulling her inside.

"Oh my god, that was crazy," she said, breathing heavily and finally looking down at the ground below.

"Crazy brilliant," Jake said. And there they were, alone in the bedroom. She relished that no one even knew they were inside the house.

He kissed her, a deep, unapologetic kiss that downgraded everything else in her life to the merest afterthought. Almost everything else.

"So how's your friend Rona?" she asked softly.

"Charlotte, I'm not seeing Rona."

His hands caressed her breasts, and he pulled her to the bed. With his mouth on hers, his hand moving under her dress to skim over her underwear, Charlotte's mind went blank, her thoughts dulled like rocks under a rushing tide.

She arched her body under his, pressing herself close until she felt his hardness against her thigh. This electrified her, and she reached down and ran her hand along the length of him. It was the boldest sexual gesture she'd ever made, and she was rewarded by him pulling off her underwear and touching his tongue to her pulsing, wet center. When she couldn't stand to wait any longer, she pulled him up.

"Come here," she said. He quickly shed his pants and she guided him inside of her, greedy to be filled by him, a sensation that gave her not only physical pleasure, but an intense sense of well-being. In the shadow of his body, she felt more safe than she'd ever felt in her life.

Afterward, she knew they didn't have the luxury of holding each other.

"You should go," she said.

"I feel so used," he said with a smile. "Don't you want to know why I showed up here today?"

She nodded.

"For this," he said, grabbing her bottom.

She laughed and pulled the sheet around herself. "No, seriously—did something happen?"

"The business deal I'm working on is looking up. I want you seriously thinking about getting out of here."

"I am," she said, reaching under the bed and pulling out a shoebox. "Can you get down the ladder holding this?"

He took it from her, weighing it in his hands.

"Sure. But why do I need to?"

She removed the lid off. Sunlight caught one of the items on the top of the pile, a sapphire and diamond cuff bracelet that dazzled even in its sad state of imminent discard. Charlotte couldn't stand to look at it. "Jeez. That's a lot of loot," Jake said.

"I need you to sell it for me."

"All of it?"

She nodded. "And then take the cash, and open a bank account."

"In my name?"

"Yes."

"You trust me to do that?"

"I trust you more than anyone else right now. And I need to know that money will be waiting for me. I can't risk leaving that stuff here in the safe for him to confiscate on a whim. He knows this marriage is over . . . that the only thing keeping me here is money."

Jake handed the box back to her. "I get it. But Charlotte, don't sell all of it. You'll regret it one day. I'll help you as soon as my deal comes through—and it's going to be moving fast now. And you're smart and educated, so you'll find a job. Everything will be fine. But once you leave this house and this family, chances are you'll never have jewelry like this again."

Her jaw was set. "Sell all of it."

Chapter 5

ROGER WARREN SKIMMED the twenty-page deposition, and felt himself getting hard by the third paragraph.

The defendant in question was charged with two counts of soliciting prostitution, three counts of lewd and lascivious behavior, and one count of resisting arrest. Considering he had been handcuffed with his trousers still down around his ankles, Roger couldn't very well blame the guy.

Apparently, the poor sod had been caught at a house on Wooster Street known to be one of the last remaining French brothels, a place where the sex being brokered was very much a one-way street: In this particular instance, that street was the mouth of a young lady of ill repute.

The detailed interview with the woman (much more detailed than was necessary for any legal purposes, in Roger's opinion) brought to mind the very experienced hands—and mouth—of Fiona Sparks.

"Roger, Mr. Buckner wants to see you in his office," said his boss's secretary, peering around the doorway of his office. Roger jolted as if he'd been caught with his own pants down.

He closed the deposition.

"I'm on my way."

Great. The last time his boss had summoned him that early in the morning, he'd dragged him to that warehouse raid that got Paul McLaren shot. But then, the raid had also landed them one of Buckner's coveted "big fish"—the bootlegger Bill Sugarfield.

Roger shuffled down the hall, and found Emory Buckner with his feet up on his desk, smoking his cigar as usual.

"You wanted to see me, sir?"

"Sit down, Warren," Buckner growled. "How many weeks have you been on this vice patrol?" he asked once Roger was seated.

"A few," Roger said, not happy about the direction this conversation no doubt was headed.

"And how many names have you given me?"

"Uh . . . none."

"I don't like that math," said Buckner, stubbing out his cigar and leaning forward. "Do you?"

"No, sir."

"So what the hell are you doing out there every night, Warren? Enjoying the music?"

Roger pushed the image of Fiona, her legs spread, out of his mind.

"There is some decent music, sir."

Buckner smacked his palm on his desk so loudly it made Roger jump.

"I want names at the end of this week. That booze is coming from somewhere, and someone, if given the right incentive, will talk. You should be seen as a regular. You should be getting to know the staff. You should be asking questions late at night, when the booze is expensive and talk is cheap."

"Yes, sir."

Satisfied, Buckner sat back in his chair. He appraised Roger with his unnervingly direct gaze. "I know you didn't ask for this job, Warren. But just remember: Greatness is often achieved not by those who seek it, but by those who are forced to rise up and meet it face-to-face."

Roger nodded, feeling suddenly that his great guilt was going to rise out of his stomach and land at Buckner's feet along with his breakfast.

"Will you excuse me, sir?" he managed to say, before running off to the men's room.

FOR THE FIRST time since she had been forced to move into the Astor mansion, Mae ventured out of her room of her own free will. A beautiful spring morning was irresistible, no matter how dire her own circumstances.

She sat on a stone bench in the middle of the rose garden behind the house. Closing her eyes, she tilted her face toward the sun, and inhaled deeply.

"There you are!" Amelia's voice jarred her out of her fleeting moment of peace.

"What now?" Mae said.

"That's the thanks I get?" said Amelia.

Mae rolled her eyes. "I assume you're talking about my date?"

Amelia sat next to her on the bench. Mae knew she should move over to offer more room, but on principle, she stayed put— despite it forcing her to be in closer proximity to Amelia than she would ever care for. "That's right, missy. Apparently, my cousin is quite smitten with you. I commend you on your ability to hide your base nature."

Mae closed her eyes again.

"I'm not done," Amelia said.

"I know," said Mae dryly.

"If you are successful in pulling off more evenings like last night, you just might have a future."

"And what's in it for you?" Mae murmured.

"Excuse me?"

Mae turned to her with a sudden directness that clearly startled Amelia. "Why do you care so much about what I do?"

"Not that it's any of your business, but I happen to care very much about your brother. You know how long we've been friends."

Mae nodded. "Yes. Long enough that if he had wanted you, he would have chosen to marry you long before Charlotte ever showed up in this city."

Amelia made an odd sound of a half cough, half gasp. Mae couldn't help but smile.

"Yes, well, everyone makes mistakes," Amelia spat. "Especially in one's youth. But we're giving you a chance to correct yours, you ungrateful little bitch."

"Don't hold your breath waiting for a thank-you note."

Amelia stood. "Jonathan will pick you up at seven this evening. I hope for your sake, he doesn't figure out that you're damaged goods."

BOOM BOOM APPRAISED her supply room, hands on her hips, cigarette dangling from her mouth. The cigarette was the only thing holding back a tide of expletives.

Her liquor stock had dwindled twice as fast as she'd anticipated when her supplier got pinched. She'd known it was a serious problem; she just hadn't thought it would be nearly fatal. But now it looked like the feds or the New York DA wouldn't necessarily have to storm the front entrance to put her out of business. They could simply take out all the key people around her.

But it was her own fault for putting all her eggs in one basket with Fiona's contact, that speakeasy owner. She'd been so worried about discretion and keeping it all in the family, she'd failed to think of a backup. And now Mr. Late Night Party was taking his good old sweet time. If you couldn't count on a bootlegger, who could you count on?

"God damn it!" she kicked an empty beer keg.

She wondered if she had made a huge mistake in switching from the brothel business to the club business. Five years ago, it would have seemed a safe bet. Sure, there was the little problem of Prohibition. But unlike prostitution, no one really thought drinking was all that bad. And running the brothel had given her experience in paying off law enforcement. Compared to prostitution, the Vesper Club made Boom Boom feel almost legit. But now, she was afraid she had bet on the wrong horse.

She heard someone walking down to the basement from the floor above. She retreated from the room, locking the door behind her.

"I hate when you call me here in the middle of the day," Fiona said, her long legs the first thing Boom Boom saw when she looked up at the stairs. "Couldn't this have waited till I started my shift?" She looked astonishingly pretty. The word "fetching" came to mind. Her hair looked even more extravagantly red, and Boom Boom wondered if she was doing something to enhance the color.

"Since when is four o'clock the middle of the day?" said Boom Boom. Then, remembering that she shouldn't be antagonizing her, considering the conversation she was about to have, she continued, "When we're done talking you can go upstairs and order yourself an Irish coffee on the house."

"You spoil me," Fiona said, lighting a cigarette.

Boom Boom had already decided her tactic: best to start with Fiona on the defensive. Then dangle the financial incentive.

"Why do you always leave with the same one or two fellas every night? How is that helping my business?"

"Isn't that what you told me to do?"

"You should spread yourself around a bit more."

Fiona smirked and Boom Boom realizes she might have a selected a better turning of phrase than one that included the word "spreading."

"Maybe *you* should find some other girls to help out—carry the load, so to speak. I have my income to consider, and the guys who pay are the ones who get to play, in my book. Call me old-fashioned."

Lord in heaven, this girl was a piece of work.

"Yes, I've thought of that, Fiona. I am a businesswoman, after all. But I've thought of an alternative to that scenario. First, do you really want me to bring in a bunch of new girls to work here? Competition for you? I think you like your perch on the top of the heap here."

"I've earned my perch at the top. Do your customers ask for anyone else by name?"

Boom Boom knew it was time to shift into tactic number two: flattery. "No, they don't. Everyone wants Fiona Sparks. You're the hottest item on the menu, dollface. And I want to keep it that way. That's why I'm proposing that instead of you having to leave to keep the high rollers entertained, it would be smarter for you to keep them on the premises."

Fiona's face registered probably as much shock as she was capable of feeling. "Are you sayin' I should . . . take care of men here? At the club?"

"Yes. That way you could, shall we say, make an impression on more than one a night. More money, and more happy customers."

"And where is all this supposed to be happening? The bathroom?"

"Accommodations are my worry, not yours."

"Well, I have 'accommodations' of a different kind to consider: What makes you think I want to fuck more than one guy a night?" The fact that euphemism had given way to blunt language suggested to Boom Boom that Fiona was taking the conversation seriously.

"I've thought of that. And here's where my expertise comes into play: When I was running my place on West Fourth Street, I had girls who were my 'buck a roll' workers. Then I had my girls who were more money but actually performed in a . . . limited capacity. I learned from some of the French girls that men are actually willing to pay more for a little . . . lip service. And it's quicker and less of a hassle for the girls. No chance of pregnancy. The girls who were proficient at it were my 'money makers.' And I think it's something for you to consider."

Fiona sank back into the chair. "You're serious about this. In the club."

"Yes," Boom Boom said. "I am."

"What's your take?" said Fiona.

"We go fifty-fifty."

"No dice," said Fiona.

"I've got all the operational expenses," said Boom Boom.

"I don't need to split the money with you; I could just do this out of my apartment."

"And who is going to bail you out of jail when you get busted? I'm giving you a venue, liquor, a steady stream of customers, and protection. And I take half."

Fiona pursed her lips. Boom Boom went in for the kill. "I have a feeling the days of flowing booze are coming to an end. If I lose my liquor sources—if Larkin doesn't come through—my backup is 'client services.' That's how I made the money to open this place. It's always been my bread and butter. And I think you have what it takes to make it yours, too."

Chapter 6

JONATHAN ASTOR PARKED his Rolls-Royce on Forty-eighth and Broadway, a block away from their dinner destination.

"Is this really where you want to eat?" he said, clearly not impressed with Lindy's Restaurant and Deli.

"It's close to the Vesper," said Mae. And it also happened to be the place where Fiona picked up a cup of coffee every night before her shift.

"I have a car. I wish you'd prioritized food quality over walking distance."

"What do you care? Is this to be our first lover's quarrel?"

"Very funny. I care because my girlfriend is joining us, and apparently unlike you, she has a refined palate."

Girlfriend! Mae had known this wasn't a real date. Still, the presence of an actual girlfriend was a bit much, even for her.

"I wish I'd known," Mae said, trying not to sound huffy. "I would have invited a friend along, too."

"Oh, don't you worry. We won't leave you out of our fun."

Jonathan slipped the hostess a few bills, and she led them past the crowd of waiting people straight to a window booth.

"So what does your girlfriend think of all this?"

"She is a very practical creature, as you will soon see for yourself." Mae's back was to the front door, but when Jonathan waved to someone behind her, she turned around.

The woman had to be six feet tall, and her hair was blond, unkempt, and unfashionably long. Her blue eyes were rimmed with charcoal-black liner, smudged and thick. She wore a fur coat even though it was sixty degrees outside.

She was one of the sexiest women Mae had ever seen.

Jonathan stood up to greet her, and when she reached the table they kissed passionately.

"Ursula, this is Mae Delacorte. Mae, this is Ursula."

"A pleasure to finally meet you," the woman said. At least, that's what Mae thought she said. Her European accent was so thick it was impossible to be sure.

The blond giant slid into the booth next to Jonathan, shrugging off her coat to reveal a tight beaded dress. She immediately lit a cigarette.

"Fancy place," she said, wrinkling her nose. And then, to Mae, "How can you date a man who takes you to a place like this?" She laughed uproariously at her own joke.

Mae forced herself to laugh.

"That's what happens when you're rich, Ursula—you think it's amusing to slum it."

"Ah, yes," Ursula said, "Jonny told me you are hairless."

Mae looked at Jonathan.

"She means an *heiress*," Jonathan said.

"Isn't that what I said?" Ursula glared at him

"Say, Ursula—why don't you come sit next to me? That way we can get to know each other better," Mae said. And all the better for Fiona to see when she walked in the door.

Ursula shrugged, and joined Mae on the opposite side of the table.

"Now isn't that cozy. Clearly, I have made an excellent choice in a fiancée," said Jonathan.

"I didn't know you two were engaged," said Mae.

"Not her—you."

"Um, last I checked, we're not engaged."

"I'm hoping that will change when I propose to you next week."

Mae looked up sharply. She couldn't say the thought hadn't

crossed her mind; she understood the endgame. "Isn't that a bit . . . quick?" she said.

"Who can argue with true love?" Jonathan and Ursula laughed. And then Fiona walked in. Mae flung her arm around Ursula.

"I'll take that as a yes," said Jonathan.

"We should go back to Jonny's for champagne," Ursula said.

Mae caught Fiona's eye, and the flash of surprise, jealousy, and longing on her face expressed feelings that Mae had all too often felt herself around Fiona.

"I think that's a swell idea," said Mae. She was ready to celebrate.

ROGER WARREN KEPT looking at the living room clock.

His wife noticed.

"Do you have to be there at a certain time tonight?" she asked, picking up their son's scattered toys.

"The usual. Maybe a little earlier."

Every minute he had to wait before seeing Fiona was like a small death. It took every ounce of control he had left just to stay home last night. He wished he hadn't told Elizabeth his schedule for the vice investigation. If he'd been smart, he would have told her he had to go out *every* night. But how could he have known he would be struck with this fever, a curse if there ever was one?

"When will this come to an end? He can't expect you to do this indefinitely. You're a lawyer, not an investigator. I just don't understand this."

It was the most impassioned expression he'd heard from Elizabeth in years—and the most terrifying: The thought of his nights at the Vesper coming to a close made his blood run cold.

"I have to go," he said, standing abruptly.

"Roger, what exactly do you do there?"

"Where?"

"At the clubs?"

"I've explained this to you, Elizabeth. I just stand around, keeping my eyes and ears open."

"You don't talk to women?"

Roger looked at her, wondering where all of this was coming from. For her entire pregnancy and since the birth of their son, she'd barely paid him any attention when he was standing right in front of her. Now she was suddenly interested in what he was doing when he was out of her sight.

"Don't be silly," he said, retrieving his overcoat from the hall closet. Down the hall, his son—no doubt unable to fall asleep, as usual—started to cry for Elizabeth. Distracted, she dropped her line of questioning.

Roger slipped out the door.

IT WAS THE worst night Fiona'd had since she started working at the Vesper.

The evening began with her spotting Mae sitting beside some Amazonian blonde at Lindy's Deli. Fiona had pretended not to see her, of course. She did have her pride.

But then she couldn't even keep an eye on the door of the Vesper to see if Mae showed up there afterward; she was too busy running back and forth to a tiny room Boom Boom had set up for her in the back of the first floor: an extra-wide supply closet now furnished with two chairs and a dim lamp. There, Fiona had begun her new enterprise of sucking guys off for four dollars a pop.

It was easier than she had imagined, until she tried to sell Roger Warren on the change in operations.

"Do you have any idea how illegal that is?" he said, his face turning purple. What, she wondered, did he think had been taking place back at her apartment all those nights? An expensive date— minus the dinner and dancing?

"No one's twisting your arm to spend time with me," she said, walking away.

"Wait," he said, running after her. "I'm sorry. I just . . . that's not how I want to be with you. Let's go back to your place."

"I can't leave in the middle of my shift anymore," she said.

"What's the sudden change?" he said, a little more suspiciously than she would have liked.

"That's just the way it is, Roger. Take it or leave it."

He then planted himself at the bar, not talking to anyone or even drinking.

When Mae was a no-show, Fiona decided she must have gone straight to Jake's. By midnight, she couldn't wait any longer to find her. She cashed out her tips—including the back-room take—with Boom Boom.

"How did it go tonight?"

"It went," Fiona said. She considered stiffing her a few bucks, but decided it was too soon for that. She dutifully counted out Boom Boom's cut and handed it to her. "I still could make more leaving with one guy a night."

"But then you leave, and that's it. And now you have this cash, and you can still leave. This is a money-making venture, Fiona. You might not like it, but you can't argue with the facts."

Fiona took her money, stuffed it in her bag, and climbed the stairs back to the first floor, suddenly exhausted.

"Are you leaving now?" Roger said, appearing by her side.

"Yes, Roger. But I'm not going home, so why don't you just call it a night."

"I'll give you a ride—wherever you want to go."

She hesitated for a minute. A ride to Jake's would save her the trouble of finding—not to mention paying for—a cab. But she had to be careful who she introduced to Jake's operation. She looked at Roger, at his puppy-dog-like willingness to please her. He'd been hanging around for weeks now. Clearly, he was only interested in her, not nosying around.

Roger Smith was harmless.

"We're going down to the Village," she said.

COLE PORTER WAS in his living room.

When Jake recovered from the realization that one of the greatest young songwriters of his generation was drinking at his bar, he immediately worried that his speakeasy would prove to be a disappointment. Jake was very aware Cole Porter was a man who had once hired the entire Ballets Russes to perform at one of his house parties abroad. His parties were legendary.

"Can I impose on you to play a little something?" Jake asked Louis Armstrong. He hated to do it, but he was feeling insecure. It wasn't just the presence of a luminary—everything felt particularly precarious, not just the balance of entertainment in his speakeasy.

He needed that deal to go through with Boom Boom.

"Hey—can I talk to you for a second?"

Fiona Sparks had appeared out of nowhere. She grabbed his arm and looked just a hair shy of frantic.

"I'm a little busy right now—is something wrong?"

"Have you seen Mae?"

Behind her lurked a guy in an expensive suit. He seemed to be appraising Jake, and this made him uncomfortable.

"No, I haven't seen Mae," said Jake. "Is this guy with you?"

"Oh, yeah—Roger, this is Jake Larkin. Jake, Roger Smith."

"This your place?" said Roger Smith.

"What's it to you?" said Jake, before walking away.

Jake saw Fiona and the guy disappear into the bathroom. He started after them to tell them to find someplace else to go, but then Louis Armstrong and Cole Porter struck up a duet, and all was forgiven and forgotten.

Chapter 7

THE BREAKFAST TABLE had become an agonizing exercise in politely ignoring one another. Charlotte was loath to break the silence, but the alternative was not getting out of the house.

"I would like to visit my mother again," she said. William looked up from *The New York Times* long enough to shake his head.

"I have to go on a business trip for the next few days, and when I get back I have pressing business to attend to. There's no time for me to take you to Philadelphia."

"Really, William. I'm just going to see my parents. You can trust that they will not let me get into any trouble."

"And how will your parents keep an eye on you, when I'm barely able? The answer is no, Charlotte. The problem is that I don't trust *you*. So you'll stay here and help Amelia with the benefit planning. And sort all those books—how many boxes arrived yesterday? It's a lot to be done. You don't have any excuse to be running around."

"My excuse is that my mother is extremely ill. If you keep me from seeing her, and something happens, how could you live with yourself? Don't you have a conscience?"

This seemed to set him thinking, which she knew it would. In there, somewhere, there had to be a shred of the person she'd thought she'd married.

"Fine," he said. "You can go for two days. But Rafferty is going with you."

"Rafferty?"

"Yes. You can go to Philadelphia while I'm in Boston. I won't be here, so I can spare Rafferty to travel with you. It's time for him to prove his worth."

She knew Rafferty would not get in her way. And the truth was, she just wanted to see her parents, not to pull any funny business with Jake.

That could wait until she got back.

ELIZABETH WARREN PICKED her husband's clothes off the floor and tossed them in the wicker laundry basket. They stank of cigarettes. She wrinkled her nose, wondering if they would taint the baby's clothes.

She looked at Roger, still sleeping. She'd heard him creep in during the earliest hours of the morning, though he didn't know he'd woken her.

With Roger and the baby asleep, she left the apartment for the basement, where she could do the wash. The one thing she loved most about their building was the washing machine in the basement. The Maytag washer was a cylindrical blue enamel tub on four castered legs with a drainpipe, motor, and wringer. She couldn't imagine how she would have managed that first year with the baby without the amazing innovation.

She found the washer available and unloaded the pile of clothes into it, starting with Roger's shirt. She frowned, a streak of bright red catching her eye. Her first thought was that it was blood, and concerned, she looked closer. But on further inspection, she realized it was, in fact, lipstick.

And her concern turned to rage.

"THANKS FOR COMING by on such short notice," Amelia said, beaming with delight at William's appearance in her sitting room.

"I would have been here sooner, but I got pulled into a conversation with Charlotte at breakfast, and then I was late to the office and had to take care of a few things there."

"Not to worry—this is news that does not spoil."

"Well," he said, smiling at her in way that made all of her machinations completely worth the effort. "Don't keep me in suspense."

Amelia drew a deep breath. "It seems my cousin is absolutely smitten with your sister. I sense that a proposal is imminent."

"Can you be sure?"

"He asked for me to set a meeting with you. 'As soon as possible,' he said. Those were his exact words."

To her absolute delight and amazement, William pulled her into an embrace, and then kissed her on the mouth.

"You, Amelia Astor, are a magician."

She scarcely dared to look at him. Was it possible that the universe would actually tilt in her favor? After all of these years? Perhaps, from her place in heaven, Geraldine was finally able to accomplish what she had not been able to on earth.

"I'll set the meeting with Jonathan."

"The end of this week is best. Charlotte will be away. I don't want her in Mae's ear. It's up to you and me to bring this ship home."

"You are my captain," she said happily, taking his hand. It was the boldest romantic gesture of her entire life.

ELIZABETH WARREN HAD only been to the District Attorney's office once before, and that had been for a holiday party.

It was a striking building—very bright and modern. The first time she'd seen it, she had been overcome with pride that it was her husband's place of business.

But not today.

She was thankful for the elevator. Otherwise, she never would have been able to get Henry's carriage up to the office.

"Is Mr. Buckner expecting you?" the secretary said, scanning a calendar on which she was clearly not listed.

"No, I'm afraid not," Elizabeth said.

She hoped she did not have to wait long. Henry was peaceful in the carriage, but that might not last for long. Even at just fourteen months old, she was starting to get a glimpse of the spirited boy he would soon become.

The secretary told her to have a seat, and then disappeared inside an office. In her smart charcoal gray suit and double strand of pearls around her neck, the older woman made Elizabeth feel downright dowdy in her housedress. Even if she'd had the time or inclination to change, she wouldn't have wanted to arouse Roger's suspicion. After all, she told him she was going to visit her mother, and that hardly merited a fresh outfit.

"Mr. Buckner will see you now," the secretary told her with a kind smile.

"Thank you."

Elizabeth awkwardly wheeled the carriage into the office, barely fitting the pram through the doorway.

"Mrs. Warren. What a pleasant surprise." He pulled out a chair for her to sit, and then he took his place behind his desk.

Her husband's boss was a commanding figure. She had met larger men, but no one filled a room quite like Emory Buckner. His eyes were sharp, and extremely focused when he looked at you. She remembered from the last time she met him how this somehow made her feel like everything out of her mouth should be important. And since nothing she said could be of any importance to a man like Emory Buckner, this had the effect of making her silent in his presence.

But silence was a luxury she could not afford today.

"I'm terribly sorry to trouble you, Mr. Buckner."

"It's no trouble, I assure you."

Emory Buckner did not get where he was by being stupid. And so, like any shrewd person, he waited for her to speak first. And he waited a good full minute before she could find her voice.

"I'm concerned about my husband," she said. "I'm afraid this nighttime work is taking a toll on him, and I'm wondering when it might be finished."

"I know the late hours are rough, Mrs. Warren—on him, and no doubt on you. But that's why I'm giving him the days off during the week so he can get some rest and work from home. I assure you, the business your husband is doing is very important. I can't discuss the particulars with you, but you should know he's doing a great service to this city."

Elizabeth nodded, her hand already reaching into her bag.

"I understand that our city might be better off. But I'm not so sure about my marriage."

With that, she slid the lipstick-stained shirt across Buckner's desk.

Chapter 8

THE TRAIN ROCKED gently, almost lulling Charlotte to sleep. If it weren't for Rafferty sitting beside her, she would have nodded off. But it felt inappropriate to sleep in front of her employee, though he had caught her napping many times in the parlor. Still, everything felt different outside the confines of the house.

"We should be there soon, then?" Rafferty said. It had been an hour since he spoke, and the sound of his voice startled her.

"Oh—yes. We're maybe a little more than halfway there."

She folded over the pages of *The New York Times,* scanning for an article to hold her interest. Beside her, Rafferty looked straight ahead.

"Would you like to read a section?" she asked.

"No, thank you, Mrs. Delacorte."

She put the paper down in her lap. "I hope you don't find this ride too terribly boring. I felt badly that Mr. Delacorte imposed this trip on you."

He turned to look at her, flashing a genuine smile.

"It's my pleasure."

Suddenly, the train gave a lurch that sent them crashing into the seatbacks directly in front of them.

"Are you all right?" Rafferty said. Charlotte was too stunned to speak. And then the entire car shook as if the train were traveling at full speed over a path of rocks. She grabbed Rafferty's hand and with her other, braced herself against the seat in front of her. After what seemed like an interminable amount of time but was probably less than a minute, the train stopped completely.

The cabin was silent—then Charlotte realized that people were actually speaking loudly, but her ears were ringing so much that she hadn't registered the sounds.

"Charlotte, are you okay?" Rafferty was still holding her hand.

"I . . . think so. Are you?"

"Yes," he said. "Wait here. I'm going to look for a steward and find out what's happened."

"I'll go with you," she said.

"No—stay here. I'm more likely to get an honest answer if he's not worried about upsetting a lady."

Charlotte watched him walk through the passage to the next car, and then she looked around at the other passengers. To her horror, some men and women were bleeding, their faces smashed from the impact with the seats in front of them. An elderly man was sprawled out in the aisle, and two men were trying to help him back in his seat while a woman urged them not to move him until medical help arrived.

It took all of her will not to run off to look for Rafferty, but she knew he was right. The train crew would be more candid with him if he weren't accompanied by a distraught woman from the first-class cabin. She was thankful Rafferty was there . . . though she wished Jake were there instead.

Rafferty returned and sat back in his seat before speaking.

"There's been a derailment," he said quietly.

ROGER COULD SCARCELY believe the irony. He had to spend his day prosecuting a fellow who was unfortunate enough to get caught with his dick in the mouth of a Bowery street prostitute, while Roger himself was spending his nights in a similar state of compromised satisfaction.

He thought about the way in which Fiona had pulled him into the bathroom at the speakeasy, yanking down his pants with the same resigned dutifulness one might use to take care of a sink full of dirty dishes. It had been exciting, he couldn't say otherwise. She certainly knew what she was doing. He probably would have enjoyed it if it weren't such a departure from the way she had opened her entire body to him those nights at her apartment. Once he'd had that, there was no going back.

"Roger!" Buckner barked from the doorway, startling Roger so much that he gasped. "Are you working or daydreaming? I've been standing here for a full minute."

"I'm sorry. I guess I'm not getting enough sleep."

Buckner was clearly not happy, and after a moment of panic, Roger reminded himself that no one could read minds.

He sat up straight as his boss closed the office door.

"I'm taking you off the vice investigation," Buckner said.

"No! I mean—not when I'm so close to serious information."

"It's not open for discussion. I want a report by Monday on any potential leads. But I don't want to hear that you're at the clubs anymore."

"You're giving up the investigation?"

"No. Coughlin will be going out in the field in your place. I believe he will be more effective."

"If I give you names by the end of the week, will you change your mind about my effectiveness?"

"If you give me some names, I might change my mind about letting you keep your job—and I mean here in the office."

With that, he walked out.

THE SMALL COLONIAL house looked like it predated the Civil War era. If it weren't for the small wooden sign out front that read, LODGING, Charlotte would never have realized it was an inn.

"You really think we should stay here?" she said to Rafferty. The cab had already driven away.

"It's the closest place," Rafferty said. "We're lucky we didn't have to wait longer or travel farther."

"Well, that's what a twenty-dollar tip to the train crew gets you," she said. The injured passengers had been taken to the nearest hospital. The others had to wait for the train stewards to organize the arrival of cabs, and call ahead to hotels and other lodgings in the surrounding areas. Charlotte and Rafferty, after slipping some money around, were among the first to leave; other passengers were surely still waiting on the embankment, uncertain where they would be spending the night.

They were greeted at the door by an elderly couple, who introduced themselves as Josephine and Tom Marsden.

"When the Rail called to inquire about room vacancies because of the accident, I can't say I was surprised," said Mr. Marsden. "It was just a matter of time. A dangerous mode of transportation. No need for such speed. The only way I travel to this day is by horse."

"You're lucky it's our slow time of year," said his wife. "As soon as the hot weather hits, we're very busy with travelers."

"You were on your way to Philadelphia?" said Mr. Marsden. "You should stop by Gettysburg. Pay honor to the Union victory."

"We should," Charlotte agreed, glancing at Rafferty. "But for now we're extremely tired."

"Of course! You've been through an ordeal. Let me show you upstairs. Mr. Marsden will bring up your luggage shortly."

"Allow me to get it, Mrs. Marsden," said Rafferty.

"Oh, what a gentleman. If you insist," she said. "And I just love your accent. We don't get many Irish around here."

The stairwell ceiling was low enough that Rafferty had to duck as they walked up to the second floor. Mrs. Marsden opened the door to a room barely large enough for the double bed and dresser it contained.

"Here you go. Make yourselves at home. And the bathroom is down the hall to the right. Just don't run the water and flush toilet at the same time."

Before she could retreat down the hall, Charlotte called after her.

"Mrs. Marsden—I'm afraid there's been a mistake. We're not . . . we aren't staying in the same room." Charlotte felt her cheeks turn red, although she knew there was nothing to be embarrassed about. But just the thought of sharing a bed with Rafferty was outrageous.

"Oh! I beg your pardon," said Mrs. Marsden. "How terrible of me to assume. But I'm afraid I already have another lodger. This is my only available bedroom until later in the week."

Charlotte had immediate visions of another cab ride, and a fruitless search for another place to stay.

"I could sleep on the couch downstairs?" Rafferty suggested.

Mrs. Marsden nodded. "That's fine. But can you wait until after supper to retire to the couch? I'll have it made up with blankets by then. But up until seven it's a common area for all the guests."

"Of course. Not a problem," said Charlotte, after Rafferty glanced at her questioningly.

"Supper is at five thirty."

With that, Mrs. Marsden retreated into the recesses of the hall-way. Charlotte closed the door. The room felt even smaller.

"I'll take a walk and meet back in an hour for dinner," Raf-ferty said.

"Don't be silly," Charlotte said. "I know you're just as tired as I am. What a disaster! Or, near disaster, really. We got off lucky. I have to admit, I didn't like William insisting on a chaperone for this trip. But now I'm actually thankful. I don't know what I would have done without you, Rafferty."

She meant her words to be complimentary, but they resulted in an inexplicably vulnerable look on her servant's face.

"I'm . . . happy that I was here, too, madame."

"Oh, please call me Charlotte."

"I don't think Mr. Delacorte would find that right."

"That doesn't really matter to me at the moment, Rafferty," and then, realizing that contradicting his boss no doubt put him in an uncomfortable position, she added, "Look, we're so far from the house. It just seems silly." She began opening her suitcase, hop-ing she remembered to pack a book. She would no doubt have a difficult time falling asleep in this strange, new environment.

"Since we are so far from the house, as you said, may I take the liberty of saying something I wouldn't say ordinarily?"

Charlotte looked up in surprise. She left the suitcase and sat on the edge of the bed. "Of course. Please . . . speak freely."

"I know you don't always agree with Mr. Delacorte. And I can see other people have caused some . . . distraction. I don't think those people are right for ya."

She didn't know what to say. Could he possibly be talking about Jake?

"I appreciate your concern, Rafferty. But there's no need to worry about me."

"I wasn't worried about Miss Mae, and now look at her."

"What? Staying at Mrs. Astor's house? That won't last for long."

Rafferty shook his head. "I mean, the marriage."

Charlotte froze. "What marriage?"

Now Rafferty truly looked uncomfortable. "I thought you knew."

"Knew what? Tell me!"

He hesitated.

"Rafferty, you damn well better tell me what's going on with Mae." He focused his bright blue eyes on her, and she realized for the first time that he was remarkably handsome. How had she never noticed that before?

"They're marrying her off to one of Mrs. Astor's cousins."

Charlotte gasped. "How do you know this?"

"I see their butler on my days off for poker night."

Charlotte began pacing the tiny room. "I won't let it happen," she said. "We have to go back to New York tomorrow so I can put stop to this while William is in Boston."

CHARLOTTE SAT UP in the soft and lumpy bed, disoriented.

Her heart was pounding. For a moment, she thought she was still on the train—that she'd been paralyzed in the accident and was waiting to be rescued. But after her initial moment of waking panic, she could see it was morning, and she was safely at the inn.

She sank back against her pillows. Her mouth was dry. She wished she'd thought to keep some water in the room. And then, a knock at the door. It was the same sound as the one that had roused her from the terrifying dream.

Charlotte pulled on her robe and opened the door. Rafferty stood in the hall, fully dressed.

"Oh!" Charlotte said, embarrassed by her disheveled state. "What time is it?"

"It's nearly ten. I know you said you wanted to get back to

New York. I need to go to the train station to find a schedule for our return. It could take a while. I didn't want you to wake up and just not find me here."

"That's thoughtful of you, Rafferty. Come in."

She sat back on her unmade bed. Even with the bright sunlight coming through the flimsy window curtain, even with Rafferty standing there, waiting to help her get back to New York, the dream clung to her like perspiration. She couldn't shake the images of bloodied and twisted faces, broken limbs with the bones protruding from the flesh. . . .

"Are you all right?" he said, sitting next to her.

"Yes. I just had terrible dreams all night long. I kept waking up and falling back asleep and they'd start up again, like an endless loop."

"The accident?"

"Yes."

"It was bad. We were lucky."

She nodded, thinking yet again how thankful she was that he had been with her for the ordeal. Sitting there, she felt an intense urge to feel his arms around her. And in that moment she realized that not all of the dreams had been violent and centered around the accident; at least one of them—the one that was sure to haunt her the longest—was the one in which Jake made love to her in that very bed. But as he was entering her, she looked up to see his face and saw Rafferty instead.

She jumped up. "I should get ready to leave. Why don't you wait for me downstairs and then we can go straight to the station together. The sooner we get back to New York, the better."

Rafferty stood, his blue eyes bright and focused.

"I'll be ready when you are," he said.

Chapter 9

IT SEEMED LIKE any other night at the club. But Roger knew otherwise. It was the beginning of the end, at least for him.

"I'll have a gin and tonic," Roger told the bartender.

He wasn't comfortable sitting at a table. Buckner had demanded he turn in all of his office-issued suits, and tonight he was at the Vesper, wearing clothes unbefitting his alias, the wealthy businessman Roger Smith.

His former alias.

Roger was taking a tremendous risk.

It didn't help matters that Fiona was clearly avoiding him. He wished he could blame it on his less-than-impressive wardrobe, but he had a sinking feeling her lack of attention was due to something much more damning. He tried, repeatedly, to get her to sit with him, but she would barely take the time to say a word to him before taking off with strange men to the back of the club. It was agony.

Roger took a hefty swig of his drink. And then, across the room, he saw something that almost lifted his spirits: It was the man who owned the speakeasy, making his way across the room and heading right for Boom Boom. Immediately, Boom Boom took the man aside.

What was his name? Jake something or other. He would remember. He had to remember: His job depended on it.

And he realized he had something more than a name to save his job: He had what he needed to get Fiona back right where he wanted her.

Roger ordered another drink, and waited impatiently for Fiona to return to the barroom. He tried not to imagine what was keeping her so long.

And then the man from the speakeasy made his way back through the room. Roger left his seat and hurried to intercept him before he reached the exit.

"What a coincidence to run into you again, Mister . . ." he said.

Jake looked at him like he was a cockroach in his cupboard. He turned away from him and left without a word.

Arrogant bastard, Roger thought. He could ignore him, but it wouldn't be long before he was talking to Buckner. Just how long would depend on Fiona.

By the time Roger made his way back to his seat at the bar, Fiona was working a fresh group of gentlemen at a table in the corner. Her red hair was pulled back with a black velvet ribbon, and she wore dangling earrings that called attention to her long, elegant neck. Her dress plunged low in the back, and she wore a long necklace that dangled a tassel just above the curve of her ass.

"I need to talk to you," he said, grabbing her by the elbow.

AFTER A LONG day of travel, Rafferty finally delivered Charlotte to the front entrance of Amelia Astor's house.

As soon as they'd made it back to New York City, Charlotte had insisted they get her car and go straight to see Mae. By then, it was twilight, and the plan that had seemed so obvious during the daylong journey back from Pennsylvania suddenly seemed ill-advised. Still, Charlotte was determined.

"I insist on going in with you," Rafferty said.

Charlotte was tempted to agree with him. He'd been such a steadfast companion during the past twenty-four hours.

"No need to get yourself into trouble," Charlotte said. "It's best if you just stay out here. I hope to be leaving with Mae, and you're my getaway vehicle." She smiled at him, but he remained stone-faced and serious.

"I don't feel good about this," he said.

"Rafferty, I appreciate that you told me about what dire straits Mae is in. But you couldn't have thought that I wouldn't intervene." She opened the car door. He stepped out of the driver's side, and they glared at each other across the width of the car.

"That woman might behave herself better if there's a witness," he said.

"I'll take my chances, Rafferty. Now please—just indulge me and wait here."

"Charlotte, if you're not out in fifteen minutes I'm coming in after you." His blue eyes were so intense and commanding, she couldn't help but relent.

"Make it a half hour."

FIONA LED ROGER to the small back room. He said he just needed to talk to her, but she knew that was just his pathetic ploy to get her attention. Boom Boom had been right: It was more lucrative—not to mention less annoying—to service a few men quickly at the club than having to cope with the burdensome intensity of dealing with one reliable but demanding john.

She was ready to freeze Roger out altogether. But then he said he needed to talk to her about Jake—that he'd just seen Jake in the club—and that got her attention. What could he possibly know or care about Jake?

"What is it?" she said, closing the door and crossing her arms.

"Please—sit down," he said.

"I don't want to sit. I want to get back to work."

"And this is what your work entails now?"

"What is it your business? You didn't seem to mind my work the other night in the bathroom."

"The bathroom of the speakeasy, you mean?" Roger sneered. For the first time since knowing him, Fiona felt a prickle of unease.

"What do you want?" she said.

"I'm in love with you," he said.

"Don't be ridiculous."

"I want you to stop bringing men back to this room. And I want you to take me back to your apartment again so we can be together like we used to be."

"That's not going to happen," she said, reaching for the door. He grabbed her arm.

"I work for the District Attorney's office," he said. "I've been investigating this place undercover this entire time."

Fiona felt her entire body go cold. "You're lying."

But as she watched him reach confidently into his wallet, she knew with a terrible sinking feeling that he wasn't. Sure enough, he flashed his office identification card.

"So . . . what? You're going to arrest me?"

"That's up to you," he said. "Will you do what I asked?"

For the first time, Fiona felt like a whore.

"Go fuck yourself," she said. She wanted to spit in his face, but instead just rushed out of the room. The sound of the band starting up reminded her that she was still at work. She had to hold it together.

"Jake Larkin, that's his name. Right?" Roger said from behind her.

She turned around.

"Bootlegging is a serious crime," he continued. "Maybe even more serious than prostitution."

Fiona didn't move.

"How many years in prison do you think your friend Jake will get for his little speakeasy—not to mention whatever business he

has with Boom Boom. I saw them talking tonight. I should thank
you, Fiona. You really brought me into the thick of things." He
moved closer to her, and she could smell the gin on his breath.
"Now, shall we go back to your place?"

Chapter 10

MAE HEARD LOUD voices coming from the entrance hall. She
put down her copy of *Photoplay,* and walked to the foot of the stairs.
She could hear the conversation more clearly now, and she recognized Charlotte's voice. She hurried down to the first floor, nearly
tripping on her long silk robe.

"Charlotte! Is something wrong?" Mae said when she was halfway down, far enough to hear her sister-in-law yelling, "I'm not
leaving until I talk to her!"

Neither woman noticed Mae.

"Your husband is going to hear about this," said Amelia.

"Oh, I'm sure you'll love that," Charlotte responded sarcastically.

"Charlotte," Mae said again. Both women turned to look at her.

"Go back upstairs," said Amelia. "This doesn't concern you."

Charlotte ran over and threw her arms around her. "It's so
good to see you," she said. "Are you all right?"

"Yes, yes, I'm fine," Mae said, shocked to see tears brimming
in Charlotte's eyes.

"The sooner you let us talk, the sooner I'll be out of your way,"
Charlotte said to Amelia.

Mae could see Amelia considering her options. Since Mae was,
by all appearances, following orders, it had been a few days since
they'd had a skirmish. While it was vaguely amusing to see her
getting fired up again, it didn't really help matters. She just needed

to, as Jonathan put it, "get to the finish line." Then she would have her money, her freedom, and maybe even Fiona. But Charlotte didn't know any of that.

"Amelia, won't you let us talk in the parlor for a minute? It's really harmless," said Mae.

Amelia glared at Charlotte. "You have five minutes, and then I want you out of my house."

Mae led Charlotte down the hall, and along the way they passed Mumson.

"Rafferty is waiting for me outside in the car," Charlotte said to the butler. "Can you please tell him I'm talking to Miss Delacorte and that everything is fine?"

"Certainly, madame."

"Why did Rafferty drive you?" said Mae, closing the parlor door.

"It's a long story, and I haven't come to chat. We're leaving. Don't worry about your clothes. The important thing is to get you away from this woman."

"Charlotte, no. There's no point in running away. It doesn't solve the problem."

"I won't let them force you into a marriage."

"They're not. No one is forcing me; it's my choice."

Charlotte shook her head. "This is *me,* darling. I'm on your side. You don't have to keep up appearances. Have you been here so long that you've forgotten that?"

Mae put her finger to her lips, then walked quietly to the parlor door. She opened it slowly, and then closed it again quietly. No one was listening. Still, she would have to be careful.

She beckoned for Charlotte to sit with her on the couch. Charlotte moved close to her. Mae spoke in a whisper.

"Jonathan Astor is doing it for the same reason I am: to keep our families happy so we aren't cut off financially. We'll both be living our own lives. He has a girlfriend—I've met her."

Charlotte looked at her skeptically. "I don't know if this is the most modern arrangement I've ever heard, or the most archaic."

"He's going to talk to William when he gets back on Friday."

Charlotte stood up and paced in front of the couch.

"Are you certain about this?"

"Yes. I don't mind faking it for the money. But how much longer are *you* going to?"

CHARLOTTE WAITED UNTIL Rafferty pulled out of the Astor driveway before asking him to drop her off at Jake's.

"It was bad enough I agreed to drive you to that troublemaking woman's house. But this is where I draw the line," he said.

Charlotte sighed, and put her hand on Rafferty's arm. "I appreciate your concern. But this isn't your 'line' to draw. I need you to just do your job and drive me where I ask."

She regretted her words as soon as she saw the look on Rafferty's face.

"My apologies, Mrs. Delacorte," he said in a clipped, formal way. She winced. It hurt a little to hear him address her so properly after everything.

"How will you be getting home?" he asked once they pulled up to the quiet street. There was no hint of the speakeasy just two buildings away.

"I'll take a cab. Or get a ride. Don't worry about me," she said. She hopped out of the car and closed the door, then immediately opened it again and poked her head back inside. "And Rafferty, thanks for everything. I don't know what I would have done without you on that trip. And I won't forget it."

He nodded, but it was joyless, and there was no hint of the friendship that had been burgeoning between them. Maybe that was for the best, she thought.

INSIDE, THE NOISE and smoke enveloped her, and a few friendly faces greeted her and offered her drinks. But Charlotte politely demurred and kept moving through the room until she found Jake. He was speaking animatedly to a man in a well-cut suit. He was not a terribly attractive man, with dark, slicked-back hair, and thin lips below a slightly bulbous nose. Still, there was an air about him that commanded attention, and he clearly held Jake in a thrall. The man turned to Charlotte, as if sensing her stare.

"Charlotte!" Jake jumped up and pulled her into his arms. She inhaled the smell of tobacco and that particular scent he had of spice and citrus. He held her for a full minute before she pulled herself away. "How did you get out?"

"William is away—I was supposed to be in Philadelphia for a few days but there were . . . train problems," she said.

"I want to introduce you to someone," he said, and she sat next to him in a chair where the dark-haired fellow was watching them with quiet interest. "Charlotte, Mr. Cole Porter. He's visiting New York for the week."

"Oh! I'm a huge fan, Mr. Porter," she said, amazed to find the well-known music writer just sitting around Jake's barroom. Aside from his professional reputation, Charlotte was well aware of Cole Porter's social extravagance. The Porters' home on the rue Monsieur near Les Invalides was well known in certain circles, palatial in size and outrageous in décor, with platinum wallpaper and chairs upholstered in zebra skin. The parties they hosted there were infamous, with a circuslike atmosphere that included everything from actual tightrope walkers to rumors of bisexual orgies. Charlotte had unfortunately missed the opportunity to experience one of these parties firsthand early in her marriage when she and William had been abroad. William had declined the invitation.

"Well, I never tire of those words, so thank you," he said.

"Cole, excuse us for just a minute," Jake said.

He took her by the hand and they scurried up to his bedroom like two teenagers on the run. When he closed the door behind them, she laughed, feeling drunk with happiness.

"Dare I ask what Cole Porter is doing here?" she said as he pulled her close again.

"He stopped by last night, and told me he'll be here every night until he has to go to L.A. I think the word is getting out that the best music in town is being played in a small Village basement," he said. "Makes me more confident that I can expand into real business."

"And not a moment too soon; I'm ready to tell William I'm leaving him. I don't have to worry about Mae—she's gotten herself taken care of. I'm not sure I entirely agree with what she's doing, but I have to admit there's some logic to it."

"I would ask you for details, but I can't say I'm interested in anything but hearing about you. What's been going on at the house? Is he leaving you alone?"

She nodded. "For the most part. But he insisted Rafferty accompany me to Philadelphia."

Jake scowled. "I'm not sure I trust that fellow," he said. Charlotte refrained from saying that the feeling was quite mutual. She also decided now wasn't the best time to mention their sojourn to a rural inn.

"Any arrangement that gets me out of the house is fine by me," she said. "Did you open the bank account?"

He nodded, and separated from her long enough to pull papers out from under his bed.

"This is the account information. I didn't put your name on it so as not to draw attention to it, but we can change that anytime you want. But until then, you'll need me to access it."

Charlotte examined the sum in the account, and nodded. She felt more encouraged than ever that she could make it a few

months until Jake was in better shape with business and she could
find a job.

As if he knew what she was thinking, he said, "Don't do anything until I have the deal in place. It shouldn't be long now. My
meeting with the source is Friday night."

Charlotte shuddered with dread.

"Please be careful," she begged softly.

"It's just a business meeting."

"There are shady characters mixed up in all of this business
now. Criminals," she said. He smiled at her and ruffled her bangs.

"I love this haircut," he said.

"I'm serious—don't be dismissive."

"I'm not. I appreciate your worry, baby—I do. But it's just
business. We're meeting at Cavanaugh's on the Bowery. It's a public place. There's nothing to worry about. If anything, this guy
wants to check *me* out to make sure I'm not a shady character."

"Well," she said, reaching up to put her arms around his neck.
"Perhaps this boss character is right to be concerned. You *are* a little shady."

Jake kissed her neck, and she felt a delicious chill run through
her. He unbuttoned the back of her dress with one hand, and
whispered in her ear, "Give me a few minutes and I'll get a lot
shadier," he said.

Chapter 11

AMELIA HAD NEVER felt a greater sense of accomplishment.

There, in her living room, William and Jonathan shook hands,
William having just granted permission for her cousin to propose
marriage to Mae.

Amelia knew that Jonathan held, in his pocket, the ten-carat, emerald-cut diamond that had once belonged to Amelia's mother. While it pained her to see it go to such a trollop as Mae Delacorte, she was, in a sense, using the diamond ring to secure her own future, so it was fitting.

"Shall I summon Mae?" Amelia said, smoothing the bottom of her dress, a blue silk chiffon dress by Lanvin, low-waisted and with a scalloped hemline. She had chosen her attire carefully; she felt this night was as much hers—no, *more* hers—than Mae's. With that in mind, she wanted to look her best. The Lanvin was an obvious choice, but she missed the traditional silhouette terribly— much more flattering to her rather pear-shaped figure. But if she didn't wear the new clothes of the season, people would talk. So she was forced to choose between fashionable or flattering.

It was no matter, she told herself. William was not interested in her for anything as trivial as her appearance. He had turned to her because he finally recognized her as his true ally.

"I'm ready," Jonathan said, straightening his tie.

"Mumson," Amelia said, "please call Miss Delacorte to join us."

Amelia opened an oak chest, and retrieved a bottle of champagne.

"I haven't seen champagne since before the war," said Jonathan.

"Perhaps we should wait for her response before we uncork it," William said. "Lord knows my sister is not the most predictable."

Amelia smiled at him.

"I'm confident," she said. She had advised Mae to dress for dinner, and that both her brother and William would be joining them. The girl certainly understood what was happening, and yet she seemed in good spirits. Amelia had to hand it to herself that the entire episode was going smoother than she had dared hope. She attributed this to the fact that it was the right thing for everyone involved, and truly a stroke of genius that she had the vision to put it all together. Not that she'd ever get a proper thank you out of Mae. But the look on William's face was all the thanks she needed. For now.

Mae walked down the stairs, dressed in a virginal white silk frock that was scandalously short even for the current fashions. She wore a white silk flower in her hair, and pearls around her neck. Amelia was certain that the outfit was a mockery of wedding attire.

"I hate being the last one to the party," Mae said.

"The last, but not the least," Jonathan said with a smile. Was it Amelia's imagination, or were the two of them stifling laughter? "Come join me in the parlor for a minute," he said, casting a look at his cousin for permission. Amelia nodded encouragingly.

"Allow me," William said when they were alone, extending his hand for the bottle.

"I thought you wanted to wait to be certain," she said, smiling.

"There's one thing I am certain about, and I'd like for us to toast before my sister and your cousin return to distract us."

With a pop and a whoosh, the bubbly was unleashed. He poured two glasses nearly full, and handed one to Amelia before raising his own.

"To a perfect union," he said.

"To a perfect union." They touched glasses, and she felt certain he was talking about them, not Mae and Jonathan.

"We have news!" Mae said, bursting back into the room. Amelia had never detested her more.

She and William stood side by side as Mae extended her left hand and waved the Astor diamond as if Amelia had never seen it before.

"Well, congratulations are in order," William said.

Amelia dutifully retrieved two more glasses.

"Amelia, how naughty of you," Mae said, taking a glass. "But I do love champagne."

"To Mae," Jonathan said, raising his glass. "You will be the most beautiful bride."

Everyone smiled, and the room was filled with the clink of crystal against crystal and the sound of congratulations.

Yet somehow, Amelia felt unsettled.

"YOU'RE SURE THIS is where you want to celebrate?" Jonathan said, paying the cover at the door of the Vesper. "I had dinner reservations for us at the St. Regis. Ursula loves their caviar."

"But this is where we had our first date. Really, Jonathan— we're not even married yet, and already you've lost all sense of romance."

Mae breathed in the heady scent of the place: the alcohol and tobacco, the expensive perfume, and, in the crowded back room, the smell of perspiration. Every few minutes, she glanced down at her left hand. The ring, although meaningless as a symbol of love and fidelity, was dazzling nonetheless. She couldn't wait to show Fiona.

Yes, now that the plan with Jonathan was secure, she would let Fiona in on their secret. After all, why should Jonathan and Ursula have all the fun?

"Gin?" Jonathan asked her.

"I don't think so. Tonight I've got the taste for champagne."

"I'll get a bottle."

"And I'll get a table."

It's too bad, Mae thought, that she didn't like men and that Jonathan didn't like her in that fashion. They might have been a perfect couple.

Then she spotted Fiona nearby, and all thoughts of happy coupledom with Jonathan Astor evaporated in a cloud of Chanel No. 5 and a flourish of pale green silk.

Fiona had clearly seen her first, and was already by her side, wrapping her cool fingers around Mae's wrist before Mae could get a word out.

"Thank god you're here," she said. "I need to talk to you."

It was then that Mae noticed that Fiona's eyes were not bright with their usual coquettish mischief, but instead darting about in an uncharacteristic panic.

"Everything's okay," Mae said. "I have good news—for us."

"No, you must let me talk first. But we have to stay out of Boom Boom's sight: She might smile when your golden boy flashes his billfold, but if she sees you with me she'll toss you out faster than yesterday's garbage."

"Okay, okay. Calm down."

"Listen to me: There's a gray door that is two away from the showroom. Wait five minutes, then go to it and knock three times. Got it?"

"Yes—yes, I've got it."

Both women noticed Jonathan heading toward them with a bottle.

"And come alone, for god's sake."

There was no time to ask any questions. Fiona took off in the crowd, and Mae turned to face Jonathan with a bright smile.

"Why did she run off? There's plenty here to go around," he said, setting the bottle on the table and pulling a few glasses out from under his arm.

"You know what? I'm going to go ask her to join us," Mae said nervously. She knew Fiona said five minutes, but once she started drinking with Jonathan it would be harder to find an excuse to immediately jump up again.

"Fantastic. The more the merrier."

The club was as full as she'd ever seen it, and more than a few people she knew tried to pull her into conversation or hand her a drink. She waved them off, careful to hide the rock on her left hand. The last thing she needed was to get sidetracked with conversation about her engagement.

She passed the show room and peeked inside. A band was setting up, and she recognized Maxwell from Jake's place. But she didn't want to call out to him and then have to chitchat for ten minutes.

Mae found the gray door. Looking around to make sure no one was watching, she knocked three times. The door sprung open and Fiona yanked her inside so fast it was as if she was pulling her out of the path of a speeding train.

"What took you so long?" Fiona hissed.

"So long? I thought I was early. And what is this? A closet?" The room was tiny, with just two bar stools and a lamp. And it smelled funny.

"Listen to me: We have big trouble. You know that guy I've been hanging around with? Roger?"

"Which guy?"

"Never mind who he is. But I've been hanging out with a guy and he's been spending a lot of time here and I even took him to Jake's one night hoping to find you there. . . ."

Mae smiled. "You were looking for me?"

"Focus!" Fiona said, snapping her fingers. "So now the guy tells me he's undercover. And he's going to turn in Jake for bootlegging. And it's all my fault."

"How do you know he's not just saying that? Bragging . . . trying to look important to impress you?"

Fiona shook her head. "I wish that was the case," she said. "But he works for the DA's office."

Mae sat on one of the stools.

"Do you think we should tell Charlotte?" Fiona asked.

"Yes. Absolutely. She'll know what to do. At the very least, she can get him a lawyer." Mae jumped up and took Fiona by the hand. "Let's go."

They moved quickly back to the barroom.

"What the hell is this?" Fiona said, feeling the rock on Mae's finger and then examining it.

"It's my ticket to my inheritance," Mae said. "I'll explain later." She waved to Jonathan in the corner as they rushed by, and he waved her over. She shook her head and kept moving.

The doorman helped them get a cab.

"Sixty-fifth Street and Fifth Avenue," Mae said.

"What if your brother is there?"

"That's a chance we'll have to take. But I think he's at Amelia Astor's. He was there earlier, and I doubt he was in any rush to leave."

"Who was that blonde you were with at the diner the other night?" Fiona asked suddenly, crossing her arms.

Mae smiled. "Wow. Don't tell me you, Miss No Strings Attached, are—dare I say it—jealous?"

"Not jealous, just curious," Fiona said with a pout.

Mae reached for her hand. "She's no one—just my fiancé's girlfriend."

Fiona looked at her. "I'm sure you're joking about some part of that—I'm just not sure which part."

"Oddly enough, I couldn't be more serious."

Fiona glared at her. "You have some nerve! You give me hell because I can't be your devoted girlfriend, and a week later you're engaged?"

"Oh, please. That's nothing compared to what you've been up to. I shudder to even think about it—"

"Just shut up," Fiona said, leaning over and kissing her hard on the mouth. Mae held her close, holding her just a minute so that they were cheek to cheek. Mae relished the softness of her skin, the familiar scent that made her twitch between her legs.

"Leave me alone," Mae said, feebly.

Fiona kissed her neck, her small hand slipping into Mae's blouse just between the buttons. She played with Mae's nipples until she moaned softly.

"Ahem," the driver cleared his throat pointedly. "I need this fare, but I am a Christian and won't hesitate to put you both out on the street."

Fiona laughed, but returned to her side of the backseat, putting a respectable few inches between them. Mae concentrated on normalizing her breathing. They didn't speak again until the cab pulled up to the Delacorte mansion.

"I can't believe the likes of you have any business here," the driver said after Mae paid the fare. Fiona slammed the door.

Giggling, they scampered up to the front door. Then, remembering why they were there, they quieted down and Mae knocked on the door.

"What are you two troublemakers doing here?" Rafferty said upon seeing them.

"Takes one to know one," Fiona said. "Tell Charlotte we need to talk to her."

"Miss Mae, you should know better by now," he said, shaking his head.

"It's important, Rafferty. Please."

He reluctantly stepped aside, and the two of them walked inside. It felt, to Mae, as if she had been gone from the house much longer than she actually had been.

"What's with that guy?" said Fiona. "If I didn't know better, I'd think he was snogging her."

"Who? Charlotte? Don't be such a bitch."

They sat on a velvet-covered settee. The house was so quiet, Mae could hear the grandfather clock ticking from the parlor.

"What are you two doing here?" Charlotte said, appearing in hall, wrapped in a purple floral robe, still holding the book she had obviously been reading.

"We need to talk to you. William's not here, is he?" said Mae.

"No—luckily for you. So what is it? Oh, good heavens, Mae—I see you're going through with it." Charlotte said, looking at her left hand.

"Listen, Charlotte: Jake's in trouble," said Mae.

That got Charlotte's attention. All color seemed to drain from her face.

"What is it?"

Mae and Fiona exchanged a look.

"It seems that a . . . fellow I know . . . is an investigator of some kind and he is going to turn Jake in for bootlegging," Fiona said.

Charlotte pressed her hand to her chest. "How do you know this?"

"He told me," Fiona said.

"I don't understand. Why would he tell you? And how long do you think we have before Jake gets arrested?"

"I don't know. I can maybe hold him off for a little while."

"This is a nightmare. And Jake is meeting with someone tonight who will get him in even deeper."

"Who?"

"I don't know who—but I do know where. Have Rafferty pull the car around. We have to stop him before it's too late."

Chapter 12

JAKE RARELY SPENT time walking around the Bowery. It wasn't far from where he had grown up, and really, the only thing the neighborhood was good for was serving as a reminder of where he didn't want to end up. In that sense, it was a perfect place to meet

O'Brian's boss. It was hard to be nervous about moving forward when going back was not an option.

Cavanaugh's, established in 1854, was small and dark and apparently hadn't done much with its décor since its opening day. Jake trudged across the sawdust-covered floor to the last booth on the right, as instructed.

As he was about to sit, a barrel-shaped man with a thick beard put his hand out.

"Not so fast, gent. What's yer name, there?"

"What's it to you?" Jake said.

"That table there is saved. So if you think you're the one it's for, y'better tell me your name."

"Larkinowski."

The man consulted a piece of paper in his hand, then looked him up and down.

"Make yourself at home. Can I get ya a bottle of pop?"

"Sure. Whatever you've got would be fine." Jake sat with his back to the bar, facing the front door. He looked at his watch. The Boss was one minute late, but Jake knew that didn't mean anything. A man in his position would never be early and risk having to wait for someone—a position of weakness.

The door opened and he looked up. It was just a kid, delivering a package to the bar.

"Here ya go." The man slid a warm bottle of Coca-Cola across the table.

Jake turned to the front door as it opened again, and his heart almost stopped.

William Delacorte had walked in.

Jake ducked his head down, hoping to go unnoticed. And if William headed straight back to the tables in the rear, he might have. Instead, William walked right up to his booth.

"*You* again?" William spat.

"Look, I don't want to get into any of this right now," Jake said evenly. "I'm just meeting someone and then I'm leaving."

William narrowed his eyes. "You're going to have to move. This booth is reserved."

Jake glanced at the door. "Yeah, it's reserved for *me*."

The two men glared at each other, until the slow horror of comprehension hit them both at the same time.

Part V

Dangerous Games

It's the loose ends with which men hang themselves.
—Zelda Fitzgerald

Chapter 1

THE OTHER PATRONS in the restaurant glanced at them anxiously, as if sensing the violence crackling in the air. The two men stared at each other, their eyes cold.

"It's you?" Jake said. "You're the one who's been selling me booze all this time?"

"Looks that way," William said, an arrogant smile on his face. Still, Jake could tell he was just as rattled as he himself was. "Quite an unfortunate turn of events for you, wouldn't you agree, *Larkinowski?*"

Jake swallowed hard. He could see his dreams of expanding the business going down the drain faster than bad moonshine.

"I'd say more unfortunate for you," he bluffed. "You just lost the chance to do a big deal." Jake realized people were staring at them, so he slid into the booth for the sake of discretion. William followed his lead.

"You're only the middleman," William hissed. "I don't need you to do this deal."

"You don't know who the buyer is."

"I didn't get in this position by not knowing things, Larkin. I

knew Boom Boom needed booze before you did. I knew it the day
Lenny Sugarfield got busted. I just didn't know if it was worth my
time and effort."

"And what do you think Charlotte will say when she finds out
her so-called upstanding husband is a liar and criminal?"

"I'd say when it comes to my wife, money talks, nobody
walks."

Just then, Charlotte, Mae, and Fiona burst through the door
into the restaurant, stunning both men.

"What the hell is going on?" William said.

He took the words right out of Jake's mouth. Jake moved quickly
to Charlotte's side to protect her.

"What is *he* doing here?" she said, her hand covering her mouth
and her eyes wide with fright when she saw William.

"What are *you* doing here? Go—just get the hell out of here.
Go to my place. I'll meet you there," Jake said.

But it was too late. William had Charlotte firmly by the arm.

"Speak of the devil—if it isn't my lovely wife. Let's go."

"Don't leave with him, Charlotte. Trust me on this. . . ."

William turned around and shoved Jake hard enough that he
lost his footing. He recovered fast enough to throw a punch that
landed squarely on William's jaw. William grabbed him by the
neck.

"Okay, you two—that's enough!" The barrel-shaped man
who had seated them, accompanied by two burly sidekicks, swiftly
and roughly hustled them out the door.

IF MAE HADN'T dragged her out of the restaurant, Charlotte
didn't know if she would have had the wits about her to move.
Nothing made any sense. She'd rushed down there in a panic to stop
Jake from getting into a risky deal, and instead found him talking

heatedly to William. She immediately thought of their acrimonious exchange the day he'd caught her talking to Jake in the parlor. *Do you, or do you not, want me to write that check every month?*

Oh god, what would he do to her now?

Outside on the street corner, everyone looked at one another warily.

"Charlotte—listen to me," Jake said urgently, his eyes completely focused on her. "Do not go home with him. Now is the time to make your stand," The look on Jake's face stopped her cold. He was not asking her—he was telling her.

"Please . . . just leave it alone for now," she said, turning away from him. She needed to make her own decisions now.

William grabbed her roughly by the arm, pulling her to the car as Mae and Fiona looked on helplessly. He shoved her into the passenger seat and slammed the door. She turned to see Jake staring after her. She mouthed, *the ladder.*

"Well, Charlotte, you've outdone yourself this time," William said, aggressively steering the car through the side streets of the Bowery. She knew it was best to say nothing. Even if she had wanted to speak, she was too busy piecing together a dozen far-fetched scenarios to try to come to a logical conclusion as to how William and Jake ended up in the same random restaurant. And nothing she imagined could have prepared her for William's inadvertent clarification.

"Who told you?" he said.

"Told me what?"

"Don't play with me, Charlotte. Who told you I was doing the deal with Jake? Or do you expect me to believe that the three of you just showed up there by coincidence? Was this a trap you set for me?"

A vein bulged out of his forehead.

Cold washed over her as she felt the blood drain from her face.

Now she understood why Jake had been so adamant that she not leave with William.

"How long"—she paused—"how long have you been doing this?"

He glanced at her, then turned his eyes back to the road. "A few years."

"A few *years*?"

"Yes, Charlotte," he said, exasperated.

"But . . . why?"

He shrugged. "Because I could. There were guys at Harvard from Canada. We had the contacts. It was fast money. Easy money."

"You have the family business . . . you don't need money!"

"A little extra on the side never hurt. And as for the family business—I never had any interest in real estate. I never had any interest in working, period. My father never should have made me take over when he got sick. Even then, I thought it would be temporary."

"When he had his stroke, you mean?"

William nodded. "I thought he'd recover, and go back to making our family a fortune. But it didn't turn out that way."

Charlotte suddenly wanted to escape. Who was this man she was married to?

"I'm taking you back to the house," William said. "Go to your bedroom and do not leave it. I have some business to take care of."

"I'll bet," she mumbled.

"What did you say?" One of his hands flew from the steering wheel to grip her around her neck.

"Nothing." She coughed as he released her.

"And Charlotte? If I ever catch you with Larkin again, I will kill him."

Chapter 2

IN ALL THE time that she had known Jake Larkin, Mae had never seen him look so defeated. And he didn't even know the worst of it yet.

Jake sat silently on the curb, his head in his hands. He hadn't moved since Charlotte took off with William. The street was empty, and the few people who did stroll by took little notice of the man and two women loitering on the street corner.

"Jake," Mae said, resting her hand lightly on his shoulder, trying again to get him to respond. "Jake, what was my brother doing here?"

He looked up, as if surprised to see them still standing there. "More important, what did you two think you were going to accomplish, running down here like this?"

"Charlotte didn't want you getting deeper into trouble," Mae said.

"I'm not in trouble."

"Yes," Fiona said, "you are." She glanced at Mae before sitting down next to him with a heavy sigh. "That guy I brought to your place? Roger? He's a cop."

"A cop? Jesus, Fiona!"

"He's not a cop," Mae corrected. "You said he works for the DA's office."

"Is there a difference?" said Fiona.

Jake jumped up and began pacing nervously. "How do you know?"

"He told me," she said. "But he promised not to give you up."

Jake threw his hands up. "Oh—well *that's* comforting. And why wouldn't he?"

"Because he's in love with me."

CHARLOTTE SAT ON the edge of the guestroom bed, staring at the wall.

Now it all made sense: the cash. The business trips.

The gun.

The thing that really got her was the hypocrisy of it all; he was the one always making her feel that she didn't measure up to his high society standards. And the way he punished and controlled Mae! And there he was, sneaking around, lying, deceiving her, breaking the law—behaving worse than Charlotte or Mae on their worse day . . . or night.

If she had any qualms about divorcing him, they were gone. Should she just walk away with nothing? And it would be nothing. The hope she had that Jake might be able to help her was gone. So much for the big business deal. . . .

Someone knocked on the door. She jumped up, straightening her robe over her nightgown. The knock had been tentative, so it clearly wasn't William. He no doubt would have pounded the locked door so hard it would fall off the hinges.

She opened to find Rafferty. She resisted the inappropriate—but not altogether surprising—urge to throw herself into his arms.

"Is everything all right?" he said. She was achingly tempted to confide in him, but knew that it would be crossing a line. She said nothing, but her pause told him everything he needed to know.

"Yes, Rafferty. Thank you. I'm fine." His blue eyes bore into hers deeply. "Just one thing—is Mr. Delacorte still at home?"

"No. He left a few minutes ago."

Charlotte wondered if it was worth the risk to venture downstairs. William had warned her not to leave the bedroom, but how seriously was he holding her to that? She shuddered, thinking of the gun, and decided she didn't want to find out. "Rafferty, I need for you to do me a favor."

"Anything," he said.

Charlotte retrieved a pen from the desk and wrote on a party invitation Mae had left behind in a pile of mail.

"Please call this number. It's my father. Tell him I need him to visit me here as soon as possible. Tell him not to leave mother if she needs him, but if he can spare a day, to come immediately."

Rafferty nodded. "I'll take care of it," he said.

"And Rafferty—do it now. Before Mr. Delacorte returns."

Something small and hard pinged against the window, grabbing their attention. Charlotte hurried over to it, with Raffety right behind her. She looked down, and there was Jake, tossing small rocks. She pushed the window open.

"Come down," he said.

"Don't," said Rafferty, touching her lightly on the shoulder.

"Please, don't get involved," she said. "Just do as I asked and call my father."

"I can't let you go down there—he's trouble," Rafferty said.

Any feelings of comfort she had when he came to the door were gone. Now, he was just another obstacle in her way.

"So now you're on William's side?"

"I'm on your side."

"Then prove it by letting me do what I have to do," she said sharply.

She didn't wait for a response, and climbed down the ladder quickly, faster than she might have if Rafferty had not been trying to stop her. The night seemed dramatically dark, and the ladder swayed slightly in the wind. Clutching the thick, burly rope of the ladder, she had a false sense of freedom, but also a very real sense of danger.

"Take it slow," Jake called from the ground. "And don't look down."

Chapter 3

CHARLOTTE HEEDED HIS instructions, even though the descent seemed to take forever. When she finally touched her right foot to the grass, she exhaled a ragged breath.

Brushing off her hands, she turned and faced Jake in the darkness. She wanted him to hold her close, to reassure her, but he just looked at her warily.

"Why did you leave with him?" he asked quietly.

"I didn't realize . . . I didn't *understand* what was going on," she stammered, feeling like somehow she was the one who had done something wrong. She glanced up at the window. Rafferty was no longer in sight.

"You could have trusted me. I wouldn't have asked you to do something rash. I know you didn't plan to leave your marriage without money in place. But don't you see that this changes everything? I know it's a shock. But now you've had time to think about it."

"I'm still trying to make sense of it," she said, wondering why she suddenly felt defensive. "I'm glad you're here so we can talk."

"I didn't come here to talk. I came to take you with me."

"What?"

"My car is parked on the next street."

"You want me to leave now?"

"Yes. I want you to literally leave with just the shirt on your back. There's nothing to hold on to here, Charlotte. Your husband isn't who you thought he was. And I'm still going to find a way to do the deal with Boom Boom so I can help you with money."

"Jake, you have to slow down. I still have parents to think about—a future to think about. I'm not going to give William the satisfaction of divorcing me as an adulteress. I'm not going to leave this marriage with nothing. I won't get much, but I won't throw it all away just for the sake of some ridiculous dramatic gesture."

"You think that's what this is?"

Jake was as upset as she'd ever seen him.

"You keep finding excuses not to leave," he said, his voice low but shaking with emotion. "If what happened tonight doesn't push you out the door, I don't think anything will."

"That's not fair," she said, her eyes filling with tears so quickly her vision blurred.

"So prove me wrong," he said, holding out his hand. "Come with me right now. Not tomorrow, not in a week. Prove it to me *now*."

"You're not the only person I have to prove things to, Jake."

The look of disappointment on his face cut deeply into her. She tried to think of something to say that would convey to him that she loved him, but that she couldn't be impulsive with her future— and her parents' future—at stake. Instead, a heavy and sad silence hung between them.

Without another word, Jake walked away, leaving her alone in the darkness. She looked at the ladder. The climb back up seemed very steep.

BOOM BOOM DRUMMED her fingers restlessly on her desk. Upstairs, she could hear the faint sounds of Jake's jazz band, the clacking of heels on the hardwood floors, and the dull hum of three hundred voices talking, flirting, laughing, and above all, ordering drinks. And the liquor they were being served was the last of her stash.

She looked at the phone. Jake should have called by now with news of his meeting with the supplier. And if that wasn't enough to worry about, Fiona Sparks had taken off with no explanation.

Boom Boom assumed she'd met some john who made her an offer she couldn't refuse. Not that it took much. She'd yell at her for leaving in the middle of her shift, of course. But, in yet another crap turn of events for Boom Boom, Fiona had become too valuable to her to strong-arm, punish, or even vaguely threaten.

A knock on her door interrupted the quick downward spiral of her thoughts.

"There's a gentleman 'ere to see ya," said the bar maid, Horace. Jake. Finally.

"Send him down," Boom Boom said.

"He's right 'ere . . . followed me," said Horace.

Boom Boom stood warily. The man who emerged from the shadow of the hallway was not Jake Larkin. This man had pock-marked skin and a short, military-style haircut.

"Who the hell are you?" said Boom Boom.

"Name's O'Brian," the man said without a smile, extending his hand. Boom Boom ignored it. If she were the type of person to get nervous, she'd be shaking by now. She didn't know who this creep was, but it was clear that he meant business.

"I'm going to have to ask you to go back upstairs. We can talk at the bar."

"I don't think you want to have this conversation where our business could be overheard," the man said.

"And what business do you think that is?"

"I have it on good authority that you're running dry."

"I have it covered. So if you'll just see yourself out . . ."

"Jake Larkin is done. My boss is cutting him off."

Boom Boom sat back in her chair. "Close the door." The man moved farther into the room, and stood in front of her desk with his arms behind his back. "I don't understand," Boom Boom said.

The man nodded. "You don't need some two-bit middleman. My boss will service you directly. Through me—for security reasons."

Boom Boom pressed her fat fingers into a steeple and bounced her hands off her forehead. She didn't know what Jake did to piss these guys off, and she didn't care. This was even better. Even if there was a price increase, she wouldn't have to cut him in, and she would have more control. And if there was anything Boom Boom liked, it was control. "If the price is right, I'm ready to do business," said Boom Boom.

"Our price is our price. But I'll tell you we can have this place wetter than the ocean by tomorrow night."

Boom Boom nodded. "I'll have the cash for you first thing in the morning."

Chapter 4

AMELIA ASTOR STOOD at her bathroom sink, beating the egg white and lemon juice mixture until it was slightly frothy. That was the exact instruction from Frances Frick, who told her this was a sure way to get a glowing complexion. And with William's marriage on the brink of disaster, she needed to *glow*.

Dipping a piece of cotton into the bowl, she then applied the egg white to her face. In less than a minute, she felt the sensation that her skin was being tightly pulled. Incredible. It must be working.

"Madame Astor?" her maid called from outside the door.

"What is it? I'm busy," she said, careful not to move her face too much. Frances told her not to crack the mask until at least five minutes had elapsed.

"You have a visitor. Mr. Delacorte is downstairs."

Blasted timing!

"I'll be right there." She ran the hot water and scrubbed off the egg whites with a washcloth. Her complexion looked pinched and red, like the hide of a plucked chicken. But she reminded herself again that beauty was an arena in which she did not have to compete.

Besides, there was no time to fuss.

She threw on a deep purple housedress, silk and hand-embroidered in Paris, and fastened a necklace with pearls the size of grapes around her neck.

William was waiting for her in the parlor. She noticed immediately that he looked pale and tense.

"Is something wrong?" she said, closing the parlor door and focusing her concerned eyes on him.

He turned to her as if he'd forgotten where he was.

"No. Not at all," he said.

"Would you like a drink?" she asked, already making her way toward the liquor cabinet.

"Yes."

She poured two glasses of scotch. She handed him one and sat in a chair facing the couch, where he was sitting. After downing his drink, he gestured for her to come closer to him.

"How quickly can we reasonably plan the wedding?" he asked.

Her heart skipped a beat, until she realized he was talking about Mae and Jonathan. "Oh—I suppose the fall."

"Let's make it summer. And I want to announce the engagement in the society pages this week," he said. "What's the soonest we can have the party?"

"A few weeks?" she said, but even that would be pushing it. "I'll have to call the Union Club to see what dates are available." She knew Charlotte would hate the very idea of it. The Union Club had a way of making even the most entrenched insider feel like they didn't belong. Charlotte would feel like a leper. Amelia smiled to herself at the thought.

"Don't ask—tell them we're doing it on the sixteenth. I don't care who they have to bump. Unless the Vanderbilts are using the ballroom, I'd say they won't give us much trouble."

Amelia took a large swallow of her drink.

"Are you afraid Mae has changed her mind?"

William shook his head, slowly and pensively. "It's not Mae I'm worried about."

Amelia knew she should tread carefully. There was a fine line between friendly conversation and prying. And she certainly didn't want to slip, in a moment of weakness, into gauche behavior.

"Charlotte, then?"

William sighed deeply, and then said, with apparent reluctance, "I suspect she knows I'm unhappy with her. She's acting very strangely, and is accusing me of ridiculous things I won't even bother to bore you with. The point is, I want to give the gossip and society pages something positive to focus on: the first marriage between the Delacortes and the Astors. They won't bother with the whispers of an estrangement between Charlotte and myself."

Amelia could barely contain her smile. This was moving faster than she'd dare to imagine.

She heard the sound of people talking in the front hall.

"That's probably Mae and Jonathan just now," said Amelia.

"She wasn't with Jonathan tonight," William said, almost to himself.

"What?"

"I mean, was she out with Jonathan tonight?"

Amelia walked to the parlor door and called out to her. Mae appeared.

"Is Jonathan with you?"

"No," said Mae. She glanced at William. "You certainly do get around."

Amelia wondered what she meant by that.

"Good night," William said dismissively. Mae turned on her heels without another word.

Amelia was used to the animosity between them. But there

was something about the way Mae looked at William tonight. It was almost a look of contempt.

A pall lingered over the room.

"I should be going," William said, abruptly setting down his empty glass. He didn't look at Amelia before he left.

Chapter 5

IT WAS STRANGE to see the Vesper Club during the daytime. Jake wouldn't have been altogether surprised to find that in the light of day, it was just an unmarked storefront—and that passersby would never imagine the decadence and drama that unfolded there after dark.

But there it was, the neon sign unlit but still broadcasting the club's name in enormous letters, the pavement just in front littered with cigarette butts.

Jake pulled on the door but it was locked. He rang the delivery bell. When no one responded, he rang again two times in succession.

"Deliveries go 'rind back," answered Horace.

"I'm here to talk to Boom Boom."

The girl opened the door. It took him a minute to adjust to the darkness inside. He followed her to the bar, where Boom Boom was bent over a stack of papers. She looked up as soon as he walked into the room.

"Don't waste any more of my time." She looked back down, shuffling her papers.

"I'm sorry I didn't call last night. The source fell through. But I have a new plan . . ."

She snorted. "Fell through? More like he cut you out."

Jake ignored the sinking feeling in his gut. "It was a conflict of interest. . . ."

"The only interest I care about is my own," she said, turning her ample body to face him. "Your source contacted me directly."

Jake looked at her incredulously. William would never expose himself. "He called you?"

"He sent his man to see me. The deal is done. You're out."

Of course—O'Brian. He realized he had been kidding himself to think that he could salvage the deal . . . that he was ever going to do business in that town again. He was done.

"I did my end of the bargain; your guys played here. But you didn't deliver on your end. So don't think you or your musicians will see a penny from me."

"Don't punish the musicians. . . ."

"You should have thought of that when you wrote a check to me you couldn't cash. Now get the fuck out of my club."

ROGER WARREN SAT facing his boss. Emory Buckner leaned back in his chair, his hands behind his head, staring pensively at the ceiling. Roger squirmed in his seat.

"I'm waiting," Buckner said,

"Waiting?" Roger didn't know what he was expected to say. Had Buckner discovered he had returned to the Vesper even after he was warned not to—after he had unceremoniously been pulled off of the vice investigation? He didn't know how Buckner would have heard, but of course it was possible. He'd known that night that it was possible, and it was the chance he'd taken. And he was glad he did it, because at least for now, he still had Fiona on the line. As long as she knew Roger could ruin her and her friends, she couldn't refuse to see him.

And now he wouldn't even have to pay her for it.

"What do you have for me? I told you that if you wanted to keep your job, I expected some intel after all your nights at the club. So let's hear it."

"Yes, of course," Roger chose his words carefully as he began to perspire. Taking a deep breath, he responded, "I discovered that there is prostitution taking place at the club."

Buckner nodded. "And you wouldn't happen to have any *first-hand* knowledge of this activity, would you?"

Roger felt his face turn hot. He almost stammered his reply, choosing to ignore the pointed question. "I don't recommend busting them yet. One of the girls is talking and I think she is close to telling me more about the operations. I just need a little more time."

Emory pulled a cigar from his desk drawer. He unwrapped it slowly, then put his feet up on the desk.

He looked at Roger with all the weight and authority a man in his position could command. "I've given you too much time already. I want names. Right here, right now."

For a few seconds, Roger actually debated whether or not he should save his leverage over Fiona, or his job. And then he thought of his son, and he knew that God was being merciful, and had given him a way out.

"Jake Larkin," Roger said.

Chapter 6

CHARLOTTE AND HER father smiled at each other awkwardly across the small end table in the parlor, waiting until Penny was out of the room before they spoke. Charlotte gestured to the pitcher of mint iced tea and tray of sandwiches.

"Are you hungry?" she said.

"Charlotte, I didn't come here to eat. Or to make small talk," he father said, moving to sit next to her on the couch.

"Oh, Dad. I can hardly believe you're here," she said, feeling like she might cry.

"Of course I'm here. You knew that as soon as Rafferty called I would be on the next train."

Charlotte shook her head. "I didn't know if it was possible. I hope you didn't leave mother at a bad time."

Black Jack sighed. "Unfortunately, there is no good time. But sitting there helplessly won't change that."

Charlotte poured him a glass of tea.

"Where's William?"

"He's at the office," she said automatically. But now, for the first time, she understood that she never really knew where he was or what he was doing. "Or, actually, I don't know where he is. I never know."

"What's that supposed to mean?" said her father.

Charlotte broke down in a sob. It was the last thing she wanted to do in front of her father, but the stress of the past few weeks was finally too much.

"Charlotte, honey, it's okay." Black Jack squeezed her hand. "Tell me what's going on so I can help you." He passed her a handkerchief.

She dabbed at her eyes and nose, not sure where to start. She told him about the discovery of William's bootlegging, and saying the words aloud made the truth all the more real and frightening.

"I don't know what to do," she cried.

"This family is richer than God," her father said. "Why would he mess around with that?"

"I don't know!"

"Well, let's take a step back for a minute. I know this might be hard for you to understand, but as someone who's dealt with the

ups and downs of business, I've seen people do whatever they have
to do to keep cash flow. I know I have. And your mother didn't
always approve, but that's life."

"It's not that I don't approve—it's that he's lied to me about
everything. Or he doesn't talk to me at all. He's been traveling a
lot, but I'm supposed to stay at home all the time. I'm only allowed
out at night for fund-raisers or society event. He tells me how to
dress, who to be friends with—who to *be*. I'm starting to feel like
a prisoner in this marriage. At least Mom was your partner in
things. I'm nothing to him."

Her father hugged her tightly. "You don't have to stay in this
marriage Charlotte. Forget the money," he said. "Come back home.
We'll make do. We always have."

She shook her head, blowing her nose into the handkerchief.
"There's more," she said. "I think I'm in love with someone else.
His name is Jake. But he's been running liquor, too. And one of
Mae's friends accidentally brought an undercover agent to his
place, and now it's just a matter of time before he is arrested. I feel
so helpless."

Black Jack had a rueful smile on his face. Charlotte couldn't
believe it.

"Honestly, Dad! After everything I just told you, I can't imagine what there is for you to be smiling about."

"I can't help but think that after all the lengths your mother
went to in order to make sure you married a different sort of man
than me . . ."

"You're nothing like William," she said bitterly. "And besides—
you're not a bootlegger."

"I wish I were. There's good money in it."

"Don't say that."

"Now listen to me, Charlotte. I may not be a bootlegger, but I
haven't always been on the right side of the law. And one thing
I've learned is that they aren't after the guys doing things on a

small scale. They want the big guns. It's when they can't get to the people at the top that they settle for the little guy until they make their way up the food chain. If you want to help your friend, you have to hand the cops a bigger fish."

He locked eyes with her. Charlotte wondered if he couldn't be saying what it sounded like he was saying.

"I think I understand you," she said slowly. "I just don't know how to do it."

THE MAGIC WAS gone.

For the first time since she first set foot in the Vesper Club, Fiona didn't want to be there.

Every smile was a duty, every drink order a chore. And as for her other job . . .

"I'm not doing *that* anymore," Fiona told Boom Boom.

"Doing what?"

"Entertaining men," Fiona said.

Boom Boom was clearly not happy, but she was smart enough to stay measured.

"Why not? You don't want to make money?"

"It's trouble," Fiona said. She wished she could tell her about Roger Smith, but if Boom Boom banned the guy from the place, there was no telling what he would do—but he'd sure as hell start by getting her and Jake arrested.

Boom Boom regarded her with great focus, as if trying to solve a puzzle.

"I can't force you," she said finally. "But I think you're making a mistake."

Now Fiona looked around the room as Boom Boom walked away, immune for once to the charms of the well-heeled patrons, the riffs of jazz, and the admiring glances of men.

"Jimmy, give me a shot of vodka," she said. The bartender

handed her a short glass and a generous pour. She turned her back to the room, and downed it.

She felt a hand on her arm, and turned to find Roger.

"Drinking on the job?" he said. He was smiling, but the comment, along with the sight of him now that she knew what she knew about him, made her feel nervous and repulsed.

"What do you want?" she said.

Unbelievably, he actually seemed hurt by her terseness.

"I came to see you," he said. She looked around to see if anyone was watching them. She moved slightly closer to him, lowering her voice.

"Let's be clear: If you want to 'see' me, you have to promise me you aren't going to turn in Jake," she said.

"Can we go back to your place?"

Oh god, she muttered under her breath. "I can't keep doing this. I mean, you have to know that."

Then, with a quick glance around her, she followed him out of the club.

"I DON'T KNOW why you're so in love with this place," Ursula sniffed, sliding into a corner table in the Vesper barroom and lighting a cigarette. With her heavy accent, the word "love" sounded like "laugh," but Mae knew what she meant. Ursula wore a red dress so short Mae could almost see the bottom curve of her ass. She smelled like body odor, but on her it was somehow sexy.

Mae didn't bother explaining that she wasn't in "laugh" with the place, she was in love with one of the waitresses.

"It's a hot club, Ursula. You're so difficult to please," Jonathan said, beaming at her.

"I like the Del Rey better," she said with a pout. She examined her new ring, a twelve-carat sapphire that Jonathan had bought her to temper her jealousy over Mae's engagement ring.

Mae's eyes pored over the entire joint, but didn't see Fiona. She wondered if she'd already left for the night.

"So let's cut out of here and head to my friend's place in the Village," she said.

"See," Jonathan said to Ursula. "Mae's a team player."

"I don't know what this 'team player' means," Ursula said. "But I do understand 'out of here.'"

Chapter 7

ROGER WATCHED FIONA close the door to her apartment, and just the click of the lock had the Pavlovian effect of making him aroused.

He hadn't thought he'd be able to go through with it. What he was doing was so beyond the pale of wrongdoing, it made his initial foray into cheating and prostitution look like the stuff of choir boys. He was an attorney, after all, and knew the only word for his behavior was "blackmail."

But now that they were alone and he was just minutes away from having her, all rational thought was once again relegated to the farthest corners of his mind. He needed to feed his desire for her, to feed the beast.

Fiona retreated to the tiny corner that she called a kitchen, and poured drinks into glasses she pulled out of the sink. She handed one to Roger. The gin was warm and not very appealing served straight up, so he gulped it.

He watched her down her own drink in one shot before walking over to the bed, where she dutifully unzipped her yellow dress. Just as quickly, she shed her delicate lace bra and bloomers, and sprawled out on the bed. The sight of her tawny pubic hair spurred him to quickly shed his clothes, which he left in a pile on the floor.

He climbed onto the bed next to her. Her alabaster skin never failed to amaze him, the pinkness of her nipples an eternal delight.

She looked up at the ceiling disinterestedly, as if she were counting sheep.

Undeterred, he ran his hand from her shoulder, over her breasts, and down to her belly. Her stomach had only the slightest roundness to it, and he bent his head to kiss her at the center of this curve. Still, she stared at the ceiling, unmoved.

Roger moved on top of her, and just as he was about to enter her, to feel that sweet warmth that haunted him relentlessly, she looked up at him with her catlike green eyes and said:

"You aren't going to get Jake in trouble, are you? You have to promise me."

Roger's erection withered like a balloon with a pinhole.

He rolled away from her. Now it was his turn to look up at the ceiling.

Fiona sat up, looking at him anxiously. "What is it?" she said.

Roger got up and started pulling on his clothes. He felt Fiona watching him, and when he turned back to her, she had the sheets gripped tightly around her.

"I gave Jake's name to my boss."

He couldn't look at her once he said it. He left her apartment for the last time, his heart like lead.

"WE ARE GOING to a basement?" Ursula said, following Mae down the stairs to Jake's place.

"Trust me, it's worth it," said Mae. Jonathan looked at her skeptically, but went along with it.

Mae knocked on the door. "Giggle water," she said. The door opened, but Jake's man Maxwell blocked their entrance.

"Who's this?" he said, sizing up Jonathan.

"They're friends of mine, Maxwell. This is Jonathan Astor. He's cool."

Maxwell stepped aside, and Mae eagerly led Ursula and Jonathan into the party. In the center of the room, a space had been cleared and a small group of men—one on saxophone, two on guitar, one on drums, and one on the trumpet—played chaotic jazz riffs while couples danced with abandon around them. Mae scanned the crowd for Fiona but didn't see her.

"Is that Colleen Moore?" Ursula said, staring unabashedly at the pretty movie star.

"Yes—are you satisfied now? Is this an adequate place for us to drink?" Mae snapped.

"Okay, ladies, let's calm down. Mae, this looks like a fine establishment. So let me go to the bar and get us a round."

Mae glanced at the bar. Jake was pouring drinks.

They made their way across the crowded room.

Jake was distracted and didn't notice her at first, but when he saw her he smiled warmly. If the warning she and Fiona had given him about Roger Smith gave him any sort of pause, he certainly didn't show it. And it was clear his business had never been better: The place was packed—a crowd filled with the hip and famous, and though she didn't know that much about music, she knew that the jazz she heard at Jake's was as good as anything she heard on the radio.

"Who's your friend?" Jake said, looking pointedly at Jonathan.

"This is Jonathan Astor. My fiancé."

"Your . . . fiancé?" Jake said.

"Yes. I didn't have a chance to tell you the other night."

Jake smiled as if she was joking, but then she fluttered her left hand.

"Jeez. This is for real?"

"What can I say? I'm a lucky man," Jonathan said, lighting a cigarette. Ursula gave him a dirty look.

"And this is Ursula," Mae offered, hoping that she could make her feel less left-out.

But Jake was distracted by one of the musicians asking for a round of whiskeys.

Mae didn't want Ursula to pout all night; it wasn't good for any of their fun.

"Let's go sit over there," Mae said, pointing to a couch in the far corner of the room. They followed her, and the three sat in a row, not speaking just sipping their drinks.

"Well, I'm going to dance," Mae said, jumping up to get away.

"No, stay," said Jonathan, pulling her back to the couch. He then rearranged the seating so he was in between Mae and Ursula. He took Mae's hand, and then started kissing Ursula. Mae watched her fiancé making out with his gorgeous girlfriend, and she had to smile at the absurdity of her situation.

Jonathan turned to her.

"What?" Mae said.

Jonathan tilted his head toward Ursula. Mae looked at her, and Jonathan pressed the two women's faces closer together. Ursula slipped her hand behind Mae's head, her mouth on hers before Mae knew what was happening. Mae felt a leap of excitement in her gut, and eagerly opened her mouth to receive Ursula's tongue. Her lips were full, and tasted as exotic as she looked.

"I hate to break up this little party."

Mae jumped back at the sound of Fiona's voice.

Chapter 8

MAE LOOKED UP to see Fiona glaring at them, hands on her hips, her angry face almost as red as her hair.

"You're here? I was looking for you all night," Mae said.

"Where did you think you would find me? Between her legs?" Fiona pulled Mae by the arm.

"Um, excuse us for a second," Mae turned to call out to Jonathan.

Fiona led her through the crowd to the bar, where she summoned Jake with a wave of her hand. He put down the drink he was pouring and trotted over to them, his face registering a concern that gave Mae her first inkling that something might be wrong.

"What's going on?" he said, wiping his wet hands on his shirt.

"I have some bad news," said Fiona.

"In that case, maybe we should talk in private."

Mae followed Jake and Fiona up the flight of stairs to his loft bedroom. Mae had never seen the space, and was busy taking in the jumble of records on the floor, the scattered clothes, the unmade bed, when Fiona blurted out,

"Roger gave your name to his boss."

Jake slammed his hand on a small wooden table. "What the fuck! You said you had him under control."

"I thought I did," said Fiona, looking to Mae for help.

"There's no sense in pointing the finger," Mae said. "The important thing is, we need to get everyone out of here."

Fiona and Jake both looked at her in surprise.

"I'm not going to start running scared," said Jake.

"There's no room for your ego in this, Jake. What about all your friends down there if you get raided? Every night you stay open puts them in jeopardy."

"She's right," Fiona said quietly.

Jake ran his hands through his hair as he paced the small room. "I can't believe this," he said.

"Look, it could have been worse," said Mae. "At least you have warning."

Jake ignored her, and walked back down the stairs.

"Is he going to listen to us?" Fiona said.

Mae shrugged. "I don't know," she said. "But we better go hustle people out of here."

"Why don't you start with that cheap blonde," said Fiona.

JAKE TOLD THE musicians first. He didn't spell out exactly what was going on, he just said he was shutting down early tonight as a precaution. His heart sank as he watched them pack up their instruments, chug their drinks, and shuffle out the door.

Next he shut down the bar. By now, everyone was drunk and rowdy, and thought he was joking when he said he wasn't doing a last call. He saw Mae and Fiona doing their best to move people out the door, and it was a good thing, because after the musicians and the bar, he didn't have the heart to keep pulling the plug over and over again.

Within twenty minutes, Mae was the only one left. Even Fiona had skipped out, no doubt feeling guilty over her role in the speakeasy's quick death.

"Do you want to go have a drink somewhere?" she asked him quietly, sitting next to him on a bar stool.

He shook his head.

"I don't think you should sit here alone the rest of the night."

"It's one in the morning, Mae. The night's over."

He hated the self-pitying sound in his voice, but it was hard to just take it all on the chin.

"Have you spoken to Charlotte?" he said.

"No. I'm not allowed to use the phone at Amelia Astor's, and it's not like Charlotte can just drop by to chat. Have you?"

He nodded. "I asked her to leave William—to come be with me. But she refused."

Mae whistled. "Bold move, Larkin. And for the record, I still don't believe that my brother is really bootlegging. None of this makes sense. Maybe he was there just to bust you . . . to get you out of the way because he knows you've been seeing Charlotte."

Jake looked at her like she was crazy. "Come on, Mae. Don't be naïve. Trust me—William was just as shocked to see me as I was to see him. And speaking of shocks—what's with you and the engagement to Mr. Fancy Pants?"

"Oh—that. Let me put it in terms you'd understand: It's a business arrangement. I don't like men, and Jonathan doesn't like the sort of women he's supposed to be with. So we're a good cover for one another. People's feathers don't get ruffled, and we live our lives. I'm also hoping my 'good behavior' will shake some change loose from William's pockets."

Jake poured himself a whiskey, and offered her a glass. She shook her head.

"Aren't you a little young to sell out for the sake of appearances?"

Judging by the way she glared at him, he knew he'd touched a nerve.

"Since you're the one about to be arrested, I don't think you should be dishing out lifestyle advice," she said.

"Fair enough," he said, sipping his drink.

Chapter 9

THE LAST PLACE Charlotte wanted to be was at Amelia's house. But with feverish decorating and other preparations underway for the library's opening night gala, the board members of the Women's Literary Alliance had moved their meeting place. And the natural choice of venue was Amelia's.

Somehow, it was unspoken that Amelia had taken over as the head of the library committee. No one seemed to blink when she strode to the front of the room, running through the agenda without so much as a nod in Charlotte's direction.

Charlotte had considered skipping the meeting altogether, but William had insisted she go. And even though she had something on him—something big—she was scared to talk back or rebel against him in any way. He was no longer the man she had married; he was a criminal who had threatened to murder Jake. Who knew how he would react if she pushed back?

Sometimes, the look in his eyes made her think he would just as soon kill her.

Her father's words kept playing in her head. She knew he had been telling her to report William to the police to take the heat off of Jake, but what he didn't understand is that it would be her word against William's, one of the most financially influential and upstanding men in New York City.

Now she understood why it was so important to William that Mae not run around in nightclubs or get caught with her cocktail waitress girlfriend: Any crack in the Delacorte armor was a crack in William's meticulously crafted persona. And he had cunningly anticipated the day when his reputation might be all that stood between him and an arrest.

"The thing we must do this week is get *all* the book donations to the Fifty-seventh Street house as soon as possible. We have volunteers shelving nearly around the clock, and I want as much done by the night of the gala as possible," Amelia said.

Charlotte thought of the collection of nearly full boxes of books she had neglected to send over. She made a mental note to take care of it when she returned home.

"But before we go any further into library business, I have a family announcement," Amelia said, her voice almost shrill with delight.

Charlotte looked up, her gut clenching. And then all eyes turned to Mae walking into the room. She was dressed almost demurely for once, in a high-necked silk dress that was the color of a ripe plum. A murmur broke out in the group.

"I wanted you to hear it here first—before the announcement in the society pages," said Amelia. "My cousin, Jonathan Astor, has asked Mae Delacorte to marry him."

Everyone turned to look at Charlotte, who reacted stone-faced. She knew she was supposed to smile, but the exclusion of her in the announcement was a stunning slap in the face.

"Yes . . . Charlotte and I are family now," said Amelia. "Isn't that right, Charlotte?"

Charlotte looked at Amelia and Mae standing next each other, and felt like the walls were closing in on her.

"Excuse me," she managed to say, before rushing out of the room.

The valet brought her car around, and she headed straight downtown.

Seeing Mae play along with William and Amelia's games terrified her. Mae knew as much as Charlotte did about William—well, nearly as much. And so she chose to become even more entrenched in the status quo? It made Charlotte all the more determined to intervene.

She parked the car around the corner from Jake's, and walked quickly to his building. It was the height of stupidity for her to risk going to his apartment, but the meeting at Amelia's had made her feel her entire world evaporating, and only Jake—and her desire for Jake—felt real.

"I'm sorry, I shouldn't be here—William will kill you if he finds out," she said by way of greeting.

But her words were lost in his kiss, his mouth bruising on her lips. She gasped at the surge of need that flooded her body.

He said nothing, but shut the door quickly and pulled her dress off of one shoulder, baring her breast, which he took greedily into his mouth. Charlotte leaned back, bracing herself against the wall. Jake slipped his hands behind her, deftly unbuttoning her dress until it dropped to the floor. She raked her hands through his hair, pulling it as his mouth moved from her breasts to her belly to the aching need between her legs.

On his knees now, he pulled off her bloomers, and the sensation of his tongue against her most sensitive point pushed a moan from her.

"Don't stop," she whispered. She kept her eyes closed, embarrassed by her wanton display but unable to control herself. When he pressed his fingers inside of her, she felt a surge of pleasure so intense it was almost pain. "Jake," she gasped as his hand moved more quickly. Just when she was on the brink, he pulled his hand away, and gently eased her to the floor, moving on top of her with such quickness and fluidity she barely had to suffer the absence of his touch between her legs. He filled her so quickly and completely that within seconds, he brought her to a full orgasm. Just as she finished, he shouted out, moving inside of her with such ferocity, it triggered another wave of pleasure.

Afterward, they lay side by side on the floor, and Jake reached for her hand.

"I hope you came here to tell me you're ready to leave him," he said.

Oh no—not this again.

"I'm working on it," she said, looking away. She knew he would tell her she was crazy if she told him what she was planning to do—or worse, he would try to stop her.

"Why don't I believe you?" he said.

She felt a flash of anger.

"I don't know. Why don't you? Jake, we've been over this. I told you I'm not just going to run away. But I have a plan. I just don't want to talk about it yet. In the meantime, I think you should shut this place down before someone turns you in."

"Too late for that," he said, so casually she wasn't sure she heard him right.

"What do you mean?"

"Fiona's friend from the DA's office."

Charlotte sat up quickly and put her head in her hands. "Jake, no."

"It's okay—I'm going to get out of town for a while. Try my luck in Chicago. Louis says it's a real scene."

"You don't have to leave. They might not even come after you—you're a . . . a . . . small fish," she said, channeling her father.

He smiled tenderly at her. "And who have you been talking to?"

"I don't want you to go. I'll help you get a lawyer. No one caught you in the act—it's just one person's word. . . ."

"Charlotte, stop. Whatever does or doesn't happen today, or tomorrow, or next week—it's all going to hell. It's time to cut loose."

She tried not to feel hurt, but her eyes filled.

"And what about us?"

He pulled her close to him. His body was cool with a thin sheen of perspiration. She touched her tongue to his shoulder and tasted salt, but then thought maybe it was her own tears.

"Charlotte, you don't want anything to change. You don't think you should leave William; you don't think I should leave New York. Without gutsy moves, there *is* no us. Don't you understand that?"

"But they should be the right decisions. Your leaving town doesn't solve anything. The authorities could see you as fleeing— they could come after you."

He shook his head. "As long as I'm not right under their noses, I'm not worth much effort on their end."

There was a knock at the door.

"Who is that? Are you expecting someone?" She jumped up and quickly slipped her dress over her head and did her best to button it. She combed her fingers through her hair so her blunt bob would fall into some semblance of order.

"No. Maybe it's the police."

"That's not funny," Charlotte said.

Jake pulled on his pants and ambled over to the door, and looked out the keyhole. He opened the door a few inches, and asked whoever was there to come back in ten minutes. He closed the door and turned to face her, his hand still on the knob.

"I take it that wasn't someone with your arrest warrant."

"No," he said. "Just a friend. But I knew you wouldn't want to be seen here like this."

She glanced at his pile of clothes on the floor. "It might be hard for me to get back here—at least for a little while. I was only able to sneak out because I was at a meeting for the library."

He walked over to her and folded her into his arms, resting his head on top of hers. She squeezed him hard, her eyes closed, her heart beating fast. He pulled away gently.

"Good-bye, Charlotte."

She knew there was no point in trying to reason with him. The time for talking was over.

It was time for action.

Chapter 10

Jake leaned with his back against the door.

He didn't know how long he would have stayed like that after Charlotte's visit if he had been left alone. But two sharp knocks jolted him out of his fog.

Out of extra caution, he checked the peephole. As expected, it was Rona Lovejoy.

"Sorry about that," he said, holding the door open.

"I saw Mrs. High Society leave, so I figured it was safe for me to come back." She sauntered in, taking off her velvet shawl and throwing it on a chair

"I need to be discreet for Charlotte's sake. She would be mortified."

"That's one way to put it," Rona said. "Another way might be . . . jealous?"

Jake shook his head. "I told her that you and I are just friends, and she knows I'm not lying."

"So what do I have to do to make a liar out of you, Larkin?"

He was surprised by her bluntness.

"Just teasing," she said. "That's not why I came to see you. I hear you're closing down shop."

He nodded, a bit warily. "That's right."

"You don't have to look at me like that, Larkin—I'm not going to give you shit about it."

He laughed. "That's good to know."

"My brother is opening a joint in Chicago," she said. "Joe Oliver's guys will play there for the opening weeks or so but after that . . ." She trailed off, holding out her hands and shrugging.

Jake knew all about Joe Oliver, the cornet player and bandleader

who left New Orleans because of all the violence and racial tension. He moved to Chicago, where he was now known as the jazz
king. Louis Armstrong raved about him.

"My brother needs someone to book musicians and generally
run the place. Interested?" she said with a smile.

"Is this for real?" he said.

"Oh, I'm for real, baby. And if you ask me, you should jump on it."

Jake wondered why everything out of her mouth sounded like
a come-on.

"It's an interesting proposition," he said.

"No shit," she said. "And don't be worrying about having no
friends in that town. I'm packing my bags already." Her chocolate
brown eyes were bright and mischievous.

"You're leaving New York?"

She nodded. "This city's beat. And what do you got to lose?"

Jake hesitated for a minute. He looked at the floor, where less
than twenty minutes ago he had been making love to Charlotte.
"I don't know anymore. Maybe nothing."

AMELIA FELT SATISFIED.

The Women's Literary Alliance meeting had been productive,
the group suitably impressed by her announcement of the Delacorte-
Astor engagement. The only unpleasantness had been Charlotte's
mad dash from the room, never to return. Of course, Amelia had
to tell William about it. That's what friends were for.

As expected, he had not sounded pleased. And then he said
he'd be right over.

She paced her bedroom, eager to see him.

When her butler announced William's arrival, Amelia smoothed
the skirt of her dress and walked down the stairs, trying to repli-
cate the regal display Mae had put on when she descended the first
night Jonathan had come to see her.

"I hope this isn't a bother," said William.

"Of course not," said Amelia.

"So let me get this straight: She just ran out of the meeting without a word to anyone?"

"That's right," Amelia said, trying not to smile.

"I checked my house and she's not there. I *told* you she's acting strangely. Her behavior is truly disturbing. Even the things she says are becoming erratic."

"Such as?"

"Oh, asking for money. She never used to, but now that Mother is gone, I think she sees it as her payday."

Amelia shook her head and made a clucking sound. "There's no substitute for good breeding. And really, no end to the damage in its absence."

"I feel like a fool."

Amelia went to his side, touching his shoulder. "You mustn't blame yourself."

And then, to her absolute shock and delight, William pulled her close to him. With her face inches from his, she could only pray that the egg-white masks were doing their job.

And then he kissed her.

How long had it been since a man had kissed her? And while William's mouth felt dry, his lips somewhat rigid on hers, her heart soared with triumph. How far she had come since the day of his wedding, when she had sat in the church pew, agonizing as Charlotte walked down the aisle, looking like a princess in her white silk Lanvin gown; Amelia had been certain that she would forever be relegated to the sidelines while some interloper stole the man she had been destined for since childhood.

He stepped back, but held on to her hands. "If she comes back here for some reason—perhaps to talk to Mae—call me immediately."

"Um, yes. Of course," Amelia was somewhat thrown by the

way he just resumed their conversation as if nothing out of the ordinary had transpired between them.

William walked to the door. "Are we all set for the engagement party next week?"

Amelia tried to reconcile herself to a universe in which a kiss—and an adulterous one, at that—segues seamlessly into banal scheduling conversation.

"The Union Club is confirmed. Oh, which reminds me: That vile gossip columnist, Greta something-or-other, called me to haggle for an invitation. I was really put off and told her it was private affair. But I can't guarantee she won't try to talk her way in at the door. You know what it's come to with the press these days."

"Let her come," William said. She was surprised not just by his opinion on the matter, but by how quickly he answered, as if there were no doubt in his mind. He saw her hesitation, and added, "In fact, I think it would be a good idea for you to go to the paper and give her an invitation."

"I don't understand," she said.

"The gossips are here to stay. If she's going to be sniffing around our party, let her come as our guest."

"If you think it's a good idea. I'll have Mumson deliver the invitation to the newsroom."

"I think you should go yourself. Make it personal. If a scandal should happen to break, we want her on our side. You know what they say, Amelia: Keep your friends close, and your enemies closer."

He smiled at her on his way out the door.

GRETA GOUCHER STORMED into the second-floor newsroom of the *New York Sun* offices. She was not happy to be summoned into her editor's office right in the middle of typing her column for the week.

She made her way across the smoke-filled room, the clattering of typewriter keys so loud she could barely think. It was funny; when she was behind her own typewriter, she didn't notice the racket. But as soon as she stepped away from her desk, she realized she was surrounded by deafening noise.

"I hope this is important, Lou. I was on a roll," she said, stalking into Lou Steinberg's office. It was stacked floor to ceiling with books and newspapers, and nearly every free surface was covered with overflowing ashtrays.

"Oh yeah?" he said, still working on his breakfast plate of runny eggs and sausage. "Are there hookers in this one?"

"Not this week," she said. No, the column she was writing was more uptown—her favorite type of story to break: a little sex, a little politics, a little money. And the fact that only about a quarter of it was based on actual facts didn't bother her a bit. Greta Goucher hadn't made a name for herself in the cutthroat world of gossip—not to mention the old boys' club of newspapers—because of facts; she was where she was because of her instincts.

Ever since she was a girl, Greta Goucher could sniff out a story. She liked to tell people that growing up as the third of seven children on the crowded Lower East Side—where she had to fight for every extra piece of bread at meals, for every inch of space in the apartment, and for every minute of attention from her overworked mother—had made her a keen observer of human nature, and a patient one: She knew when to yell to get what she wanted, but more important, she learned how to be quiet and listen. She learned the rhythms of her household and of her neighborhood, and although she was on the lookout for things she needed for basic survival, all her listening and snooping led to inadvertently picking up a lot of entertaining secrets along the way. And she held on to these little gems of hearsay: Is the widow Kaplan pregnant? Mrs. Goldfarb hasn't paid the butcher in six months and he won't sell her any meat?

The tidbits were endless, and Greta stored them in her mind like gold in the vault, only doling them out when she needed something in return. By the time she was a teenager, information became Greta's most valuable commodity.

Now, at a time when gossip columns were springing up faster than two-bit speakeasies, Greta Goucher had made a name for herself by not focusing on the easy Hollywood gossip. Instead, she won readers' devotion with what she called "flip-siders"—stories that involved both high culture and low culture, and that showed the private side of people's public personas. And she had learned that the only place to find these stories was where most people didn't think to look.

"I'm sorry to interrupt your Pulitzer-prize-winning work," he said sarcastically. "But you have a visitor."

"Who is it?"

He shrugged. "Someone fancy. Maybe she's a fan. Or maybe you ran a story about her husband." He chuckled. "Either way— she's sitting out in reception."

"Can I borrow a notepad?" she said, lifting an ashtray to take paper from his desk.

She couldn't imagine who could be asking for her. No one had ever shown up at the paper. Maybe her career was about to go up a notch.

Greta made her way to the reception area right outside of the newsroom. It was more of a corridor than a room, and just opening the door risked knocking into the two chairs. Before she opened the door, Greta gave herself a minute to peek through the glass to see if she recognized her visitor.

She was tall and broad-shouldered, with brown hair in an old-fashioned knot. She wore a maroon silk dress, obviously expensive but not entirely fashionable. The dress was rendered incidental by an enormous yellow diamond brooch in the shape of a bird. Who needed fashion when you had wealth?

Greta knew she had seen the woman before, but couldn't summon her name. She pushed open the door and the woman rose to her feet.

"Miss Goucher?" the woman said.

"Yes. Can I help you?"

"I'm Amelia Astor," the woman said. "You called me about the engagement party for Mae Delacorte?"

Greta nodded. The woman had been so rude on the phone. Had she come down here just to yell at her for making the call?

Amelia Astor reached into her handbag and pulled out a cream-colored envelope.

"Please do come as my guest," she said, handing over the envelope. Greta opened it and pulled out an invitation to the Union Club.

"Thank you, Miss Astor," Greta said, trying to act as if this sort of thing was routine. "I will certainly be there."

Amelia Astor smiled tightly and all but ran out of the room in the manner of someone who had performed a necessary but deeply unpleasant task.

Greta had no idea what was going on. But she had every confidence she would figure it out—and when she did, Amelia Astor might get more than she bargained for.

Chapter 11

THE UNION CLUB, founded in 1836, was the oldest private club in Manhattan—and a bastion of exclusivity.

It had only been in the past seven years that women were allowed to set foot into the Union Club—and only then because they needed female waitstaff when the men were called off to war.

Although William's family had been members since the beginning, Charlotte had never been inside the limestone clubhouse on the northeast corner of Fifth Avenue and Fifty-first Street. How fitting that on a night when she could not feel more like an outsider, she was finally dining in a place that existed only in service of the ultimate insiders.

The front hall was lined with portraits of members who had passed: John Alsop King, governor of New York. Ward McAllister, arbiter of society; Ulysses S. Grant; J. P. Morgan; Leland Stanford, who went on to found the university in his name; Cornelius Vanderbilt; Rutherford Stuyvesant, who built the first apartment building in New York City; and of course, the ill-fated John Jacob Astor IV, who died shockingly on the *Titanic* thirteen years ago nearly to the day.

Charlotte handed her fox stole to the attendant, and waited for William to offer his arm before they entered the dining hall. He did not.

They had not spoken in days, but she had assumed he would at least put on a front while they were out in public. The fact that he made no effort to do so was alarming to her. She realized, now more than ever, that William did not do things by chance or without calculation. If he was signaling to the most important people in New York that there was a rift between them, he was doing so for a reason—a reason that was certainly not in her favor.

Waiters in black tie circulated with silver trays filled with glasses of white wine. The Union Club had a rumored stash of fourteen years' worth of wine and liquor. Since it had all been purchased before Prohibition went into effect, it was legal to serve it.

The reception hall, with its oak paneling, was too dark to look truly festive, but Amelia had done an undeniably good job of brightening it with dozens of arrangements of peonies and lilies in wide crystal vases. The sideboards along the walls were decorated with pieces of K'ang-Hsi porcelain, and the walls were covered in portraits, the most striking of which were a Joshua Reynolds portrait of Richard Boyle, the Earl of Shannon, and a large Thomas Gainsborough painting of William IV, Duke of Clarence.

Charlotte awkwardly made her way to their designated table

by herself, while William worked the room, greeting guests according to their hierarchy of importance. She watched him with disgust: the great Mr. Delacorte, pillar of society.

If they only knew.

As she placed her evening bag on her seat, she felt someone staring at her. She looked up to find that small, horse-faced woman from the funeral reception watching her carefully.

The gossip columnist. What the hell was she doing here? This was the last thing she needed.

Charlotte got up from the table and made her way over to her.

"Excuse me—Miss Goucher, isn't it?"

"That's right. Nice to see you again, Mrs. Delacorte. Congratulations on your sister-in-law's impending nuptials."

"I don't know how you got in here, but as we told you at the funeral for my mother-in-law, this is a private affair. I'm going to have to ask you to leave."

The woman smiled. "I hate to disappoint you, but I'm a guest of Miss Astor's."

"I sincerely doubt that."

Greta glanced pointedly across the room at Amelia. "Feel free to go ask her. I'm sure she'll be happy to get you up to speed. Or maybe you can ask your husband? It might give you two something to talk about." And with that, she walked away.

Charlotte looked after her, mouth agape. The nerve! Was it really possible that Amelia wanted the horrid woman at the party? And for what?

With nothing else to do, Charlotte retreated to her seat. The table was now filling with guests, people slowly finding their place cards. Amelia had rigidly structured the seating in a manner so controlling, it made Charlotte's late mother-in-law seem lax by comparison.

A man sat next to Charlotte. He had a high forehead and a significant coif of hair—wavy on the top but short on the sides. His lips were thin, his eyes intelligent as he nodded to her.

It took a moment, but Charlotte realized she was seated next to Emory Buckner, head of the New York attorney's office. *The man who might soon be prosecuting Jake.*

She took a sip of her water.

Across the room, Mae made her entrance. She looked radiant, appearing very much the bride-to-be in love—if you didn't know any better, which Charlotte certainly did. Mae wore a pale pink, bias cut evening gown, beaded from neckline to bottom, and fringed with fuchsia feathers. It had no doubt cost a fortune, and Charlotte wondered who had paid for it. Mae wore a matching bandeau around her head, with a single feather. Around her neck were ropes of pearls. Guests clustered around her, eager to congratulate the future Mrs. Astor.

"Your family has a lot going on these days," Emory Buckner said.

"Excuse me?"

"I said, your family seems quite busy—building the library, and now a wedding." He smiled at her.

"Oh . . . yes. We're busy." He should only know how busy William is, she thought. And then she remembered her father's words, and finally saw part of the answer sitting right next to her. But how?

Emory Buckner was at the party as William's guest. She would never be able to just come out and say it. It would always be her word against William's. She couldn't *tell* Buckner; she had to show him. *Yes, Mr. Buckner. In fact, William has been exceedingly busy running a secret bootlegging operation. Would you like to stop by sometime and see his secret pile of cash at the house? Or perhaps his gun?*

The problem was that even if she wanted to blow things up like that, cash in the house did not prove anything. A gun wasn't necessarily illegal. But there had to be some sort of evidence in that locked room.

She mentally revisited the office: the file cabinets. The desk top. The desk drawer. And then she remembered the ledgers. The leather-bound books were filled with columns of numbers. Maybe they were records of William's legitimate business dealings. But maybe not.

And then she realized the perfect way to smuggle the ledgers out of the house.

"Mr. Buckner, will you be attending the library opening next week?" she said.

"I'm afraid not. My time is very limited these days."

"Well, Geraldine Delacorte always said, you can tell more about a society by its art than by its politics. Surely you can take an evening to support a new cultural institution."

He smiled faintly. "It's a nice sentiment, but then, Mrs. Delacorte wasn't practicing law enforcement during Prohibition. I can't remember the last time I had a moment to visit a library or museum."

Charlotte tried not to be deterred.

"Maybe you can make an exception," Charlotte said. And then, her heart pounding, she added unwaveringly, "You never know where you will stumble upon your next big case."

Buckner turned to look at her, but she couldn't quite meet his gaze. She feigned interest in the china set in front of her.

"Mrs. Delacorte? Just so we're clear: You're suggesting the library opening might be an event I should not miss?"

Charlotte finally made eye contact with him, looked at him directly for a long while, and nodded almost imperceptibly.

"Then I shall be sure to make an appearance," he said.

Charlotte stood, feeling shaky.

"Excuse me for a moment."

She walked quickly into the hall, fanning herself with her napkin. The air was mercifully cooler outside of the dining room.

And then she heard a familiar voice in the entrance foyer.

"Oh, I'll find my table. I don't want to be a bother."

Charlotte moved to the front door. Sure enough, Fiona was

handing the attendant her stole. She wore a demure, lavender silk chiffon gown. Her riotous hair was, for once, pulled back in a discreet French twist. She wore very little makeup, and appeared every inch a lady.

"What are you doing here?" Charlotte said, taking her by her white-gloved elbow.

"Crashing the engagement party, obviously," she replied.

"Yes, I can see that," said Charlotte. "The question is, why? Do you need to cause a fuss all the time?"

"Why? Because I realize I'm in love with her. And I'm not going to cause a fuss. No one will notice one extra person at this circus. I spent a small fortune on this dress. Do you like it?"

"Yes, it's lovely. You look lovely. But that's beside the point. Please, just stay clear of William. He might recognize you from the night we crashed his little party with Jake." Could the night get any more stressful, Charlotte wondered.

"I'll keep my distance. Don't be such a worrier." Fiona snagged a glass of wine from a passing waiter. "Nice," she said with a smile. "I wish I'd known. I wouldn't have bothered to fill my flask."

Chapter 12

AMELIA HAD TO hand it to herself: Her seating arrangement at the table was pure genius. By dividing the couples so husbands and wives were not seated next to each other—a little tip to she picked up from her grandmother, a legendary New York hostess—she was able to maneuver it so that she was seated next to William.

She felt the table deferring to them as the host and hostess of the evening. Sitting next to William, she didn't feel a sexual tension so much as the frisson of energy that comes from consolidation of power. Her decision, for years, to turn down inadequate suitors was finally validated; the way they played off of each other, buoying the conversation like a well-executed tennis match, kept everyone entertained. She had no doubt that every woman at the table would in the future make sure to seat them next to each other at their own parties to ensure a similar liveliness.

Unfortunately, their momentum was disrupted when her cousin Charles—Jonathan's father and an irritating drunk—stood to make a toast. His wife Annabeth—an imbecile—banged a spoon against her water goblet to get everyone's attention.

"Everyone, if I could have your attention for just a moment. I want us to raise our glasses to our son, Jonathan, and his beautiful bride-to-be, the lovely Mae Delacorte. I have to say, his mother and I didn't think we'd ever see this day. . . ."

In the midst of Charles's rambling speech, William leaned over and whispered in her ear, "Meet me in the card room. Upstairs, two doors down on the right. Next to the library."

She nodded, her stomach leaping in anticipation.

William left the table, and Charlotte watched him. Amelia just hoped that she didn't get up to follow.

Amelia allowed a few minutes to pass, and then excused herself.

In the interest of discretion, she waited in the front hallway for a few seconds to make sure no one was around. When she was satisfied no one took notice of her, she quickly climbed the stairs.

The noise of the party below emphasized the stillness and silence of the upper floor. Following William's direction, she made her way to the designated room.

She walked in tentatively. Well aware of the club's storied male history, she wondered if she was the first woman to see this particular room. Like most of the building, the room was dark wood, the only dashes of color coming from the green velvet draperies and carpet. The room was lit by silver walk sconces and a silver chandelier. She judged the furniture to be mostly Queen Anne pieces with some Chippendale thrown in.

William, seated in a carved mahogany armchair, looked quite at home. As if he owned the place, really.

"You did an excellent job with this party, Amelia. As always."

"I appreciate your trusting me to get it off the ground. Fortunately, Charles didn't interfere. He was just happy not to have to chip in for the bill. Is there anything worse than cheap relations?"

She sat in a chair across from him.

"Oh, I could think of a few things. Like a money-grubbing wife."

Amelia looked at him in surprise.

"Have things become that bad?" Amelia didn't know what to make of this turn. After her years of subtly working to sabotage Charlotte, to strategically reveal her shortcomings, William was suddenly finding a level of fault with his wife that was beyond the best efforts of Amelia's wildest orchestration.

"I'm afraid so," he said. "And she knows I have had it with her—that I intend to leave."

With great effort, Amelia maintained a calm facial expression. "Did you tell her so explicitly?"

"No," he said slowly, as if choosing his words with great care. "But she is smart—cunning, really. She made it clear that if I left her, she would not go easily. She will make trouble for me, Amelia."

"How can she? She's nobody," Amelia said vehemently.

"She threatened to publicly accuse me of ill-gotten gains—to say that my business is not legitimate."

"Oh, that's absurd. She's out of her mind."

William stood and paced the room. "That may be, but the truth is, there's a witch-hunt climate out there right now for anyone violating the Volstead Act."

"The Volstead Act? Oh, William. What is she going to do? Accuse you of being a bootlegger? It's so absurd I can't even say it with a straight face."

William nodded his head. "You're right. I'm sure this is just my feelings of guilt playing tricks on my sense of reason."

"Guilt? Whatever for?"

"For realizing I married the wrong woman. It was always you, Amelia. I was just young and stupid and ignored the push my mother had always given me in your direction. It was childish, and I've been paying for it ever since."

Amelia took his hand. "I'll see you through this—you know that, don't you? I will not allow a scandal." As she pledged her allegiance to him, her mind wandered to visions of herself moving into the Delacorte mansion, the new pulse of the social heart of Manhattan. Her reign would make Geraldine Delacorte—and even her own grandmother, Cecilia Von Deer Astor—dim memories.

Her days as the sidelined spinster were coming to an end. And she wasn't going to let any ninth-hour desperate machinations on Charlotte's part change that.

THERE WAS A break between dinner and dessert service, and everyone used that time to get up from their designated tables and mingle. As usually happened at such affairs, the guests seated at the host table—the most desirable table—didn't get to wander very far. The rest of the room practically tripped over themselves in their effort to get face time. Mae made an exception, however, at Amelia's prodding. She extricated herself from her table and made her way across the room to talk to Jonathan's ninety-seven-year-old great-grandmother.

Mae sat next to her, and the woman put her tiny veined hand on Mae's arm, and pronounced, "Thank goodness for you, dear girl. How many years can one be a bachelor without suspicion that one does not like women at all?" She winked one droopy eye.

Mae looked at her in surprise.

"Mae, can I borrow you for a second? Excuse us, Granny," said Jonathan.

When they were a few paces away, Mae said, "I hate to break the news, but your great-grandmother suspects you are a homosexual."

"How ironic that she should confide that in you," he said. "But speaking of—isn't that Fiona I see in the corner talking to Mr. McDonough?"

Startled, Mae followed his gaze to a slender woman wearing a demure lavender gown. Her arms were covered with long white gloves, and her hair was pulled back so tautly, it was hard to discern the flaming red color unless you knew to take notice of it.

"Oh, good lord. What is she doing here?"

"I wish you'd told me you were sneaking her in; I would have gotten Ursula in somehow."

Mae shook her head. "I had no idea she would come here. She probably just doesn't want to feel left out."

"I agree—she shouldn't be left out," Jonathan said, a devilish glint in his eyes. "So why don't you tell her to meet us upstairs in that library room. We'll have our own little party."

Chapter 13

JAKE MADE HIS way backstage at the King Club. The room was cloudy with marijuana smoke, and filled with the sweet strains of the house band, with Rona singing the blues.

He paused by the side of the stage, pulling the dark blue curtain aside to look at her. She was bathed in a violet stage light, and her angelic voice poured into the room. He thought how much more sense his life would make if Rona was the woman he was in love with.

"A sight for sore eyes, eh?"

Jake turned to find the man he had come to see: Lawrence

"the King" Lovejoy, proprietor of the most successful jazz club in Harlem.

"And ears," said Jake. "You're lucky you get the family discount for booking her; otherwise, you probably couldn't afford her."

"I don't get no discount," Lawrence said with a deep, booming laugh. "My sister is one tough negotiator. Don't let that sweet sound fool ya." Despite Jake's height, Lawrence Lovejoy still towered over him. The large man slapped a hand on Jake's shoulder, and said, "Come into my office."

Lawrence's office was surprisingly big, complete with a sofa and card table. One corner was filled with instruments. His desk was cluttered with three different ashtrays, all full.

"You know what I call that couch?" he said. Jake shook his head. "I call it Hotel Lovejoy. If I had a dollar for every musician who slept on that couch, I'd be a rich man."

"Maybe you're in the wrong business."

"No, I'm in exactly the right business, and that's what you're here to talk about, ain't it?" Lawrence gestured toward the couch with a sweep of his long arm.

"This is true," Jake said, looking up at a signed picture of a cornet player. The signature read "Bix." "Who's that?"

"That? You don't know Big B?"

Jake shook his head.

"That's Bix Beiderbecke. He just made his first recording last year, but you will know that name, mark my words. Jake, this world is filled with talented musicians. But you know what we don't got enough of?"

"I'm guessing I don't," Jake said with a smile, accepting a cigar Lawrence offered him.

"Good businessmen. But I do my best, Jake, and I think I've got a good sense and a good eye, and I know Chicago is the way to go. But I need a man on the ground and can't be at two places at once, you know what I'm talking about?"

"Yes," Jake said, knowing he should be excited by the conversation, but experiencing instead an undeniable sinking feeling. "I think I do."

"There's a few guys around here who wouldn't mind that shift, you know what I'm saying? But you come highly recommended by my sister, and I am not fool enough to think my sister is just a pretty face. Besides, I know how you is with the musicians. And I know you live and breathe this shit the same as the rest of us. So as far as I'm concerned, if you want it, the job is yours."

Jake shifted on the cushion, trying to avoid a wayward spring.

"Lawrence, I'm flattered. You know how I feel about this place—and about you and Rona, too. I just need a few days to think about it."

"Don't be thinkin' too hard," said Lawrence. "No good can come from that. Now, what you say we get back in the club? My sister would kill me if I kep' you in here fo' her entire act."

But from the sounds of it, they were already too late. Rona's sweet blues had been replaced by the frenetic jungle sound of the house band in full-jazz mode.

The office door opened.

"I thought I'd find you two in here," Rona said, her liquid brown eyes sharply focused on Jake.

"We was just finishing up," Lawrence said.

"Good timing," she said. "Because I need to borrow our man Larkin an' talk to him in private."

MAE AND FIONA followed Jonathan up the wide central staircase. They made their way down the second-floor hallway, laughing drunkenly before tumbling into a library. The room was all dark wood paneling and oak furniture, with royal blue drapery and carpets.

Jonathan closed the door and put his fingers to his lips to shush them.

"Who decorated this place? Martha Washington?" said Fiona.

"She wouldn't have been allowed in the front door," said Mae, slurring. She knew she should have stopped after the sixth or so glass of wine. But the weight of the charade, the effort it took to deal with all of those well-wishers under the ever-watchful eyes of Amelia and William . . . it was just too much. And the way everyone kept talking about her mother, "I'm certain Geraldine is smiling down from heaven." Laughing is more like it, she thought. If her mother had just given her an inheritance outright, Mae never would have been drawn into the farce of an engagement. It was no doubt exactly the result her mother had wanted, if not outright orchestrated.

And then there was Charlotte and William. They were obviously not even speaking to each other. Mae was surprised her brother would let the tension be so obvious to the casual observer. It was unnerving—he was usually much more disciplined when it came to public appearances. Mae wanted to talk to Charlotte about it, but every time she got close to her they were interrupted. The entire evening felt less like a celebration than a walk through a minefield.

Jonathan pulled a bottle of gin from his jacket.

"Where did you get that?" said Fiona.

"Smuggled it from the barroom." He opened it with a flourish.

"We don't have glasses," said Mae. Jonathan took a swig from the bottle and handed it to her. She did the same, and passed it to Fiona.

"A toast," he said, raising a phantom glass. "To my bride-to-be, and her very beautiful . . . what would you say? Lover? Girlfriend."

"All of the above," said Fiona.

"You're not my girlfriend anymore," Mae said pointedly. "You broke up with me, remember?"

Fiona rolled her eyes. "Are you still stuck on that?"

Mae thought of the day she met Fiona at the tobacco shop. She remembered the ribbon in Fiona's hair, and her careless beauty as Fiona told her that she couldn't make her any promises—that she needed to make money.

And she thought of how Fiona was making that money.

"Stuck on you telling me you don't want to be together? That you can't make any promises? Yes!"

"Well, looks like you two will just have to kiss and make up," said Jonathan.

Mae sat in one of the chairs, crossing her arms over her chest. Fiona sat on the arm of the chair.

"I do want to make up," Fiona whispered. "Don't you?" Her hair was coming undone from its twist. Mae reached up and slowly pulled one of the pins to let the glorious russet locks fall loose.

"Are you still doing that . . . business? With the men at the club?" Mae said.

Fiona's hair fell in a curtain across Mae's face as she leaned down to her.

"No," Fiona said softy. "The only business I want to do is you."

"Mmm," Mae murmured, as the room tilted.

Fiona put one finger under Mae's chin, and tilted her face up to hers. She kissed her, deeply and with possession. Mae felt her insides do a little flip, and reached her arms around Fiona, eager to feel her close, to be able to touch her and smell her after all of these weeks apart.

Fiona stroked Mae's breasts over the thin fabric of her dress, and the throbbing between her legs was immediate and insistent.

"I've missed you, baby," Fiona murmured, sliding down to the floor in front of her.

Mae was dimly aware that Jonathan was still in the room, watching them. Under different circumstances—if she were sober, or if she was not overwhelmed with pent-up sexual desire—

this would have deterred her. But as it was, she could not have stopped if the entire dinner party invaded the room.

Fiona pushed up Mae's dress, kissing the inside of her thighs. Mae lay back against the chair, closing her eyes. She felt Mae pulling down her underwear, the lacy fabric brushing her thighs on the way down, over her ankles, and then . . . the wet heat of Fiona's tongue against the throbbing center between her legs.

Mae moaned, the room tilting as the alcohol and a rush of intense pleasure worked in tandem to push her toward sweet, unconscious oblivion.

The last thing she heard, from a distance, as if filtered through water, was a vaguely familiar female voice saying, "Well, well, well—what do we have here?"

Chapter 14

FIONA JUMPED BACK with a start.

The Goucher woman was standing in the doorway, smiling with glee. She closed the door behind her and walked into the room.

"Get out!" Jonathan said. "You have no business being up here."

"Oh, I think I do. This sort of scandalous depravity is exactly my business. And I can't wait to see what the denizens of Gotham will say when they read about it in my column next week."

Fiona looked at Jonathan for help. Mae, passed out, was useless.

"Fine," he said, reaching into his jacket pocket and taking out his wallet. "What's this going to cost me?"

Greta gave a small smile. "Money might be the only thing you people care about, but it's not so for some of us. You can't put a price on this kind of scoop."

Fiona had spent her life being pushed around and hustled. Like a boxer whose muscles are always ready to defend a blow, she deflected Greta's threat before she had time to think about the words coming out of her mouth.

"I have a better one," Fiona said.

Jonathan kept his eyes on Greta, stone-faced.

"A better story? I doubt it," said Greta.

"I do. This might be . . . scandalous. But I know something that would really put you on the map. It's the scoop of the year."

It was a bluff, of course, but a good one. The only thing more irresistible to a reporter than a good story was a better one. She just had to hope Greta was a gambler at heart.

"I don't believe you," Greta said.

"Look where you are," said Jonathan. "This is a building most New Yorkers will never set foot it. The people downstairs run this town. You think we don't know things you'll never know? Things that *matter*?"

Greta watched him, but didn't say anything for a full minute.

"Fine," she said. "I'll give you forty-eight hours to give me this so-called scoop of the year. And then I start typing my own story. And I promise you, it will be *fascinating* reading."

With that, Greta Goucher turned on her heels and strode out of the room.

Jonathan hurried to the door and closed it behind her. He stood with his back to it as if warding off any more trouble.

"Oh my god," Fiona said. "This is a disaster."

"I've got to hand it to you, that was some quick thinking. I assume, of course, that you are bluffing.

"Of course! And what good did it do? In two days we'll be in the same position."

"I'd like to see you in that same position again," he said with lascivious smile.

"That's not funny. Look, this doesn't really affect me. I don't have a reputation to worry about. But Mae does. If this story runs, that crazy brother of hers will never give her another dime. . . ." And then Fiona realized she did have a real scoop—one that would not only entertain Greta's readers, but that could destroy the entire social order of Manhattan's illustrious elite. And it could get rid of Mae's brother for a good long while.

She needed to talk to Mae—and fast. Unfortunately, from the looks of her, it wasn't going to happen until morning.

RONA PULLED JAKE into the smoky corridor between Lawrence's office and the stage.

"So what do you think?" she said, in a slightly breathless way that made him wonder if she was talking about Lawrence's job offer, or the sight of her body poured into the silver lamé dress. He opted to assume the safer of the two.

"It's an interesting proposition," he said. "I'm tempted."

She licked her lips. He realized that they might be having two different conversations.

"So what's stopping you?" she said.

He broke her gaze, and knew that no matter what they were talking about—the job or her—the answer was the same: Charlotte.

As if sensing his weakness—and therefore her opening—Rona leaned forward and pressed her lush mouth against his. She smelled like cinnamon and smoke, and the feeling of her lips against his stirred an entirely animalistic desire in him. He wanted her because any hot-blooded male would want her, and he wanted her because he wondered if she could make him forget Charlotte.

Neither one of these were good reasons—especially if he was seriously considering going into business with Lawrence.

Jake pulled back, but held her hands and looked into her eyes.

"You're an incredibly sexy woman," he said, and if she felt below his belt, she would know he wasn't lying. "But this is not a good idea."

Rona was breathing heavily. He could tell that she was not only frustrated, she was mildly annoyed.

"For a smart man, you're playin' the fool," she said. "You want to be that woman's toy? Because a woman like that has no use for someone like you. But you and me—we could do something together. We could set the world on fire, Larkin. Starting with Chicago. So why don't you think about *that* when you get into bed alone tonight."

She sauntered down the hall, her hips swinging to the beat, and back toward the stage where she would get all the adulation she needed for the next few hours.

Jake looked after her, wondering if his life was destined to be as chaotic as a jazz song.

Chapter 15

THE MORNING OF the library gala broke with the hottest temperature of the spring. Charlotte didn't know if she was sweating from the heat or from her nerves, but either way she wasn't looking forward to dressing in her gown.

She stood in the doorway of the sitting room, hands on her hips, surveying the last few boxes that needed to be taken to the library. Amelia had insisted that the books be grouped in alphabetical order to make it easier for the volunteers who would be shelving them.

The boxes were sealed, all except for one.

She glanced at clock on the mantel. It was almost noon. With only had an hour before the cut-off time for books to be delivered to the library—at least those to be shelved in time for the grand opening—she had no time left. It was now or never.

Charlotte walked into the hallway, closing the door behind

her. The house was quiet. She needed to find Rafferty; enlisting
his aid was her first hurdle. But she knew he wouldn't refuse to
help her; Rafferty had been privy to her business for too long to
fail her now. He found her looking through William's office that
first time. Then, the morning when she returned after being out
all night with Mae and Jake, Rafferty signaled to her that William
hadn't found out. Then, of course, there had been that ill-fated
and stressful trip to Philadelphia when he voiced his opinion about
Jake. And most recent, the night she'd discovered the truth about
William, Rafferty had come to the guest room, and he had known
she was distraught.

She just had to hope she hadn't counted on him one time too
many.

It was at least one fortunate consequence of Geraldine's meddling; if she hadn't insisted on choosing their servants, and assigning
them the inexperienced son of her own butler, Charlotte would
have missed out on what was turning out to be her most important
ally. More than just an ally—a friend, really. She thought of her
friend Isobel's prediction that the modern attrition rate of domes-
tic servants would make the days of lifelong servants a thing of the
past. Now, servants were marrying and leaving to have lives of
their own.

The idea of Rafferty marrying someone made her stomach
churn with jealousy.

Shaking off the thought, she walked around the first floor, but
did not have to search long: The front doorbell rang, and she heard
Rafferty moving quickly down the hall to answer it.

"I was just looking for you," she said. He stopped short. "No—
please do get the door."

Charlotte waited off to the side, trying not to feel trepidation.
There was no telling who would show up at the house with the
way things were going lately. And of course, every time the doorbell sounded, she hoped it was Jake.

She watched Rafferty accept an envelope, and then close the door.

"A delivery?" she said.

He handed her an envelope, and she tucked it under her arm. She couldn't get distracted. There was no telling what time William would return home in order to get ready for the party.

"Rafferty, can you help me with something?"

"Of course," he said, "Anything."

And she knew he meant it.

"I need to do something in William's office. Can you watch the front of the house and alert me if you see him arriving?"

Rafferty nodded as if this were the most normal request in the world.

"Thank you," she said, feeling a surge of gratitude toward him. She didn't know what she'd done to elicit such devotion, but she wanted to find a way to express her gratitude.

With Rafferty watching sentry, Charlotte hurried through the parlor to William's office. She pulled a pin from her hair, and deftly went to work on the door lock. Once again, it easily yielded to the pressure of the pin. And with a quick, worried glance behind her, Charlotte let herself into the office.

Her heart immediately began to thump. She took a few deep breaths, and opened William's desk drawer. Everything looked exactly as it had the last time she was in the room. And there, sure enough, were the two leather-bound ledgers. She picked one up and flipped through it. The numbers still didn't make sense to her, but she had a feeling they would mean something to Emory Buckner. And it wouldn't be good.

She looked around the desk, wondering if there was anything else she should smuggle out and decided not. She just hoped these ledgers offered something to make it more than her word against William Delacorte's.

She knew she should just get out of the room as quickly as

possible, but she couldn't leave without checking the filing cabinet. With shaky fingers, she undid the lock, and pulled out the third drawer.

The gun was missing.

Fumbling, she closed the drawer and locked it. Clutching the ledgers to her chest, balancing the envelope that had been delivered to her on top, she hurried out of the room. She turned the lock on the office door so it would close when she shut it behind her. She waited to her the click.

Taking a minute to compose herself, she returned to Rafferty in the front hallway.

"Thank you, Rafferty. I'm finished. Now I just need for you to help me load the boxes of books into the car."

Charlotte carried the ledgers to the sitting room, and slipped them into the last box of books. She hid them under a copy of F. Scott Fitzgerald's *The Beautiful and the Damned* and, with shaking hands, sealed the box—and her own fate.

"Do you need help with that?" Charlotte looked up to find Rafferty in the doorway.

She stood up and brushed off her skirt, and the envelope fell to the floor. She hurriedly stuffed it into her purse. "These boxes are ready to go," she said.

This was it. The end of her marriage.

There had been a time when she thought she loved William. She married him thinking they would be happy together—that they would spend the rest of their lives together. And now she was about to do something that could send him to jail.

But he wasn't the man she thought she had married.

It was the end of her life as Charlotte Delacorte. The end of safety and security. But then, that hadn't really existed in the first place.

"What are you up to, Charlotte?"

She looked at Rafferty. Ever since the trip to Philadelphia, he had switched back and forth the between addressing her properly

and addressing her as a friend. At that moment, it was more welcoming and comforting than ever before.

"I'll tell you in the car on the way."

AMELIA'S DRIVER DROPPED her off at the Fifty-seventh Street
mansion, which from tonight on, would no longer be a private
home, but the grandest library in the city. The New York Public
Library might hold more books, but for elegance and cachet, it
could not compete with the Delacorte Women's Library.

She looked up at the plaque she had commissioned for place-
ment above the entranceway, inscribed with words taken from the
Latin engraving on the entrance-hall fireplace, "The house at its
threshold gives evidence of the master's good will."

Geraldine would be pleased; even more so, Amelia thought, if
she could see all that had developed between her and William.

Since the engagement dinner for Mae and Jonathan, it felt as if
she and William were a couple. That night, he had barely spoken
to his wife, and the guests, picking up the subtle social cues, treated
William and Amelia as if they were the host and hostess. Charlotte
had been completely marginalized—had it been Amelia, it would
have rendered her so humiliated she would not have been able to
appear at a public event for weeks or even months. She had hoped
maybe Charlotte would take the hint and bow out of attending
the library opening, but no such luck.

"Maybe it would be less awkward for everyone if you simply
asked her not to come," Amelia had suggested to William. He had
seemed to seriously consider this for a moment, but ultimately
decided, "I don't think it's smart to antagonize her right now."

Amelia deferred to him, of course. After all, he was the one
who had to go through the bother of a divorce.

She fished around her handbag for her key, just as another car
pulled into the circular driveway.

Amelia was not happy to find that it was Charlotte. She walked briskly over to the car.

"Why are you here so early?" The board members had all agreed to meet at six, just an hour before the guests began arriving.

Charlotte's butler disembarked from the driver's side, and walked around to open the door for her. Amelia found his height and stark good looks to be unnerving.

"I have to drop off the last of the books," Charlotte said, stepping out of the car, her shiny chestnut bob swinging against her face. The new haircut, though easy to dismiss as trendy and silly, transformed her prettiness into an ethereal, doll-like beauty that was impossible to ignore. It made her just that much more irritating.

"For heaven's sake, Charlotte. Why did you wait until the last minute? I have so much to do."

"I know you do. So don't mind us. We'll take everything inside and make sure the volunteers know the books are here."

Amelia was taken off guard by her conciliatory tone.

"Well, in that case. Fine. You'll have to get the boxes up to the second floor. Did you alphabetize them like I told you?"

"Of course," Charlotte said with a smile. Her manservant was already lifting boxes out of the backseat.

Amelia reluctantly opened the front door for them.

When they were gone, she took another sweeping look at the exterior, conscious of the fact that it would no doubt be photographed by the reporters who attended the gala. Satisfied with the entranceway presentation, she started to walk inside when another car pulled up.

"William," she breathed out softly.

Chapter 16

THE HOUSE WAS bustling with florists, housekeepers, and food delivery. Charlotte followed Rafferty up the central staircase.

"You really know your way around here," she said.

"My father worked in this house for forty years," he said.

"Oh, of course." She felt foolish for forgetting.

They found a few of the shelving volunteers in one of the smaller anterooms off of the parlor.

"Excuse me—sorry to add to your workload, but we have a few more boxes," Charlotte said.

"That's fine, Mrs. Delacorte. Just leave them here."

And then, as planned, Rafferty said, "Why don't you ladies let me help you get these on the shelves?"

"Thank you, but we're fine," said one of the girls. She was plump, with mousy brown hair in a long braid. She couldn't have been more than sixteen or seventeen. Charlotte needed to make it clear they weren't asking, they were telling.

"I'd feel much better knowing firsthand that these particular volumes made it onto the shelves. The people who donated them will be guests tonight, and I hate to imagine the insult if they look for them and don't find them. I'm sure you girls don't want to bear the brunt of that responsibility."

The girls looked at each other.

"Whatever you say, Mrs. Delacorte," said the girl with the braid.

AMELIA TOUCHED HER hair to make sure it was secure at the nape of her neck, and made her way to the car.

"What a pleasant surprise!" she said.

"I can't stay long. I just wanted to make sure everything is running smoothly."

Amelia noticed that William looked particular tense.

"It's going perfectly. The stonesmith just put the plaque above the door an hour or so ago. Come take a look."

William followed her to the front door, and read the inscription above the entranceway to the house in which he had grown up.

"Good job, Amelia." He smiled tightly. Amelia hated to be the bearer of bad news, especially since he didn't seem happy to begin with, but he would find out soon enough.

"I should warn you—Charlotte is here," she said, putting her hand on his arm.

He sighed. "What is she doing?"

"She and that odd butler of yours are dropping off more books. Honestly, William—she is so disorganized. This should have been done days ago."

"Well, she'd too busy devising ways to make my life a living hell," he said. "I'm going to go speak to her and make sure she's not holding things up."

He shrugged her hand off and walked inside, leaving Amelia disappointed. Damn Charlotte and her terrible timing. She'd no doubt robbed Amelia of her one chance to be alone with William before the big evening ahead.

Amelia's only consolation was that this was one of the last social events she would ever have to share with her.

CHARLOTTE FELT LIKE she was about to rob a bank. Her stomach was clenched in a knot, and she suspected that at any minute someone would round the corner and stop her.

"You don't have to keep lookin' around. No one's here," Rafferty said.

"Okay," she said, telling herself to just breathe. She found the

F–G stacks in the center of the room. Rafferty followed her with the box. She pulled out the copy of The *Beautiful and the Damned*, and placed it on the shelf next to the Fitzgerald novels and short story collections that had already been shelved.

"How do you know someone won't pull out the ledgers while they are looking for a book?" he said.

"Well, it's a chance I have to take. I can't very well smuggle them into the party in my small evening clutch. I have to plant them somewhere. I figure if I put them on the highest shelf directly above the Fitzgerald book, I'll remember where they're located, but casual browsers won't stumble upon them."

She looked up. The only problem was that the highest shelf was not only unreachable, it was empty. "The second highest shelf," she amended.

Still, she would need a ladder or a stepstool. They looked around, but there was nothing to stand on.

"Maybe I can reach it," said Rafferty. He stretched up his arm, and he could touch the shelf, but his reach didn't extend far enough to securely put the ledger in between two books so that it didn't stick out.

"I'll go ask Mumson for a stepladder," said Rafferty.

"No—I don't want to make a fuss. And I don't want anyone coming in here. You'll just have to lift me up." Rafferty looked at her like she was joking. "I'm serious," she said. "We can't draw attention to ourselves running all around the place looking for something to climb up on. I can reach it if you just pick me up."

With a dubious expression, Rafferty moved closer to her and put both hands firmly on her waist. At his touch, she felt a thrill that momentarily distracted her from the task at hand. She felt herself lean back against him, and then corrected herself.

He bent slightly and then hoisted her up. Her hands trembled as she pressed the first black ledger in between two books, and she wasn't sure which transgression was more unsettling: planting the evidence to bust her own husband, or allowing her butler to hold her.

She pressed the second ledger onto the shelf, and then took a moment to see if they stood out to the casual observer.

"What the hell are you doing?"

She felt Rafferty nearly drop her at the sound of William's voice. But he kept it together long enough to give her a dignified landing.

Charlotte felt like she might pass out.

"Shelving books," she said as calmly as possible, well aware her face was flushed scarlet. *Oh god, I hope he doesn't know.*

"Yes, I can see that. Tell me, Charlotte: Are you not capable of conducting yourself like a normal member of polite society?"

She had no idea how he could ask her that question with a straight face, but supposed it was for Rafferty's benefit. Or maybe William was just so used to being a fake, it was his default mode.

"I'm trying to be helpful."

William glanced at the box of books at her feet.

"Rafferty, take that upstairs to the volunteers."

Rafferty hesitated for just a fraction of a second, long enough for Charlotte to know that he was reluctant to leave her, but quickly enough to not tip their hand that they were up to something.

William waited until they were alone before speaking.

"Now, I want you to tell me what the hell you're doing, Charlotte."

His face looked murderous with rage, and she could only imagine what would happen if he knew the answer to his question.

"I'm trying to be helpful," she repeated, painfully aware of the ledgers just a few feet above their heads.

"Why don't I believe you?" he said.

"I don't know."

"Everyone is talking about us, you know," he said.

"What do you mean?"

"Our . . . estrangement."

"That's not my fault," she said. "You wouldn't even look at me at the engagement party."

"You don't understand—I'm happy people are talking. I'm glad they are wondering why we're having problems. Of course, it might be a bit embarrassing for you when they hear that you've done nothing but angle for money since Mother died, and are carrying on with a bootlegger. What choice do I have but to divorce you?"

"What are you talking about?" she said slowly.

"And it's perfectly natural that in your anger at being cut off, you concoct a laughable story about *me* being a bootlegger. It is quite sad, really. *Pathetic*."

"Why are you saying this?"

"Because I want you to know that public opinion is already turning against you, Charlotte. If you even think about breathing a word of your . . . accusation against me, it will only make things worse for you in the end."

Chapter 17

SHAKEN, CHARLOTTE WAITED outside of the library while Rafferty brought the car around.

She didn't speak until they were out of view of the house.

"Are you all right?" he asked.

She nodded. "I just hope I'm doing the right thing."

"What's the alternative? To do nothing?"

"I suppose. And that's not really an option now, is it?"

Since she had enlisted Rafferty, she wondered what she had ever done without him. She was tempted to tell him everything, but where would she even start?

Charlotte didn't know how she was going to get through the night, much less put on a front of normalcy. She reached into her handbag for her compact, wondering if she looked as shaken as she felt. Instead, her hand found the envelope that had been delivered to the house. She'd forgotten about it.

She tore off an edge and then gently opened the top to find a bank check and a note.

> Dear Charlotte:
> This is the amount I got for selling your jewelry. I had to close the bank account. I'm not going to be around to access it for you, and I didn't want your money to be out of reach.
> I know you think you are doing the right thing by not leaving your marriage, and I also know I can't change your mind. I just wish things had turned out differently for us.
> I love you and I haven't given up hope that our paths will cross again at a better time for both of us.
> —Jake

"Turn the car around," Charlotte said to Rafferty.

"What's wrong?"

"I need to go to Jake's."

He sighed. "Oh Charlotte—not that again. Not now. You have to focus."

"This isn't open for discussion, Rafferty. Head downtown. I don't know why you have it in for him, but Jake's my . . . friend. He's not the enemy here."

Rafferty's annoyance was palpable as he switched avenues to head south.

"Does he know what you're planning to do?"

"No," Charlotte said. "But I'm going to tell him right now."

Rafferty couldn't find parking on the small street.

"You can just drop me off. I'll take a cab home."

"I'll wait here for you," he said, pulling the car off to the side and turning off the motor.

"I don't know how long I'll be," she said. "What if William goes back to the house? I need you to cover for me. Tell him I went to get my hair done. Or no—tell him there was a problem with my dress and I went to the seamstress."

She got out and closed the car door but Rafferty didn't turn on the motor. "Please, Rafferty. I know you don't agree with me but this is what I need for you to do."

She didn't have time to debate him, and did not wait to see if he drove away before crossing the street to Jake's building. She hurried down the stairs, her heart thumping, and knocked on the door. The door opened so quickly, it took a moment for Charlotte to absorb the fact that Jake wasn't the one standing in front of her.

It was Rona Lovejoy.

"Is Jake here?" Charlotte said, her heart now pounding for entirely different reasons.

"No," Rona said, closing the door. Charlotte put her hand out to prevent the door from shutting.

"Excuse me—I'd like to come in," Charlotte said, pushing past the woman into Jake's living room. She gasped. The space was completely empty except for a few boxes.

"You're too late," Rona said. "Jake was arrested last night."

Part VI

Hell Hath No Fury

*He who wields the instruments of justice wields the most
powerful instruments of government.*
—from the 1941 *New York Times* obituary of
Emory Buckner

Chapter 1

CHARLOTTE STOOD IN front of the midtown police precinct, wishing she could just keep walking past. But she couldn't—not with Jake trapped behind bars inside.

She mustered her resolve and opened the heavy door, clutching her evening bag close to her body. She had no idea how much this was going to cost her, so she brought all of the money from Jake's sale of her jewelry.

Every person in the crowded room turned to look at her. She couldn't blame them; in her salmon-colored fringed and beaded gown, she was a spectacle. With the library gala in less than two hours, she'd had to dress for the night, and then run down to the police station.

"Can I help you?" asked an officer from behind the front desk. The room was loud, with ringing phones and the clatter of typewriters. Two long wooden benches were filled with people waiting.

She cleared her throat. "I'm here to post bail," she said.

"For who?" the man said gruffly. Charlotte felt embarrassed, as if she were doing something wrong. But she told herself that this was routine for them: They arrested people, and then they dealt with the bail money. She wasn't doing anything the system didn't expect.

"Jake Larkin."

The man shuffled through a pile of paper. "I don't see him here. When did they bring him in?"

Charlotte shifted uncomfortably in her high heels. "Last night."

The officer pushed away from his desk and walked out of the room. Charlotte tried to ignore the feeling of being watched. She felt very exposed in her dress, and wished she'd thought to wear a coat despite the warm weather.

The officer was gone a long time. By the time he returned to his desk, Charlotte was sweating from nerves.

"It's eight hundred for Larkin," he said.

Charlotte started taking money out of her purse.

"Not here!" the officer barked. "Go down the hall to your left."

Charlotte felt a flash of annoyance, but followed his direction.

Walking down the narrow hallway, she thought about her run-in with Rona Lovejoy. She'd panicked when she heard the words "he was arrested" coming from Rona's lips—and now shuddered to think if that mouth had been on Jake's. Why was that woman at Jake's in the first place? Had he given up on Charlotte already? Did he really believe she had no intention of finding a way to leave her marriage and be with him?

Even now, in the midst of everything, just the thought of his hands on her body was enough to quicken her pulse. She imagined his arms around her, the scent of him when she rested her head against his chest. Knowing in just minutes she would look into those dark eyes—eyes that were equally as capable of igniting passion as they were in offering comfort—was enough to put a skip in her step as she hurried to the end of the dingy police station corridor.

———

GRETA GOUCHER LOOKED up at the brass door knocker. It was in the shape of a lion, and she felt it was poetically appropriate. What was she doing if not throwing herself into the lion's den by arriving uninvited on Amelia Astor's doorstep? But everyone had their limits, and Greta had run out of patience for the juicy story that had been promised to her a week ago.

She banged the knocker as hard as a gavel at the hand of a frustrated judge. The door was opened almost immediately by an irritated-looking butler.

"Can I help you?" he asked.

"I'm here to see Mae Delacorte," Greta said.

"Miss Delacorte is indisposed at the moment. You can leave your card," he said.

"Tell her it's Greta Goucher. I bet she'll get 'disposed' very quickly."

The butler let her into the house with obvious reluctance. He instructed her to wait on a silk-covered ottoman near the front door.

She wondered if she would see the lady of the house while she was there. Even after the engagement party, Greta couldn't understand Amelia Astor's quick turnaround from practically hanging up the phone on her to showing up in person to invite her to the engagement party. Whatever the reason, Greta was thankful for the woman's strange change of heart; it had put Greta in an extremely good position.

Greta glanced up at the sound of footsteps in the hallway.

"What are you doing here?" asked Mae Delacorte harshly. She was dressed in a stunning royal-blue gown, threaded with black seed pearls and beads. Greta couldn't help but remember that the last time she'd seen the patrician-looking girl, she'd had another woman's face between her legs.

Greta shook the image from her mind.

"We have some unfinished business, Miss Delacorte."

"I'm on my way out," Mae said flippantly.

"I can see that. But I must insist on a few minutes of your time. You see, I'm *not* going out tonight. I'm going to be at my office until very late, writing my column for tomorrow."

Mae paled visibly under her face powder and rouge.

"Come into the parlor," she said. "But I only have a minute. I'm already late."

Greta followed Mae into a room grander than any she had ever been in during her entire life. This only made Greta more determined to hold Mae to her promise. She was tired of the rich thinking they were beyond the reach of scandal or the law. It wasn't fair that a working woman like herself could still barely afford more than a closet-sized apartment in a rundown building, when Mae Delacorte lived like a princess. What had she ever done to deserve the reverence and privilege she enjoyed? Nothing. Greta was tired of it, and she knew her readers were tired of it too.

"Your redheaded friend promised me a valuable scoop in exchange for not writing about your . . . relationship with her. I've tried to track her down but she's like a ghost. You, on the other hand, are quite visible. To everyone, if you get what I mean."

Mae sat on a sofa, and didn't look at Greta. When she finally glanced up, her face was steely and emotionless.

"I'm on my way to the opening of the new Delacorte Library," said Mae. "I'm sure you've read about it."

"Of course," said Greta. And she had. It was yet another glamorous event in the glossy lives of the rich. At least this one had, in the end, something to offer the public.

"Why don't you come tonight as my guest? And we will continue this conversation."

Greta knew she was being played—Mae Delacorte was stalling—but she was willing to let her. She wanted to go to the event.

She would get her story one way or another.

"In that case, I'll let myself out," said Greta. "And I will see you later tonight."

Chapter 2

"I'LL FIND A way to pay you back," Jake said brusquely as he climbed into the front seat of Charlotte's car. His eyes had deep shadows underneath them, and he needed a shave. This only added to his rugged handsomeness, and she ached to feel his arms around her. But he'd barely looked at her since the bailiff released him.

"Don't worry about it," she said, "I'm just glad you're out."

She'd thought Jake would be happy to see her. Instead, he seemed almost irritated. All she wanted was for him to touch her hand, to smile at her. Instead, he stared out the window as she drove toward his apartment.

"I appreciate you not saying I told you so," he said.

"Why would I?" she said, her heart sinking. How had she become the enemy?

He shrugged. "You warned me to be careful. And you said they would come after me. You were right, Charlotte."

"Jake, I don't want to be right. I just want to fix this mess."

"It's not your mess to fix," he responded emotionlessly.

Charlotte tried not to get too rattled by his cold detachment. But after a few blocks of silence, she pulled over and shut the car's engine.

"Why are you being like this?" she said. Her voice cracked.

"Charlotte, just drive the car. You obviously have to be somewhere." He looked pointedly at her gown.

She'd almost forgotten.

"The library opening is tonight," she said, trying not to panic at the thought of William looking for her at the house. "But I'm not going anywhere—and neither are you—until you talk to me."

He sighed, and for a split second his face relaxed enough from his tense irritation for her to catch a glimpse of sadness flicker across his face. "I don't need you to rescue me, Charlotte. I only wanted one thing from you, and you decided you can't do it and I've accepted that. I told you I think we need some time apart, and I meant it."

She looked at him in amazement. "You ungrateful bastard. I rushed down here to bail you out of jail, and all you care about is the fact that I'm not running away like the heroine of some crazy movie! Running away doesn't solve anything, Jake." She glared at him.

"So what does?"

"Doing something to divert attention off of you and onto a bigger bust—like William."

He looked at her in surprise. "And how are you going to do that?"

"By talking to the DA."

He turned to her and looked at her seriously. "This isn't a game. You shouldn't be messing around in this while you're still living with him, Charlotte. He's dangerous. You underestimate him."

"Do you have any records of your deals with him? Receipts? Anything?"

Jake shook his head. "No way. There's no paper trail, and if you're looking for one, you're wasting your time. Everything is done in person, on the phone, and in cash."

Charlotte had assumed as much. "Do you know of any other people he's selling to?"

"I know he's dealing with Boom Boom now. But I'm telling you, Charlotte, whatever you're thinking of doing is a bad idea. Just get the hell out of there, and let me worry about myself." He turned away again, resuming his cold glare out the window.

She started the engine again. "*You* underestimate *me*," she said.

The rest of the ride downtown was silent. But when she pulled onto his block, she couldn't resist saying, "I saw Rona at your place. That's how I knew you'd been arrested."

"I figured," he said.

"That's all you have to say?"

He grabbed her face and kissed her so hard his teeth clashed with hers, and her stomach flipped. "What do you want me to say?" he said huskily.

"You're infuriating!" she said, catching her breath.

Their eyes met, and she felt the same deep tremor she'd felt since the first time she saw him at her mother-in-law's funeral.

He ran his finger slowly down her neck, kissing the hollow between her collarbone and her shoulder.

"You know I only want you, Charlotte," he said, his voice low with desire. "I just don't know what *you* want."

"How can you say that?" she murmured. His hands cupped her breasts, and she felt a twinge between her legs.

"Come inside," he said.

"I can't," she breathed.

Jake pulled away from her slowly.

He got out of the car and walked to his apartment without looking back.

"THIS IS A disaster," Mae said, tossing her beaded handbag onto Fiona's bed.

At four in the afternoon, Fiona was still in her nightgown.

Even with all of the windows open in her tiny apartment, it was like an oven.

"You look gorgeous," Fiona said, stretching languidly on the bed. "I wish I could be there tonight to fuck you in the library."

"You fucked me enough at the Union Club," yelled Mae. "How could you promise Greta Goucher a story you don't have? She's so worked up over it, she showed up at Amelia's today to tell me she's going to write about what she saw at the engagement party."

Fiona pulled Mae onto the bed, further irritating her.

"Don't get me all wrinkled and smudged," Mae said. "I don't have time to fix anything. I have to be at the library in an hour."

"Just calm down about that stupid gossip. What's the big deal? You can always deny it," Fiona said, stroking her bare shoulder, her fingers skimming over the black sequined straps of Mae's dress.

"My brother will know it's true, and so will Amelia."

"Your brother is a bootlegger! Who is he to judge you?"

"I'm sure he justifies his bootlegging by thinking that at least it's a moneymaking venture. I'm just some kind of freak to him."

"I bet Jonathan's family would have something else to say about William's 'moneymaking venture.'"

"I'm sure. But my brother is clever enough not to get busted. Still, it's something else I have to worry about. So I don't need my own personal scandal on top of it."

"What's the worst that could happen if Greta runs the story?"

Mae ran her hand through her hair, agitated. "I don't know. Maybe Jonathan's parents will try to block our marriage. It will complicate everything. My marriage gives me the cover to live my private life in private. I don't want it blown up like this."

"Oh, you silly duck," Fiona said adoringly. The way she looked at her was almost enough to calm Mae. For over a year, she had longed for Fiona to gaze at her with such affection. And now she had it, but she was too cornered by her brother, Amelia, and that horrible gossip to enjoy it.

"Do you know a story I can feed her?" Mae said, her anger softening. "Anything about people at the Vesper? Anyone cheating on his wife?"

Fiona thought for a minute. "You could tell her about Roger having an affair with me. In fact, maybe you should. That bastard ratted out Jake and he deserves to get busted, too."

Mae nodded. "It's probably the only thing we have that would shut her up for a while. But it will expose you."

Fiona shrugged. "I don't care."

Mae looked at her. "You would do that for me?"

"I owe you one. I was stupid these past few months, and I almost blew the best thing I ever had."

Mae felt her eyes fill with tears. "I love you, too."

Fiona kissed her hard on the lips. "So what do you want to do about it?"

"I'm going to get this Goucher woman off of our tails. I'm going to marry Jonathan Astor. And you and I are going to live happily ever after," Mae said decisively.

CHARLOTTE TRIED TO make it through the front door unnoticed. But before she even reached the stairs, William was hot on her heels.

"Where the hell have you been?" He grabbed her arm so hard she knew it would leave a bruise.

"I had a last-minute tailoring emergency. If you'd asked Rafferty he would have told you."

William looked at her with obvious distrust. "He did tell me. And again, I'm asking you: Where have you been?"

"Please let go. You're hurting me." She said the words calmly, without emotion. Charlotte hated that she was afraid of William, and she knew if she allowed her fear to show, he would know for certain she was lying to him. She told herself that he couldn't do anything to her.

He didn't lessen his grip.

"I went to the seamstress," she said. He let go of her arm, but didn't respond. "Does it have to be like this, William?" she asked, then added daringly, "It won't do for me to have bruises on my arm at the event. People will *talk.* . . . " She waited for some glimpse of the man she had married—the man she thought she had married. And she told herself that if she saw it, she wouldn't go through with it.

"You didn't uphold your end of the deal," he said.

"What are you talking about?"

William smiled, a small grin that didn't show his teeth. "Why do you think I married you, Charlotte? I could have married any woman in New York—wealthy women, socially connected women. But I married you."

"And why was that?" she asked, feeling her heart unravel.

"I thought you were beautiful," he said. "And I thought you wouldn't give me a hard time. And maybe give me a son."

She felt the last sentence in her gut.

"At least you're still beautiful," he said.

And that's when she realized that William Delacorte deserved whatever he got.

Charlotte pushed past him and rushed up the stairs. When she was at the top and alone, she stopped to catch her breath. Her heart was pounding and her hands were sweating. For a minute she was afraid she was going to pass out. But the wave of anxiety passed over her, and she continued into the master bedroom.

She wanted to lock herself in the guest room until it was time to leave, but she needed to get the jewelry she was wearing that evening out of the safe. Out of the pieces she hadn't given to Jake to sell, she planned to wear a large emerald ring William had given her on her birthday two years ago, and a small Van Cleef & Arpels ruby broach shaped like a bird, which she had inherited from Geraldine.

Her hand shook as she dialed the combination lock, and she hoped William wouldn't come in to harass her. The safe door sprung open.

The safe was empty.

"Looking for something?"

Charlotte turned to find William in the doorway.

"I'm wanted to get my jewelry out to wear tonight." It suddenly seemed absurd to care about jewelry or appearances, but old habits died hard.

"I'll be holding on to your jewelry from now on. What pieces do you want to wear?"

Had he realized she'd been selling some of it? Or was this just part of the control mode he was in? She tried to brush past him and leave the room, but he wouldn't let her by.

"I asked you a question," he said. She was so rattled, she couldn't think of one piece of jewelry she owned. Finally, she stammered, "The emerald ring and the ruby bird . . . the broach."

"You can have the broach, not the ring," he said. "Go to the guest room and I'll send Penny to deliver it to you."

She had no idea why he would withhold the ring. And she didn't care.

She walked out the room and hurried down the hall.

"And Charlotte—don't be late to the party."

She turned around.

"You want to arrive separately? Won't people talk?"

"I'm sure they will," he said. And then he smiled.

Chapter 3

MAE BARELY RECOGNIZED the interior of the house she had grown up in.

The grand mansion on Fifty-seventh Street had been transformed from a private home into a public institution. It made her feel slightly nostalgic, but at the same time it was very liberating. The past was gone, and the future was hers to make.

She walked through the entrance foyer on the arm of Jonathan, and found herself greeted warmly by everyone she encountered. It was impossible not to notice the change in people's attitudes toward her now that she was engaged to Jonathan Astor. Before, she was simply Geraldine's wayward daughter. Now she appeared to have a future in her own right—a potentially big future in New York society. And she was starting to get a sense of the respect that future would afford her. She had to admit: It was certainly seductive.

"You didn't mention if there was a bar at this lovely little fete," said Jonathan.

"I doubt it," said Mae. Jonathan then flashed open his jacket to reveal a silver flask. She smiled, feeling more optimistic about her marriage with each passing day.

"Good lord, here comes Amelia," said Jonathan. "I'm going to go hide among the riffraff. Meet me in the history section in fifteen minutes for a quick shot before the hors d'oeuvres."

He disappeared in the crowd. Mae felt someone tap her on the shoulder.

"You didn't mention it was black tie," said a voice behind her. She turned to find the little gossip woman.

"I was hoping to see you here," said Mae.

"Somehow I doubt that," said Greta wryly.

"I first need to say hello to a few people. Then you and I can find a quiet place to talk," said Mae.

Greta looked at her dubiously.

"So you really do have something to tell me?"

Mae watched Amelia approach them. "I do. But it's going to have to wait."

CHARLOTTE'S GOWN CLUNG to her back in patches of perspiration. She felt like she'd been wearing the dress for days. She'd noticed a blue ink smudge on the side, and she assumed she had leaned into something at the police station. To conceal the stain, she awkwardly held her left arm straight down and close to her body.

She watched the guests circulate gaily, and it was as if she were viewing a show from a seat in a theater. People said hello to her; a few friends tried to engage her in conversation. But she felt detached and rigid, unable to think of anything except what she would say to Emory Buckner.

Mae circulated with a grace and ease Charlotte had never before seen in her sister-in-law. Watching her, Charlotte realized her plan would affect Mae almost as much as it would affect William.

She must warn her.

Amelia was talking to Mae, touching her arm and smiling warmly. To anyone who didn't know better, they looked like family already. And then Charlotte realized yet another ripple effect of her busting William: Amelia Astor. What would Amelia say when her precious William was revealed to be a criminal?

Amelia spotted Charlotte first as she approached them.

"Charlotte. Don't you look lovely," she said. Her smile was as fake as the color on her cheeks. When had Amelia Astor started wearing makeup?

Charlotte smiled tightly. "Mae, I need to speak with you for a minute," she said.

"Don't start in with your drama now, Charlotte. Mae needs to start learning how to be a proper hostess and you don't exactly set an example for her."

Charlotte ignored her and took Mae by the hand.

"What is it?" Mae said, clearly not happy to be pulled away from the festivities.

"Don't tell me you've bought into all of this now," said Charlotte. "Not too long ago, I'd be a welcome relief from talking to Amelia."

They made their way through the crowd and up the stairs.

"It's not personal, Charlotte. But for the first time since my mother died, I feel almost in control of my life. I don't want to rock the boat," she said.

Charlotte steered her into the room where they had once held the Women's Literary Alliance meetings.

"I hate to be the bearer of bad news, but the boat *is* going to rock. And to be honest, I'd say it's going to capsize," she said.

Mae put her hands on her hips.

"What are you talking about?"

"Sit down," Charlotte said. Mae dropped herself onto the French settee. "You know William is bootlegging. And you know he's controlling all the money—the legitimate family money included. He's also controlling you, regardless of what you say about your own motivations for your marriage. I suspect he's planning to divorce me in a very public and probably devastating way. On top of all that, Jake was arrested last night."

"No!" Mae cried, putting her head in her hands.

"I bailed him out, but he still faces prosecution. So all things considered, I'm going to have a little talk with the head of the District Attorney's office tonight. And I'm going to point him in William's direction. I'll tell him he can have evidence against

William—who is a much bigger player—if he drops charges against Jake."

Mae looked up at her, her eyes wide. "You're going to get William arrested?"

"I don't know what's going to happen. I hope so."

"Don't do it," said Mae.

"He's not helping you, Mae. He's never going to hand over your inheritance. You can play the part of the good girl all you want, but he'll always punish you because he knows the truth. And because you know the truth about him. You can't count on your marriage to provide financial stability. Take it from me."

Mae seemed to absorb this, then said, "And what about my engagement? Jonathan is interested in me because I'm allegedly more respectable than the women he really wants to date. And now I'm going to be scandalized."

As well intentioned as she had been in confiding in Mae, Charlotte wondered if she'd made a dangerous mistake.

"Mae, listen to me: You might think your marriage to Jonathan will solve all your problems . . . and maybe it will for a short while. But this family is rotting from the inside out and I'm offering a solution. Not to mention saving our friend's neck in the process," Charlotte said.

"No. William is still my brother. He's the only family I have," Mae said fiercely.

Charlotte glanced at her watch. They would be seating for dinner soon and she had to find Buckner before Mae did something to thwart her. "Please at least think about what I've said," Charlotte emplored, standing to leave. She reached over and lightly squeezed Mae's shoulder before walking away.

Chapter 4

SHAKEN, MAE MADE her way down the stairs.

She understood why Charlotte needed to do what she was about to do, but she herself didn't know if she was prepared for the fallout. She realized that until that moment, she'd taken her good family name for granted.

"I was wondering where you disappeared to," said Greta Goucher from the foot of the stairs, as if she'd been about to go up to look for her.

Mae tried not to lose her patience.

"I told you it had to wait," Mae said. "This is a public event, Greta. I can't just scurry off with you at any given moment."

"Fair enough," Greta said. "But my patience is running out."

"They will be seating for dinner soon," Mae said, looking around to find Jonathan. He was chatting up an elderly couple near the entrance to the house. Amelia was nowhere in sight, and neither was Charlotte. William was directing a waiter, no doubt dissatisfied with something.

When she was confident no one would take notice of her, she gestured for Greta to follow her up back up the stairs.

Greta took the same place on the settee that Mae had just occupied while listening to Charlotte.

"Quite a place your mother had," said Greta, looking around. "This is where you grew up?"

"Yes," said Mae.

"I can't imagine."

"It was always just a house to me," said Mae.

"Spoken like a true spoiled brat," said Greta.

Mae shook her head. "Is that what your column is all about? Sticking it to people who have more than you?"

"Not necessarily," said Greta. "It's news. It's entertainment. And most of the time, it's the truth. So what d'ya got for me?"

Mae paced in front of the woman. Compared to what Charlotte was about to do, giving up a little information about Fiona and Roger Smith wasn't a big deal. But she still felt nervous. She knew once it was done, it couldn't be undone.

"How do I know you won't print the story about me anyway?" she said. "I could tell you what I know, and then you still screw me."

"That's a good question. Part of it is that you'll just have to take my word for it. But more than that, I have my career to think about. If I blow a good source like you, I don't get more stories, and I don't get invited to events like this. In other words, I lose access. And access is what separates me from all the other hacks out there."

Mae nodded, somewhat satisfied with the answer.

"Okay. Then this is what I have to tell you: One of the lawyers working for the District Attorney's office has been paying for sex with a woman who works at the Vesper Club."

Greta's face was impassive. Mae supposed it was part of her professionalism.

"Who is it? I need names. Without names this is worth nothing."

"His name is Roger Smith. I think it's Smith—you'll have to double check."

"This better be true. Buckner's people aren't guys to mess around with. We have libel laws, you know."

"It's completely true."

Greta seemed to be deep in thought. "Still," she said, almost to herself, "I'll have to be careful with it."

"I need to get back to the party," said Mae, heading for the door.

"Frankly, Mae, this isn't as big a story as the one about you that I held back from writing."

"What are you saying?" Mae said, stopping in her tracks.

Greta didn't answer her. She was too busy scribbling on a small notepad. When she looked up, she was all smiles. "Congratulations. You're my new high-society mole. I'll let you know when I need my next story from you. In the meantime, keep your eyes and ears open."

CHARLOTTE WATCHED WILLIAM with disgust.

He stood in front of the crowd, regal in his tuxedo, his smile suggesting he didn't have a care in the world.

"I only wish my mother were here to see the fulfillment of her dream. She had a vision for this library, and I'd like everyone to give a round of applause to my dear friend Amelia Astor, for making that dream a reality."

Everyone clapped, awkwardly balancing their hors d'oeuvre plates and wineglasses filled with sparkling water. "In a short while, we'll be seating for dinner. Until then, I encourage you all to explore the latest, grand addition to the New York libraries. Be the first to borrow books from her shelf. And kick off what I hope will be a wonderful tradition of reading and thinking in these hallowed halls for generations to come."

More applause.

Charlotte searched the crowd for Emory Buckner, but didn't see him. She twitched anxiously, thinking that maybe he had decided not to come after all.

She felt as if the walls were closing in.

"Excuse me," she said, as she pushed her way through the people near the back, and out of the room. She knew people were looking at her strangely, no doubt wondering why she wasn't by William's side.

The front hall was clear of guests, and she was confident she could slip outside unnoticed. She had her hand on the cool brass knob of the front door when she heard:

"Mrs. Delacorte?"

She turned to find Emory Buckner.

"I was just looking for you," she said, her tone measured in case anyone happened to overhear them.

"My apologies for my late arrival. Nice party," he said, glancing around.

"They will be seating for dinner soon," said Charlotte. "I'd like to show you some of the collection before they do."

"After you," he said.

She walked to the room where she and Rafferty had planted William's ledgers. It seemed hard to believe it had just been earlier that day. And she hoped this time the visit to the F–G shelf would go uninterrupted.

Buckner didn't speak as they made their way through the crowded central hall. Charlotte noticed that William's friends avoided her. In her finely attenuated social universe, arriving separately was the distant thunder before the storm. And no one wanted to get wet.

The book-lined rooms felt different at night. Charlotte realized she'd never been to a public library after dark, and under different circumstances, it would have been quite fun.

"We have a complete collection of Fitzgerald," she said, for the benefit of anyone who might be lurking unseen on the other side of the stacks. Then she pointed to the high shelf, where the thin, black, and unmarked spines of the ledgers stood out from the novels on either side of them.

"Charlotte—I've been looking all over for you."

Charlotte turned to find Isobel. For once, she was not happy to see her friend. Buckner was discreet enough to feign interest in a copy of *The Great Gatsby*.

Charlotte made small talk, and she knew that Isobel sensed something was wrong but was too polite to pry. If Isobel noted her rudeness for not introducing Buckner, she didn't let on. Charlotte felt bad keeping one of her friends at an arm's length, but she told herself she was doing Isobel a favor by not confiding about the whole mess. No one in their right mind would want to be burdened with Charlotte's secrets.

"I'll see you in the dining room. I'll be there in just a minute," Charlotte said, not so subtly dismissing her. Isobel took the cue and left with a wounded expression on her face.

"I think it would be best if I visited this bookshelf when everyone else is occupied with dinner or dessert," said Buckner.

"You're probably right," said Charlotte. "I won't be able to get away, though. You won't forget to come back?"

Buckner glanced at the high shelf. "In all due respect, Mrs. Delacorte—I didn't get where I am today by forgetting anything. Or anyone."

He gave her a small smile before joining the rest of the guests in the outer hall.

Chapter 5

ROGER WARREN AWOKE from yet another feverish dream about Fiona Sparks.

In this dream, like all the others before, she appears naked, angelic, her long red hair floating behind her as if she were some sort of celestial creature. He reaches for her pale and shimmering flesh, his desire a stabbing pain, as piquant and fresh as an open wound. But as soon as his fingertips reach her, she disappears. And he is left in agony.

He rolled over and checked his watch. It was ten in the morning. Elizabeth had no doubt been up for several hours already. Henry always woke her at the crack of dawn.

He groaned softly as his feet hit the floor. It would be a long weekend. Ever since Fiona had cut him off, life felt like nothing more than a series of agonizing duties. Any faint pleasure he'd taken in his wife's company was gone. He kept telling himself that if he tried hard enough, maybe he could find his way back to that place where he wanted her, and where she had cared for him. On some days, especially during the week, he felt progress. But the weekends were the most difficult: forty-eight hours of uninterrupted togetherness.

Roger pulled on his robe and made his way to the kitchen. The apartment was strangely silent.

The newspaper was waiting at his spot at the table. This was unusually considerate of Elizabeth. It was nice to see that she was finally making an effort, too.

He made a pot of coffee, then sat down to read. The paper was folded in half, open to a page in the middle. It was not a section he usually read, but the headline caught his attention:

GRETA'S GOTHAM
Busy Days (and Nights) for the DA's Office

The District Attorney's office is working day and night to keep our fair city free of vice. One in particular is working extra, extra hard—especially at night. Word has it that this promising young lawyer—let's call him Roger—has taken it upon himself to fight not only illegal liquor sales, but yet another nightlife scourge: prostitution. This selfless gentleman has personally sampled the wares of some of the nightclub's finest young offerings—in particular, a smashing redhead at the Vesper Club that this lawyer finds more addictive than anything served up in a bottle.

His heart pounding, Roger crumpled the paper into as much of a ball as he could manage.

"Elizabeth!" he yelled, rushing into the living room.

It was empty. His son's toys, usually scattered all over the floor, were nowhere in sight. Roger opened the hallway closet. It was empty.

BOOM BOOM PICKED up her copy of the *New York Sun* and hurled it against the wall, knocking over her full coffee mug in the process.

"God damn it!" she yelled, pushing away from her desk and scrambling to retrieve the paper to use as a towel. She did her best to sop up the coffee on her desk and left the rest on the floor. She'd have one of the girls clean it up later. A wet floor was the least of her problems at the moment.

She'd been relishing the gossip columns for months, and yet never thought she could be bitten in the ass by one. Now she realized she'd made a huge oversight in her checks and balances—and she meant checks, literally.

The last thing she needed was a gossip columnist bringing heat onto the club. She never worried about it before, and that was a costly mistake. It looked like she'd have to add Greta Goucher to her list of payola. And, of course, she'd have to fire Fiona.

What a shit storm.

Boom Boom reached for her phone.

Chapter 6

CHARLOTTE COULDN'T EAT.

She pushed the strawberries around her breakfast plate, and glanced at the grandfather clock in the corner of the room. She wondered what Emory Buckner was doing at that very moment. Would he call her? Would he come to the house?

Even the salacious Greta Goucher column couldn't distract her from her worries. Although she did wonder if the redhead in question was Fiona Sparks.

"What time did William leave this morning?" she asked Rafferty as he poured her a cup of coffee.

"Not too long ago," said Rafferty. "Maybe an hour." He leaned in close as he spoke to her, his breath caressing her neck. She noticed yet again how his physical proximity gave her a rush, the feeling that her body was flooding with extra blood. She didn't know if it was because of their unconventional mistress of the house/servant relationship, or if it was something else. Something she didn't want to think about. "I could barely sleep last night, wondering what happened with your friend at the library," he said.

Of course he had been thinking about it. She should have been more considerate about giving him an update. After all, he was her partner in crime, so to speak.

"It seemed to go fine." She spoke quietly, even though there didn't seem to be anyone in the house who would know—or care—what they were talking about. "But I didn't actually see him take the ledgers. I pointed them out to him, and he said he would go back later in the night. And when I checked the shelf again, they were gone—and so was Mr. Buckner. Now I don't know what happens next."

"You wait," Rafferty said, resting his hand on her shoulder for a brief moment. "Buckner'll come to you now. The hard part is over."

Her breath caught. Was it just the stress she was under that was making her respond so to his touch this way? "You really think so?"

He nodded.

"The hard part is far from over," she said, trying to collect herself. She was sure the odd attraction she felt was only because she missed Jake.

"No matter what comes, I will be here for you," he said.

Rafferty set the coffeepot down, and took her hand, intertwining his fingers in hers. Startled by the bold gesture, she looked up at him. His eyes were ice blue and as serious as she'd ever seen on a person.

Charlotte found she was holding her breath.

AMELIA WAS BASKING in the afterglow of a successful evening. It was as if William's mother had been reaching out from the grave and handing Amelia the mantle of her legacy.

She felt the tide turning. There was a certain deference afforded her last night that she'd never experienced before—not even as an Astor. The socially astute crowd smelled the blood in the water, and it wasn't too hard for them to guess who they should align themselves with in order to avoid becoming casualties themselves.

"Mrs. Astor, a visitor. Mr. Delacorte," said her butler from the bedroom doorway.

She'd had a feeling William would visit, and so she'd had the foresight to get fully dressed by eleven a.m.

Amelia scurried quickly down the stairs in a fashion so as not to reveal she was actually in a hurry. William, already seated in the parlor, looked more relaxed than she had seen him in a long time.

"What a night," he said, smiling at her.

HELL HATH NO FURY

"A tremendous success," she said. "I think Geraldine would have been proud."

"Thanks to you," he said.

She smiled and looked away with false modesty.

"I'm quite serious," he said. "The library is elegant, it's organized, and it's welcoming but still retains an aura of exclusivity. The collection is robust even at this nascent stage. The food was delicious; the music was top-notch. Your table seating ensured that no one had a dull moment. Amelia, you truly are a wonder."

Amelia didn't tell him that the food, music, and organization were largely the product of Charlotte's early planning. The only thing Amelia had actually done was get rid of Charlotte's idea of having a theme. And Amelia had brought in a large number of books—not the least of which came from that bumbling, would-be-suitor, Claud Miroux. He's asked her to dance several times last night, but fortunately never when William was around to notice.

"I enjoyed every minute of it," she said. "Do you want something to eat? I already had breakfast but I'd be happy to have something made up for you."

"Maybe in a few minutes," he said. "And you might want to have them break out a bottle of champagne."

With that, he reached into his jacket pocket and pulled out a ring box.

"What on earth?" Amelia accepted it from him with surprise. He said nothing, just waited for her to open it. She pressed open the lid and found a large oval-shaped emerald ring nestled in the blue velvet cushion. The emerald was surrounded by pave diamonds and set in platinum. The ring was beautiful, but unsettlingly familiar.

She could have sworn she'd seen Charlotte wearing it on several occasions.

"Amelia, despite the obvious complications, I want to ask you to be my wife."

Though she had dreamed about such a moment since she was a teenager, the reality of it left her cold. She didn't know if it was the secondhand ring, or that he was still married to Charlotte. But she was not feeling the elation she should be experiencing. Still, there was only one possible response.

"I'd be honored to marry you," Amelia said. To this life-changing utterance, William kissed her on the cheek.

She brushed any petty concerns aside, and forced herself to enjoy the moment.

"Let's not flaunt this in front of Charlotte," he said. "You know what they say about a woman scorned. I'd hate to think of what lies she might concoct in retribution."

"Of course," Amelia said, glancing at the ring that would be impossible to miss—especially by anyone who had once worn it. "For now, this is just between us."

Chapter 7

CHARLOTTE FOUGHT THE urge to sneak downtown to see Jake. As she struggled to keep Emory Buckner out of her mind, she was instead plagued with recurring snippets of her car-ride conversation with Jake—and the way he had enflamed every nerve in her body before he walked away.

Couldn't he see what she was doing was so much more difficult than running away like a thief in the night? Did he still think she was enjoying her role as William's mistreated wife, trying to have it both ways? The idea that he would imagine that even for a second was enough to make her so furious, she wished she'd left him in that jail cell.

But no. She wanted to be with him right then and there, no matter what he thought of her. After all, it was those first unbelievable flickers of feeling for Jake that had opened her eyes to the truth about her marriage—about her life. He thought she was clinging to the status quo, but in all honesty, one of the reasons why she loved him was because he had set her free. Even if it didn't seem that way. Yet.

Rafferty broke through her thoughts.

"There's a telephone call for you," he said.

"Who is it?" she asked, suddenly flustered.

"He wouldn't say," said Rafferty. "And I didn't recognize the voice."

Her heart beginning to thump, she walked quickly to the phone.

"Charlotte Delacorte," she said.

"Hello, Mrs. Delacorte. It's Emory Buckner."

"Oh—hello. I'm glad you called. I didn't see you leave last night and I wondered . . ."

"Mrs. Delacorte, it's important I meet with you today. Can you get away?"

"Yes," she said, without hesitation. "Just tell me when and where."

CHARLOTTE WALKED THROUGH the art deco lobby of Emory Buckner's office building on Nineteenth Street. It was eerily quiet.

An elevator attendant escorted her up to the eighth floor. He rolled back the door of the lift and opened it to a quiet and deserted hallway. Charlotte stepped out tentatively, feeling out of place and out of sorts. Then she spotted Buckner peeking out of his office halfway down the hall.

"I'm sorry to disrupt your weekend," he said, waving her inside the surprisingly large room. Was he joking? What did he think—that she and William had just been sitting around sharing a quiet afternoon together as she waited for his call?

"Not at all, I've been anxious to hear from you. I'd assumed you got the ledgers, but since we never actually spoke again . . .

well, I got nervous. I imagined of all kinds of scenarios," she said with an uneasy laugh.

He gestured for her to take a seat. He moved behind his desk, and put his feet up. He unwrapped a cigar.

"Do you mind if I smoke?" he said.

"No," she said, even though she hated the smell of cigars.

"I'm going to give it to you straight," he said through a cloud of smoke. "The ledgers don't prove any illegal activity."

"They don't?"

He shook his head. "They show that your husband is getting the bulk of his cash flow from an enterprise other than Delacorte Properties—and that this cash flow is considerable. But there is nothing to prove that he's bootlegging. For all these books tell me, he could be a part-time traveling bible salesman."

"Do bible salesmen have filing cabinets stuffed with cash?"

He held up his hand. "Hear me out: I don't doubt you. And from the amounts I see recorded, I think you're right in your suspicion that he's doing a real high-volume business. But again, there's no proof here."

Charlotte put her head in her hand, shaking her head slowly.

"Mrs. Delacorte, I'm not saying there's nothing to go on. I'm just saying I need more."

"Like what?"

"We need to catch William in the middle of a transaction, or—at the very least—on the premises of a place where he is dealing in the trafficking of illegal alcohol."

Charlotte nodded. "Mr. Buckner, may I ask you a question?"

"Yes."

"Do you believe me?"

Emory Buckner swung his feet down from the desk, and leaned toward her so that they had optimal eye contact. "Mrs. Delacorte, I do believe you. Not out of the goodness of my heart, or because you seem to be an upstanding woman, or even because of the ledgers you showed me. I believe you because I already had my eye on your husband."

Charlotte knew she should be surprised by his pronouncement, but all she felt was a crushing sadness.

"I know you were at the house the day some of my men went to question your husband. I read it in the report."

She nodded.

"Was that when you first realized he was maybe doing something illegal?" he said.

"Not exactly," she said. "At least, not entirely. When I asked him about that, he told me that some people who were at his mother's funeral were under investigation. I believed him."

"And it's true—they were and they are. But that also made us suspicious of William. These people were putting themselves in public view to pay their respects to William's mother, and this was risky for them. They weren't doing this because of their fine up-bringing; they were doing it because the risk of offending William was as bad—if not worse—than the risk of getting seen by the authorities. We believe your husband is a dangerous man, Mrs. Delacorte."

Charlotte felt the hair pricking up on her arms.

"I need to get the ledgers back into my house," she said. Buckner nodded.

"I agree." He slid them across the desk to her, and her hands shook as she put them into her bag.

"So how are we going to catch William in the act, Mrs. Delacorte? Any ideas?"

Charlotte tried to make her brain function in a useful way. What did she know? Nothing. She was completely in the dark. Except . . .

"He's doing a deal with Boom Boom at the Vesper Club," she said.

Buckner nodded. "Are you certain?"

Charlotte knew this was her opening to get Jake out of the legal system's line of fire.

"A friend told me—a useful source of information. And he probably knows more. But if I tell you who he is, and if I help you get William, I need you to promise me you will drop the charges that are pending against this friend."

"I can't promise you that. What has he been charged with?"

"Just bootlegging—and he runs the smallest little speakeasy. It's nothing compared to what you're getting with William."

"Who is it?"

"You don't know?"

"Mrs. Delacorte, do you have any idea how many people are in the system right now for bootlegging and related charges?"

"His name is Jake Larkin," she said. If the name meant anything to him, he didn't show it.

"It's my job to prosecute, and oversee the prosecution of, people who violate the Volstead Act. I can't make exceptions for your friend, no matter how helpful you are with an ongoing investigation."

Charlotte stood, the ledgers heavy in her handbag.

"Then I guess we have nothing left to talk about. Enjoy the rest of your weekend, Mr. Buckner." Her voice was steady, but she was shaking inside.

She reached the door and was turning the handle when he called her back.

"I can't make the charges against your friend disappear," he said. "But I can get him a good public defender and have a word with the judge."

She looked back at him. "How do I know you'll follow through with this?"

"You'll know when the lawyer contacts him tomorrow to discuss his case."

Charlotte returned to her seat.

"Do you know any more information about his dealings with Boom Boom? When and where they meet? How much she has paid him so far?"

Charlotte shook her head.

"I need you to try to find out. And keep me informed. The lines of communication between us must be open, Mrs. Delacorte. It's critical. I'm on your side."

She nodded. Again, she headed for the door.

"And Mrs. Delacorte? One more thing I thought you should know: If what I'm seeing in those ledgers is accurate, you and your husband have no legitimate source of income."

"What are you saying?" Charlotte said, trying to remain calm.

"In layman's terms? You're broke."

Chapter 8

RAFFERTY MUST HAVE been waiting for her, because he was at the front door of the house the minute she walked through it.

"Is William here?" she said.

"No."

"Please be on the lookout and let me know the second you see a car. I have to return these ledgers to his office."

Rafferty clearly wanted to talk to her, and if she gave herself time to think about it, she wanted very much to confide in him. But there was no time.

Charlotte ran through the house, her movement constricted by the tightness of her dress. She jammed a hairpin into the lock on William's office door, but twisted too aggressively for it to work.

"Calm down," she told herself, trying again until she heard the click. She pushed into the room.

"Charlotte!" Rafferty called out. "Get out of there!"

"Damn it," she muttered, shoving the ledgers into the drawer. A bunch of papers got stuck as she tried to close it, and she had to rearrange the ledgers so as not to push things out of place.

Stumbling in her haste, she relocked the door and sprinted to the parlor. She dove onto the couch, her heart beating so hard she was sure it was visible through her dress.

She heard William greet Rafferty, and then his footsteps on the stairs. Relieved, she sat still for a minute and collected herself.

How was she going to get more information for Buckner? William was a complete mystery to her, and the office in the house only yielded so much information—and what it did provide wasn't enough. As for catching him in the act, William was too smart—and now probably too careful—to get caught with anybody or at any place that would incriminate him.

She heard footsteps outside of the parlor, moving closer. She lay down and closed her eyes, feigning sleep.

She sensed the person come next to the couch—could feel his eyes on her. It went against all instinct not to open her own eyes and look.

Time seemed to stop. How long had he been standing there? And then she had a terrible thought, a panicked thought that made it hard for her to breathe. She imagined William standing over her with a pillow, bringing it down over her face, and holding it. Would she be able to scream loud enough for Rafferty, or would it be muffled?

Just when she thought she couldn't take it anymore, when she was ready to spring upright, she heard him retreat.

She waited a few seconds past when the footsteps were gone and slowly sat up. Her heart was pounding so hard it hurt.

The front door closed heavily.

Maybe Jake was right—she was crazy to stay in the house. Especially now that Emory Buckner's help was not proving to be a quick fix.

Charlotte felt paralyzed. She wanted to get up but didn't know where to go or what to do. Everything that had seemed so clear to her just a day ago was now clouded with uncertainty.

The front doorbell sounded. Her first thought—or hope, rather—was that it was Jake. If it was Jake, she told herself, it was a sign that everything was going to be ok.

She stood and began pacing. And then Mae walked into the room.

"What are you doing here?" said Charlotte, surprised. "You barely missed William. He was just here a minute ago."

"I know," said Mae. "When I left Amelia's house he was there, so I thought I was in the clear. But then I got here and saw the car so I waited a few minutes and luckily, he left."

"Do you have any idea what he was doing there?" said Charlotte.

"No," said Mae, sitting on the couch. "They were behind closed doors. And I didn't stick around to find out."

"Well, you shouldn't stay here long. I don't need him getting in a state over the two of us talking. He's so paranoid lately."

"Is it paranoia when there's actually something going on behind one's back?"

Charlotte glared at her. "If you're going to start in on me about this, then you might as well leave now. I don't want to hear it."

Mae shook her head. "I'm not here to argue. I just want to know what's going on. I've been on pins and needles since we talked last night. I'm going to see the florist for the wedding this afternoon with Amelia, and for all I know the newspaper headlines by then will say that my brother is a bootlegger. Is he going to be arrested?"

Charlotte sat next to her. "Can I trust you, Mae?" she said, looking directly into her sister-in-law's bright blue eyes.

Mae nodded, so faintly it was barely noticeable. "Yes."

"If you feel caught in the middle out of some sense of loyalty to William—he is your brother, after all—I understand. But if that's the case we should just stop the conversation right here. And you should know that I would never do anything to intentionally hurt you."

"I *do* know that, Charlotte. You've saved my sanity these past few months. But this thing with William—the family will never recover. It will be true disgrace. I'm not sure that exposing him is the right thing to do."

"Mae, Emory Buckner told me something that's difficult to believe but he has no reason to lie: He said William is broke. The only money seems to be the illegal money from the bootlegging. Delacorte Properties is near bankruptcy. I don't know what the status of your inheritance is. If William was the executor of your mother's will, he could have squandered any money. I don't know how it all works. But what we need to do is get William out of the way so I can get in there and figure out how bad it is and find a way to fix it. So you see, the biggest danger to the Delacorte family is keeping William in charge."

Mae shook her head. "I can't believe it."

"Is that just a figure of speech, or do you really doubt me?"

"I don't doubt you," Mae said.

Charlotte hesitated, then realized she needed help badly enough to gamble by enlisting Mae.

"Look, I need to find a way to catch William in the act—either at a club like the Vesper where he is doing business, or taking another meeting like the one he was having with Jake. Except this time, with someone we don't mind getting busted alongside William."

Mae seemed to consider this.

"Will you help me?" said Charlotte.

"Yes. How?"

"I'm not sure yet," Charlotte said. "That's what we need to figure out."

"What are things like between the two of you?"

"He hit me the day he found Jake talking to me here in the parlor. He told me if he catches me with Jake again he will kill him."

Mae visibly shuddered. "Oh, Charlotte! I didn't know it was this bad."

"I'm sleeping in your old room. And I look forward to the day I get out, just like you did."

FIONA SURVEYED HER apartment, which had essentially become a walk-in closet that she happened to sleep in.

Almost every visible surface was covered with dresses, scarves, shoes, hats, and tangled bunches of beaded necklaces in every color and shape. She'd spoken to one of the building handymen about putting up some metal rods so she could hang the dresses, but he seemed more interested in jumping on her than jumping on the task.

She knew there was probably something she should be doing with her money other than spending it on clothes and accessories, but for the life of her she couldn't imagine what that would be. She was making money in tips, and had saved some money from when she had been sleeping with johns, but it wasn't enough to travel or get a bigger apartment. It was just enough to buy dresses, though—and that was fine by her. As far as she was concerned, any money spent on making herself look better was an investment in her future.

There was a knock at the door, and she wondered if the handyman was finally showing up. Cautious as ever, she looked out the peephole.

Roger Smith. Or, Roger Warren, as she now knew he was really named.

"What are you doing here?" she called through the locked door. Her first thought had been to ignore the knock, but the last thing she needed was another scene where he knocked like a lunatic the way Mae had that night—until the cops had come and arrested her.

"I need to talk to you."

He had to be kidding.

"You should have thought of that before you busted my friend," she said. "Fuck off."

"Please, Fiona—let me in. Did you see the paper today? My life is ruined! My wife left, I was fired from my job. . . ."

Oh, good lord. Greta Goucher's column. She'd forgotten all about it.

"Do you have a copy of the paper with you?" she said.

"What? No—no, I don't have it with me. I never want to see that rag again."

"Go get a copy for me," she said.

She watched him hesitate a minute, then retreat down the stairs. A tedious conversation with him was a small price to pay for paper delivery service. And it might be amusing to hear his take on Greta's juicy exclusive.

Now back to the wardrobe dilemma.

Fiona picked a black silk chiffon imitation Chanel dress off of her bed, and held it against herself. She wished she had a full-length mirror. Maybe that should be the next thing she bought.

Another knock on the door.

"Are they selling papers at the bottom of the building stairs?" she grumbled. But when she peeked out, she saw Mae. "You must be psychic," she said, opening the door with a smile. "I need some-one to help zip me up." Fiona waved the black dress like a flag.

Mae crossed her arms in front of her chest and scowled. She walked into the apartment like someone marching into battle. Fiona knew something was amiss but at least it wasn't her fault this time. She would just have to cheer her up. "Or maybe you'd rather help *un*dress me," she said saucily, pulling off her night-gown.

"Why did that guy Roger just walk out of this building?" Mae asked angrily.

"Oh, no! . . . It's not what you think. I didn't even let him in—though I did send him to get me a newspaper."

"What?" Mae said, wrinkling her nose like she smelled something bad. Clearly she did not believe her.

"He came knocking on my door, saying he needed to talk—that his life was ruined. I forgot all about that Greta Goucher column, to be honest."

Mae pulled a newspaper out of her handbag and tossed it on Fiona's bed. She still didn't look happy. Fiona took her hand. "Mae, we're a team now. No more funny business, okay?"

Mae's eyes softened, and she sat on the bed.

Fiona picked up the newspaper and flipped through until she found Greta's column. "'A smashing redhead at the Vesper Club that this lawyer finds more addictive than anything served up in a bottle.'" She laughed. "I like that. That woman can really write." She looked at Mae, who clearly wasn't amused.

"What's with you today?"

"This whole thing with Jonathan is about to blow up."

"Why? Don't tell me he's changed his mind?"

"Not yet. But he will." Mae told her about Charlotte's plot against William, and how it would expose him as a criminal.

Fiona responded with a single word.

"Good."

"Maybe. But my marriage will be a casualty of it."

"You don't need Jonathan Astor. Once William's out of the way you will have more control of your life."

Another knock at the door.

Mae jumped up and, ignoring Fiona's protest, opened it.

"Where's Fiona?" she heard Roger ask.

"Fuck off, Roger. Unless you want to be in the paper again tomorrow." With that, Mae slammed the door.

Fiona covered her mouth to stifle her laughter. "Wow. I've never seen you so angry. It's kind of hot," she said.

Mae glared at her. "I'm glad you find all of this so amusing."

Fiona pulled her down onto the bed, kissing her neck and

running her hands over her breasts until she felt Mae's small frame tense with excitement. Mae took one of Fiona's hands and pushed it between her legs. Fiona slipped her fingers inside Mae's underwear, rubbing and pressing with practiced strokes, until Mae shuddered in climax. Mae put her head in Fiona's lap, and Fiona stroked her hair.

"I think we should help Charlotte," Fiona said.

Mae shifted so that she was looking up at her. "I'm willing to help her. I just don't know how. And frankly, I'm still worried about keeping that crazy bitch Greta under control. She told me that column we fed her isn't a big enough story—that she wants me to be her mole."

Fiona reached for the newspaper, and skimmed Greta Goucher's column. "I'd say we have another story for her. A huge one."

Mae looked at her questioningly, then understanding dawned on her, and she shook her head.

"We're *not* publishing a gossip item about William—that will only tip him off and make it impossible for Charlotte to get evidence for the DA."

"I'm not talking about publishing a gossip item. I'm thinking we use her as bait."

Chapter 9

JAKE WAS JOLTED out of a deep, hungover sleep by the knocking on his door.

It had been days since he'd had a visitor. He hadn't spoken to anyone since Charlotte bailed him out of jail three days earlier.

With the legal charges against him, he was in limbo. He'd never accepted Lawrence Lovejoy's job offer in Chicago, but he'd never officially turned it down, either. Still, he was sure Rona had told her brother about Jake's arrest, and Lawrence would know that meant Jake wasn't leaving town anytime soon. So the decision had been made for him.

And that was never a good thing in life.

He made his way to the door, tripping over an empty beer bottle he had left in the middle of the living room.

"Who is it?" he said.

"Mr. Larkin? My name is John Kellman. I'm a defense attorney."

"You picked the wrong case, buddy. I can't afford an attorney." Jake, bewildered, spoke through the closed door.

"My services won't cost you a penny," the guy called.

Jake hesitated a minute, then let the guy inside.

"Okay, you've got my attention," he said.

The lawyer walked into the apartment with just the hint of hesitation, as if expecting it to be booby-trapped. Jake got the distinct sense the visit was not the lawyer's own idea.

"So what brings you by, Kellman?" said Jake.

"A strong suggestion from your friend."

"And what friend is that?"

"Emory Buckner," said Kellman.

Jake froze on the spot.

What the hell was Charlotte up to?

THE AMBER ROOM was a private dining club. Mae had read about them springing up all over the city, luxurious, opulent spaces that resembled the dining rooms of the finest houses in the city, but were accessible to the select few who could afford the annual fee. She had never been inside one before.

Mae knew her mother had detested them, and would have looked down on Jonathan's parents for lowering themselves to dine in one.

"They're worse than restaurants," her mother had said. "Because with a restaurant, you know you are dining among the riffraff and there is no two-ways about it. But these 'clubs' have the pretense of exclusivity."

The New Yorker and *Vanity Fair* did not agree with her, and had made a point of saying that they were the preferred luncheon spots for the young and chic.

Mae caught Jonathan's mother watching her.

"Lovely room, isn't it?" she said.

"Yes, it is," said Mae.

"Now Mae, dear, I'm just going to come out and say that we think the wedding reception should be at the Waldorf-Astoria."

"That makes sense," said Jonathan amiably, winking at Mae.

"It doesn't look right if we don't use the family's hotel," his father said to Mae, as if holding the wedding at the luxurious Waldorf-Astoria would be a disappointment to her. Maybe he thought the Delacortes viewed using hotels rather than family estates as gauche.

"The family has never fully gotten over that nasty feud," said Annabeth. "With every occasion at the hotel, we keep hoping it's one step closer to putting it all behind us."

"No need to get into all that now, dear," said Charles, patting her hand.

"The Waldorf-Astoria were originally two competing hotels owned by two Astor cousins. Then they merged," Jonathan explained.

"Cousin Amelia is *strongly* suggesting we do a summer wedding. I think the earliest we can reasonably pull off is July."

"July? No one has a July wedding," said Jonathan.

"Well, we won't make June. And Amelia was adamant we not stretch this out until the fall." She looked pointedly at Mae.

"Oh—I'm . . . no, there's no rush from me," she stammered, realizing what the Astors were thinking.

"That's good to know," said Annabeth, glaring at her son.

"Don't worry, Mother. There'll be no scandals here," he said, taking Mae by the hand. His parents nodded approvingly, and Annabeth smiled with warmth.

"We are happy to hear it," Annabeth said. "And we welcome you to the family, Mae."

"To family," Charles said, raising his glass of sparkling water.

"To family," they said, touching glasses.

No one seemed to notice that Mae couldn't look them in the eyes.

CHARLOTTE WOKE TO a knock on the window.

Her breathing felt shallow, and she wondered for a minute if she were still asleep and dreaming. Her mind drifted to Jake, and in her state of half wakefulness, she imagined him slipping into bed with her, his hands roaming underneath her nightgown. . . .

She heard the knock again. This time, she jumped out of bed and pulled back the curtain.

"Mae?"

Charlotte opened the window as quickly as her hands, stiff with sleep, would allow.

"What are you doing here?" she said quietly. "And how did you know this ladder was back in place?"

"I didn't," said Mae. "I was just going to throw rocks at the window. But I was pleasantly surprised to find my old resourcefulness put to good use."

"The few times I used that thing I was certain I would fall to a shameful death. Now get inside. You're making me nervous."

She pulled Mae through the window and into her dark bedroom.

"Were you sleeping? It's only eleven."

"There's not much for me to do after dinner these days," said Charlotte. "Now what's going on?"

"You mean aside from the dinner I just had with the Astors, planning the wedding that will never happen?"

Charlotte sighed. "Did you come here just to make me feel bad?" She sat back on her bed, and Mae sat next to her.

"No. I have an idea . . . well, actually Fiona had the idea—"

"You told Fiona about this?"

Mae ignored the question and pushed ahead, her words coming out in a rush. "William is keeping a low profile, right? He knows that we all know, and he probably feels really exposed, and he's not going to do anything stupid. So you're never going to find anything lying around, and he's not going to go anywhere incriminating. But what if he slipped up in a fit of anger?"

"I don't want to make him angry," Charlotte said. "I'm scared of him, frankly."

"You don't have to be anywhere near him for this to work; we get Greta to call him and provoke him. She asks him to confirm if it's true his wife is having an affair with a speakeasy owner. He gets enraged, and then Greta tells him you're at the Vesper Club with Jake right now. William runs down there, and Buckner is waiting. Voilà—he's on the premises of the place where he's dirty dealing." Mae smiled.

"The problem with that idea is I think William would be perfectly happy for me to disgrace myself in public. I'm not sure what he's planning, but I'm afraid the idea of my publicly cuckholding him plays right into it."

Mae shook her head. "I know my brother. His ego could never let a phone call like that go unanswered. He'll be at the Vesper faster than you can say busted bootlegger."

Charlotte hugged her knees to her chest.

"I don't know. . . ."

"Charlotte, you're the one who sold me on the idea that something has to be done. Are you getting cold feet?"

"Maybe," Charlotte said.

"I told you, I'm on your side, okay?" Mae said. "And Fiona is, too. Whatever happens, we'll make it together."

Chapter 10

THE MORNING WAS bright and hot, and Fiona was up and out much too early. But she had been summoned by Boom Boom. She could only imagine what had her in a snit this time.

She headed uptown on Houston Street, wishing she'd worn more sensible shoes. And then she noticed a familiar face heading in her direction.

"Larkin!" she said. "I heard you were in the clink."

"I was," he said. "And now I'm not. Turn around—we're going to your place for a little chat," he said grimly.

"Oh, now what?" she said. "You'll have to get in line—Boom Boom already called me to her office."

"Boom Boom can wait. You need to tell me what Charlotte is up to."

"Why don't you ask her?"

"I'm not exactly welcome at the Delacorte house these days."

"I'll bet," Fiona said. "How are you so sure I know something?'

"Don't play games with me, Sparks. I'm sure Mae knows something, and if Mae knows, you know. I've been around you crazy birds long enough to know that much."

They locked eyes, and she blinked first. "Fine. But you have to make it worth my while. Keeping Boom Boom waiting is going to make my life miserable. Why don't you take me for breakfast?"

"As you might have noticed, I'm out of business these days. Why don't you take *me* for breakfast."

"Because *I'm* not the one looking for information," she said.

He sighed with exasperation, and she led the way to her favorite coffee shop on Jane Street, Buckles and Barrels. Jake went to the counter to order, and Fiona squeezed into a small table in the corner.

"So spill it," he said, sitting down, placing some food in front of her.

Fiona eyed him as she ate, silent until she was finished and patting her mouth carefully with a napkin.

"Now, look Jake, I appreciate the breakfast. So I'm gonna give you some friendly advice. Leave Charlotte alone. Get out of town, and consider yourself lucky not to be in jail."

Jake reached for her hand across the table. When she met his eyes, they were filled with worry.

"I know something is going on," he said.

"Nothing that involves you," she said.

"Fee, you and I have to stick together. We're the outsiders in this whole thing, but we have a lot at stake, too, don't we?"

She stood up and put two dollars on the table.

"That's for breakfast. I'm late for my meeting."

GRETA GOUCHER LIKED to pride herself that she never forgot a voice. And so when she answered her phone just minutes before she was going to leave to get fresh coffee, she recognized the caller as Boom Boom Lawrence before she even identified herself.

"What can I do for you?" Greta said.

"I noticed that fine piece of work you had in the paper yesterday," Boom Boom said. The sarcasm was not lost of Greta.

"Always nice to hear from one of our readers, Miss Lawrence. But I was just on my way out."

"I won't take much of your time. In fact, I was just calling to see if we could meet for coffee later today. I have a little business proposition for you."

"Journalism is all the business I need, Miss Lawrence."

"Well, I wouldn't be so sure about that. Everyone knows that writers make peanuts."

Greta sighed. She knew she was being baited, and that she should just hang up the phone. But the writer in her just couldn't resist hearing what the crazy woman had to say next.

"What are you suggesting, Miss Lawrence," said Greta.

"I think I might know of a way to pad your monthly income," Boom Boom said. "And you don't even have to do anything. In fact, I'm willing to pay you to *not* do something."

Greta knew where this was going. "I hope you're not suggesting that I refrain from writing about your club in exchange for money."

"I never said that. What time can you meet this afternoon?"

"Unlike cheap liquor and cheap women, the press can not be bought and sold, Miss Lawrence," Greta said, and hung up the phone.

"What was that all about?" said Lou, startling her. She turned around in her seat.

"Wrong number," said Greta dryly. "What brings you up here?"

"You've got a visitor. Again," he said.

Her coffee run would have to wait. She followed him downstairs.

"What hot little number do you have cooking up this week, Goucher? You're making our paper famous," he said.

"I need a raise," she said, following him down to the first floor. There, sitting in his smoke-filled and cluttered office, was

Charlotte Delacorte. This surprised Greta more than the day she found Amelia Astor in the office, because out of all the society women she'd encountered lately, Charlotte had always seemed the most wary of her.

With her ultra-chic haircut and expensive clothes, Charlotte looked as out of place in the *Sun* offices as most of the journalists would look at a society ball.

Greta noted, not for the first time, Charlotte Delacorte's regal prettiness. Unlike most people she encountered, it was difficult for Greta to gauge what was going on behind those wide gray eyes.

"Hello, Mrs. Delacorte. What brings you here?" Greta tried to seem nonchalant, but she was practically salivating at the thought of what gem of information was about to fall into her lap.

"I was hoping we could talk in private," Charlotte said, turning her back to Lou. "Perhaps we can go to your office?"

Greta didn't want to admit that it would be a cold day in hell before she had her own office.

"Well, we're already here. Lou, maybe you could step out so we can use your office for a few minutes?"

She could tell that her boss was about to tell her she was out of her mind, but then she saw the gears shift in his mind. Her column on the DA's office prostitution scandal had finally earned her some clout at the paper.

"Okay, yeah, why not," he said, groaning slightly as he heaved himself out of his chair. "But not too long. I've got work to do, too, ya know."

Greta forced herself to smile at him. "Thanks, Lou. We'll just be a few minutes."

She waited until he was out of the office—and out of earshot—before turning back to Charlotte.

"Welcome, Mrs. Delacorte," Greta said, sitting in the chair behind Lou's desk, covering his plate of cold eggs with a sheet of paper. Charlotte sat in the stiff wooden chair by the office door.

Her discomfort was obvious. Greta knew that the first rule of getting people to talk was putting them at ease. "Now that you've seen where I spend my days, you can imagine why I'm so happy to get invited to your parties at night."

Charlotte laughed. "I guess you can say that."

Greta knew it was her turn to speak, but she refrained. Charlotte fidgeted in silence for a few more minutes. "I know that Mae told you the information you used in that column about the lawyer and the prostitute," Charlotte finally said.

Greta nodded. "Maybe she did, and maybe she didn't. I'm not discreet with what I publish in my column, Mrs. Delacorte, but I never divulge a source."

Charlotte nodded. "I appreciate that. But I happen to know that you're putting pressure on Mae to give you an even bigger story in exchange for not writing something salacious about her."

Greta kept silent.

"I have a big story for you. But I'm only giving it to you if you promise to leave Mae alone. And if you take the story and don't leave Mae alone, the next story you write will be about how the DA is investigating you for blackmail."

Greta swallowed hard. "Well, when you put it that way, Mrs. Delacorte—I'm all ears."

"My husband suspects I am having an affair," Charlotte said. "Tonight, he will show up at the Vesper Club looking to catch me there with my presumed lover. All hell will break loose. And you can be there to report on it firsthand."

Greta coughed. "And how do you know your husband will go to the Vesper tonight?"

"Because you're going to call him and tell him he can find me there."

Chapter 11

FIONA RANG THE bell at the Vesper for her meeting with Boom Boom.

The big woman herself opened the front door, looking as distressed as Fiona had ever seen her. Her yellow hair was askew, and her makeup looked more clownish than usual. And Fiona suspected she'd already started hitting the bottle.

"You're late," she growled.

"I hadn't planned on being here at all today. I have things to do outside of this place, you know."

"Yes, clearly. And does one of them involve talking to gossip columnists?" Boom Boom said, waving the newspaper in front of Fiona's face.

"I had nothing to do with that. I'm as surprised as you are," she lied.

"Did you know one of your johns was part of a sting operation?"

Fiona feigned indignation. "You're the one who told me to get into all that. I'm lucky I wasn't arrested! I should be the one mad at you."

Boom Boom seemed to consider this. She turned and walked to the bar, and Fiona followed. Maybe she'd get a free drink out of this.

Boom Boom heaved herself up on a bar stool, and gestured for Fiona to do the same.

"I'm going to have to fire you, you know," Boom Boom said. Fiona could tell she was genuinely upset about it.

"I understand," said Fiona, sighing heavily. The truth was, she knew she was going to be out of a job soon anyway. They all were.

"You do?" Boom Boom said in surprise.

HELL HATH NO FURY

"Yes. Just let tonight be my last night. My farewell shift, okay?" She had to see the raid go down. There was no way she'd miss that kind of action.

Boom Boom nodded. "I'm not paying you severance," she said.

"You're the boss," Fiona said. It took all of her effort to keep a straight face.

GRETA HAD NEVER had a story dropped in her lap before. It was highly suspicious, and she wasn't going to go chasing a story that would make a fool out of her.

And so she had no choice but to track down Jake Larkin to verify it.

She walked down the narrow stone stairway to the basement apartment. Her source said he ran a speakeasy out of the place, but in the harsh light of day, it was difficult to imagine.

The man who answered the door was darkly handsome. Greta knew she shouldn't be surprised by his good looks; after all, he was Charlotte Delacorte's alleged lover. And her husband was no slouch in the looks department.

"Jake Larkin?" she said.

He looked at her warily. "Who are you?"

"I'm Greta Goucher. Reporter for the *New York Sun*."

Jake began closing the door.

"I want to verify a conversation I had with Charlotte Delacorte," she said. And lo and behold, the door stopped closing.

Jake Larkin looked at her more closely. "And what conversation is that?" he said.

"She mentioned that you are meeting her tonight at the Vesper Club."

Greta couldn't quite read the expression on Larkin's face. Confusion? Surprise?

"Oh she did, did she?" he said.

"Yes. Can you verify that this is true?"

Larkin's face was a storm of emotion, and she knew in that moment she was onto something—the high and mighty Charlotte Delacorte was giving her the goods.

"Yes," he said slowly. "I think I *will* be at the Vesper Club tonight."

Greta smiled at him, though he seemed a million miles away and wasn't looking at her. "Thank you, Mr. Larkin. Have a nice day."

CHARLOTTE COULDN'T TELL if Emory Buckner was doubtful about her plan, or merely contemplating the logistics. Either way, she fidgeted nervously in her seat in his office.

"How sure are you that he'll show up? Fifty-fifty?" he finally said, leaning back in his seat, his hand behind his head.

"I'd say slightly more than fifty-fifty."

"When can you get him there?"

"Um, tonight?"

Buckner shook his head and lit a cigarette. "I need to put a team in place. It'll be a push, but we'll do it."

"How will it work, exactly? I mean, on your end."

"This is how it's going to go: You get to the club. Bait William into showing up. Meanwhile, I'll have the police covertly waiting in the front and back of the club. Who did you say is helping you with this?"

"My sister-in-law. Mae Delacorte."

"Okay, when William shows up, Mae has to walk out of the front the club and signal for my guys to go in. We'll decide on what that signal is. I need you inside, keeping William distracted and in place. The police will enter the premises and commence with the arrests."

"Will they arrest everyone?"

"Yes. That's how a raid works. And that's why we don't go around doing it every night. It's a burden on the system. But tonight we have a good reason, and so we'll arrest everyone, then sort out who is worth prosecuting. Of course, we all know in this case it's just William and Boom Boom."

"Will you be able to keep William in jail? He's going to realize I set him up and I don't want him coming back to the house until I've had time to make other arrangements and get out."

"I won't let them set bail."

Charlotte contemplated this. She still had one question, though she was almost afraid of the answer.

She hesitated before asking, "What if you don't find any evidence that William was selling to Boom Boom?"

"If I was just hoping to 'find' evidence, that would be a legitimate concern. But the goal tomorrow night is to get Boom Boom, too. I'll give her a plea deal if she gives us the goods on William."

Charlotte nodded, absorbing this. For the first time, the idea of William being arrested seemed real.

"Okay then. I guess we're set," Charlotte said, standing. Buckner held his hand out to shake her hand.

"By the way, I sent the public defender to see your friend, Mr. Larkin. But he declined his services."

"Why?" Charlotte said, dismayed.

"Don't know," said Buckner. "But it wasn't a smart move."

Chapter 12

A GOSSIP'S JOB was never done.

Greta curled up on her living room sofa, her cat purring by her feet. Her dirty dinner dishes were still on the dining room table, her laundry piled in a basket untended. But everything would have to wait: The day's most challenging—and unexpected—task was still ahead of her.

She lit a cigarette, and inhaled deeply. She hadn't been this nervous to make a call since her first job.

Sure, she'd been strong-armed into making the call for Charlotte Delacorte. But truth be told, it was something she would have happily done just for sport.

The phone rested on her left, atop a table she found discarded out on West Fourth Street. She reached for it.

"Here it goes, Boots," she said to the animal.

She dialed the number Charlotte Delacorte had written on a piece of paper. She had been warned the butler would answer, and that she would have to ask for William. Charlotte had instructed her to have the butler say it was a friend of Charlotte's calling—just to increase the odds that William would take the call.

The phone rang three times before it was answered. Greta ran through the verbal script, then waited for William Delacorte to get on the line. She found herself nervously perspiring, then told herself to calm down. She had nothing at stake here. But for some reason, she felt the weight of it.

"William Delacorte here," said a low, somewhat irritated voice on the other end.

"Hi, Mr. Delacorte," she said, her words coming out in a nervous rush. She told herself to slow down. "This is Greta Goucher. We met a few times—"

"What is this regarding, Miss Goucher?"

"Your wife. Are you aware that she is having an affair with a speakeasy owner?"

There was a pause. When he didn't say anything, she just plowed ahead. "In fact, she's out with him tonight. Everyone's just amazed by their blatant behavior."

"And where is this blatant behavior taking place, Miss Goucher?"

"The Vesper Club," she said.

"That's just fine," said William. "My wife is free to make a fool of herself, if that's what she chooses to do." Then she heard a click on the other end. She shrugged and replaced the phone receiver.

JAKE STARTED FOR the front door, and heard thunder rolling in the distance. He considered trying to find a hat in his closet, then just as quickly dismissed the idea. There was no time to worry about weather-appropriate apparel.

He'd barely been able to sit still in the hours since that woman appeared at his front door. He was just thankful she was crazy enough to show up like that. Fiona hadn't made things easy on him when she refused to say what was going on, but it seemed fate meant for him to intervene. He just never imagined fate would appear in the form of a pushy little newspaper reporter.

Jake's hand was on the doorknob when someone knocked. Startled, he looked out of the peephole.

He opened the door.

"I was just on my way out," he said to Rona. She looked beautiful in a bright red dress, her hair wild.

"I'll go with you," she said with a smile.

"That's not a good idea. You can stay here if you want. I just don't know how long I'll be."

She pouted playfully. "Where are you going?"

"I have to run up to the Vesper Club to find Charlotte."

Rona stiffened, all playfulness gone. She put her hand on his arm. "When are you going to stop chasing that woman?"

"Never," he said. Then, seeing the hurt expression on her face, he softened. "Rona, you're welcome to hang out here, but I don't have time to talk about all this right now. I'll see you later."

Jake brushed past her as the first raindrops started to fall.

THE THUNDER AND lightning started as soon as Charlotte pulled the car up to the front of the Vesper Club. Mae glanced at her nervously.

"I hope that's not a bad omen," she said. She didn't really believe in omens, but she did want Charlotte's reassurance.

"Everything will be fine," Charlotte said. "When you see William walk in, you walk out. And that's it—you're done. You won't be arrested as long as you stay out of the club once the police head in." Charlotte waited for Mae to get out of the car.

"Where are you going?" Mae said.

"I have to see Jake," Charlotte said. "Now that this is happening and he can't try to stop me, I can finally tell him what's happening."

"Can't it wait?" Mae said, hating how weak she sounded. But knowing that Charlotte was nearby would make her feel so much better.

"No. He has to know that today is the day I'm free from William. All this time, he's doubted me. He needs to know before it's too late." Charlotte smiled comfortingly at her. "Don't worry. Everything will be fine."

And with that, she drove off.

The doorman nodded to Mae, who handed over the cover charge, which she noticed had gone up a dollar.

Inside, the Vesper seemed somehow brighter and busier than she remembered. It was as if the universe recognized this fateful night in the life of the club, and brought all of its intangible glamour and excitement to bear.

The jazz music washed over it all, a soundtrack to the pulsing crowd. The trombone and sax were among the best she'd ever heard. Mae thought wistfully of how much this place had meant to her the past year or so, her escape, the place where she'd met Fiona. It was sad to think of it all coming to an end.

And then she spotted Fiona heading toward her.

"What are you doing here?" Mae said, dismayed. "I thought you had tonight off." Before she could warn Fiona that she had to stay by her side and leave with her when she told her to, Boom Boom sidled up to them.

"Well, if it isn't the soon-to-be Mrs. Astor. I hear congratulations are in order for you, Mae. Suffice to say, no one is more surprised than I am to hear of your marriage plans," she said with a smirk.

"Yes, well, don't hold your breath for a wedding invitation," said Mae.

Boom Boom seemed to barely hear her; her eyes were always moving around the club almost nervously. "What the hell is he doing here?" she muttered.

That's when Mae turned to see Jake.

Chapter 13

CHARLOTTE COULD SEE that the lights were on inside of Jake's apartment. She smiled in anticipation as she knocked on the door. He might halfheartedly reprimand her for not letting him in on her plan, but she knew any irritation would quickly disappear. She could already feel his arms around her, his mouth on hers . . . The door opened.

"What are you doing here?" said a clearly put-out Rona Lovejoy.

Charlotte was momentarily stunned into silence. This particular scenario had never entered her mind. When she recovered, she said, "I need to talk to Jake."

"He ain't here," said Rona, her big dark eyes cold and wary.

"Don't play games with me, Rona. This is important."

"I *said* he ain't here."

Charlotte sighed. "Then where is he?"

"Looking for you," said Rona.

It didn't make any sense. She was sure the woman was messing with her. "Really? And where is he looking for me?"

"The Vesper Club."

Charlotte turned and ran quickly back up the stairs to her car, praying that she could reach him in time.

MAE PUSHED THROUGH the crowd, and grabbed Jake by the arm.

"You have to get out of here," she said. He looked at her warily. They were surrounded by laughing women; a cocktail waitress in a slinky dress handed her a drink she never ordered.

"You're in on this, too?" Jake said. "Tell me what's going on!"

She thought of what Charlotte said in the car, *you won't be arrested as long as you stay out once the police head in.*

Now she had to get Jake *and* Fiona out with her.

"Please—just go."

"Not without Charlotte."

Mae would have to tell him the plan—it would be the only way to get him out of the club. But before she could say a word, Boom Boom was on top of them.

"You have some nerve showing up here, Larkin," she said.

Mae was about to tell Boom Boom to just leave them alone, when a sharp push sent her flying into a table. It took her a few seconds to recover, but she stood up in time to see William grab Jake by the collar and punch him in the face.

"Break it up, you two!" Boom Boom yelled, trying to restrain William. She distracted him long enough for Jake to land a blow on his jaw.

Mae's instinct was to jump in and help Jake, but she knew this was her time to get outside and signal for the police to head in.

"Let's go," she said as she grabbed the hand of a shocked Fiona.

"I'm not going anywhere! Can you fucking believe this?" Fiona said.

"Come on!" Mae yelled, frantically pulling her to the front door.

CHARLOTTE SHOVED A handful of bills at the doorman and ran inside the club. Out of the corner of her eye, she saw Mae rushing out, with Fiona trailing closely behind.

The room was in chaos, and for a minute she thought the raid was already underway, but soon realized the cause of the frenzy: A brawl had broken out in the center of the barroom, with Boom Boom and two security men trying to break it up.

She had a terrible sinking feeling in her gut and as she drew closer to the action, her fear was confirmed.

"Jake!" Charlotte yelled. She didn't know how she was going to get close enough to him to pull him outside. The security guard had him with both arms twisted behind his back, but Jake looked up to see her.

Their eyes met and the connection sent an electric crackle straight through her.

"Raid!" someone shouted, and Charlotte turned to see police pouring into the club from every direction. For a moment, it was as if the entire room froze. And then, all at once, people began to scream and run for the exits. Tables and chairs went flying as people tried to clear a path to the door. She turned to see William pulling free from the security guard's hold, and he headed toward her with murderous rage. He knew.

She turned to run from him, swept up in a tide of people desperate to reach an exit. She felt a hand pulling on her shoulder, and she screamed and pushed it away until she realized it was Jake.

"Come with me," Jake said, taking her by the hand. Immediately, she felt calmer.

He rushed her toward the back of the club.

"The police will be at the side exit, too," she shouted.

"That's not where we're going."

She looked behind her and saw Boom Boom hit a police officer with a liquor bottle as another tried to cuff her.

"Oh my god!" Charlotte said.

"This is going to get dangerous," said Jake.

"It's going to *get* dangerous?"

He pulled her to a doorway and opened it to a narrow set of wooden stairs.

"We can only fit one at a time. Go down and I'll follow."

"We'll get trapped down there with no way out." The sounds of screaming and breaking glass made her feel frantic. She was more afraid of running into William than of getting caught up in the sweep.

"There's a doorway—a tunnel down there that leads to the neighboring store. Go!" He let go of her hand, and she resisted the urge to grab onto him again.

Charlotte started down the stairs, but before she could descend more than a few feet, she heard someone yell, "Freeze! Hands up."

Jake slammed the door closed behind her. She started back up but then realized he was busted.

Chapter 14

AMELIA NEARLY CHOKED on her morning coffee.

She sat up in bed, and held the *New York Times* front page closer to her eyes, as if she had misread it. There, under the headline, POLICE RAID MIDTOWN NIGHTCLUB; DOZENS ARRESTED was the sentence, "Among those taken into police custody was William T. Delacorte."

"Mumson!" she yelled, throwing on her robe and bellowing out her bedroom door. "Bring me my telephone number book."

Once she had the slim, leather-bound volume in hand, she hurried downstairs to the telephone in the sitting room. She flipped through her address book and turned quickly to the Ps. Then she dialed the Delacorte family lawyer, Andrew Paulson.

"Has William been arrested?" she said.

"Yes, Miss Astor."

"Well, we have to rectify this immediately. I'll bring a check to your office and you must go down there and get him out. Frankly, I'm surprised I have to tell you this—"

"Miss Astor, if you would give me a moment to speak: I have already been to midtown. There is no bail set for William."

"No bail? Why in god's good name not?"

"I don't know."

"Well, what has he been charged with?"

"I'm not at liberty to discuss my client's case with you, Miss Astor."

"You're useless!" she said, slamming down the phone. Her heart pounding with indignation, she reopened the address book. Who to call? This was a disaster. It looked bad, and she could only imagine how humiliated William must feel. But he had done nothing wrong, and everyone surely knew there was a witch-hunt climate out there—anyone could become a victim of it. Surely this was not the sort of thing that would dim the sheen of their social status. It would fade into a colorful anecdote—a story they would cheerfully tell at cocktail parties for decades.

The phone rang, startling her. She wasn't used to answering it herself. But there was no use waiting for Mumson since she was standing right there.

"Hello?" she said tentatively. She hated the telephone. A necessary evil, that's what William's mother had called it. And she had been right—as she had been about everything.

"Amelia, it's me," said Margaret Cavendish. "Have you seen Greta Goucher's column today?"

"Not now, Margaret—I'm in the middle of something." She slammed down the phone.

"Mumson! Bring me the rest of the newspapers."

Her servant appeared and nervously handed her the *New York Sun* and a few magazines. "Just the paper," she said, tossing the magazines back at him. She flipped to the gossip page:

GRETA'S GOTHAM
A First-Class Raid

The DA's office cast a wide net when it raided the midtown Vesper Club last night—and caught itself one very big fish. Among the dozens arrested was none other than Fifth Avenue's William Delacorte, heir to the real estate fortune and—rumor has it—suspected rum runner. Sources say the next piece of property Mr. Delacorte looks at will have very few windows, but plenty of bars.

This couldn't be happening. How could such trash be allowed to be printed? She would own that rag by the time she was finished with her lawsuit!

If only Geraldine were alive. Then none of this nonsense ever would have been printed in a newspaper. Or, if it had, the mayor and the owner of both newspapers would both be issuing public apologies by now.

Then she realized who she needed to call.

Amelia quickly flipped through the address book again until she found the number for Jimmy Walker's campaign office. For the first time, she would be asking a favor of the mayoral hopeful— not the other way around.

CHARLOTTE SAT UP in bed. For the first time in weeks, she was back in the master bedroom. And she was blissfully alone.

It had worked. She could scarcely believe it. William was in jail, and now she would find out exactly what he was up to. And she was free. There was little question of a divorce going favorably for her—or at least, fairly. And in the meantime, the finances would be sorted out. Buckner had said they were broke—that Delacorte Properties was bankrupt and they had no legitimate income. But Charlotte knew that couldn't be the full picture. There was money somewhere—even if it was just what Geraldine had left to Mae. Now William would have to sort it out properly.

But she couldn't rest easily until she saw Jake. The first thing she had to do was get back to the midtown police precinct.

Penny reappeared with a tray of food and the newspaper.

"Thank you, Penny. Is Mae awake?"

Penny nodded and Charlotte asked that she send her in.

"I couldn't sleep a wink," Mae said, walking into the room.

"Thanks so much for staying here last night."

Mae smiled. "Of course. Though I have to admit it's a shock to the system to do things of my own free will around here."

"What does the newspaper say?"

"*The New York Times* only mentions that William was

arrested among dozens of other people. But the *New York Sun* has quite a different take on it." Mae smiled slyly.

"Greta?"

Mae nodded and handed her the paper.

Charlotte read it and smiled.

"She doesn't waste any time." She gestured for Mae to hand her the paper, wanting to see the words herself. "I have to go to the police station and try to bail out Jake," she said.

"Do you have the cash to do it?"

"I don't know!" Charlotte said, not having considered the financial reality of getting Jake out of jail. "It will probably be a lot since this is his second arrest. And I don't know how much access I have to money until Buckner sorts out this mess with William."

"I'm going to meet Jonathan for breakfast," Mae said. "I'll borrow money from him. Then you and I can go get Jake together."

"Don't even waste the time coming back here. If Jonathan will give you the money, just go straight to the jail. I don't want Jake there a second longer than necessary. Promise me?"

"I promise," said Mae.

JAKE LOOKED OUT from the bars of his cell, wishing he hadn't told that defense attorney to take a hike. At least he'd have someone to call.

He paced in his confined space, wishing he'd just listened to Charlotte when she implored him to leave. Not for his own sake, but for hers. He knew he'd be in custody indefinitely, but he doubted William would have the same problem. And there was no telling what that guy would do when he was out.

This was all his own fault. Jake had underestimated Charlotte; assuming all along that she had been hesitating to leave her marriage out of fear. Now, he saw that she'd done the most fearless thing imaginable.

If he'd known she was going to set William up and actually get him arrested, he would have helped to make sure that her hand in it did not show. He doubted she understood the true risk she had taken; Charlotte still, on some level, saw William as the man she had married—the wrong man, but still not someone to truly fear. But Jake had seen the real evil lurking in those aristocratic eyes.

Now, his failure to see the big picture had put him in a position of weakness just when Charlotte needed him the most. Instead of using his one phone call to try to get himself bailed out, he needed to warn Charlotte to leave the house and go to a place where William couldn't find her.

"Guard!" Jake called. The guard, an older man with a weathered face who kept himself busy with a deck of cards, either did not hear him or chose to ignore him. Jake banged on the bars, hitting the metal so hard he knew he was bruising his hand. He called out to the man again, and this time the guard turned lazily in his direction, his hand poised midair as he dealt himself a card.

And then, just as lazily, he turned back to his desk.

Chapter 15

AMELIA WAS SHOCKED at how disheveled William looked after just one night spent in jail. His complexion was ashen, and it looked like he hadn't shaved in a week. She wondered if he had been mistreated, and suspected there might be a lawsuit in the near future. This type of law enforcement error was completely unacceptable.

Jimmy Walker had told her who to ask for, and that although the bail he had managed to arrange sounded exorbitant, she should consider herself lucky it wasn't higher.

"I don't understand," she had said. "On what basis can they hold him without bail?"

"They must see him as a flight risk," Walker had said. "You owe me for this, Amelia. I expect some big checks in the coming months—checks that will buy me the election if it comes down to it."

Amelia had barely heard him. She was not a dumb woman. He was right: The authorities had to view William as some kind of threat to justify not setting bail. It was probably a misunderstanding, but she had to get to the bottom of it, nonetheless.

She glanced at the emerald ring on her finger.

William smiled at her, but did not speak until they were out of the station house.

"You never cease to amaze me, my darling," he said, opening the passenger door for her.

"I have to admit, this did take a bit of string-pulling," she said. "You want to drive?"

"Yes," he said, getting behind the wheel. "I need to get my Rolls. It's still parked in midtown where I left it last night."

"Don't worry about your car at a time like this, William. I'll send someone to get it later. I'm taking you back to my house so you can clean up and get some rest."

William shook his head. "I need to get home."

"Why? What's so important?" She felt a tug of jealousy. Was he eager to see Charlotte for some reason?

He didn't answer her, his eyes locked on the road.

"You know, they refused to post bail for you initially," she said. "I had to call on Jimmy Walker." Again, he said nothing. She began to feel a tension in her gut, a flutter of worry that began to spread throughout her body. "William," she said, "I think I deserve to know what is going on."

"You do, Amelia. If we're going to be partners moving forward, which I believe we are, I'm going to need your support." He paused, and it felt like the longest half minute of her life. She looked at his regal profile, reminding herself how long she had wanted him, and steeled herself to hear something that was unpleasant, problematic, but ultimately fixable. "I've been charged with violations of the Volstead Act—liquor distribution, trafficking, and sales."

"Why?" she said, her mind already racing about how to keep this from going public. She would shoot that damn Goucher woman if she had to!

"Because it's true," he said.

She thought her heart would stop. And she realized that clearly she was not the only one with this information—that somehow, Charlotte knew it too. But Charlotte was not rushing to his defense.

And then a chill washed through her as the past few weeks started piecing together in an entirely different way, like a kaleidoscope turned in the opposite direction.

William pulled the car onto West Fifty-fourth Street, and she saw his Rolls-Royce on the corner. He put Amelia's car in park and turned to look at her.

"They have no evidence, I'm certain," he said, tilting her chin up with his finger. "Charlotte set me up. That raid last night was not a coincidence."

Amelia looked away coldly, pulled the emerald ring off of her finger, and handed it to him.

MAE WATCHED THE front door of Lindy's Restaurant and Deli from the same booth where she'd sat with Jonathan on one of their early dates—a night that seemed like a million years ago.

She knew he wasn't an early riser, and it was asking a lot of him to meet her for breakfast. But she didn't want him to learn about William's arrest from the newspapers. Maybe it was already too late.

Fiona arrived first, dressed in a white blouse and flouncy yellow skirt. She looked like a schoolgirl, with her face free of makeup and her hair tied up in a high ponytail. She slid next to Mae with a smile.

"I can't believe you dragged me out of bed this early. I'm exhausted after all the excitement last night," she said.

Mae wanted to kiss her, but refrained. After everything, she'd lost her taste for scandal and provocation.

"Thanks for coming. I have to break the news to Jonathan, and it's easier with you here."

"For the record, I'm glad you're not going through with the marriage. We'll find our own way to make money."

Mae nodded, unconvinced. "It won't be easy."

"Come on," Fiona said. "I didn't spend all this time working for Boom Boom without learning a few things."

Jonathan walked in, looking slightly dazed.

"This is like the crack of dawn to him," Mae said.

"I know the feeling," said Fiona.

Mae waved him over, and Jonathan smiled and waved a waitress over along with him.

"I am in dire need of coffee," he told the woman, making a gesture to convey "large." He turned to Mae and Fiona.

"Two for the price of one." He winked at them. "What a pleasant surprise. How are you, Fiona?"

"Tired," she said.

"Indeed. As much as I adore hearing from my future wife, I can't imagine what would require meeting at such an ungodly hour. If I didn't know better, I'd fear you were about to tell me you're in the family way. But we both know that's not possible." He laughed.

"Did my phone call wake you?" Mae said. "Because you're probably the only one I know who hasn't read the paper yet this morning." She slid both *The New York Times* and the *Sun* across the table.

The waitress appeared with coffee.

"Yes, yes, I know all about it. My mother called me. A morning of scandal for the Delacorte family," he said with a grin. He lit a cigarette and offered one to her.

"I'm glad you're taking it so well," Mae said, surprised.

"Taking what so well?"

"The whole point of your marrying me was to put on an unblemished front. Carry on the good Astor name and all that. Now my family is disgraced. You might as well be walking down the aisle with Ursula."

He scoffed. "That's not going to happen. Ursula left me for a duke."

"A duke?"

"Yes. Apparently, titles are more important than money these days."

Mae and Fiona looked at him in sympathy. "Oh, don't give me those sad puppy eyes. Not everyone is looking for true love like you two romantics."

Mae squeezed Fiona's hand. "Well, now that you mention it, we are going to make a go of it. So scandal or not, I think we need to call off our engagement." She slid the diamond ring across the table to him. He pushed it back to her.

"Oh, keep it, doll. At least for a while. I'm in no rush to use it, that's for damn sure. And I think you're being hasty. I'm not ready to concede that our faux nuptials have lost their usefulness. My mother will get over the bootlegging scandal, and so will the rest of the city once tomorrow's headlines are printed. But Mae, we're talking about the future. And the world will look much more kindly upon us as a respectable couple than they will look at us as two renegades."

"Maybe we want to be renegades," said Fiona.

"There's nothing for you to be threatened by, Fiona. There's plenty of room for you in this equation."

Fiona lit a cigarette. "The equation is me and Mae—and *we* don't have room for *you*."

"What do you plan to do for money? Rumor has it Mae here is broke."

Fiona shrugged. "We might start a little nightlife venture. Maybe something that will make the Vesper Club look like a two-bit speakeasy."

Jonathan nodded, smiling.

"I might be interested in steering a bit of cash toward that. A different type of partnership than I had envisioned for us, Mae, but maybe one that will pay off even more." He pulled out a gold cigarette case and opened it for Mae.

She removed a cigarette, and he lit it for her. She exhaled her first drag, and said, "Well, since we're talking about partnership, there's one favor I have to ask of you."

"Name it."

"I need your help bailing my friend Jake out of jail."

Chapter 16

CHARLOTTE PACED HER bedroom nervously, waiting either for Mae to show up with Jake, or for her to return with news about him.

She'd made two calls to Buckner, but both times his secretary told her he was in a meeting. She not only wanted to make sure bail was set for Jake, she also had to prepare herself for what would happen next with William's case. With all of her focus on the details and logistics of the raid, she hadn't asked questions about how the investigation would play out once William was behind bars. She wanted to know everything they learned about his operation, and she wondered if maybe she shouldn't be looking to hire her own attorney.

And then she heard the front door open and close. She quickly pulled on her shoes, and ran a brush through her hair. She walked outside of the bedroom, but before she could reach the top of the stairs, she saw William heading up them.

She let out a scream, and ran back to the bedroom. She slammed the door closed, and fumbled with the lock on the door. Before she could get it to latch, William pushed through the door, sending her flying onto the ground.

The way he looked at her made her blood run cold.

"You ungrateful bitch," he said. "What did you tell them? What do they know?" He grabbed her by the hair and pulled her so she was sitting upright. She felt the cold, blunt tip of a gun pointed at her temple.

"Nothing," she whispered, her heart pounding so hard she thought she would die from that alone. "William, using that gun is only going to make things worse for yourself. Do you want to be in jail for the rest of your life?"

"Oh, but I'm not using the gun." His laugh cut through her. "Unfortunately, you just can't handle the stress of your husband's disgrace, and the dwindling fortune . . . and since you'd been snooping around my office, you helped yourself to my gun."

She realized in that moment Jake had been right, and her failure to listen to him had been even more foolish than his failure to listen to her. And their stubbornness would cost them everything.

"William, please. Put the gun down," she begged, her voice wavering.

He smacked her hard across the face, releasing her so she fell and hit her head on the hardwood floor.

"What did you tell them?" he said.

Her thoughts became faint clouds. She closed her eyes, wanting to slip into some kind of sleep. But she knew she had to fight that urge with all her being.

A sudden commotion wrenched her eyes back open.

Rafferty had William by one arm, twisting it behind his back. Charlotte didn't know if he realized William had a gun, so she yelled it out, her voice so shrill and tight she barely recognized it as her own.

"Move out of the way!" Rafferty said. She scrambled to the side of the bed, looking for something to use as a weapon to help fell William.

A shot thundered through the room.

"Rafferty!" she screamed, her panic quelled by the realization that Rafferty was standing, and William was on the ground.

She rushed to Rafferty and threw her arms around him. He drew her in tightly for a second, his lips brushing her temple, and then released her.

"Go call an ambulance," he said.

She stood immobile, staring at William on the floor. Blood pooled out from under him.

"Charlotte—go!" Rafferty said.

This time, she listened.

Chapter 17

CHARLOTTE KNEW THAT William was dead even before the medical examiner told her.

But she didn't have the wherewithal to fully process the information. Her immediate concern was the aggressiveness of the police officers' questioning of Rafferty. The two of them were seated in the parlor, surrounded by men in blue uniforms and suits. Penny had made mint iced tea, which everyone was drinking except for Rafferty.

"It doesn't look good when a butler shoots the master of the house—in the bedroom no less," one of them said, gesturing for Rafferty to stand up. "You're coming with us."

"What are you doing?" Charlotte cried. "I *told* you, he saved my life. My husband came here to kill me." The police officers ignored her. "Don't talk to them, Rafferty. Don't say a word. I'm going to get you a lawyer."

The front doorbell rang, and Charlotte ran to answer it. She hoped it was Mae, though she had a key and wouldn't have to ring. What was keeping her so long?

And then she realized she would have to break the news to Mae about William. Even when she told Mae exactly how things unfolded, it would no doubt be difficult for Mae to believe that her brother had intended to kill his wife. He was her brother; how could she not despise Charlotte after what happened to him?

She opened the door to find Emory Buckner.

"Mrs. Delacorte—my condolences." He walked into the foyer and removed his hat.

"Mr. Buckner! Thank god you're here. They're arresting my . . . my butler, and he saved my life."

As if on cue, the police appeared in the room with Rafferty in handcuffs.

Charlotte turned to Buckner, her tension releasing into anger.

"This is an outrage. What was William even doing out of jail? You assured me no bail would be set for him! I could have been killed."

"Charlotte, it's okay," Rafferty said soothingly. Buckner looked at him strangely, no doubt startled by a servant addressing her by her first name.

She glanced back at Rafferty with concern. "Let me handle this," she said softly.

Buckner sighed, and put his hands on his hips. He surveyed the police and Rafferty standing in front of him.

"Is there a place we can talk privately?" he asked Charlotte.

She led Buckner back to the sitting room. She sat on a chair near the telephone, and had a flashback to the day Mae had arrived unexpectedly, suitcase in hand. Charlotte remembered trying to reach William on his business trip, thinking that he must have a simple explanation for everything. That when she spoke to him, everything would be all right.

She suddenly felt like she was going to vomit.

Charlotte bent over and put her head in hands, breathing in quick shallow breaths.

"Mrs. Delacorte, are you alright?"

She ignored him, breathing deeply in and out, in and out, until after a minute, the feeling passed. When she felt composed, she turned back to Buckner.

"William knew I set him up," she said. "He came here to kill me. My butler was just trying to get the gun away from him. What the hell was he doing out of jail?"

Buckner nodded. "Your husband's release was arranged behind my back. Strings were pulled by someone, and I intend to get to the bottom of it."

"You can't arrest my butler."

"He just killed a man, Mrs. Delacorte."

"Look, I helped you—I handed you William on a silver platter. Now you have to help me. My butler is innocent."

"First of all, a dead bootlegger is of no help to me. How am I supposed to find out who he worked for? How do I leverage this to stop the chain of sales? The answer is, I can't. So you are free of William, and I am back to square one."

"You have Boom Boom in custody, don't you?"

"Yes," he conceded. "But I mainly have her on prostitution and resisting arrest. She's not the lynch-pin seller I need for my bootlegging case. So as I was saying, the main problem we have today is your husband is dead, and your butler shot him."

"My attorney is on his way," she lied, wondering if he had any idea she didn't have one. Mr. Paulson certainly wasn't going to come to her aid. "You will advise my butler of his rights?"

"Of course," Buckner said, standing up.

"Just give me a minute to speak with him, please. The man did just save my life. And I'd appreciate your removing the hand-cuffs."

THE POLICE OFFICERS filed out of the house.

"I'll be waiting for you outside," Buckner said to Rafferty.

Charlotte closed the door behind Buckner. She turned to face Rafferty, and it took everything she had not to burst into tears. She didn't want to alarm him. Trying to sound confident, she began, "I'm going to get a lawyer. Don't worry. . . ."

Suddenly Rafferty pulled her to him. He held her so close she could feel his heart beating against her own chest. "You saved my life," she whispered, looking up at him. His pale blue eyes were clouded with an intensity she'd never seen before. He brushed a lock of her hair from her eyes, and the intimacy of the gesture flooded her with shocking desire. She stood on her tiptoes, and urgently pressed her mouth against his. He held the back of her head with his large hands, his mouth unabashedly eager for hers, kissing her with ferocity.

The doorbell sounded.

Charlotte pulled away. "Damn Buckner," she said breathlessly, her shaking hands fumbling with the doorknob.

"Charlotte! Thank God," Jake said, rushing inside. "The front of your house is swarmed with police. Is everything all right?"

She was too shocked to speak.

He pulled her to him, and she felt the prickly stubble against her cheek. The smell of him was so familiar and comforting, it brought a fresh wave of tears. "William is dead," she said. He pressed her head to his chest, holding her as if to let go would be to lose her.

"Are you all right? That's all that matters," he said.

"I'm fine," she said, and looked up at his concerned face. A vivid purple bruise from where William had punched him was visible on his jaw under the shadow of his faint beard.

"Excuse me, Mrs. Delacorte." Buckner walked in with two officers, and they cuffed Rafferty.

Rafferty turned back to look at her, his eyes a complicated mix of strength and longing that she knew would keep her awake at night.

And then he was gone.

Jake closed the door behind the officers and pulled her into his arms. He held her close, and kissed the top of her head.

"I'm so sorry I underestimated you," Jake said.

"What?" Charlotte said, trying to bring her focus back to him. He took her face delicately in his hands, and kissed her not just with passion, but tenderly, with love. She felt her body relax, almost wilting against him.

"I thought you were taking the easy way out, and the whole time you were doing the riskiest thing of all. Charlotte, I'll spend the rest of my life making it up to you—if you'll let me."

At those words, she let everything else fall away.

"Will you let me make it up to you?" he whispered, pulling her chin up gently, forcing her to meet his gaze. She looked into his familiar dark eyes, the same ones that on a spring day not so long ago, had challenged her to dream of something other than the life she was living.

"Yes," she said. And for the first time in a very long time, she felt herself smile.

GRETA'S GOTHAM
A Bang in the Bedroom

What happens when a butler ends up in the bedroom with the mistress of the house—and is caught by her husband? Someone usually ends up dead. At least, that's what happened yesterday when recently jailed William Delacorte returned home to find his wife and butler making good use of his absence. Shots were fired, and now the city has lost its classiest bootlegger. As for the butler, one can only wonder if he will hang . . . or move permanently into the master bedroom.

Time will tell.